THE WATER OF THE
WONDROUS
ISLES

William Morris

WITH A NEW INTRODUCTION BY
NORMAN TALBOT

THOEMMES PRESS

Published in 1994 by

Thoemmes Press
85 Park Street
Bristol BS1 5PJ
England

ISBN 1 85506 256 9

This is a reprint of the 1913 Edition

Publisher's Note

These reprints are taken from original copies of each book. In many cases the condition of those originals is not perfect, the paper, often handmade, having suffered over time and the copy from such things as inconsistent printing pressures resulting in faint text, show-through from one side of a leaf to the other, the filling in of some characters, and the break up of type. The publisher has gone to great lengths to ensure the quality of these reprints but points out that certain characteristics of the original copies will, of necessity, be apparent in reprints thereof.

INTRODUCTION

The scales of literary irony have been loaded against *The Water of the Wondrous Isles* from the start. On one hand the romance has been robbed of its poignant significance as the last major work of its author's life, because Mackail, his official biographer, manages to avoid mentioning the book at all. Instead he emphasizes how, some three weeks before his death in November 1896, Morris struggled with the disappointing *Sundering Flood*.[1] Although Morris had lamented that 'the rough of my tale' of *Water* was nearly completed in August 1895, he seems to have been working on the proofs, the Fair Copy for the Kelmscott printers, both then and later.

Later biographers all follow Mackail, and ignore May Morris's very specific record of her father's last labours:

> My father saw the first two Parts of the *Water* in proof, and that is all. His Fair Copy of the tale breaks off in the middle of Part IV, chapter 14 page 174 of this volume. Thereafter we are dealing with the first manuscript, and it must be understood that wonderful and clean as this manuscript is – page after page flowing smoothly off the pen, without a correction – in half a dozen places there are certain

---

[1] J.W. Mackail, *Life of William Morris*, 2 volumes, London 1899, II p. 348. In fact, *The Sundering Flood* had not been completed, though Morris had supplied a final chapter. Most of the book only exists in clear, but brief and perfectly pedestrian, summary.

repetitions of words or repetitions of sound and one or two awkward sentences, all of which the author would have put right when he overlooked his work.[2]

The evidence of the Manuscripts, held in the British Library,[3] confirms May Morris's account, down to the very page she nominates, though she conveys nothing of the extent and extraordinary quality of Morris's revisions.

On the other hand, *Water*, perhaps the crowning achievement of an extraordinary life, had no critical reception in its own right, but merely obituary notices. Theodore Watts-Dunton's review may be taken as representatively well-intentioned,[4] in that he decides to say almost nothing about the book but to put on record his enthusiastic admiration of its author. He recommends the romances in general as 'artistic poetry' in prose, never hinting that there is any power or purpose in them as stories. It was perfectly possible for him to praise Morris for imaginative brilliance, magnanimity and independence of temperament, and vehement courage in his convictions, without looking for these qualities in the text before him.

One reason used for neglecting the romances is the tiresome chestnut that their language is mock-medieval 'Wardour Street English',[5] decorative

---

[2] May Morris, Introduction to volume XX *Collected Works* p. xix.

[3] See Textual Note. p. xxvii.

[4] Unsigned review, *Athenaeum* December 1897. Reprinted in Peter Faulkner (ed.) *William Morris, the Critical Heritage* (Routledge & Kegan Paul, London 1973) pp. 418–426.

[5] First employed in an anonymous review of *The Roots of the Mountains*, *The Spectator*, 65, 8 February 1890, pp. 208–9; reprinted in Peter Faulkner (ed.) *William Morris, the Critical Heritage* (Routledge & Kegan Paul, London 1973), p. 335–8.

fakery.[6] This odd misdescription still occasionally appears in spite of the lucid rebuttal by C.S. Lewis in his essay 'William Morris' in 1938:

> most of the detractors when they talk of Morris' style are really thinking of his printing: they expect the florid and the crowded, and imagine something like Sidney's *Arcadia*. In fact, however, this style constantly departs from that of modern prose in the direction of simplicity. Except for a few archaic words...it is incomparably easier and clearer than any 'natural' style could be, and the 'dull finish', the careful avoidance of rhetoric, gloss, and decoration, is of its very essence.[7]

A second group of adverse reviewers, more discerningly, recognized that somehow or other these romances were at the heart of Morris's case against the Victorian age, his concern for the cultural and ecological inheritance of England and Europe, his fierce longing for a more just, self-regulating and beautiful society. Some were not clear how the romances managed to subvert contemporary social and moral standards, but their instinct was correct. Some were respectable, and alienated by extra-marital sex and other indecorums; others were aesthetes, to whose sophistication Morris loudly preferred barbarism.

Since the demise of Empire Morris's fiction has been discussed mostly by those sympathetic with his

[6] I have discussed the language of *Water* in my article 'Whilom, as Tells the Tale' *Journal of the William Morris Society*, VIII, 2 (Spring 1989), pp. 16–25.

[7] Reprinted in *Rehabilitations and Other Essays*, London, OUP 1939, p. 220.

political perspective. Yet many of these too have felt betrayed: these pointlessly pretty archaic idylls did not seem to forward the cause of the workers' republic at all. Even if *Water* were comprehensible, they felt uneasily, it would merely obscure the proletariat's comprehension of the class-struggle and present no indictment of the status quo: it was neither stimulant nor emetic. Surely Morris had 'gone soft in the head',[8] through overwork, disappointment, senility or insufficient grounding in economic theory!

That fuzzy, mean-minded label 'escapist' has been especially malign in limiting and misguiding Morris's audience. It implies that there is one natural form of story, called 'realistic'; that it is cowardly, immoral or sentimental of an author to invent, and a reader to become interested in, improbable or impossible contexts and events; and that a Gradgrindish reverence before circumstance ('facts' or statistical probabilities) is both rational and healthy. All these things are untrue, and the criteria implied by the label 'escapist' would be self-destructive when applied to the major stories of any culture; of course, they are not so applied, either to traditional or to 'classic' works.

More subtle discomfort is betrayed by those critics, conscious of profound implications in Morris's narration, who list the romances (whether or not with

---

[8] The quoted phrase, intended more in sorrow than in anger, appears in E.P. Thompson's *William Morris: Romantic to Revolutionary* (1955), and was adopted – with different motives – as the title 'Had Morris Gone Soft in the Head?' of an aloof essay by Robert Currie in *Essays in Criticism*, XXIX, (October 1979), pp. 341–56. In his 1977 Merlin Press revision Thompson adds a far more apposite 'Postscript 1976'.

honorific intentions) as 'high fantasy'.[9] The atheistic
Morris is certainly not 'high' in the 'High Church' or
Heaven-focussed sense that pious, even pietistic,
writers like Macdonald, Lewis and Williams are.

Gender-bound critics have found *Water* especially
confusing. Morris is famous for preferring medieval
European society to that of his own day, and for being
very much 'a man's man', delighted to be mistaken for
a ship's captain. How can this rugged William Morris
have written a story in which a female character is
'the hero', obstructing the proper ending of a good
healthy medieval quest-romance? Wouldn't she make
the deeds of noble knights more or less irrelevant?

As to the female hero, Morris was an enemy of his
age in its patriarchal as well as its economic, aesthetic
and ethical assumptions. That he refused the role of
righteously-wrathful betrayed Victorian husband is
well-known, and his radicalism in matters of gender is
consistent. His early childhood was dominated by a
mother and two older sisters, and his delight in story,
which began so early that he could not remember a
time when he could not read, was formed among
them. Probably his preference for reading aloud,
rather than being read to, stems from childish
determination to make his contribution to the family
entertainment. Throughout his life (though monarchy
of any kind often roused his scorn or fury) his country
was ruled by a Queen. His own family, once the
obnoxious Rossetti had left Kelmscott Manor, was all-

[9] Auden intends high praise by the term in his interesting essay 'The
Quest Hero' (*Texas Quarterly*, IV, 1962, pp. 81–93). Rosemary
Jackson dismisses Morris into pious company in the 'Victorian
Fantasists' chapter of *Fantasy: the Literature of Subversion* (Methuen
New Accents, 1981), and castigates them all as authors of 'high fantasy'
on page 153.

female, and his closest extra-familial relationships always included women of vigour, vision and personality.[10]

Women play a major role in all Morris's late romances except the very short time-travel novella *A Dream of John Ball*, and are central to all his important fiction. This was necessarily true of the title poem to his first collection, *The Defence of Guenevere*, and almost all the verse narratives within *The Earthly Paradise* frame, whether or not orthodox 'love stories'. Signy, Brunhild and Gudrun similarly dominate *Sigurd the Volsung*. Morris was consistently aware, too, of the necessary conflict between goddess-vision and mortal women.[11]

As to quest-romance, Morris was temperamentally aligned with the stubborn courage of uncourtly – even barbarian – warriors of northern story, rather than either vowed or errant knights. Two of his romances have privileged boy-heroes who go out 'at a venture', but the others are called, or driven, into their adventure. Moreover, even Goldmane and Ralph are ambitious of folktale deeds rather than knightly achievements; the social, cultural and sexual realities that surround his protagonists, threatening both mind and body, are quite unlike those of a Malory or Chretien tale. Morris well understood why

[10] The admirable work of Linda Richardson in her 1990 Oxford D.Phil Thesis, *William Morris and Women: Experience and Representation*, remains unpublished due to her untimely death in that year. A copy is held by the William Morris Society at Kelmscott House, Hammersmith. Two significant essays based on that thesis have also been printed in the *Journal of the William Morris Society* ('Louise Michel and William Morris', VIII, 2, Spring 1989, pp. 26–9, and 'William Morris' Childhood and Schooling', ix, 1, Autumn 1990, pp. 15–19).

[11] See my article (written early in my acquaintance with Morris romance) 'Women and Goddesses in the Romances of William Morris', *Southern Review* (Adelaide), III, 4, pp. 339–57, 1969.

Tennyson's King Arthur sees the Grail-quest as destructive of Camelot, just as he understood, and abominated, Arthur's view of female sexuality.

Medieval courtly love or religious allegory did not much attract Morris. An expert translator and redactor of saga, epic and other traditional and popular narrative forms, he interweaves these with folk conventions in his last-decade stories. His protagonists, though physically pleasing and mentally stable, have no extraordinary wisdom or power; they respond to their ordeals in organic but innocent rituals of personal fulfilment. They are not representatives of or refugees from our homocosmic reality, but contend with a world that has its own phenomenal laws – including magic, which they never really understand, though helpers or lovers may do so.

Morris's romances are an expansive English, adventurous form of the psychological fantasy, as in the German novella, where plot, setting and character offer radical analogies to inward self-knowledge. These late romances hive up wonder and relish into unparaphrasable recognitions. They offer self-renewal, through vicarious joy, to an attentive audience and celebrate, yet defy, the mortality of the individual and the brevity of social harmony. These 'radical analogies' can as readily be expressed in rhetorics derived from Freud or Jung as in the terms of social psychologists like Marx.

Only during this century, with the growth of heterocosmic fantasy into a major literary field, have audiences become conscious of the skills appropriate to reading these romances. Morris exploited the quasi-familial female audiences of his own life to represent this implied, attuned audience, but predominantly he aimed at audiences of the far future, in an energetic and responsive society like his Nowhere.[12]

A brief introduction cannot do justice to the many aspects of this magnificently original fantasy. The emphasis here comes from my amazement, on my latest re-reading, at reaching the all-male Castle of the Quest and realizing that (apart from a toddler and a very old man) the story had travelled a hundred pages, a vast lake and two whole books without introducing a single male character. I have recently discussed the heroine's brilliant subversion of quest-romance convention.[13] Here I celebrate her over-turning of other static institutions, including audience expectation.

Birdalone, so improbably and naturally named, is both an interrogation and a reconciliation of several traditional images of women. Like Rapunzel (on whose story Morris wrote a brief verse-play), she is brought up by a wicked witch. Like Cinderella, Catskin, and other hardworking poor girls she can, given the opportunity, excel in aristocratic contexts. Like Snow-White (of the Seven Dwarfs) she is hated by a powerful, implacable woman, and like Snow-White and Rose-Red she is tested and protected, loved and hated, in a woodland context far from all the resources of civilization. Like the sister of the Seventh Swan she plies her needle in silent determination to contribute something to the world around her.

But these are all folktales. When Birdalone escapes from her ruthless fosterer she enters the world of

[12] See my 'A Guest in the Future: *News from Nowhere*', in Boos and Silver, eds. *The Political Writings of William Morris*, Minnesota 1991, pp. 38–60.

[13] 'Heroine as Hero: Morris' Case against Quest-Romance', in Kath Filmer (ed.) *The Victorian Fantasists*, London, Macmillan 1991, pp. 25–44.

magical quest, of heroic knight-errantry, where (before *The Lord of the Rings*) folktale conventions were rarely allowed entrance. Up to the point where Morris's Fair Copy revision stops, his psychomyth is a complex interweaving of ironic Bildungsroman, magical wonder folktale, and pastiche of chivalric adventure, satiric of Victorian social conventions as of male world-views.

The first chapter is Bildungsroman, describing Birdalone's kidnapping by the witch-wife from Utterhay, a microcosm of urban capitalism. The baby can be stolen because here money can do most things, even defy and outrage nature, while poverty can hardly keep itself alive. Only as the witch hurries fearfully through the almost trackless forest Evilshaw with her prize does the narrative first hint at its wonder-tale aspects.

The enmity between wood and witch-wife here foreshadows a struggle for Birdalone's will between wild nature and the solitary power-woman. But the ill-named woods are kindly, constantly offering the lonely girl the beauty and abundance of nature, and the woman is all cold, fierce, witch-crafty ego. As Birdalone grows up, between natural magic and arcane ritual knowledge, the participation of the wood-spirit Habundia in her life seems entirely benevolent, but her human society is limited to one human being, the wicked stepmother as remorseless tyrant, far more obviously powerful and magical than the inhuman spirit. The witch shackles the child to hard day-labour in her cottage and fields by the shore of the Water of the Wondrous Isles, enforcing obedience, mostly by beatings but also by menacing her slave's physical form by magical shape-changing.

Habundia, by contrast, opens the life of the wildwood to the child's wondering gaze, and – by appearing in her image – also reveals to her her own body, a natural perspective more wonderful than anything in *Twelfth Night.* The wood-spirit may not understand human love or tears, but she definitely understands delight in beauty.

Why does the witch want Birdalone, apart from slave-labour? Here the interlacement of irony-based Bildungsroman and delight-based wonder tale is eloquent. She is to be a sexual bait for men, and eventually to be taught witchcraft, to be the core of another generation of wickedness. But before her hideous training begins, Birdalone flees from her tutor's fury, naked and alone, carried off across the Water in the witch's own sinister magical boat, which can be propelled (but not steered) by a smear of her blood.

The Sending Boat takes this graceful, candid, naked, teenage fugitive, whom not even King Lear in his madness could call sophisticated, to the Isle of Increase Unsought, earthly paradise of the Queen of all the Wondrous Isles that give the lake its name. She steps ashore into the complex world of courts, classes, knight-errantry, lovers' vows and sexual longing, prison, and other social constraints, and meets three beautiful and heraldically colour-coded upper-class girls, Viridis (green), Aurea (gold) and Atra (black). These maiden heroines of a fine chivalric romance, shamefully enslaved by the Queen, send her as messenger to their three brave, handsome true-love knights. They each provide an emblematic garment which, offered to the knights with appropriate information, will stimulate them to the last phase of their amorous quest, heroic rescue and victory. After that satisfactory climax, she can go away, presumably, and the three couples settle down to live happily ever after.

Of course, that pattern is subverted by the very fact that the messenger is here the central character, and the ladies, initially at any rate, mere graceful figures in tapestry poses around her sublime nudity. The most perceptive of the three, Atra, recognizes almost at once that this is a female hero, not a helper, adjuvant, auxiliary at all! She has every right to be apprehensive, especially when they have to explain about sex to this naked teenager:

> They were silent now a little, and it was as if some sweet incense had been burned within the chamber. For Birdalone, the colour came and went in her cheeks, her flesh quaked, her heart beat quick, and she was oppressed with the sweetness of longing. More daintily she moved her limbs, and laid foot to foot and felt the sleekness of her sides; and tender was she of her body as of that which should one day be so sorely loved (II, 5, 66–7).

This passage and its heroine could hardly be less Victorian.

The ludicrous name of the Isle and the hilarious incompetence of its Queen's mingled malevolence and voluptuosity help to deconstruct the audience expectation of quest-romance patterns of closure. Whom will these gallant knights, personifications of chivalry, have to joust with to rescue their darlings? And with what weapons?

If the misnaming of the lovely *Evilshaw* and the destructively ambiguous *Wondrous* Isles invites interrogative rather than trusting responses, so does the unforgettable Queen of those Isles. She is splendidly built, with abundant golden hair, but when Birdalone is brought into her royal presence her effect is spoiled by her vicious expression,

> a look both proud, foolish, and cruel; terrible indeed, sitting in judgment in that place on a shrinking naked creature (II, 3, 58).

Her impact is like that of Swinburne's chant 'Dolores', though the tone is contempt rather than perverse fascination:

> Thou art fed with perpetual breath,
> And alive after infinite changes,
> And fresh from the kisses of death;
> Of langours rekindled and rallied,
> Of barren delights and unclean,
> Things monstrous and fruitless, a pallid
> And poisonous queen.

Birdalone indeed sees the palace of the Queen's artificially maintained glamour as 'The House of Death'.

The Queen has magical resources, yet not from any personal qualities; they come from either an inexhaustible chest of 'Increase Unsought', the Wonder-Coffer, or an *aqua vitae*, the Water of Might (names clearly connected with the book's title and the lake-realm she rules), or her big sister. She has power, for example over the three ladies who are her servants, and feels intense erotic pleasure at her dominating them, yet because it was her sister who captured them for her, she is forbidden to maltreat them physically while they are obedient. However, this constraint does not apply to her new, naked captive, since the Queen's powerful sister is the very witch-wife from whom Birdalone has 'stolen herself'.

But much as the Queen looks forward to torturing such a young, beautiful female, Birdalone is not in such very great danger when she is brought before the throne: the Queen's memory is so bad that she will have forgotten the event the next day. Her combination of spite and smug incompetence caricatures the ruling class of the British Empire. Thus her Increase Unsought and condescending cruelty equate with capitalism's unearned income and colonial tyranny; her pomp and her magnificent island palace correspond to the fineries and the lovely country-houses of England's aristocracy; her ignorance, stupidity and amnesia are necessary attributes of the Tory reactionaries, pretending to conserve a cultural tradition they neither respond to nor care about.

This ornate double of Birdalone's 'terrible mother' rules an Earthly Paradise where there is no work but a ruthless reign of pleasure and a constant production of commodities; she needs a supply of cultured slaves to amuse her (and to keep track of things). Her elder sister spoils her with expensive presents. Her coffer is like a factory system, invisible from the windows of the Big House; her wondrous wealth, like the profits of usurers, brokers and bankers, is unsought by either joy or labour.

High Tory capitalism is a hypocrisy not even very skilfully maintained. The gracious and beautiful ladies Viridis, Aurea and Atra, taking their ease in the sunlit garden, are in fact slaves. The pleasure-house is a prison and the gorgeous chest holds instruments of torture. The breaking of her spells is long overdue.

Like the real-life authorities on church architecture
who marred and desecrated the buildings they claimed
to 'restore', she discounts other people's active human
experience as worthless; like the fictional Bounderby,
she projects her selfishness onto those subject to her
power, blinding herself to indomitable energies of
class-solidarity, fidelity and pity, the active love that
sets Birdalone free.

In all this the Queen is the 'civilized' antonym of
ecologically sustainable nature. Where the nature-
spirit Habundia gives wealth, the Queen wields riches
(Morris was fond of this distinction); Habundia
celebrates and reflects Birdalone's human beauty, but
the Queen hates, fears and would mar it. She later
usurps Birdalone's place as Arthur's bedfellow; later
still it is Habundia who restores his sanity and leads
him to Birdalone's bed. Obviously, the Queen's
splendours are no natural abundance, but a disguise
for her island's foul and unnatural blight.

On this theme of sexuality, of love and the right true
end of love, the wonder-tale is as perceptive and
forthright as the Bildungsroman or the chivalric satire.
The Queen affects the role of *femme fatale, la belle
dame*, who can give her *merci* to her adorers or
withhold it. But she is no irresistible, quasi-
unattainable courtly-love queen, merely a lecherous,
proud, domineering and insecurely promiscuous
seductress. None of the castaways that have come to
the island have fallen in love with her, so in mortifi-
cation she has tortured and destroyed them – and of
course forgotten them. Her blatant lust to get the
three questing knights into her bed (true lovers all,
though Arthur's emotions are in upheaval) is what
destroys her: rather than ruling a Court of Love she is
condemned by its laws and executed by its justice.

Birdalone's four-lobed journey is the structure of the
book. To deliver the emblem-clothes and messages of
Viridis, Aurea and Atra to their knights, she must sail
to each of the Queen's Isles that give the book its title.
All are beautiful, stupid, malevolent traps, worthy of
their mistress, and forbidden change while she lives.
The Sending Boat ends at the Castle of the Quest,
built where the maidens were abducted. Like the tales
of *The Earthly Paradise* (but much more briefly
evoked) each isle has its own mystery and implied
narrative, and on both visits Birdalone glimpses
fragments of each story as it pierces the frame, so to
speak, of her own.

When Birdalone retraces this *imram,* well after the
Queen's death, the other Isles are radically alive and
changing, but Increase Unsought is totally
deconstructed. The Tory paradise is now revealed as
a waste land, its only life thorns, lizards and beetles,
adders and 'great carrion flies'. On this sterile shore
the Sending Boat breaks up and Birdalone has to try
to swim several miles of the Lake unaided. Only by
Habundia's aid does she survive, returning to the
witch's house as naked as she had left.

The Isle of the Young and the Old obscenely
preserves the innocence of childhood and the poignant
incompetence of second childhood: the permanent
children have been reduced to 'images', scarcely more
human than the rabbits in the grass, and their
guardian to a useless alternation of maundering and
senile content with maundering and maudlin
fragments of displaced memory. When change rushes
upon them, the old man is released into restful death
and the young begin to grow up. Birdalone's second
visit may stimulate some structure and vision of a

good society to direct towards wisdom their thronging
human impulses.

The Isles of Queens and of Kings are obviously a
pair, both dominated by imposing castles. The first
has a congregation of noble and beautiful ladies
appropriate in pathos and passion to its magnificence,
the second an all-male garrison of martial dignity to
match its stern and warlike grandeur. Both are
parodic of the 'Sleeping Beauty' folktale – and not
only of its gender stereotypes. Every inhabitant is
immobilized, but would awaken from the magical
trance if the central figure in the tableau were kissed
awake. But there will be no happy endings: the lovely
woman in the Kings' castle and the tall king in the
Queens' are emphatically dead, not sleeping. It may
be that they killed each other in some neurotically
formal version of the war of the sexes.

When Birdalone revisits these islands, the Kings' is
inhabited by a group of nubile and man-hungry virgin
huntresses, the Queens' by a similar throng of virile
hunters. Both try to trap her into joining them; the
maidens use contemptuous and spiteful giggling at her
male armour, because they assume any male is
superior to the bravest woman; a man tries to capture
her, with cheerfully cynical lechery, but another
prevents him, expressing a youthful and healthily
idealistic chivalry. These Isles have unreassuring
implications for single-sex education systems, clubs
and associations....

The last Isle of the five, the Isle of Nothing, is a
wide, low featureless bank of gravel, and when
Birdalone ventures inland an equally featureless grey
mist grows and thickens around her. By natural
magic, burning a lock of hair Habundia had given her,

she conjures upon the mist a vision of the spirit – or of herself, since Habundia always appears to her in her own image – and escapes by following it back to the shore. Natural beauty is, it seems, the antidote to metaphysical doubt and nihilistic isolation.

Birdalone finds this Isle intensely different on her return. Though only five years have passed, tall young trees crowd much of the island, and a small pastoral tribe pastures its sheep, goats and cattle there, and of course breeds children. They recognize her visit as a blessing by their very own goddess, because Habundia had been the first power evoked here, and in the image of Birdalone.

Between these two *imrams*, Birdalone has delivered her message to the Castle of the Quest, built and garrisoned by the heraldically yearning but helpless knights, betrothed to Viridis, Aurea and Atra. Once she also gives them the blood-drinking magic boat and tells them precisely what to do, and where, they sail off to rescue their ladies. Their serio-comic, largely accidental success is what destroys the Queen. This male triumph is told in a fairly straight-faced flashback chapter, as a mere episode in Birdalone's foregrounded story.

But what story? What can a female hero actually do? According to audience expectations shaped by male quest, her role is over with her message. Can healthy, passionate Birdalone be trapped in an all-male castle, being taught to read, write, embroider, and be a lady? Of course she soon sickens, confined by the Norman-French expectations of aristocrats and clergy.

The sickness is love: she has fallen in love with Arthur, the betrothed of her friend Atra. And she is expected to wave him prettily goodbye as he sails off to be united with Atra! Perhaps a well-bred young lady would have repressed desire, or at least suppressed her natural activity of spirit to pine picturesquely, but neither slavery under the witch nor communion with wood-spirits is conducive to this skill. Instead Birdalone acts – and bears the blame for female wiles, broken oaths, death, ghosts and ruin, and madness. No better test of individuation and maturity than such autonomy could punctuate a Bildungsroman!

Birdalone learns of an ancient earth-magic area, the Black Valley of the Grey-Wethers (one of Morris's superb Icelandic landscapes), and escapes there to intercede for her love. She lays her hand on the huge kingstone, praying with absolute directness:

> O Earth, thou and thy first children, I crave of you
> that he may come back now at once and loving me.
> (IV, 9, 159.)

Her prayer is granted, literally and immediately, but she does not realize this. The prayer is also instantly answered in travesty: from behind the stone steps an ironically different Black Knight, emphatically 'at once' in love with Birdalone!

He is a bad Black Knight, lieutenant to a wicked and depraved mage, the Red Knight, who rules the loathsome Red Hold. Though contact with Birdalone quickly turns Sir Thomas from evil, the Red Knight viciously murders him before he can do specific good. When the heroes of the quest, including her love Arthur, come to rescue her, they see her at the nadir of her young life, walking tethered behind the murderer's horse, soaked with blood because Sir Thomas' severed head hangs from her neck.

They ambush and kill the Red Knight, but the noble Golden Knight, Baudoin, is also killed. The chivalrous company of knights and ladies is broken. Aurea's love is dead and Atra's alienated: no one has any doubt that Arthur loves Birdalone rather than his official fiancée. Viridis and Sir Hugh have each other, but necessarily share the general mourning.

Is this all Birdalone's fault? Definitely not. The innocent maiden from the wildwood cannot be bound by male-centred rules or the expectations of upper-class courtly lovers, however neatly colour-coded. Without her the ladies would still be slaves, and the knights still gazing out across the lake in futile postures of devotion. Now, as Arthur, Hugh and their allies plan to exterminate the remaining vermin of the Red Hold, at last employing their warrior prowess for the benefit of their neighbours inland, Birdalone is assured by all, including Aurea and especially Atra, that she is not to blame. This is when she and Arthur confess their love and exchange their first caresses of love (once she has reassured him about her relationship with Sir Thomas).

After Hugh's charming account of the unheroic expedition that rescued the ladies from the Isle of Increase Unsought, the war against the Red Hold begins. At once Birdalone acts again, rebelling against that other courtly-love staple, the eternal triangle, by stealing away secretly to hide from both Arthur and Atra. She survives, in fact succeeds brilliantly, as a craftswoman in a middle-class mercantile city. She even meets her true mother, and brightens her last years.

It must be admitted at this point that Morris's revisions for the printers' Fair Copy of *Water* make a very great difference to the quality of the writing. He may have pretended that he could toss off romances with careless ease, but in fact he revised industriously and often brilliantly, with keen awareness of both cadence of expression and nuance of meaning. The Fair Copy emendations stop at Birdalone's dealings with Sir Thomas, and there is a certain thinness about some later episodes, especially Birdalone's reunion with her mother. A convenient dream sends her back to the Castle of the Quest, and she resolves to seek Habundia again, thus completing the water-lobe of her journey. This is when she sees the Isles in the throes of change, ending with the prospect of a lonely and pointless death on the dead Queen's own blasted Isle.

After her epic swim and the natural-magical aid of the floating tree, Birdalone finds her witch-wife mistress dead, and humbly begins to render the cottage livable again, while waiting to meet Habundia. The spirit still looks identical to Birdalone, which makes precarious the task of bringing her lover back to sanity, for after a savagely successful military campaign Arthur has suffered a breakdown: he emulates Tristan and Lancelot, wandering skinclad and wildwood-mad, a starved but dangerous harper. To see plural Birdalones would have unhinged a much less unstable lover.

Birdalone was un-Victorian enough in her frequent nudity and her courageous activity, but when clear narratorial approval is given to her leadership in enthusiastic extramarital sex, she is at her most alien to public versions of Morris's contemporary audience:

> Then Birdalone drew in her love, and went about lighting the candles and quickening a little cooking-

fire on the hearth, till the yellow light chased the
moon away from the bed of their desire.

(VI, 27, 353.)

After this Bildungsroman climax (in books III–V she
was wooed by many contrasting men, as is but
natural given that she is physically beautiful and
exudes 'naturalness'), she and Arthur live and work
together until he is physically strong again, and are
then comrades-in-arms in a Robin-Hood style rescue
of Viridis, Hugh, Aurea and Atra.

The story ends anticlimactically. Birdalone
completes the fourth lobe of her life's journey,
returning to her birthplace as a pledge allying the
townspeople with her husband and his aristocratic
allies. Given the Utterhay attitude to human values in
the first chapter, Morris would undoubtedly have
sharpened the ironies of this 'happy ending' when he
came to its Fair Copy revision. As it is, not only has
the town turned, non-satirically, into a Good Place,
but the female hero seems almost subjugated to both
political exigency and her husband's prowess in
generalship.

First, the Bildungsroman element requires no return
to Utterhay: Birdalone's competence with urban,
mercantile and maternal realities has been proved in
her exile in Five Crafts. Second, the aristocratic
masculinist elements so fiercely satirized in earlier
episodes are now acceptable to the bourgeoisie.
Third, the wonder-tale aspect, the strife between
Habundia's natural magic and the Witches' control-
magic, has been resolved, and the victorious ecology
can now be thought of again as 'out there', where it
always had been for the burghers of Utterhay.

Still, the achievement of this extraordinary book cannot be lessened by the mortality of its author. With typical rediscovery of the energy intrinsic in a set medieval phrase, he gives his characters the epitaph appropriate to himself:

> their love never sundered, and...they lived without shame and died without fear (VII, 4, 387).

Norman Talbot
University of Newcastle,
New South Wales, 1994

TEXTUAL NOTE

The Water of the Wondrous Isles was published posthumously by the Kelmscott Press in April 1897, in quarto, in an edition of 250 copies (with six on vellum).

It was reset in crown octavo and published by Longmans in October 1897; this first popular edition was reprinted in 1902 and again in 1909.

This edition reproduces the text of Volume XX of the *Collected Works of William Morris*, published by Longmans in September 1913.

The MSS are all held in the British Library's Manuscript Room as Additional Manuscripts 45,322 to 45,325 as volume XXX of the May Morris bequest. 45,322 (438 pages long, with 5 pages of outline) is the 'first manuscript' May Morris refers to in the editorial comment quoted early in the introduction. 45,323 (201 pages) is the Fair Copy for the printer that Morris was working on, which breaks off at page 174 of this edition. 45,324 (47 pages) is the earlier version, *The Widow's House by the Great Water*, that Morris abandoned in favour of *Water*, and 45,325 (17 pages) is a false start to *Water*, in verse.

All printed editions follow MS45,323, transferring, when that breaks off, to 45,322. After the first two books, which Morris saw in proof, not all chapter divisions are marked, and not all have titles: May Morris probably supplied them. In the Kelmscott first edition and occasionally in MS and Fair Copy, a leaf emblem is sometimes used instead of a full stop. Quotation marks for speeches are not used until the crown octavo edition.

CONTENTS

THE SECOND PART: OF THE WONDROUS ISLES

THE THIRD PART: OF THE CASTLE OF THE QUEST

THE FOURTH PART: OF THE DAYS OF ABIDING

THE SEVENTH PART: THE DAYS OF RETURNING

THE WATER OF THE
WONDROUS ISLES

THE WATER OF THE WONDROUS ISLES. THE FIRST PART: OF THE HOUSE OF CAPTIVITY.

CHAPTER I. CATCH AT UTTERHAY.

WHILOM, as tells the tale, was a walled cheaping-town hight Utterhay, which was builded in a bight of the land a little off the great highway which went from over the mountains to the sea.

The said town was hard on the borders of a wood, which men held to be mighty great, or maybe measureless; though few indeed had entered it, and they that had, brought back tales wild and confused thereof.

Therein was neither highway nor byway, nor wood-reeve nor way-warden; never came chapman thence into Utterhay; no man of Utterhay was so poor or so bold that he durst raise the hunt therein; no outlaw durst flee thereto; no man of God had such trust in the saints that he durst build him a cell in that wood.

For all men deemed it more than perilous; and some said that there walked the worst of the dead; othersome that the Goddesses of the Gentiles haunted there; others again that it was the Faery rather, but they full of malice and guile. But most commonly it was deemed that the devils swarmed amidst of its thickets, and that wheresoever a man sought to, who was once environed by it, ever it was the Gate of Hell whereto he came. And the said wood was called Evilshaw.

Nevertheless the cheaping-town throve not ill; for whatso evil things haunted Evilshaw, never came they into Utterhay in such guise that men knew them, neither wotted they of any hurt that they had of the Devils of Evilshaw.

Now in the said cheaping-town, on a day, it was market and high noon, and in the market-place was much people thronging; and amidst of them went a woman, tall, and strong of aspect, of some thirty winters by seeming, black-haired, hook-nosed and hawk-eyed, not so fair to look on as masterful and proud. She led a great grey ass betwixt two panniers, wherein she laded her marketings. But now she had done her chaffer, and was looking about her as if to note the folk for her desport; but when she came across a child, whether it were borne in arms or led by its kins-women, or were going alone, as were some, she seemed more heedful of it, and eyed it more closely than aught else.

So she strolled about till she was come to the outskirts of the throng, and there she happened on a babe of some two winters, which was crawling about on its hands and knees, with scarce a rag upon its little body. She watched it, and looked whereto it was going, and saw a woman sitting on a stone, with none anigh her, her face bowed over her knees as if she were weary or sorry. Unto her crept the little one, murmuring and merry, and put its arms about the woman's legs, and buried its face in the folds of her gown: she looked up therewith, and showed a face which had once been full fair, but was now grown bony and hag-gard, though she were scarce past five and twenty years. She took the child and strained it to her bosom, and kissed it, face and hands, and made it great cheer, but ever woe-fully. The tall stranger stood looking down on her, and noted how evilly she was clad, and how she seemed to have nought to do with that throng of thriving cheapeners, and she smiled somewhat sourly.

At last she spake, and her voice was not so harsh as might have been looked for from her face: "Dame," she said, "thou seemest to be less busy than most folk here; might I crave of thee to tell an alien who has but some hour to dwell in this good town where she may find her a chamber where-in to rest and eat a morsel, and be untroubled of ribalds and ill company?"

Said the poor-wife: "Short shall be my tale; I am over poor to know of hostelries and ale-houses that I may tell thee aught thereof." Said the other: "Maybe some neigh-bour of thine would take me in for thy sake?" Said the

2

mother: "What neighbours have I since my man died; and I
dying of hunger, and in this town of thrift and abundance?"

The leader of the ass was silent a while, then she said:
"Poor woman! I begin to have pity on thee; and I tell thee
that luck hath come to thee to-day."

Now the poor-wife had stood up with the babe in her arms
and was turning to go her ways; but the alien put forth a
hand to her, and said: "Stand a while and hearken good
tidings." And she put her hand to her girdle-pouch, and
drew thereout a good golden piece, a noble, and said:
"When I am sitting down in thine house thou wilt have
earned this, and when I take my soles out thereof there will
be three more of like countenance, if I be content with thee
meanwhile."

The woman looked on the gold, and tears came into her
eyes; but she laughed and said: "House-room may I give
thee for an hour truly, and therewithal water of the well,
and a mouse's meal of bread. If thou deem that worth three
nobles, how may I say thee nay, when they may save the life
of my little one. But what else wouldst thou of me?"

"Little enough," said the alien; "so lead me straight to
thine house."

So went they forth of the market-place, and the woman
led them, the alien and the ass, out of the street through the
west gate of Utterhay, that, to wit, which looked on Evilshaw, and so into a scattering street without the wall, the end
of which neared a corner of the wood aforesaid: the houses
there were nought so evil of fashion, but whereas they were
so nigh unto the Devil's Park, rich men might no longer
away with them, and they were become wares for poor folk.

Now the townswoman laid her hand on the latch of the
door that was hers, and threw the door open; then she put
forth her palm to the other, and said: "Wilt thou give me
the first gold now, since rest is made sure for thee, as long
as thou wilt?" The ass-leader put it into her hand, and she
took it and laid it on her baby's cheek, and then kissed both
gold and child together; then she turned to the alien and

said: "As for thy way-beast, I have nought for him, neither
hay nor corn: thou wert best to leave him in the street." The
stranger nodded a yea-say, and the three went in together,
the mother, the child, and the alien.

Not right small was the chamber; but there was little
therein; one stool to wit, a yew-chair, a little table, and a
coffer: there was no fire on the hearth, nought save white
ashes of small wood; but it was June, so that was of no
account.

The guest sat down in the yew-chair, and the poor-wife
laid her child down gently on the floor and came and stood
before the stranger, as if abiding her bidding.

Spake the alien: "Nought so uncomely or strait is thy
chamber; and thy child, which I see is a woman, and therefore belike shall long abide with thee, is lovely of shape,
and fair of flesh. Now also thou shalt have better days, as I
deem, and I pray them on thine head."

She spake in a kind wheedling voice, and the poor-wife's
face grew softer, and presently tears fell down on to the table
from her, but she spake no word. The guest now drew forth,
not three nobles, but four, and laid them on the table, and
said: "Lo, my friend, the three nobles which I behight thee!
now are they thine; but this other thou shalt take and spend
for me. Go up into the town, and buy for me white bread of
the best; and right good flesh, or poulaine if it may be, already
cooked and dight; and, withal, the best wine that thou mayst
get, and sweetmeats for thy baby; and when thou comest back,
we will sit together and dine here. And thereafter, when we
be full of meat and drink, we shall devise something more
for thy good speed."

The woman knelt before her weeping, but might speak
no word because of the fullness of her heart. She kissed the
guest's hands, and took the money, and then arose and caught
up her child, and kissed her bare flesh eagerly many times,
and then hastened out of the house and up the street and
through the gate; and the guest sat hearkening to the sound
of her footsteps till it died out, and there was nought to be

4

heard save the far-off murmur of the market, and the chir-
rup of the little one on the floor.

Then arose the guest and took up the child from the floor,
who kicked and screamed, and craved her mother as her
broken speech might; but the alien spake softly to her, and
said: "Hush, dear one, and be good, and we will go and find
her;" and she gave her therewith a sugar-plum from out of
her scrip. Then she came out of doors, and spake sweetly to
the little one: "See now this pretty way-beast! We will ride
merrily on him to find thy mother."

Then she laid the child in the pannier with a soft cushion
under, and a silk cloth over her, so that she lay there happily.
Then she took her ass's rein and went her ways over the waste
toward Evilshaw; for, as ye may deem, where the houses
and the street ended, the beaten way ended also.

Quietly and speedily she went, and met but three men on
the way; and when these saw her, and that she was making
for Evilshaw, they turned their heads away, each one, and
blessed themselves and went past swiftly. Not one sought
to stay her, or held any converse with her, and no foot she
heard following after her. So in scarce more than the saying of a low mass she was in amongst the trees, with her ass
and her wares and her prey.

No stay she made there, but held forward at her best before the night should fall upon her. And whatsoever might
be told concerning the creatures that other folk had met in
Evilshaw, of her it must needs be said that therein she happened on nought worser than herself.

CHAPTER II. NOW SHALL BE TOLD OF THE HOUSE BY THE WATER-SIDE.

FOUR days they wended the wood, and nought befell
to tell of. The witch-wife (for even such was she) fed
the stolen child well and duly, and whiles caressed her
and spake sweetly unto her; whiles also she would take her
out of the pannier, and set her on the ass's back and hold

5

her thereon heedfully; or, otherwhiles, when they came upon
grassy and flowery places, she would set her down on the
ground and let her roam about, and pluck the flowers and
the strawberries. And whoso might be sorry, the child was
glad, so many things new and fair as she came upon.

At last, when the fifth day was waning, and they had been
a long while wending a wood set thick with trees, it began
to grow grey betwixt the distant boles, and then from grey
to white, and it was as if a new world of light lay before them.
Thitherward went they, and in a little, and before the sun
was set, came they to the shore of a great water, and thence was
no more land to be seen before them than if it had been the
main sea itself, though this was a sweet water. Albeit, less than
a half mile from the shore lay two eyots, as it might have been
on the salt sea; but one of these sat low down on the water,
and was green and well bushed, but the other, which lay
east of it, and was nigher to the shore, was high, rocky,
and barren.

Now the ending of the wood left a fair green plain betwixt
it and the water, whiles more than a furlong across, whiles
much less; and whiles the trees came down close to the
water-side. But the place whereas they came from out the
wood was of the widest, and there it was a broad bight of
greensward of the fashion of the moon seven nights old,
and a close hedge of thicket there was at the back of it; and
the lake lay south, and the wood north. Some deal of this
greensward was broken by closes of acre-land, and the tall
green wheat stood blossoming therein; but the most was
sweet meadow, and there as now was a gallant flock of goats
feeding down it; five kine withal, and a tethered bull.
Through the widest of this meadow ran a clear stream
winding down to the lake, and beside a lap of the said
stream, two bow-shots from the water, was a knoll, whereon stood, amidst of a potherb garden, a little house strongly
framed of timber. Before it the steep bank of the lake broke
down into a slowly-shelving beach, whose honey-coloured
sand thrust up a tongue in amongst the grass of the mead.

6

Went the witch-wife straight to the door of the said house as if she were at home, as was sooth indeed. She threw the door open, and unladed the ass of all his wares, and first of the youngling, whom she shook awake, and bore into the house, and laid safely on the floor of the chamber; nor did she wait on her wailing, but set about what was to be done to kindle fire, and milk a she-goat, and get meat upon the board. That did she, and fed both herself and the child plenteously: neither did she stint her of meat ever, from that time forward, however else she dealt with her.

CHAPTER III. OF SKIN-CHANGING.

ONE thing must here be told: Whenas the said dame stood forth clad amidst of the chamber the next morning, the child ran up to her to greet her or what not, but straightway when she saw her close, drew aback, and stood gasping with affright; for verily she deemed this was nowise she who had brought her last night into the fair chamber, and given bread and milk to her and put her to bed, but someone else. For this one had not dark hair, and hooked nose, and eyen hawk-bright; stark and tall was she indeed, as that other one, and by seeming of the same-like age; but there came to an end all her likeness to last night's house-wife. This one had golden-red hair flowing down from her head; eyes of hazel colour, long and not well-opened, but narrow and sly. High of cheek-bones she was, long-chinned and thin-lipped; her skin was fine and white, but without ruddiness; flat-breasted she was, and narrow-hipped.

Now she laughed at the babe's terror, and said, but in her old voice at least: "Thou foolish little beast! I know what scares thee, to wit, that thou deemest me changed: now I tell thee that I am the one who brought thee here last night, and fed thee; neither is my changing a matter of thine, since at least I am the one who shall keep thee from hunger and weather henceforward; that is enough for thee to know as now. Now thou hast to eat and sleep and play and cry out,

7

that thou mayest the sooner wax, and grow into the doing of my will."

Therewith she led her out into the sunshine, and tethered her to an ash sapling which grew anigh the door, that the child might be safe the while she went about her work in acre and mead.

But as for that matter of changing of aspect, the maiden came to know thereafter that the witch durst not go into the wood in the same skin as that which she wore at home, wherefore she had changed it for the journey to Utterhay, and changed back again in the night-tide before she arose.

CHAPTER IV. OF THE WAXING OF THE STO-LEN CHILD.

THIS little one, who is henceforth called Birdalone, though the witch called her but seldom so, nor indeed by any name, dwelt there betwixt the Water and the Wood, and saw none save the said witch-wife, who, as aforesaid, fed her well, but scarce meddled with her else for a long while; so she wandered well-nigh as she had will, and much in the wood; for she had no fear thereof, nor indeed of aught else save of the dame. She learned of the ways and the wont of all the creatures round about her, and the very grass and flowers were friends to her, and she made tales of them in her mind; and the wild things feared her in no wise, and the fowl would come to her hand, and play with her and love her. A lovely child she was, rosy and strong, and as merry as the birds on the bough; and had she trouble, for whiles she came across some ugly mood of the witch-wife, she bore it all as lightly as they.

Wore the years thus, till now she was grown tall and thin, and had seen twelve winters, and was far stronger and handier than at first sight she looked to be. That found her mistress, and would not forego the using of her deftness. For indeed the maiden knew all matters of wood and field full well, and somewhat of the water also (though no boat had she ever
8

seen there), for she learned herself swimming, as the ducks
do belike.

But now her mistress would learn her swinking, and hard was the lesson, for with twiggen rods and switches was she learned, and was somewhat stubborn with this woman, who she deemed loved her not; and, however it were, there began to grow in her an inkling that all was not well with the dame, and howsoever she might fear her, she trusted her not, nor worshipped her: otherwise she had learned her lesson speedily; for she was not slack nor a sluggard, and hated not the toil, even when it pained and wearied her, but against the anger and malice she hardened her heart.

It is to be said, that though there she dwelt alone with the witch-wife, she had somehow got to know that they two were not alone in the world, and she knew of male and female, and young and old. Thereof doubtless the witch herself had learned her, would she, would she not; for though she were mostly few-spoken, yet whiles the tongue of her would loosen, and she would tell Birdalone tales of men and women, and kings and warriors and thralls, and the folk of the world beyond them, if it were but to scare the child. Yea, and when she rated Birdalone, or girded at her, words would come forth which the maiden stored up, and by laying two and two together gat wisdom howso it were. Moreover she was of the race of Adam, and her heart conceived of diverse matters from her mother's milk and her father's blood, and her heart and her mind grew up along with her body. Herein also was she wise, to wit how to give wrath the go-by, so that she oft found the wood a better home than the house: for now she knew that the witch-wife would enter it never; wherefore she loved it much, and haunted it daily if she might.

Amidst all this she lived not unmerrily; for the earth was her friend, and solaced her when she had suffered aught: withal she was soon grown hardy as well as strong; and evil she could thole, nor let it burden her with misery.

9

CHAPTER V. OF BIRDALONE, AND HOW SHE IS GROWN INTO MAIDENHOOD.

WEAR the years and the years amidst such days as these, and now is Birdalone grown a dear maiden of seventeen summers; and yet was her life not unhappy; though the mirth of her childhood was somewhat chastened in her, and she walked the earth soberly and measurely, as though deep thoughts were ever in her head: though, forsooth, it is not all so sure that her serious face and solemn eyes were but a part of the beauty which was growing with the coming forth of childhood into youth and maidenhood. But this at least is sure, that about this time those forebodings which had shown her that she had no call to love and honour her mistress took clearer shape, and became a burden on her, which she might never wholly shake off. For this she saw, that she was not her own, but a chattel and a tool of one who not only used her as a thrall in the passing day, but had it in her mind to make of her a thing accursed like to herself, and to bait the trap with her for the taking of the sons of Adam. Forsooth she saw, though dimly, that her mistress was indeed wicked, and that in the bonds of that wickedness was she bound.

One thing, moreover, had she noted now this long while, that once and again, it might be once every two moons, the witch-wife would arise in the dead of night and go forth from the house, and be away for a day, or two or three, or whiles more, and come back again weary and fordone; but never said she any word to Birdalone hereof. Yet oft when she arose to go this errand, before she left the chamber would she come to Birdalone's truckle-bed, and stand over her to note if she were asleep or not; and ever at such times did Birdalone feign slumber amidst of sickening dread. Forsooth in these latter days it whiles entered the maiden's head that when the dame was gone she would rise and follow her and see whither she went, and what she did; but terror constrained her that she went not.

Now from amidst all these imaginings arose a hope in her
that she might one day escape from her thralldom: and whiles,
when she was lonely and safe in the wood, to this hope she
yielded herself; but thereof came such tumult of her soul
for joy of the hope, that she might not master her passion;
the earth would seem to rise beneath her, and the woods to
whirl about before her eyes, so that she might not keep her
feet, but would sink adown to earth, and lie there weeping.
Then most oft would come the cold fit after the hot, and the
terror would take her that some day the witch would surprise
the joy of that hope in her eyes, and would know what it
meant, or that some light word might bewray her; and therewith came imaginings of what would then befall her, nor were
that hard to picture, and it would come before her over and
over again till she became weary and worn out therewith.

But though they abode ever with her, these troubling
thoughts pricked not so oft at the keenest, but were as the
dull ache of little import that comes after pain overcome:
for in sooth busy and toilsome days did she wear, which
irked her in nowise, since it eased her of the torment of
those hopes and fears aforesaid, and brought her sound
sleep and sweet awaking. The kine and the goats must she
milk, and plough and sow and reap the acre-land according to the seasons, and lead the beasts to the woodland pastures when their own were flooded or burned; she must
gather the fruits of the orchard, and the hazel nuts up the
woodlands, and beat the walnut-trees in September. She
must make the butter and the cheese, grind the wheat in
the quern, make and bake the bread, and in all ways earn
her livelihood hard enough. Moreover, the bowman's craft
had she learned, and at the dame's bidding must fare alone
into the wood now and again to slay big deer and little, and
win venison: but neither did that irk her at all, for rest and
peace were in the woods for her.

True it is; that as she wended thicket or glade or wood-
lawn, she would at whiles grow timorous, and tread light
and heedfully, lest rustling leaves or crackling stick should

arouse some strange creature in human shape, devil, or god
now damned, or woman of the Faery. But if such were there,
either they were wise and would not be seen, or kind and had
no will to scare the simple maiden; or else maybe there were
none such in those days. Anyhow, nought evil came to her
out of Evilshaw.

CHAPTER VI. HEREIN IS TOLD OF BIRD-ALONE'S RAIMENT.

LANK and long is Birdalone the sweet, with legs that
come forth bare and browned from under her scant
grey coat and scantier smock beneath, which was all
her raiment save when the time was bitter, and then, forsooth, it was a cloak of goat-skin that eked her attire: for
the dame heeded little the clothing of her; nor did Birdalone
give so much heed thereto that she cared to risk the anger of
her mistress by asking her for aught.

But on a day of this same spring, when the witch-wife was
of sweeter temper than her wont was, and the day was very
warm and kindly, though it was but one of the last of February days, Birdalone, blushing and shame-faced, craved
timidly some more womanly attire. But the dame turned
gruffly on her and said: "Tush, child! what needeth it? here
be no men to behold thee. I shall see to it, that when due
time comes thou shalt be whitened and sleeked to the very
utmost. But look thou! thou art a handy wench; take the
deer-skin that hangs up yonder and make thee brogues for
thy feet, if so thou wilt."

Even so did Birdalone, and shaped the skin to her feet;
but as she was sewing them a fancy came into her head; for
she had just come across some threads of silk of divers colours; so she took them & her shoon & her needle up into the
wood, and there sat down happily under a great spreading
oak which much she haunted, and fell to broidering the
kindly deerskin. And she got to be long about it, and came
back to it the next day and the next, and many days, when-

12

so her servitude would suffer it, and yet the shoon were

So on a morning the dame looked on her feet as she moved
about the chamber, and cried out at her: "What! art thou
barefoot as an hen yet? Hast thou spoilt the good deerskin
and art yet but shoeless?"

"Nay, our lady," said Birdalone, "but the shoon are not
altogether done."

"Show them to me," said the dame.

Birdalone went to her little coffer to fetch them, and
brought them somewhat timorously, for she knew not how
her mistress would take her working on them so long, if perchance she would blame her, or it might be chastise her, for
even in those days the witch-wife's hand was whiles raised
against her. But now when the dame took the shoes and
looked on them, and saw how there were oak-leaves done into
them, and flowers, and coneys, and squirrels, she but smiled
somewhat grimly on Birdalone, and said: "Well, belike
thou art a fool to waste thy time and mine in such toys; and
to give thee thy due would be to give thee stripes. But thou
doest herein after the nature of earthly women, to adorn thy
body, whatsoever else is toward. And well is that, since I
would have thee a woman so soon as may be; and I will help
thy mind for finery, since thou art so deft with thy needle."

Therewith she went to the big coffer and drew forth thence
a piece of fine green cloth, and another of fine linen, and said
to Birdalone: "This mayest thou take, and make thee a gown
thereof and a new smock, and make them if thou wilt as gay
as thy new shoon are gotten to be; and here is wherewithal."
And therewith she gave her two handfuls of silken threads
and gold, and said: "Now I suppose that I must do the more
part of thy work, while thou art making thee these gaudy
garments. But maybe someone may be coming this way ere
long, who will deem the bird the finer for her fine feathers.
Now depart from me; for I would both work for thee and
me, and ponder weighty matters."

Who was glad now but Birdalone; she grew red with new

13

pleasure, and knelt down and kissed the witch's hand, and then went her ways to the wood with her precious lading, and wrought there under her oak-tree day after day, and all days, either there, or in the house when the weather was foul. That was in the middle of March, when all birds were singing, and the young leaves showing on the hawthorns, so that there were pale green clouds, as it were, betwixt the great grey boles of oak and sweet-chestnut; and by the lake the meadow-saffron new-thrust-up was opening its blossom; and March wore and April, and still she was at work happily when now it was later May, and the hare-bells were in full bloom down the bent before her.

All this while the witch had meddled little with Birdalone, and had bidden her to no work afield or in the stead which was anywise grievous, but had done all herself; yet was she few-spoken with her, and would oft behold her gloomily. And one evening when Birdalone came in from the wood, the witch came close up to her and stared her in the face, and said suddenly: "Is it in thine heart to flee away from me and leave me?"

A sharp pang of fear shot through Birdalone's heart at that word, and she turned very red, and then pale to the lips, but stammered out: "No, lady, it is not in mine heart."

The dame looked grimly on her and said: "If thou try it and fail, thou shalt rue it once only, to wit, lifelong; and thou canst but fail." She was silent a while, and then spake in a milder voice: "Be content here a while with me, and thereafter thou shalt be more content, and that before long."

She said no more at that time; but her word clave to Birdalone's heart, and for some time thereafter she was sorely oppressed with a burden of fear, and knew not how to hold herself before the witch-wife. But the days wore, and nought betid, and the maiden's heart grew lighter, and still she wrought on at her gown and her smock, and it was well-nigh done. She had broidered the said gown with roses and lilies, and a tall tree springing up from amidmost the hem of

14

the skirt, and a hart on either side thereof, face to face of each other. And the smock she had sewn daintily at the hems and the bosom with fair knots and buds. It was now past the middle of June, hot and bright weather.

CHAPTER VII. BIRDALONE HATH AN ADVENTURE IN THE WOOD.

O N a day she went to the wood, and sat down under her oak-tree, and it was far and far out of sight of anyone standing in the meadow by the lake; and in the wood Birdalone looked to see nought at all save the rabbits and squirrels, who were, forsooth, familiar enough with her, and fearless, so that they would come to her hand and sport with her when she hailed them. Wherefore, as the day was exceeding hot, she put off from her her simple raiment, that she might feel all the pleasure of the cool shadow and what air was stirring, and the kindness of the greensward upon her very body. So she sat sewing, covered but by a lap of the green gown which her needle was painting.

But as she sat there intent on her work, and her head bent over it, and it was now at the point of high noon, she heard as if some creature were going anigh to her; she heeded it not, deeming that it would be but some wandering hind. But even therewith she heard one say her name in a soft voice, and she leapt up trembling, deeming at first that it would be the witch come to fetch her: but yet more scared she was, when she saw standing before her the shape of a young woman as naked as herself, save that she had an oak-wreath round about her loins.

The new-comer, who was now close to her, smiled on her, and said in a kind and sweet voice: "Fear nought, Birdalone, for I deem thou wilt find me a friend, and it is not unlike that thou wilt need one ere long. And furthermore I will say it," said she smiling, "that since I am not afraid of thee,

15

thou needest not be afraid of me." Said Birdalone, she also
smiling: "True it is that thou art nought fearsome to look
on."

The new-comer laughed outright, and said: "Are we not
well met then in the wildwood? and we both as two children
whom the Earth loveth. So play we at a game." "At what
game?" said Birdalone. Spake she of the oak-wreath: "This;
thou shalt tell me what I am like in thine eyes first, because
thou wert afraid of me; and then when thou art done, I will
tell thee what thou seemest to me."

Quoth Birdalone: "For me that will be hard; for I have
nought to liken thee to, whereas save this sight of thee I
have seen nought save her that dwelleth in the House by
the Water, and whom I serve."

"Nay," said the other, "then will I begin, and tell thee
first whatlike thou art, so that thou wilt know the better how
to frame thy word concerning me. But tell me, hast thou
ever seen thyself in a mirror?"

"What thing is that?" said Birdalone. "It is a polished
round of steel or some other white metal," said the wood-
maiden, "which giveth back in all truth the image of whatso
cometh before it."

Said Birdalone, and reddened therewith: "We have at
home a broad latten dish, which it is my work, amongst other
things, to brighten and keep bright; yet may I not make it
so bright that I may see much of mine image therein; and
yet—"

"What wouldst thou?" said the wood-woman. Said Birdalone: "I shall tell thee presently when thy part of the play
is done."

Laughed the new-comer, and said: "It is well; now am I
to be thy mirror. Thus it is with thee: thou standest before
me a tall and slim maiden, somewhat thin, as befitteth thy
seventeen summers; where thy flesh is bare of wont, as thy
throat and thine arms and thy legs from the middle down,
it is tanned a beauteous colour, but otherwhere it is even as
fair a white, wholesome and clean, and as if the golden sun-

16

light, which fulfilleth the promise of the earth, were playing
therein. Fairer and rounder shall be thine arms and thy
shoulders when thou hast seen five more summers, yet scarce
more lovesome, so strong and fine as now they are. Low are
thy breasts, as is meet for so young a maiden, yet is there no
lack in them; nor ever shall they be fairer than now they are.
In goodly fashion sits thine head upon thy shoulders, upheld
by a long and most well-wrought neck, that the sun hath
tanned as aforesaid. The hair of thee is simple brown, yet
somewhat more golden than dark; and ah! now thou lettest
it loose it waveth softly past thy fair smooth forehead and on
to thy shoulders, and is not stayed by thy girdlestead, but
hideth nought of thy knees, and thy legs shapely thin, and
thy strong and clean-wrought ankles and feet, which are with
thee as full of thine heart and thy soul and as wise and deft as
be thy wrists and thine hands, and their very fellows. Now as
to thy face: under that smooth forehead is thy nose, which is
of measure, neither small nor great, straight, and lovely carven at the nostrils: thine eyen are as grey as a hawk's, but
kind and serious, and nothing fierce nor shifting. Nay, now
thou lettest thine eyelids fall, it is as fair with thy face as if they
were open, so smooth and simple are they and with their long
full lashes. But well are thine eyen set in thine head, wide
apart, well opened, and so as none shall say thou mayst not
look in the face of them. Thy cheeks shall one day be a snare
for the unwary, yet are they not fully rounded, as some would
have them; but not I, for most pitiful kind are they forsooth.
Delicate and clear-made is the little trench that goeth from
thy nose to thy lips, and sweet it is, and there is more might
in it than in sweet words spoken. Thy lips, they are of the
finest fashion, yet rather thin than full; and some would not
have it so; but I would, whereas I see therein a sign of thy
valiancy and friendliness. Surely he who did thy carven chin
had a mind to a master-work and did no less. Great was the
deftness of thine imaginer, and he would have all folk that see
thee wonder at thy deep thinking and thy carefulness and thy
kindness. Ah maiden! is it so that thy thoughts are ever deep

and solemn? Yet at least I know it of thee that they be hale
and true and sweet.

"My friend, when thou hast a mirror, some of all this shalt
thou see, but not all; and when thou hast a lover some deal
wilt thou hear, but not all. But now thy she-friend may tell
it thee all, if she have eyes to see it, as have I; whereas no man
could say so much of thee before the mere love should overtake him, and turn his speech into the folly of love and the
madness of desire. So now I have played the play, and told
thee of thee; tell me now of me, and play thy play."

For a while stood Birdalone silent, blushing and confused,
but whiles casting shy glances at her own body, what she
might see of it. At last she spake: "Fair friend, I would do
thy will, but I am not deft of speech; for I speak but little,
save with the fowl and wild things, and they may not learn
me the speech of man. Yet I will say that I wonder to hear
thee call me fair and beauteous; for my dame tells me that
never, nor sayeth aught of my aspect save in her anger, and
then it is: Rag! and Bag-of-bones! and When wilt thou be a
woman, thou lank elf thou?"

The new-comer laughed well-favouredly hereat, and put
forth a hand, and stroked her friend's cheek. Birdalone looked
piteous kind on her and said: "But now I must needs believe
thy words, thou who art so kind to me, and withal thyself so
beauteous. And I will tell thee that it fills my heart with joy
to know that I am fair like to thee. For this moreover I will
tell thee, that I have seen nought in field or woodland that is
as lovely to me as thou art; nay, not the fritillary nodding at
our brook's mouth, nor the willow-boughs waving on Green
Eyot; nor the wild-cat sporting on the little wood-lawn, when
she saw me not; nor the white doe rising up from the grass to
look to her fawn; nor aught that moves and grows. Yet there
is another thing which I must tell thee, to wit, that what thou
hast said about the fashion of any part of me, that same, setting aside thy lovely words, which make the tears come into
the eyes of me, would I say of thee. Look thou! I take thine
hair and lay the tress amongst mine, and thou mayst not tell

18

which is which; and amidst the soft waves of it thy forehead
is nestling smooth as thou saidst of mine: hawk-grey and
wide apart are thine eyen, and deep thought and all tenderness is in them, as of me thou sayest: fine is thy nose and of
due measure; and thy cheeks a little hollow, and somewhat
thin thy lovely lips; and thy round chin so goodly carven, as
it might not be better done. And of thy body else I will say
as thou sayst of mine, though I deem these hands have done
more work than thine. But see thou! thy leg and mine as they
stand together; and thine arm, as if it were of my body. Slim
and slender thou art, or it may be lank; and I deem our Dame
would call thee also bag-of-bones. Now is this strange. Who
art thou? Art thou my very own sister? I would thou wert."

Spake then to Birdalone that image of her, and said, smiling kindly on her: "As to our likeness, thou hast it now; so
alike are we, as if we were cast in one mould. But thy sister
of blood I am not; nay, I will tell thee at once that I am not of
the children of Adam. As to what I am, that is a long story,
and I may not tell it as now; but thou mayst call me Habundia,
as I call thee Birdalone. Now it is true that to everyone I show
not myself in this fair shape of thee; but be not aghast thereat,
or deem me like unto thy mistress herein, for as now I am, so
ever shall I be unto thee."

Quoth Birdalone, looking on her anxiously: "Yea, and I
shall see thee again, shall I not? else should I grieve, and wish
that I had never seen thee at all." "Yea, forsooth," said Habundia, "for I myself were most fain to see thee oft. But now
must thou presently get thee back home, for evil as now is
the mood of thy mistress, and she is rueing the gift of the
green gown, and hath in her mind to seek occasion to chastise
thee."

Now was Birdalone half weeping, as she did on her raiment
while her friend looked on her kindly. She said presently:
"Habundia, thou seest I am hard bestead; give me some
good rede thereto."

"That will I," said the Woodwife. "When thou goest
home to the house, be glad of countenance, and joyous that

thy gown is nigh done; and therewith be exceeding wary. For I deem it most like that she will ask thee what thou hast seen in the wood, and then if thou falter, or thy face change, then she will have an inkling of what hath befallen, to wit, that thou hast seen someone; and then will she be minded to question thy skin. But if thou keep countenance valiantly, then presently will her doubt run off her, and she will cease grudging, and will grow mild with thee and meddle not. This is the first rede, and is for to-day; and now for the second, which is for days yet unborn. Thou hast in thy mind to flee away from her; and even so shalt thou do one day, though it may be by way of Weeping Cross; for she is sly and wise and grim, though sooth it is that she hateth thee not utterly. Now thou must note that nowise she hindereth thee from faring in this wood, and that is because she wotteth, as I do, that by this way there is no outgoing for thee. Wherefore look thou to it that it is by the way of the water that thou shalt fare to the land of men-folk. Belike this may seem marvellous to thee; but so it is; and belike I may tell thee more hereof when time serveth. Now cometh the last word of my rede. Maybe if thou come often to the wood, we shall whiles happen on each other; but if thou have occasion for me, and wouldst see me at once, come hither, and make fire, and burn a hair of my head therein, and I will be with thee: here is for thee a tress of mine hair; now thou art clad, thou mayst take a knife from thy pouch and shear it from off me."

Even so did Birdalone, and set the tress in her pouch; and therewith they kissed and embraced each other, and Birdalone went her ways home to the house, but Habundia went back into the wood as she had come.

CHAPTER VIII. OF BIRDALONE AND THE WITCH-WIFE.

IT went with Birdalone as Habundia had foretold, for she came home to the house glad of semblance, flushed and light-foot, so that she was lovely and graceful beyond her wont. The dame looked on her doubtfully and grimly a while, and then she said: "What ails thee, my servant, that thou lookest so masterful?" "Nought ails me, lady," said Birdalone, "save that I am gay because of the summer season, and chiefly because of thy kindness and thy gift, and that I have well-nigh done my work thereon, and that soon now I shall feel these dainty things beating about my ancles." And she held up and spread abroad the skirt with her two hands, and it was indeed goodly to look on.

The witch-wife snorted scornfully and scowled on her, and said: "Thine ancles forsooth! Bag-o'-bones! thou wisp! forsooth, thou art in love with thy looks, though thou knowest not what-like a fair woman is. Forsooth, I begin to think that thou wilt never grow into a woman at all, but will abide a skinny elf thy life long. Belike I did myself wrong to suffer thee to waste these three or four months of thy thrall's work, since for nought but thrall's work shalt thou ever be meet."

Birdalone hung her head adown, and blushed, but smiled a little, and swayed her body gently, as a willow-bough is swayed when a light air arises in the morning. But the witch stood so scowling on her, and with so sour a look, that Birdalone, glancing at her, found her heart sink so within her, that she scarce kept countenance; yet she lost it not.

Then said the witch sharply: "Wert thou in the wood to-day?" "Yea, lady," said the maiden. Then said the dame fiercely: "And what sawest thou?"

Quoth Birdalone, looking up with an innocent face somewhat scared: "Lady, I saw a bear, one of the big ones, crossing a glade." "And thou without bow and arrow or wood-

PART I
Chap. 8

knife, I warrant me," said the witch. "Thou shalt be whipped, to keep thee in mind that thy life is mine and not thine."

"Nay, nay, I pray thee be not wroth!" said the maid; "he was a long way down the glade, and would not have followed me if he had seen me: there was no peril therein."

Said the witch-wife: "Didst thou see aught else?" "Yea," said Birdalone, and was weeping somewhat now; which forsooth was not hard for her to do, over-wrought as she was betwixt hope and fear: "yea, I saw my white doe and her fawn, and they passed close by me; and two herons flew over my head toward the water; and—"

But the witch turned sharply and said: "Thrall! hast thou seen a woman to-day in the wood?" "A woman?" said Birdalone, "and what woman, my lady?" said Birdalone. "Hath any woman come to the house, and passed forth into the wood?"

The dame looked on her carefully, and remembered how she had faltered and changed countenance that other day, when she had charged her with being minded to flee; and now she saw her with wondering face, and in no wise confused or afraid of guilt, as it seemed; so she believed her tale, and being the more at ease thereby, her wrath ran off her, and she spake altogether pleasantly to Birdalone, and said: "Now I have had my gird at thee, my servant, I must tell thee that in sooth it is not all for nothing that thou hast had these months of rest; for verily thou hast grown more of a woman thereby, and hast sleekened and rounded much. Albeit, the haysel will wait no longer for us, and the day after to-morrow we must fall to on it. But when that is done, thou shalt be free to do thy green gown, or what thou wilt, till wheat harvest is toward; and thereafter we shall see to it. Or what sayest thou?"

Birdalone wondered somewhat at this so gracious word, but not much; for in her heart now was some guile born to meet the witch's guile; so she knelt down and took the dame's hands and kissed them, and said: "I say nought, lady, save that I thank thee over and over again that thou art

22

become so good to me; and that I will full merrily work for
thee in the hay-field, or at whatsoever else thou wilt."

And indeed she was so light-hearted that she had so escaped from the hand of the witch for that time, and above all,
that she had gotten a friend so kind and dear as the wood-
woman, that her heart went out even toward her mistress, so
that she went nigh to loving her.

CHAPTER IX. OF BIRDALONE'S SWIMMING.

FULL fair was the morrow morn, and Birdalone arose
betimes before the sun was up, and she thought she
would make of this a holiday before the swink afield
began again, since the witch was grown good toward her.
So she did on her fair shoes, and her new raiment, though
the green gown was not fully done, and said to herself that
she would consider what she would do with her holiday when
she was amidst of her bathing.

So she went down to the waterside, and when she was
standing knee-deep in the little sandy bight aforesaid, she
looked over to Green Eyot, and was minded to swim over
thither, as oft she did. And it was a windless dawn after a hot
night, and a light mist lay upon the face of the water, and
above it rose the greenery of the eyot.

She pushed off into the deep and swam strongly through
the still water, and the sun rose while she was on the way,
and by then she had laid a hand on the willow-twigs of the
eyot, was sending a long beam across the waters; and her
wet shoulders rose up into the path of it and were turned
into ruddy gold. She hoisted herself up, and climbing the
low bank, was standing amongst the meadow-sweet, and
dripping on to its fragrance. Then she turned about to the
green plain and the house and the hedge of woodland beyond, and sighed, and said softly: "A pity of it, to leave it!
If it were no better otherwhere, and not so fair?"

Then she turned inward to the eyot, which had done her
nought but good and which she loved; and she unbound

her hair, and let it fall till the ends of the tresses mingled with the heads of the meadow-sweet, and thereafter walked quietly up into the grassy middle of the isle.

She was wont to go to a knoll there where the grass was fine, and flowery at this time with white clover and dog-violet, and lie down under the shade of a big thorn with a much-twisted bole: but to-day some thought came across her, and she turned before she came to the thorn, and went straight over the eyot (which was but a furlong over at that place) and down to the southward-looking shore thereof. There she let herself softly down into the water and thrust off without more ado, and swam on and on till she had gone a long way. Then she communed with herself, and found that she was thinking: If I might only swim all the water and be free.

And still she swam on: and now a light wind had been drawn up from the west, and was driving a little ripple athwart the lake, and she swam the swiftlier for it awhile, but then turned over on her back and floated southward still. Till on a sudden, as she lay looking up toward the far-away blue sky, and she so little and low on the face of the waters, and the lake so deep beneath her, and the wind coming ever fresher from the west, and the ripple rising higher against her, a terror fell upon her, and she longed for the green earth and its well-wrought little blossoms and leaves and grass; then she turned over again and swam straight for the eyot, which now was but a little green heap far away before her.

Long she was ere she made land there, and the sun was high in the heavens when she came, all spent and weary, to the shadow of the hawthorn-tree; and she cast herself down there and fell asleep straightway. Forsooth her swim was about as much as she had might for.

When she awoke it lacked but an hour of noontide, and she felt the life in her and was happy, but had no will to rise up for a while; for it was a joy to her to turn her head this way and that to the dear and dainty flowers, that made the

24

wide, grey, empty lake seem so far away, and no more to be
dealt with than the very sky itself.

At last she arose, and when she had plucked and eaten
some handfuls of the strawberries which grew plenteously
on the sweet ground of the eyot, she went down to the land-
ward-looking shore, and took the water, and swam slowly
across the warm ripple till she came once more to the strand
and her raiment. She clad herself, and set her hand to her
pouch and drew forth bread, and sat eating it on the bank
above the smooth sand. Then she looked around, and stood
up with her face toward the house, to see if the dame would
call to her. But she saw the witch come out of the porch and
stand there looking under the sharp of her hand toward her,
and thereafter she went back again into the house without
giving any sign. Wherefore Birdalone deemed that she had
leave that day, and that she might take yet more holiday; so
she stepped lightly down from her place of vantage, turned
her face toward the east, and went quietly along the very lip
of the water.

CHAPTER X. BIRDALONE COMES ON NEW TIDINGS.

SOON she had covered up the house from her, for on
that eastern end, both a tongue of the woodland shoved
out west into the meadow, and, withal, the whole body
of the wood there drew down to the water, and presently
cut off all the greensward save a narrow strip along by the
lake, off the narrowest whereof lay the rocky eyot aforesaid,
nigher unto the shore than lay Green Eyot.

Now never had Birdalone gone so far east as to be over
against Rock Eyot. In her childish days the witch had let her
know that she might go where she would, but therewith had
told her a tale of a huge serpent which dwelt in the dark wood
over against Rock Eyot, whose wont it was to lap his folds
round and round living things that went there, and devour
them; and many an evil dream had that evil serpent brought

25

to Birdalone. In after days belike she scarce trowed in the tale, yet the terror of it abode with her. Moreover the wild-wood toward that side, as it drew toward the water, was dark and dreary and forbidding, running into black thickets standing amidst quagmires, all unlike to the sweet, clean upland ridges, oak-begrown and greenswarded, of the parts which lay toward the north, and which she mostly haunted.

But this summer day, which was so bright and hot, Bird-alone deemed she might harden her heart to try the adven-ture; and she had a mind to enter the wood thereby, and win her way up into the oakland whereas she had met Habundia, and perchance she might happen on her; for she would not dare to summon her so soon after their first meeting. And if she met her, there would be the holiday worthily brought to an end!

On went Birdalone, and was soon at the narrowest of the greensward, and had the wood black on her left hand, for the trees of it were mostly alder. But when she was come just over against Rock Eyot, she found a straight creek or inlet of the water across her way; and the said creek ran right up into the alder thicket; and, indeed, was much overhung by huge ancient alders, gnarled, riven, mossy, and falling low over the water. But close on the mouth of the creek, on Bird-alone's side thereof, lay a thing floating on the dull water, which she knew not how to call a boat, for such had she never seen, nor heard of, but which was indeed a boat, oarless and sailless.

She looked on it all about, and wondered; yet she saw at once that it was for wending the water, and she thought, might she but have a long pole, she might push it about the shallow parts of the lake, and belike take much fish. She tried to shove it somewhat toward the lake, but with her little might could make nothing of the work; for the craft was heavy, like a barge, if there were nothing else that withstood her.

About this new thing she hung a long while, wondering that she had never heard thereof, or been set to toil there-

26

with. She noted that it was mostly pale grey of hue, as if it
had been bleached by sun and water, but at the stem and
stern were smears of darker colour, as though someone had
been trying the tints of staining there.

Now so much did this new matter take up all her mind,
that she thought no more of going up into the wood; but
though she had fain abided there long to see whatever might
be seen, she deemed it would go ill with her did the witch
happen on her there; wherefore she turned about, and went
back the way she had come, going very slowly and pondering
the tidings. And ever she called to mind what Habundia had
said to her, that it was by water she must flee, and wondered
if she had sent her this thing that she might escape therein;
so different as her going would be thereby to swimming the
lake with her wet body. Then again she thought, that before
she might let herself hope this, it were best, if she might, to
find out from the witch what was the thing, and if she knew
thereof. Yet at last she called to mind how little patient of
questions was her mistress, and that if she were unheedful
she might come to raise an evil storm about her. Wherefore
she took this rede at the last, that she would keep all hidden
in her own breast till she should see Habundia again; and
meanwhile she might steal down thither from time to time
to see if the thing still abode there; which she might the
easier do by swimming if she chose her time heedfully, and
go thither from Rock Eyot, which now and again she visited.

CHAPTER XI. OF BIRDALONE'S GUILT AND THE CHASTISEMENT THEREOF.

BY this she was come back to the sandy bight, and the
sun was westering; and she looked up toward the house
and saw that it was the time of their evening meal, for
the blue smoke of the cooking-fire was going up into the air.
So she went thither speedily, and entered gay of seeming.
The witch looked on her doubtfully, but presently fell to
speaking with her graciously as yesterday, and Birdalone was

27

glad and easy of mind, and went about the serving of her; for
always she ate after the dame; and the mistress asked her of
many matters concerning the house, and the gathering of
stuff.

So came the talk on the fishing of the brook that ran before
their door, and how the trouts therein were but little, and not
seldom none at all; and even therewith came these words into
Birdalone's mouth, she scarce knew how: "My lady, why do
we not fish the lake, whereas there be shoal places betwixt us
and the eyots where lie many and great fish, as I have seen
when I have been swimming thereover? And now in that
same creek whereas the serpent used to lurk when I was little, we have a thing come, which is made to swim on the water;
and I, could I have a long pole to shove withal—"

But no time she had to make an end, ere the witch-wife
sprang up and turned on her with a snarl as of an evil dog,
and her face changed horribly: her teeth showed grinning,
her eyes goggled in her head, her brow was all to-furrowed,
and her hands clenched like iron springs.

Birdalone shuddered back from her and cringed in mere
terror, but had no might to cry out. The witch hauled her up
by the hair, and dragged her head back so that her throat lay
bare before her all along. Then drew the witch a sharp knife
from her girdle, and raised her hand over her, growling and
snarling like a wolf. But suddenly she dropped the knife, her
hand fell to her side, and she fell in a heap on the floor and lay
there hushed.

Birdalone stood gazing on her, and trembling in every
limb; too confused was she to think or do aught, though some
image of flight through the open door passed before her: but
her feet seemed of lead, and, as in an evil dream, she had no
might to move her limbs, and the minutes went by as she
stood there half dead with fear.

At last, (and belike it was no long while) the witch-wife
came to herself again, and sat up on the floor, and looked all
about the chamber, and when her eyes fell upon Birdalone,
she said in a weak voice, yet joyfully: "Hah! thou art there

28

still, my good servant!" Then she said: "A sickness fell upon
me suddenly, as whiles it is wont; but now am I myself again,
and presently I have a word for thee."

Therewith she rose up slowly, Birdalone helping her, and
sat in her big chair silent a while, and then she spake: "My
servant, thou hast for the more part served me well: but this
time thou hast done ill, whereas thou hast been spying on my
ways; whereof may come heavy trouble but if we look to it.
Well is it for thee that thou hast none unto whom thou mightest babble; for then must I needs have slain thee here and
now. But for this first time I pardon thee, and thou hast escaped the wrath."

Her voice was soft and wheedling; but for Birdalone the
terror had entered into her soul, and yet abode with her.

The witch-wife sat a while, and then arose and went about
the chamber, and came to a certain aumbrye and opened it,
and drew forth a little flasket of lead and a golden cup scored
over with strange signs, and laid them on the board beside
her chair, wherein she now sat down again, and spake once
more, still in the same soft and wheedling voice: "Yet,
my servant, thy guilt would be required of me, if I let this
pass as if to-day were the same as yesterday; yea, and of thee
also would it be required; therefore it is a part of the pardon
that thou be corrected: and the correction must be terrible
to thee, that thou mayst remember never again to thrust
thyself into the jaws of death. And what may I do to correct
thee? It shall be in a strange way, such as thou hast never
dreamed of. Yet the anguish thereof shall go to thine heart's
root; but this must thou needs bear, for my good and thine,
so that both we may live and be merry hereafter. Go now,
fill this cup with water from the spring and come back with
it." Birdalone took the cup with a sinking heart, and filled it,
and brought it back, and stood before the witch more dead
than alive.

Then the witch-wife took up the flasket and pulled out
the stopple and betook it to Birdalone, and said: "Drink of
this now, a little sip, no more." And the maiden did so, and

29

the liquor was no sooner down her gullet than the witch-wife and the chamber, and all things about her, became somewhat dim to her; but yet not so much so as that she could not see them. But when she stretched out her arm she could see it not at all, nor her limbs nor any other part of her which her eyes might fall upon. Then would she have uttered a lamentable wail, but the voice was sealed up in her and no sound came from her voice. Then she heard the witch-wife how she said (and yet she heard it as if her voice came from afar), "Nay, thou canst not speak, and thou canst not see thyself, nor may any other, save me, and I but dimly. But this is but part of what I must lay upon thee; for next I must give thee a new shape, and that both thyself and all other may see. But, before I do that, I must speak a word to thee, which thy new shape would not suffer the sense thereof to reach to thine heart. Hearken!"

CHAPTER XII. THE WORDS OF THE WITCH-WIFE TO BIRDALONE.

SAID the witch-wife: "When thou comest to thyself (for it is not my will that thou shouldest never have thine own shape again), doubtless the first thing which thou shalt do with thy new-gained voice and thy new-gained wit shall be to curse me, and curse me again. Do as thou wilt herein; but I charge thee, disobey me not, for that shall bring thee to thy bane. For if thou do not my bidding, and if thou pry into my matters, and lay bare that which I will have hidden, then will it be imputed unto thee for guilt, and will I, will I not, I must be avenged on thee even to slaying: and then is undone all the toil and pain I have had in rearing thee into a deft and lovely maiden. Deem thou, then, this present anguish kind to thee, to keep thee that thou come not to nought.

"Now since I have begun speaking, I will go on; for little heretofore have I spoken to thee what was in mine heart. Well I wot that thou thinkest of me but as of an evil dream, whereof none can aught but long to awake from it. Yet I would have thee look to this at least; that I took thee from poverty and pinching, and have reared thee as faithfully as ever mother did to child; clemming thee never, smiting thee not so oft, and but seldom cruelly. Moreover, I have suffered thee to go whereso thou wouldest, and have compelled thee to toil for nought but what was needful for our two livelihoods. And I have not stayed thy swimmings in the lake, nor thy wanderings in the wood, and thou hast learned bow-shot there, till thou art now a past-master in the craft: and moreover thou art swift-foot as the best of the deer, and mayest over-run any one of them whom thou wilt.

"Soothly a merry life hast thou had as a child, and merry now would be thy life, save for thine hatred of me. Into a lovely lily-lass hast thou grown. That I tell thee now, though my wont has been to gird at thee for the fashion of thy body; that was but the word of the mistress to the thrall. And now what awaiteth thee? For thou mayst say: I am lonely here, and there is no man to look on me. Of what avail, therefore, is my goodliness and shapeliness? Child, I answer thee that the time is coming when thou shalt see here a many of the fairest of men, and then shalt thou be rather rose than lily, and fully come to womanhood; and all those shall love and worship thee, and thou mayst gladden whom thou wilt, and whom thou wilt mayst sadden; and no lack soever shalt thou have of the sweetness of love, or the glory of dominion.

"Think of it then! All this is for thee if thou dwell here quietly with me, doing my will till thy womanhood hath blossomed. Wherefore I beseech and pray thee put out of thy mind the thought of fleeing from me. For if thou try it, one of two things shall be: either I shall bring thee back and slay thee, or make thee live in misery of torment; or else thou wilt escape, and then what will it be? Dost thou know how it shall go with thee, coming poor and nameless, an outcast, into the world of men? Lust shalt thou draw unto thee, but scarce love. I say an outcast shalt thou be, without worship or dominion; thy body shall be a prey to ribalds, and when

31

the fine flower thereof hath faded, thou shalt find that the words of thy lovers were but mockery, that no man shall love thee, and no woman aid thee. Then shall Eld come to thee and find thee at home with Hell; and Death shall come and mock thee for thy life cast away for nought—for nought. This is my word to thee: and now I have nought to do to thee save to change thee thy skin, and therein must thou do as thou canst, but it shall be no ugly or evil shape at least. But another time maybe I shall not be so kind as to give thee a new shape, but shall let thee wander about seen by none but me."

Then she took the cup and took water in the hollow of her hand and cast it into Birdalone's face, and muttered words withal; and presently she saw herself indeed, that she was become a milk-white hind; and she heard and saw again, but not as she, the maiden, was wont to hear and see; for both her hearing and seeing and her thought was of a beast and not of a maiden.

Said the witch-wife: "It is done now, till I give thee grace again; and now be off into the field; but if thou stray more than half a bowshot from the brook, it shall be the worse for thee."

And now the day was done and night was come.

CHAPTER XIII. BIRDALONE MEETETH THE WOODWOMAN AGAIN.

IT was fifteen days thereafter that Birdalone awoke lying in her bed on a bright morning, as if all this had been but a dream. But the witch-wife was standing over her and crying out: "Thou art late, slug-a-bed, this fair-weather day, and the grass all spoiling for lack of the scythe. Off! and down to the meadow with thee."

Birdalone waited not for more words, but sprang out of bed, and had her work-a-day raiment on in a twinkling, and stayed but to wash her in a pool of the brook, and then was amidst the tall grass with the swathe falling before her. As

she worked she thought, and could scarce tell whether joy at
her present deliverance, or terror of the witch-wife, were the
greatest. Sore was her longing to go see her friend in the
wood, but the haysel lasted more than a week, and when that
was done, whether it were of set purpose or no, the dame
forgat her other promise, to give Birdalone more holiday,
and kept her close to her work about meadow and acre.
Otherwise her mistress nowise mishandled or threatened
her, though she had gone back to the surliness and railing
which was her wont. At last, on a morning when the dame
had bidden her to nought of work, Birdalone took her bow
in her hand and cast her quiver on her back, and went her
ways into the wood, and forgat not the tress of Habundia's
hair; but she had no need to use it, for when she was come to
the Oak of Tryst, straightway came Habundia forth from
the thicket, and now so like to Birdalone that it was a wonder,
for as her friend she bare bow and quiver, and green gown
trussed up till her knees were naked.

So they kissed and embraced, and Birdalone wept upon
her friend's bosom, but was ashamed of the words which
would have told her of her case. Then Habundia set her
down upon the greensward, and sat down beside her, and
caressed her and soothed her; then she smiled on Birdalone,
and said: "Thy tale is partly told without words, and I
would weep for thee if I might shed tears. But thou mayest
tell me wherefore thou didst suffer this; though forsooth I
have an inkling thereof. Hast thou happened on the witch's
ferry?"

"Even so it was, sister," quoth Birdalone. And therewith
she plucked up heart, and told her all the tale of the vanishing
of her body and the skin-changing. And Habundia answered:
"Well then, there is this to be said, that sooner or later this
must have happened, for thereby lieth thy road of escape;
wherefore it is better sooner than later. But tell me again:
was she fierce and rough in words with thee? for what she
said to thee thou hast not yet told me."

Said Birdalone: "In her first fury, when she was like to have slain me, she had no words, nought but wolfish cries. But thereafter she spake unto me strangely, yet neither fiercely nor roughly; nay, it seemed to me as if almost she loved me. And more than almost she besought me rather than commanded me not to flee from her." "And wert thou beguiled by her soft speech?" said Habundia. "Nowise to cast aside my hope of escape, nay, not even in that hour," said Birdalone; "but amidst all the confusion and terror somewhat was I moved to compassion on her."

Spake Habundia, looking anxiously on her: "Dost thou deem that thou art somewhat cowed by what she hath done to thee?" Said Birdalone, and flushed very red: "Oh no, no! Nought save death or bonds shall come betwixt me and my utmost striving for escape." "That is better than well," said Habundia; "but again, canst thou have patience a little, and be wary and wise the while?" "So meseemeth," said the maiden.

Said Habundia: "Again it is well. Now is the summer beginning to wane, and by my rede thou shalt not try the flight until May is come again and well-nigh worn into June; for thou wilt be bigger then, little sister, and tidings are waxing that shall get matters ready for thy departure: moreover, thou must yet learn what thou hast to do meanwhile, and thereof shall I tell thee somewhat as now. For that boat, the thing which thou didst find, and for which thou didst suffer, is called the Sending Boat, and therein thy mistress fareth time and again, I deem to seek to some other of her kind, but I know not unto whom, or whereto. Hast thou noted of her that whiles she goeth away privily by night and cloud?"

"Yea, verily," said Birdalone, "and this is one of the things which heretofore hath made me most afraid."

Said Habundia: "Well now, that she wendeth somewhither in this ferry I wot; but as I wot not whither, so also I know not what she doth with the Sending Boat to make it obey her; whereas, though I know all things of the wood, I

34

know but little of the lake. Wherefore, though there be peril
to thee therein, follow her twice or thrice when she riseth up
for this faring, and note closely what is her manner of dealing
with the said Sending Boat, so that thou mayst do in like
wise. Wilt thou risk the smart and the skin-changing, or
even if it were the stroke of the knife, to gather this wisdom?
And thereafter thou shalt come hither and tell me how thou
hast sped."

"With a good heart will I, dear sister," said Birdalone.

Then Habundia kissed her and said: "It is a joy to me to
see thee so valiant, but herein may I help thee somewhat;
here is a gold finger-ring, see thou! fashioned as a serpent
holding his tail in his mouth; whenso thou goest on this
quest, set thou this same ring on the middle finger of thy left
hand, and say thou above thy breath at least:

> To left and right,
> Before, behind,
> Of me be sight
> As of the wind!

And nought then shall be seen of thee even by one who
standeth close beside. But wear not the ring openly save at
such times, or let the witch have sight thereof ever, or she
will know that thou hast met me. Dost thou understand, and
canst thou remember?"

Laughed Birdalone, and took the ring and set it on her
finger, and spake aloud even as Habundia had given her the
words. Then quoth Habundia, laughing: "Now have I lost
my friend and sister, for thou art gone, Birdalone. Take off
the ring, sweetling, and get thee to thine hunting, for if thou
come home empty-handed there will be flyting awaiting
thee, or worse."

So Birdalone took off the ring and came back to sight
again laughing; then the wood-woman kissed her and turned
her heels to her, and was gone; but Birdalone strung her
bow, and got to her wood-craft, and presently had a brace of

hares, wherewith she went back home to the dame; who indeed girded at her for her sloth, and her little catch in so long a while; but there it ended.

CHAPTER XIV. OF BIRDALONE'S FISHING.

NOW were the days wearing toward wheat-harvest, and nought befel to tell of, save that on a morn the witch-wife called Birdalone to her, and said: "Now is little to be done till the wheat is ready for the hook, and thy days are idle; or what is that word that fell from thee that other day, that there be good swims for fish about the eyots? Canst thou swim across bearing thine angle, and back again therewith, and thy catch withal?"

"Yea certes," said Birdalone gaily; "with one hand I may swim gallantly, or with my legs alone, if I stir mine arms ever so little. I will go straightway if thou wilt, lady; but give me a length of twine so that I may tie my catch about my middle when I swim back again."

Therewith she went forth lightly to fetch her angle, which was in a shed without; but just as she took it in her hand, a sudden thought came to her, so wary as she was grown. She undid the bosom of her gown, and took forth her serpent-ring; for she bore it next to her skin, made fast to the bosom of her smock; but now she hid it carefully in the thickest of her brow-hair, which was very thick and soft. Withal the tress of Habundia's hair she bore ever mingled with her own.

No sooner had she done it, but she was glad; for she heard the dame calling her, who, when she came to the house-door, spake and said: "Now shall I fare with thee down to the water, and look to thy garments lest they be fouled by some straying beast." And therewith she looked curiously on Birdalone, and knit her brows when she saw that the maiden changed countenance in nowise.

Down to the water went they, and the witch sat down close to where Birdalone should take the water, and watched

36

her do off her raiment, and eyed her keenly when she was
bare, but said nought. Birdalone turned her head as she
stood knee-deep, and said: "How long shall I abide, lady, if
I have luck?" "As long as thou wilt," said the dame: "most
like I shall be gone by then thou comest back, even if thou
be away no long while."

Fell Birdalone to swimming then, and when she was
more than half over, the witch, stirring no more than need
was, got hold of her raiment, which was but the old grey
coat over a smock, and ransacked it, but found nought, as
well ye may wot. And when she had done, she sat down again
in heavy mood as it seemed, and watched Birdalone swimming, and when she beheld her body come forth out of the
water, and pass out of sight amongst the flowers of the eyot,
she arose and went her ways home.

Birdalone looked through the willow-boughs, and saw
her turn away; then she fared to her fishing with a smile,
and soon had plenteous catch from under the willow-boughs.
Then, whereas the day was very calm and fair, and the dame
had given her holiday, she wandered about the eyot, and
most in a little wood of berry-trees, as quicken and whitebeam and dog-wood, and sported with the birds, who feared
her not, but came and sat on her shoulders, and crept about
her feet. She went also and stood a while on the southern
shore, and looked on the wide water dim in the offing under
the hot-weather haze, and longed to be gone beyond it.
Then she turned away, and to the other shore, and gat her
fish and strung them on the string, and made them fast to
her middle, and so took the water back again to the yellow
strand, where now was no one awaiting her. But before she
did on her garments, she looked on them, and saw that they
lay not as she had left them, whereby she knew well that the
witch-wife had handled them.

Amidst all this the day was wearing to an end, and again
she saw the smoke of the cooking-fire going up into the air
from the chimney of the house; and she smiled ruefully,
thinking that the witch might yet find an occasion for ran-

37

sacking her raiment. But she plucked up heart, and came home with her catch, and the dame met her with a glum face, and neither praised her nor blamed her, but took the fish silently. Such ending had that day.

CHAPTER XV. BIRDALONE WEARETH HER SERPENT-RING.

AFTER this she went once and again fishing on to Green Eyot by the bidding of the dame, who went not again to the shore with her. These times she had half a mind to go see the Sending Boat, but durst not, lest the thing itself might have life enough to tell of her.

And now was come the time of wheat-harvest, and Birdalone must wear her days swinking in the acre-land, clad but in smock and shoes; and the toil was hard, and browned her skin and hardened her hands, but it irked her not, for the witch let her work all alone, and it was holiday unto the maiden if her mistress were not anigh, despite those words which had somewhat touched her heart that other day.

But when wheat-getting was done, there was again rest for her body, and swimming withal and fishing from the eyot by the witch's leave. And again by her own leave she went to seek Habundia in the wood, and spent a happy hour with her, and came back with a fawn which she had shot, and so but barely saved her skin from the twig-shower. Then yet again she went into the wood on the witch's errand as well as her own, and was paid by her friend's sweet converse, and by nought else save the grudging girding of her mistress.

But on a night when September was well in, and the sky was moonless and overcast, somewhat before midnight the dame came and hung over Birdalone as she lay abed, and watched to see if she waked; forsooth the witch's coming had waked her; but even so she was wary, and lay still, nor changed her breathing. So the witch turned away, but even therewith Birdalone made a shift to get a glimpse of her, and this she saw thereby, that the semblance of her was changed,

38

and that she bore the self-same skin wherewith she had come
to Utterhay, and which she had worn twice or thrice afterwards when she had an errand thither.

The witch now glided swiftly to the door, and out into the
night. Birdalone lay still a little, lest she should fall into
a trap, and then arose very quietly and did on her smock,
which lay ever under her pillow with the ring sewn thereto
again, and so went out adoors also, and deemed she saw the
witch some way on ahead; but it was nothing for her light
feet to overtake her. So she stayed to take the ring from her
smock, and set it on her finger; then in a low voice she said:

> To left and right,
> Before, behind,
> Of me be sight
> As of the wind!

Then boldly she sped on, and was soon close on the heels of
the witch, who made her way to the edge of the lake, and
then turned east, and went even as Birdalone had gone when
she came across the Sending Boat.

So fared the witch-wife straight to the creek-side, and
Birdalone must needs stick close to her, or she had known
nought, so black was the night amongst the alder-boughs.
But the witch-wife fumbled about a while when she was
stayed by the creek, and presently drew somewhat from
under her cloak, and the maiden saw that she was about
striking flint upon steel, and quaked somewhat, lest her
charm had played her false. Presently the tinder quickened,
and the dame had lighted a lantern, which she held up,
peering all about; and full she looked on the place whereas
was Birdalone, and made no show of seeing her, though
well-nigh the maiden looked for it to see her drop the lantern
and spring on her.

Now the witch, holding the lantern aloft, steps over the
gunwale of the boat, and sits down on the thwart; and it was
a near thing but that Birdalone followed her into the boat,
but she feared the getting forth again, so she but hung over

39

it as close as she might. Then she saw the witch draw out of
her girdle that sharp little knife which Birdalone had seen
raised against her own throat; and then the witch bared her
arm, and pricked it till the blood sprang from that barren
white skin. Thereat she stood up, and went to the bows of
the craft and hung over them, and drew her arm to and fro
over the stem to bloody it; and went thereafter to the stern,
and took blood into her right hand and passed it over the
place of the steerage (for there was no rudder), and came
back and sat down on the thwart again; and, so far as Birdalone might see, busied herself in staunching the little wound
on her arm. Then deemed Birdalone that she knew what
manner of paint was that which had made the rusty smears
which she had seen on the boat by daylight.

But now as the witch sat there, a harsh voice began to stir
in her throat, and then words came out of her, and she sang
in a crow's croak:

> The red raven-wine now
> Hast thou drunk, stern and bow;
> Then wake and awake!
> And the wonted way take:
> The way of the Wender forth over the flood,
> For the will of the Sender is blent with the blood.

Therewithal began the boat to stir, and anon it glided
forth out of the creek into the waters of the lake, and the
light of the lantern died, and it was but a minute ere Birdalone lost all sight of it. She abode a little longer, lest perchance boat and witch might come back on her hands, and
then turned and went swiftly back again. She would have
drawn off her ring straightway, but the thought came on
her, that she had seen the witch depart in her second semblance; how if she were abiding her at home in her wonted
skin? So she came to the house even as she was, and opened
the door, and looked in, quaking; but there was no image of

40

a child of Adam therein, and no living thing, save the cat drowsing before the fire; wherefore Birdalone took the ring from her finger and went to the hearth, and stirred up the cat with her foot till he arose and fell to rubbing himself against her legs, and she was fain of him.

Thereafter she made her ring fast to her smock again, and set the smock under her pillow as her wont was, and betook herself to bed, and fell asleep sweetly, leaving all troublous thoughts for the morrow; and that the more as she was free of the witch-wife for that night at least.

CHAPTER XVI. BIRDALONE MEETETH HABUNDIA AGAIN; AND LEARNETH HER FIRST WISDOM OF HER.

WHEN morning was, Birdalone arose, and longed sore to go into the wood to seek Habundia again, but durst not, lest the witch-wife should come to hand again earlier than might be looked for. So she abode quiet and did what was toward near about the house. All that day the witch came not back, nor the next; but the morrow thereafter, when Birdalone arose, she found the wonted aspect of her mistress in the wonted place, who, when she saw the maiden, greeted her, and was somewhat blithe with her; and Birdalone would have asked her leave to go to the wood, but she trusted little in her unwonted soft mood; which yet lasted so long that on the third day she herself bade Birdalone go take her pleasure in the wood, and bear back with her what of venison she might.

Forthwith went Birdalone as glad as might be, and met her friend at the Oak of Tryst, and told her closely how all had betid; and Habundia said: "Here, then, thou hast learned how to sail the lake. But hast thou learned enough to try the adventure and not to fail?" "Even so I deem," said Birdalone; "but this I would say, that meseemeth it better that I follow the witch down to the boat one more time at least;

41

for this first time it was dark; and moreover shall I not be surer of the spell if I hear it said oftener, lest it be not ever the same words? What sayest thou?"

She said: "Thou art right herein, and since the adventure may not be tried till next June is at hand, there is time enough and to spare. And now for this hour that is we need talk no more of it. Only, my sweet, I beseech thee be wary; and above all suffer not the witch-wife to set eye or hand on the ring. Truly mine heart oft aches sorely for thy peril; for therein the image of thee abideth rather as of my daughter than my friend. Yea, now thou laughest, but kindly, so that the sound of thy laughter is as sweet music. But know that though thou art but a young maiden, and I in all wise like unto thee of aspect, yet have I dwelt many and many a year upon the earth, and much wisdom have learned. Trowest thou me?"

"Yea, yea," said Birdalone, "with all my heart." Then she hung her head a while and kept silence, and thereafter looked up and spake: "I would ask thee a thing and crave somewhat of thee, as if thou wert verily my mother; wilt thou grant it me?" "Yea, surely, child," said Habundia. Said Birdalone: "This it is then, that thou wilt learn me of thy wisdom." Habundia smiled full kindly on her, and said: "This of all things I would have had thee ask; and this day and now shall we begin to open the book of the earth before thee. For therein is mine heritage and my dominion. Sit by me, child, and hearken!"

So the maiden sat down by her likeness under the oak, and began to learn her lesson. Forsooth forgotten is the wisdom, though the tale of its learning abideth, wherefore nought may we tell thereof.

When it was done, Birdalone kissed her Woodmother and said: "This is now the best day of my life, this and the day when first I saw thee. I will come hither now many times before the day of my departure." "Yea, but, sweet child," said Habundia, "beware of the witch and her cruelty; I fear me she shall yet be grim toward thee." "So will I be wary," said Birdalone, "but I will venture some little peril of pain but if thou forbid me, mother. And I pray thee by thy love to forbid me not. And this I pray thee the more, because after one of these grim times then mostly doth she meddle the less with me for a while, wherefore I shall be the freer to come hither."

Habundia kissed her and embraced her, and said: "Valiant art thou for a young maiden, my child, and I would not refrain thee more than a father would refrain his young son from the strokes of the tilt-yard. But I pray thee to forget not my love, and my sorrow for thy grief."

Therewith they sundered, and it was drawing toward evening. Birdalone sought catch, and brought home venison to the dame, who was yet blithe with her, and spake that evening as she eyed her: "I cannot tell how it is, but thou seemest changed unto me, and lookest more towards thy womanhood than even yesterday. I mean the face of thee, for wert thou stripped, lean enough I should see thee, doubtless. But now look to it, I beseech thee, to be both deft and obedient, so that I may be as kind to thee as I would be, and kinder than I have been heretofore."

CHAPTER XVII. THE PASSING OF THE YEAR INTO WINTER.

WORE the days now, till on a night of October, toward the end thereof, the witch went a-night-tide to the Sending Boat, and Birdalone followed her as erst. This time the night was wild and windy, but the moon was high aloft and big, and all cloud save a few flecks was blown from off the heavens; so that the night was as light as could be; and even at the tree-hung creek it was easy to see all that was done. And so it was that the witch did and spake in all wise as she did before.

Another time, when November was well-nigh out, the dame arose for her lake-faring; but this night the snow lay deep betwixt house and water, and Birdalone thought that

43

it would scarce do to follow. Forsooth she knew not whether
her feet would the less leave their print in the snow because
they were not to be seen. When she asked Habundia thereof,
she laughed and said: "Once more thou hast been wise, my
child, for though it had been no harder to put this might into thy ring, that whoso wore it should not touch the ground,
yet it hath not been done."

It must be told, that in this while Birdalone went oft to
the Trysting Tree, and called on her mother (as now she
called her) to come to her, and ever more and more of wisdom
she won thereby. Though the witch was oft surly with her,
and spared not her girding, yet, the needful work done, she
meddled little with her. But on a day she straightly banned
her the wood, and Birdalone went notwithstanding, and
when she was there with the woodmother nought she told
her thereof, but was blithe and merry beyond her wont. She
came back home thereafter empty-handed, and stepped into
the chamber proudly and with bright eyes and flushed
cheeks, though she looked for nought save chastisement;
yea, it might be even the skin-changing. Forsooth the witch
was sitting crouched in her chair with her hands on the
elbows and her head thrust forward, like a wild beast at point
to spring; but when her eye fell on Birdalone, she faltered
and drew back into herself again, and muttered somewhat
unheard; but to Birdalone spake nought of good or bad.

Now was winter-tide upon them, when there was nought
to do in field and acre, and but a little in the byre. In years
bygone, and even in the last one, the witch had not spared
Birdalone toil any the more, but had made errands for her
amidst the snow and biting winds, or over the lake when it
was laid with ice. But now she bade her to nought save what
she had a will to; whereby she lost but little, whereas Birdalone was well willing to strive against wind and weather
and the roughness of the winter earth, and overcome if she
might, so that all were well done that had to be done about
the stead.

Still did the witch give her hard words and rail at her for

44

the most part, but from the teeth outward only, and because
she was wont thereto. Inwardly indeed she began to fear
Birdalone, and deemed that she would one day have the
mastery; and this led her into fierce and restless moods; so
that she would sit staring at the maiden's beauty handling
her knife withal, and scarce able to forbear her. And in such a
mood she once made occasion to chastise her as her wont had
been erst, and looked to see Birdalone rebel against her; but
it fell out otherwise, for Birdalone submitted herself to her
meekly and with a cheerful countenance. And this also was a
terror to the witch, who deemed, as indeed it was, that the
purpose was growing in her thrall. So from that time she
meddled with her no more. All this while, as may be thought,
Birdalone went yet oftener to the Oak of Tryst, despite
frost and snow and wind, and gat much lore of her Woodmother, and learned wisdom abundantly. And her days were
happy.

CHAPTER XVIII. OF SPRING-TIDE AND THE MIND OF BIRDALONE.

NOW was the winter gone and the spring-tide come
again, and with the blossoming of the earth blossomed Birdalone also. Nought sweeter of flesh might
she be than erst, but there was now a new majesty grown into her beauty; her limbs were rounded, her body fulfilled,
her skin sleeked and whitened; and if any mother's son had
beheld her feet as they trod the meadow besprinkled with
saffron and daffodil, ill had it gone with him were he gainsaid the kisses of them, though for the kissing had he fared
the worse belike.

That spring-tide, amidst of April, she followed the witch-
wife down to the Sending Boat for the third time; and there
went everything as erst, and she deemed now that the lesson
was well learned, and that she was well-nigh as wise as the
witch herself therein.

But the day after she went about somewhat pensive, as

though a troublous thought were on her; and when, three days thereafter, she met the Woodmother, she spake to her even as they parted, and said: "Mother, much wisdom hast thou learned me, and now this at the last withal, that hitherto there has been shame in my life; and now fain were I to be done with it." "Fair child," said Habundia, "little is the shame though this woman hath had the upper hand of thee and hath used thee cruelly: how mightest thou, a child, strive with her? But now I see and know that there is an end of that; that she feareth thee now, and will never again raise a hand against thee save thou fall wholly into her power; as thou shalt not, my child. Be comforted then for what is gone by!"

"Nay, mother," said Birdalone, "it is not that which troubleth me; for, as thou sayest, what else might I do? But thy wisdom which thou hast set in my heart hath learned me that for these last months I have been meeting guile with guile and lies with lies. And now will I do so no more, lest I become a guileful woman, with nought good in me save the fairness of my body. Wherefore hearken, sweet mother! What is done, is done; but when it cometh to the day, which is speedily drawing nigh, that I must part from thee, it may be for a long while, then will I not fare to the Sending Boat by night and cloud and with hidden head, but will walk thither in broad day, and let that befall which must befall."

Changed then Habundia's face and became haggard and woeful, and she cried out: "O if I could but weep, as ye children of Adam! O my grief and sorrow! Child, child! then will betide that falling into her hands which I spake of e'en now; and then shall this wretch, this servant of evil, assuredly slay thee there and then, or will keep thee to torment thee till thy life be but a slow death. Nay, nay, do as I should do, and fare with hidden head, and my ring on thy finger. Or else, O child, how wilt thou hurt me!"

Birdalone wept; but presently she fell to caressing the mother's hand, and said: "This is thy doing, wherein thou hast made me wise. Yet fear not: for I deem that the witch-wife will not slay me, whereas she looketh to have some gain

46

of me; moreover, in the evil of her heart is mingled some
love toward me, whereof, as erst I told thee, I have a morsel
of compassion. Mother, she will not slay me; and I say that
she shall not torment me, for I will compel her to slay me
else. It is my mind that she will let me go." Said the mother:
" Yea, mayhappen, yet but as a bird with a string to its leg."
"If it be so," said Birdalone, "then let my luck prevail
over her guile; as well it may be, since I have known thee, O
wise mother!"

The Woodwife hung her head and spake nought for a
while; then she said: "I see that thou wilt have it so, and
that there is something in thine heart which we, who are not
children of Adam, may not understand; yet once wert thou
more like unto us. Now all I may say is, that thou must rule
in this matter, and that I am sad."

Then she looked down again and presently raised a
brighter face, and said: "Belike all shall be better than I
thought." Then she kissed Birdalone and they parted for
that time.

CHAPTER XIX. THEY BID FAREWELL, BIRD-ALONE AND THE WOODMOTHER.

NOW April was gone, and May was come with the
thorn a-blossoming, and there was Birdalone waxing
still in loveliness. And now the witch had left all
girding at her even, and spake to her but little, save when
she needs must. But to Birdalone it seemed that she watched
her exceeding closely.

Birdalone went oft to the wood, and learned yet more of
lore: but of the matter of the Departure, how it was to be
gone about they spake no more, and great was the love betwixt them.

At last when May was worn nigh to June came Birdalone
to the Oak of Tryst, and found the Woodmother there; and
when they had talked a while, but ever from the teeth out,
spake Habundia: "Though thou be now the wiser of us

two maybe, yet have I wisdom to wot that this is the hour of
our sundering, and that to-morrow thou wilt try the adventure of the Sending Boat: is it not so?" "Yea, mother," said
Birdalone; "I bid thee farewell now: woe is me therefor!"
Said Habundia: "And thou wilt deliver thyself into the
hands of the witch, wilt thou, as thou saidst that other day?"
Quoth Birdalone: "Is it not wisdom, dear mother, if I trust
in my goodhap?" "Alas," said the Mother, "it may be so
when all is said. But O my sad heart! and how I fear for
thee!"

"My mother, my mother!" said Birdalone, "that I should
make the days grievous unto thee! and thou who hast made
my days so joyous! But now canst thou not say of thy wisdom
that we shall meet again?"

The Woodwoman sat down, and let her head fall over her
knees, and was silent a long while; then she rose up and stood
before Birdalone, and said: "Yea, we shall meet again, howsoever it may be. Let us depart with that sweet word in the
air between us. Yet first thou shalt give me a tress of thine
hair, as I did to thee when first we met; for by means of it may
I know to-morrow how thou hast sped."

Even so did Birdalone, and this was the end of their talk,
save broken words of lamentation as they said farewell. And
therewith for that while they sundered.

CHAPTER XX. OF BIRDALONE AND THE SENDING BOAT.

BIRDALONE woke up in the morning, and arose and
clad herself, and she saw not the witch-wife in the
chamber, though her bed looked as if it had been slept
in. Birdalone accounted little thereof, whereas the dame
would oft go on one errand or another much betimes in the
morning. Yet was she somewhat glad, for she was nowise
wishful for a wrangle with her. Withal, despite her valiancy,
as may well be thought, she was all a-flutter with hopes and

fears, and must needs refrain her body from overmuch quak-PART I
ing and restlessness if she might.Chap. 20

Now she mingled the tress of the Woodmother's hair with her own hair, but deemed it nought perilous to leave the ring yet sewn to her smock: she set some deal of bread and flesh in her scrip, lest her voyage should be long, and then all simply stepped over the threshold of the House of her Captivity.

She went straight to the strand aforesaid, seeing nought of the witch-wife by the way; and when she came there, was about to turn straightway to her left hand down to the creek, when it came into her mind that she would first swim over to Green Eyot for this last of times. For the eyot indeed she loved, and deemed it her own, since never had her evil dream, the witch, set foot thereon. Moreover, she said to herself that the cool lake would allay the fever of her blood, and make her flesh firmer and less timorous for the adven-ture. And again, that if the witch should see her from afar, as she could scarce fail to do, she would deem the maiden was about her wonted morning swimming, and would be the less like to spy on her.

So now, when she had let her garments slip from off her on to the sand close to the water's edge, she stood a while, with her feet scarce covered by the little ripple of the bight, to be a token of safety to her mistress. To say sooth, now it was come so nigh to the deed, she shrank aback a little, and was fain to dally with the time, and, if it might be, thrust something of no import betwixt her and the terror of the last moment.

Now she took the water, and rowed strongly with her lovely limbs till she came to the eyot, and there she went aland, and visited every place which had been kind to her; and kissed the trees and flowers that had solaced her, and once more drew the birds and rabbits to sport with her; till suddenly it came into her head that the time was wearing overfast. Then she ran down to the water and plunged in, and swam over to the strand as fast as she might, and came

aland there, thinking of nothing less than what had befallen.

For lo! when she looked around for her raiment and her
scrip, it was nowhere to be seen; straightway then it came
into her mind, as in one flash, that this was the witch's work;
that she had divined this deed of the flight, and had watched
her, and taken the occasion of her nakedness and absence
that she might draw her back to the House of Captivity. And
this the more as the precious ring was sewn to Birdalone's
smock, and the witch would have found it there when she
handled the raiment.

Birdalone wasted no time in seeking for the lost; she looked
down on to the smooth sand, and saw there footprints which
were not her own, and all those went straight back home to
the house. Then she turned, and for one moment of time
looked up toward the house, and saw plainly the witch come
out adoors, and the sun flashed from something bright in
her hand.

Then indeed she made no stay, but set off running at her
swiftest along the water-side toward the creek and the Sending Boat. As is aforesaid she was as fleet-foot as a deer, so but
in a little space of time she had come to the creek, and leapt
into the boat, panting and breathless. She turned and looked
hastily along the path her feet had just worn, and deemed she
saw a fluttering and flashing coming along it, but some way
off; yet was not sure, for her eyes were dizzy with the swift-
ness of her flight and the hot sun and the hurry of her heart.
Then she looked about a moment confusedly, for she called
to mind that in her nakedness she had neither knife, nor
scissors, nor bodkin to let her blood withal. But even therewith close to hand she saw hanging down a stem of half-dead
briar-rose with big thorns upon it; she hastily tore off a length
thereof and scratched her left arm till the blood flowed, and
stepped lightly first to stem and then to stern, and besmeared
them therewith. Then she sat down on the thwart and cried
aloud:

50

The red raven-wine now
Hast thou drunk, stern and bow;
Then wake and awake!
And the wonted way take:
The way of the Wender forth over the flood,
For the will of the Sender is blent with the blood.

Scarce had she time to wonder if the boat would obey her spell ere it began to stir beneath her, and then glided out into the lake and took its way over the summer ripple, going betwixt Green Eyot and the mainland, as if to weather the western ness of the eyot: and it went not a stonecast from the shore of the said mainland.

Hither to meet it now cometh the witch, running along the bank, her skirts flying wild about her, and a heavy short-sword gleaming in her hand. Her furious running she stayed over against the boat, and cried out in a voice broken for lack of breath:

Back over the flood
To the House by the Wood!
Back unto thy rest
In the alder nest!
For the blood of the Sender lies warm on thy bow,
And the heart of the Wender is weary as now.

But she saw that the Sending Boat heeded her words nothing, whereas it was not her blood that had awakened it, but Birdalone's. Then cried out the witch: "O child, child! say the spell and come back to me! to me, who have reared thee and loved thee and hoped in thee! O come back!"

But how should Birdalone heed her prayer? She saw the sax; and withal had her heart forgotten, her flesh might well remember. She sat still, nor so much as turned her head toward the witch-wife.

Then came wild yelling words from the witch's mouth,

E2   51

and she cried: "Go then, naked and outcast! Go then, naked fool! and come back hither after thou hast been under the hands of the pitiless! Ah, it had been better for thee had I slain thee!" And therewith she whirled the sax over her head and cast it at Birdalone.

But now had the boat turned its head toward the ness of Green Eyot and was swiftly departing, so that Birdalone but half heard the last words of the witch-wife, and the sax fell flashing into the water far astern.

There the witch stood tossing her arms and screaming, wordless; but no more of her saw Birdalone, for the boat came round about the ness of Green Eyot, and there lay the Great Water under the summer heavens all wide and landless before her. And it was now noon of day.

HERE ENDS THE FIRST PART OF THE WATER OF THE WONDROUS ISLES, WHICH IS CALLED OF THE HOUSE OF CAPTIVITY. AND NOW BE-GINS THE SECOND PART, WHICH IS CALLED OF THE WONDROUS ISLES.

THE WATER OF THE WONDROUS ISLES. THE SECOND PART: OF THE WONDROUS ISLES.

CHAPTER I. THE FIRST ISLE.

SO glided Birdalone over the Lake and was come forth from the House of Captivity; it might well be that she was but swimming unto death; naked as she was, fireless, foodless, and helpless, at the mercy of mere sorcery. Yet she called to mind the word of the Woodmother that they should meet again, and took heart thereby; and she was glad in that she had had her will, and shaken off the guile and thraldom of the witch. Much she thought of the Woodmother, and loved her, and wondered had she yet sought into and seen her welfare by the burning of a hair of that tress of hers; and therewith she looked on that tress of Habundia's hair and kissed it.

All day the Sending Boat sped on, and she saw no land and nought to tell of. It was but wave and sky and the familiar fowl of the lake, as coot, and mallard, and heron, and now and then a swift wood-dove going her ways from shore to shore; two gerfalcons she saw also, an osprey, and a great erne on his errand high up aloft.

Birdalone waked in her loneliness till the day was spent, and somewhat worn of the night; then she fell asleep for weariness; but so it was, that before dusk she had deemed that a blue cloud lay before her in the offing which moved not.

She slept the short night through, and was awakened by the boat smiting against something, and when her eyes opened she saw that she was come aland and that the sun was just risen. She stood up, and for the first minute wondered where she was, and she beheld her nakedness and knew not what it meant; then she loosened her hair, and shook its abundance all about her, and thereafter she turned her eyes on this new land and saw that it was fair and goodly. The flowery grass came down to the very water, and first was a fair meadow-land besprinkled with big ancient trees; thence arose slopes of vineyard, and orchard and garden; and, looking down on all, was a great White House, carven and glorious. A little air of wind had awakened with the sunrise, and bore the garden sweetness down to her; and warm it was after the chill of the wide water. No other land could she see when she looked lakeward thence.

She stepped ashore, and stood ancle-deep in the sweet grass, and looked about her for a while, and saw no shape of man astir. She was yet weary, and stiff with abiding so long amongst the hard ribs of the boat, so she laid herself down on the grass, and its softness solaced her; and presently she fell asleep again.

CHAPTER II. BIRDALONE FALLETH IN WITH NEW FRIENDS.

WHEN she next awoke, the sun was not yet high, and the morning young, yet she stood upon her feet much refreshed by that short slumber. She turned toward the hill and the gay house, and saw one coming over the meadow to her, a woman to wit, in a shining golden gown, and as she drew nigh Birdalone could see that she was young and fair, tall, white-skinned and hazel-eyed, with long red hair dancing all about her as she tripped lightly and merrily over the greensward.

Now she comes up to Birdalone with wonder in her eyes, and greets her kindly, and asked her of her name, and Birdalone told it all simply; and the new-comer said: "What errand hast thou hither, that thou art come thus naked and alone in this ill-omened ferry?"

Birdalone trembled at her words, though she spake kindly to her, and she said: "It is a long story, but fate drave me thereto, and misery, and I knew not whither I was bound. But is there no welcome for me in this lovely land? I lack not deftness wholly; and I will be a servant of servants, and ask no better if it must be so."

54

Said the new-comer: "Unto that mayst thou come; but
sore will be thy servitude. I fear me thy welcome here may
be but evil." Said Birdalone: "Wilt thou not tell me how
so?" Quoth that lady: "We know thy ferry here, that it is
the craft wherein cometh hither now and again the sister of
our lady the Queen, into whose realm thou art now come,
and who liveth up in the white palace yonder, and whom we
serve. And meseems thou wilt not have come hither by her
leave, or thou wouldst be in other guise than this; so that
belike thou wilt be the runaway of thy mistress. Wherefore
I fear that thou wilt be sent back to thy said mistress after a
while, and that that while will be grievous to thee, body and
soul."

Birdalone's heart sank, and she was pale and trembling;
but she said: "O dear lady, might I then depart as I have
come hither, without the wotting of this Queen! after thou
hast given me a morsel of bread, for I am hungry."

Said the gold-clad one, looking on her pitifully: "Nay,
maiden, I cannot choose but bring thee before our mistress,
whereas most like she hath already seen thee from above
there. For she is far-sighted beyond the wont of folk who
be more manlike. But as for the bread, see thou! I have
brought a manchet in my pouch, and cheese withal, as I came
hurrying; for I thought, she will be hungry." And she
reached the victual out to her. And Birdalone took it and
kissed the golden lady's hands, and she might not refrain
her tears, but wept as she ate.

Meanwhile the golden lady spake unto her and said:
"Nevertheless, thou poor maiden, somewhat may be done
for thine helping, and I will presently speak to my sisters
thereon, who are, both of them, wiser than I. Sisters by blood
are we not, but by love and fellowship. And I doubt not but
that as we go up into the house we shall happen upon them
in the garden. But now I look upon thee, how fair a woman
art thou!"

"Thou art kind and friendly," said Birdalone, smiling
amidst of her tears; "might I know by what name to call so

55

dear a woman?" "Thou shalt call me Aurea," said the other;
"and my next sister is Viridis, and the third, Atra; for that
is according to the hues of our raiment, and other names we
have not now. And lo! here cometh Viridis over the meadow."

Birdalone looked, and saw a woman coming toward them
clad all in green, with a rose-wreath on her head. And she
drew nigh, and greeted Birdalone kindly, and she also was a
very beauteous woman; not great of body, whereas Aurea
was tall and big-made, though excellently shapen. Light
brown and goodly waved of hair was Viridis, her eyes brown,
and rather long than great; her lips full and ruddy, her cheeks
soft and sweet and smooth, and as rosy-tinted pearl; her
hands small and delicate of fashion; her whole body soft-
shapen as an egg; a kind, wheedling look her face bore.

When she had looked a while on Birdalone, she kissed
her, and said: "I would thou wert happier, for thou art
beauteous, and all but the evil must love thee." Therewith
she drew a cate from her pouch, and said: "Eat somewhat,
for thou wilt be hungry; and let us go meet our other sister,
who is wiser than we."

So they went, all three of them, and came from off the
meadow on to the garden-slopes, and at the entry thereof
was come Atra to meet them; she was clad all in black, a tall
slim woman, with the grace of the willow-bough in the wind,
with dark plenteous hair and grey hawk-eyes; her skin
privet-white, with but little red in her cheeks. She also
greeted Birdalone kindly, but sadly withal. She gave her
strawberries to eat laid on a big kale-blade; and she said:
"Sisters, here are we hidden by the trees, and cannot be seen
from the house; therefore we may sit here for a minute or
two, while we talk together as to what may perchance be
done for the helping of this unhappy maiden, who is so fair
and lovely, and hath strayed into so ugly a trap." Then she
said to Birdalone: "Thou must know, poor wanderer, that
this Queen, our mistress, who is sister to the Witch Under
the Wood, is big and strong, well-made, and white-skinned,

56

so that she deems herself a Queen of all beauty: keen-eyed
is she to see a fly where others would see nought smaller than a coney; fine-eared withal; wise in wizardry; not altogether dull-witted, though she be proud, and crueller than the cruellest. But herein she faileth, that her memory is of the shortest for matters of the passing hour, albeit she remembers her spells and witch-songs over well. But other matters will scarce abide in her head for four and twenty hours. Wherefore, sisters, if we may keep this maiden out of her sight (after she hath seen her and given doom upon her) till the dead of to-morrow night, we may perchance do some good for her; and it is in my mind that then she may do good for us also."

Now they rejoiced in this word of Atra the wise; and Atra prayed Birdalone to tell them somewhat more of her story; and she told them much; but, whyso it were, she said nought concerning the wood-wife, whose outward semblance was the same as hers. Then they pitied her, and caressed her; but Atra said: "We must tarry here no more, but go straight up to the lady, or maybe we shall lose all."

So they went their ways and came into the pleasance, and trod the sweet greensward betwixt the garland flowers and the beauteous trees; which now indeed, though Birdalone saw them all clear and over-clear, were become nought to her. Those three also spake gently to her, and now and then asked her somewhat, as if to show her that she was one of themselves; but she spake not, or answered at random, and to say sooth scarce heard their words: forsooth she was now become heart-sick, and was half dead for fear; and her nakedness, which would have troubled her little across the water, was now grown a shame and a terror unto her, and every deal of her body quivered with the anguish thereof.

CHAP. III. BIRDALONE IS BROUGHT BEFORE THE WITCH-WIFE'S SISTER.

SO came they at last to the very house, and whereas it stood high on the bent, a great stair or perron of stone went up to it, and was of much majesty. They went through the porch, which was pillared and lovely, and came into a great hall most nobly builded, and at the other end thereof, on a golden throne raised upon a dais, sat a big woman clad in red scarlet. The three damsels led Birdalone to some four paces of the great lady, and then stood away from her, and left her standing there alone, the scarlet-clad woman before her; on the right and the left the tall pillars going up gleaming toward the roof, and about her feet the dark polished pavement, with the wallowing of strange beasts and great serpents and dragons all done on the coal-blue ground.

When she was so left alone, at first she tottered, and went nigh to falling; but then came back some little heart to her, as she said to herself that now she should verily die once for all, and that no long while would be the passing from life into death. She looked up and beheld the Lady-witch, that she was somewhat like to her sister, white-skinned and of plenteous golden-hair as was she, but younger of aspect, and nowise so ill-looked as that other had now become; for somewhat well-shapen of body she was; but her face forbidding; her lower lip thrust out, her cheeks flaggy and drooping, her eyes little more than half open; to be short, a face both proud, foolish, and cruel; terrible indeed, sitting in judgment in that place on a shrinking naked creature.

Now she spake; and if there were no majesty or solemnity in the voice, there was ugly glee and malice therein; but she said to those damsels: "Is this the woman that my keen eyes beheld come aland from my sister's Sending Boat e'en now?" Aurea knelt on one knee, and said: "Yea, so please you, my Lady."

58

Then said the witch: "Ho thou! Wilt thou plead some
errand hither from my sister? Dost thou deem me so wit- less as not to know that if she had sent thee hither thou wouldst not have come in this plight? Nay, I know; thou hast stolen thyself from her: thou art a thief, and as a thief shalt thou be dealt with."

Spake Birdalone in a clear voice: "No errand do I feign from thy sister, Lady: when I could bear my life there no longer, I took occasion to flee from her: this is all the tale. Yet once and again it hath been in my mind that it was thy sister who stole me from them that loved me."

"Hah, thrall!" said the Lady, "thou art bold; thou art over-bold, thou naked wretch, to bandy words with me. What heed I thy tale now thou art under my hand?" Her voice was cold rather than fierce, yet was there the poison of malice therein. But Birdalone spake: "If I be bold, lady, it is because I see that I have come into the House of Death. The dying may well be bold."

"The House of Death!" cried the stupid lady; "and wilt thou call my noble house the House of Death? Now art thou no longer bold, stripped thrall, but impudent."

Scorn rose into Birdalone's heart at this word, but she re- frained her, and spake: "I meant that I have stirred the wrath in thee, and that thou wilt slay me therefor; and that it avail- eth not to crave mercy of thee."

Laughed the Lady: "Thou art a fool, thrall," said she; "if a sparrow fled hither from my sister, I should not wring its neck, but keep it for her. So shall I do with thee. I shall not slay thee, and so destroy my sister's chattel; nor shall I spoil thee, and spoil her possession. I shall send thee back unto her, the stolen thrall in the stolen boat, when I have learned thee a lesson here. Forsooth it was for that cause meseemeth that she let thee slip through her fingers, for she is wise enough to have stayed thee from this holiday had she willed it. But she is tender-hearted, and kind, and soft, and might well deem that if thy chastisement were done to her hand here, it

59

were better done than by her mercy. Now, thrall, I have
spoken enough to thee, or more than enough: get thee back
out of earshot! "

CHAPTER IV. THE WITCH'S PRISON IN THE WAILING TOWER.

BIRDALONE did as she was bidden, and the witch
called unto her Atra, who came and stood humbly on
the footpace beside her, and held converse with her
mistress a while. Then she went backward from her a little,
and then came to Birdalone, and in a somewhat harsh voice
bade her come with her. Birdalone followed her, quaking, and
they came out of the hall and into a long passage, which led
to a wide stair winding round a newel; and all was builded
exceeding fair, had Birdalone's heart suffered her eyes to see
it; but her flesh was weak, and quaked before the torment to
come, so that her knees well-nigh failed her.

But now Atra lays a hand kindly on her shoulder and
stays her, and says: " Now meseems the walls of the Wailing
Tower, for so it hight, have no ears to hear, and we may talk
together. Wottest thou why I have brought thee hither?"
Said Birdalone in a faint voice: "Hast thou been bidden to
whip me?" "And if I had been so bidden, dear maiden,"
said Atra laughing, "nowise would I do it. Hold up thine
heart! For all hath gone well so far, and now meseems betwixt us three we shall save thee."

Birdalone's spirit came back to her at that word, and she
put her hands to her face and fell a-weeping. But Atra was
kind to her and made much of her; and she kissed her and
wiped her tears, and Birdalone smiled again amidst her sobs,
and she thanked Atra; who said to her: " First of all I must
tell thee that I am taking thee to prison by the witch's bidding."

"Yea," said Birdalone, "and what is prison?"

Said Atra: "A prison is a grim place where poor folk who
have done that which pleaseth not rich folk are shut up, that

they may be grieved and tormented by not being able to fare
abroad, or go where they would; and by suffering whatsoever their masters may lay upon them, as darkness, and cold,
and hunger, and stripes. Somewhat so, or worse, our lady
would have it for thee; but so would not we. Therefore for
thee shall this prison be a place where thou shalt be safe till
we may bring thee forth when the night hath worn towards
its ending. For she will have forgotten thee by to-morrow;
and this she knoweth; wherefore just now, when thou stood-
est out of earshot, she was bidding me, amongst other matters, to bring thee before her to-morrow morning, and tell
her the tale of thee, that she might call it to mind then what
she had will to this morning."

"Yea," said Birdalone, "but will she not remember that
she hath given thee a charge concerning me?" "But little
thereof," said Atra, "and with a few words I may easily con-
fuse her memory so that speech thereon will fail her. Keep up
thine heart, sweetling; but let us up this stair now forthwith,
for I were fain to have thee hid away in this prison, and then
will I down to her and tell her that thou art lying therein in
all misery and terror, lest it come into her head to send for
thee ere her memory is grown dim."

Again did Birdalone take heart, and they hastened a long
way up the stair, till Atra stayed at last at a door all done
with iron, endlong and overthwart. Then she took a leash of
keys from her girdle, one big and two little, and set the big
one in the lock and turned it, and shoved the heavy door
and entered thereby a chamber four-square and vaulted;
and the vault was upheld by a pillar of red marble, wherein,
somewhat higher than a man's head, were set stanchions of
latten, that could be clasped and unclasped. This chamber
was in a way goodly, but yet grim to look on; for the walls
were all of black ashlar stone close-jointed, and the floor
black also, but of marble polished so wholly that it was as
dark water, and gave back the image of Birdalone's dear feet
and legs as she went thereon. The windows were not small,
and the chamber was light in every corner because of them,

61

but they were so high up under the vaulting that none might see thereout aught save the heavens. There was nought in the chamber save a narrow bench of oak and three stools of the same, a great and stately carven chair dight with cushions of purple and gold, and in one corner a big oaken coffer.

Now spake Atra: "This is our lady's prison, and I fear me we cannot make it soft for thee, dear stranger. Yea, I must tell thee" (and she reddened therewith) "that it is part of my charge to set thee in irons." Birdalone smiled on her, and was over weary to ask what that meant, though she knew not. But Atra went to the big coffer and opened it and thrust in her hands, and there was a jangling therewith, and when she turned about to Birdalone again she had iron chains in her hands, and she said: "This shameth me, dear friend; yet if thou wouldst wear them it might be well, for she may have a mind to go visit her prison, and if she find thee there unshackled she shall be wroth, and oftenest her wrath hath a whip in its hand. And these are the lightest that I might find."

Birdalone smiled again, and spake not, for she was very weary, and Atra did the irons on her wrists and her ancles; and said thereafter: "Yet, bear in mind that it is a friend that hath the key of these things. And now I will go away for a little, but I shall be on thine errands; for first I shall tell the mistress that thou art lying here shackled and in all wanhope; and next, by the will and command of her, I am to see that thou be well fed and nourished to-day that thou mayst be the stronger for to-morrow. Now if I may give thee rede, it is that thou forbear to open the coffer yonder; for ugly things shalt thou find there, and that may dishearten thee again."

Therewith she kissed her kindly on the cheek and went her ways, and the great key turned in the lock behind her.

There then was Birdalone left to herself; and she was over weary even to weep; true it is that she made a step or two
62

towards the coffer, but refrained her, and took two of the
pillows from the great chair and turned aside into the other
corner, her chains jingling as she went. There she laid herself
down, and nestled into the very wall-nook, and presently
fell asleep, and slumbered dreamlessly and sweetly a long
while.

CHAPTER V. THEY FEAST IN THE WITCH'S PRISON.

BIRDALONE was awakened by the sound of the key in the lock, and the door opened, and there was Atra bearing dishes and platters, and behind her Viridis with the like gear, and beakers and a flagon to boot, and both they were smiling and merry.

Birdalone's heart leapt up to meet them, and in especial was she gladdened by the coming of Viridis, who had seemed to be the kindest of them all.

Viridis spake: "Now is come the meat for the dear sister, and it is time, for surely thou art famished, and it is now long past high noon. Do off her irons, Atra." Said Atra: "Maybe it were well to let the fetters abide on her ankles, lest the mistress should come; but for the wrists, reach out thine hands, wayfarer." So did Birdalone, and Atra laid her things on the ground, and unlocked the hand-shackles, and did them off: and meanwhile Viridis spread forth the banquet, partly on the floor, and partly on that ill-omened coffer. Then she went up to Birdalone and kissed her, and said: "Now shalt thou sit in our lady's throne, and we shall serve thee, and thou shalt deem thee a great one."

Nought else would they have, and Birdalone laid her nakedness on the purple cushions, and then they fell all three to the feast. The victual was both plenteous and dainty, of venison and fowl, and cream and fruits and sweetmeats, and good wine they had withal: never had Birdalone feasted in like manner, and the heart came back unto her, and her cheeks grew rosy and her eyes glittered. But she said: "How if your lady were to come upon us here, and we so merry?"

Said Atra: "Out of the chair must thou when thou hearest the key in the lock, and then is all well, and she would have nought against us; for she herself bade us, and me in special, to keep thee company here, and talk with thee; and Aurea also would have been here, but that she is serving the lady as now." "Hath she then some pity on me," said Birdalone, "that she hath bidden thee do by me what is most to my pleasure?"

Laughed Viridis thereat, and Atra said: "She hath no pity, nor ever shall have; but so hard of heart is she, that she may not deem that we could love thee, a stranger, and unhappy, who can serve us in nowise; so she feareth not the abatement of thy grief from any compassion of us. Rather she hath sent us, and me in especial, not to comfort thee, but to grieve thee by words; for she biddeth me tell thee fair tales, forsooth, of what to-morrow shall be to thee, and the day after; and of how she shall begin on thee, and what shall follow the beginning, and what thou mayst look for after that. For by all this she deemeth to lower thy pride and abate thy valour, and to make every moment of to-day a terror to thy flesh and thy soul, so that thereby thou mayest thole the bitterness twice over. Such is her pity for thee! And yet belike this cruelty hath saved thee, for but for that she had not refrained her from thee to-day, and to-morrow thou shalt be far away from her."

"Meanwhile," said Viridis, in her soft sweet voice, "none of all these things will we talk over with thee, but things comfortable and kind; and we will tell each to each of our story. Will we not, Atra?" "Yea, verily," said she.

Birdalone looked upon them and said: "Wondrous is your compassion and loving-kindness unto me, and scarce do I know how to bear the burden thereof. But tell me one thing truly; will ye not suffer in my place when this witch cometh to know that ye have stolen me away from her?"

64

"Nay," said Atra, "I have told thee that by to-morrow she will have altogether, or at least almost, forgotten thee and thy coming hither. Moreover, she is foreseeing, and hath come to know that if she raise a hand against any of us three, it will lead her to her bane, save it be for heavy guilt clearly proven against us. Forsooth, in the earlier days of our captivity such a guilt we fell into, and did not wholly escape, as Viridis can bear me witness. But we are now grown wiser, and know our mistress better, and will give her no such joy."

Viridis cast her eyes down at those words and Atra's smile, and turned red and then pale, and Birdalone looked on her wondering what ailed her; then she said: "Do ye sisters work in the field and the garden? I mean at milking the kine and the goats, and digging the earth, and sowing and reaping, and the like?"

"Nay," said Atra; "either our mistress, or someone else who is of marvellous might, hath so ordained, that here everything waxeth of itself without tillage, or sowing or reaping, or any kind of tending; and whatso we need of other matters the mistress taketh it for us from out of her Wonder-coffer, or suffereth us to take it for ourselves. For thou must know that this land is one of the Isles of the Lake, and is called the Isle of Increase Unsought."

"Meseemeth then," said Birdalone, "were the mistress of you to gainsay you the gifts of the Wonder-coffer, ye were undone." "Yea, verily," said Atra; "then would be but the fruits of the earth and the wild creatures for our avail, and these, we have not learned how to turn them into dinner and supper." And they all laughed thereat; but Birdalone said: "See ye then how I was right to offer myself unto you as a servant, for in all matters of the house and the byre and the field have I skill. But since ye would not or could not have me, I wonder not that ye be ill at ease here, and long to be gone, for as plenteous and lovely as the isle is, and though ye live here without present mishandling or pining. For, sooth to say, ye have over you a tyrant and a fool."

Viridis answered: "Yet is there something else, dear friend, that whets our longing to depart. Tell her thereof, Atra."

Atra smiled and said: "Simple it is: there are they who long for us and for whom we long, and we would be together." Said Birdalone: "Be these kinsfolk of yours, as fathers, mothers, sisters, brothers, or the like?"

Reddened Viridis again; but Atra spake, and she also blushed somewhat, though she smiled: "Those whom we love, and who love us, be not queans, but carles; neither be they of our blood, but aliens, till love overcometh them and causeth them to long to be of one flesh with us; and their longing is beyond measure, and they desire our bodies, which they deem far fairer than belike they be. And they would bed us, and beget children on us. And all this we let them do with a good will, because we love them for their might, and their truth, and the hotness of their love toward us."

Looked up Viridis thereat, and her eyes gleamed amidst the flushing of her cheeks, and she said: "Sister, sister! even in such wise, and no other, as they desire us do we desire them; it is no mere good will toward them from us, but longing and hot love."

Now must Atra blush no less than Viridis; yet she but said: "I have told thee hereof, Birdalone, because I deem that thou hast lived simply and without the sight of men; but it is what all know in the world of the sons of Adam." Said Birdalone: "Thou sayest sooth concerning me. Yet about this love have I learned somewhat even ere to-day, and now, as ye speak and I, meseems the lore of it comes pouring in on me and fills my heart with its sweetness. And O, to have such love from any, and with such love to be loved withal!"

"Dear sister," said little Viridis, "fear not; such as thou shalt not fail of the love of some man whom thou must needs love. Is it not so, sister Atra?" Said Atra: "Yea; such love shall come unto her as surely as death."

They were silent now a little, and it was as if some sweet
66

incense had been burned within the chamber. For Birdalone,
the colour came and went in her cheeks, her flesh quaked,
her heart beat quick, and she was oppressed by the sweetness
of longing. More daintily she moved her limbs, and laid foot
to foot and felt the sleekness of her sides; and tender she was
of her body as of that which should one day be so sorely
loved.

Now she spake timidly to the others, and said: "Each one
of you then has a man who loves her, and longs for her and
for none else?" "So it is," said Viridis. "How sweet that
shall be!" said Birdalone; "and now all the more I wonder
that ye could trouble yourselves over me, or think of me
once; and the kinder I think it of you."

Said Atra smiling on her: "Nay, now must the cat be out
of the bag, and I must tell thee that thou art to think of us as
chapmen who with our kindness would buy something of
thee, to wit, that thou wouldst do an errand for us to those
three lovers of ours."

"Surely," said Birdalone, "it were a little payment to set
against your saving of my life and my soul; and had I to go
barefoot over red gleeds I would do it. And yet, if I may go
hence to your lovers, why not all three of you along with
me?"

Said Atra: "For this reason; thy ferry, the Sending Boat,
wherein ye came hither, is even somewhat akin to thy mistress and ours; and the mistress here hath banned it against
bearing us; and now, were we so much as to touch it, such
sore turmoil would arise, and such hideous noise as if earth
and heaven were falling together; and the Lady would be on
us straightway, and we should be undone; and, as thou shalt
hear presently, this hath been proved. But thou, thou art free
of the said ferry. Forsooth I wot not why thy mistress banned
it not against thee; maybe because she deemed not that thou
wouldst dare to use it or even go anigh it."

Birdalone considered, and thought that even so it was;
that the witch deemed that she would not dare use the Sending Boat, nor know how to, even if she came upon it, and

F2   67 that if she did so find it, she would sicken her of the road thereto. So now she told her friends the whole tale thereof more closely than she had afore, save again what pertained to Habundia; withal she told every word of what her mistress had said to her at that time when she changed her into a hind. And Viridis heard and wondered, and pitied her. But Atra sat somewhat downcast a while. Then she said: "However this may be, we will send thee forth to-morrow in the dawn, and take the risk of what may befall thereafter; and thou shalt bear a token for each of those three that love us. For we deem that they have not forgotten aught, but are still seeking us."

Birdalone said: "Whatsoever ye bid me, that will I do, and deem me your debtor still. But now I pray you, pleasure a poor captive somewhat more."

"Wherein?" said they both; "we be all ready thereto." Said the maiden: "Would ye do so much as to tell me the tale of how ye came hither, and then how it hath been with you from your first coming until now?"

"With a good will," said Atra; "hearken!"

CHAPTER VI. ATRA TELLS OF HOW THEY THREE CAME UNTO THE ISLE OF INCREASE UNSOUGHT.

WE were born and bred in the land that lies south-west along this Great Water, and we waxed happily, and became fellows when we were yet but children, and thus grew up dear friends into maidenhood and womanhood. We were wooed by many men, but our hearts turned to none of them save unto three, who were goodly, kind, and valiant; and thou mayst call them the Golden Knight, who is Aurea's man; the Green Knight, who is man of Viridis; and my man, the Black Squire. But in this was unhap, that because of certain feuds which had endured from old time, this love was perilous unto them and us; so that we lived in doubt and unrest.

"Came a day, now three years ago, when the king of the
68

whole land brought his folk into our lake-side country, and there held a court and a mote in a fair great meadow anigh to the water. But even as the mote was hallowed, and the Peace of God proclaimed at the blast of the war-horn, came we three woeful ladies clad in black and knelt before the lord king, and prayed him hearken us. And he deemed that we were fair, so he had compassion on us, and raised us up, and bade us speak.

"So we told our tale, how that strife and wounds and death stood betwixt us and love; and we wept, and bewailed it, that our love must be slain because men were wroth with each other and not with us.

"The king looked on us kindly, and said: 'Who be the swains for whom these lovely damsels make such a piece of work?' So we named them, and said that they were there in the mote; and the king knew them for valiant men who had done him good service; and he cried out their names, and bade them stand forth out of the throng. So forth they stood, the Golden Knight, the Green Knight, and the Black Squire (and he also was now a knight); but now were they all three clad in black, and they were unarmed, save for their swords girt to their sides, without which no man amongst us may come to the mote, be he baron or earl or duke, or the very lord king himself.

"So the king looked upon us and them, and laughed and said: 'Fair ladies, ye have got me by the nose, so needs must my body follow. Do ye three knights, whom I know for valiant men and true, take each his love by the hand, and let the weddings be to-morrow.' Who then were joyful but us? But even at the word the king spake arose great turmoil in the mote, for they smote the feud and contention awake, and men thronged forward against each other, and swords were drawn and brandished. But the king arose in his place and spake long and deftly, and waxed exceeding wroth, while none heeded him nor hearkened. And there stood our three men, who laid no hand to hilt, but abode heart-whole by seeming amid the tumult. And lovely they were to look

69

on. At last the wise men and old barons went between, and by fair words appeased the trouble, and the mote grew hushed. Then spake the king: 'What is this, my thanes? I had deemed that my foemen were far away, and that ye that here are were all friends unto me and unto each other. But now must we try another rede.' Therewith he turned unto our men and said: 'Ye champions, are ye so much in love with Love that ye will fight for him?' They all yeasaid that, and then the king said: 'Then do I declare that these three will hold the field against all comers from matins till high noon, and that he who vanquisheth any one of them shall have his lady and wed her if he will, and, if he will, shall ransom her. And this field shall be foughten after two months' frist in these fair meadows, when I return from the outermost marches of the south, whereto I am now wending. But when the battle is done, then let all men bow to the judgment of God, whether he be well content or not, and this on peril of life and limb. And now let there be deep peace between all men meanwhile; and if any break the peace, be he high or low, rich or unrich, churl or earl, I swear it by the souls of my fathers that he shall lose nought save his life therefor.'

"At these words was there a rumour of yeasay, and all men were content, save we three poor maidens, into whose hearts had now entered fear of loss and death.

"But our kindreds on both sides were glad and proud, and they were not so bitter against us as they had been; they put hand to pouch, and let rear for us a fair pavilion of painted timber, all hung with silk and pictured cloths and Saracen tapestry, by the very lake-side; and gay boats gaily bedight lay off the said pavilion for our pleasure; and when all was done, it yet lacked a half month of the day of battle, and thither were we brought in triumph by the kindreds on a fair day of May, and there was not a sword or a spear amongst the whole company, and peaceful and merry was all by seeming. But we were not suffered to meet our lovers all this while, from the time when the mote was.

"Now on a day came a messenger on the spur, and did us

70

to wit that the king would be with us on the morrow, and that the day after, the fateful field should be foughten. Then, though the coming of this day had been so longed for by us, yet now it was at hand it cast us into all unrest and trouble, so that we scarce knew whether to go, or stand, or sit, or what to do with our bodies. Our folk, and all other men withal, were so busy making ready for the morrow of to-morrow, that they left us alone to wear through the day as we might.

"Now it was afternoon, and the day hot and hazy, and we stood on the very lip of the land wearied with hope and fear, and striving to keep good countenance to each other; and there came a boat unto the shore gaily painted and gilded, and bedight with silken cloths and cushions; and the steerer thereof was a woman, not young, by seeming of fifty winters; red-haired she was, thin-lipped and narrow-eyed, flat-breasted and strait-hipped; an ungoodly woman, though her skin was white and smooth as for her age. Hast thou ever seen such an one, guest?" Said Birdalone, smiling: "Forsooth that have I; for such an one is my mistress to behold."

"Well," said Atra, "this dame stretched out her hands to us, and said: 'Will not the pretty ladies, the dear ladies, who have nought on hand this afternoon, come into my boat and look on the face of the water, so calm and fair as it is, and let their lovely hands go over the gunwale and play with the ripple, and so beguile this heavy time for a two hours; and then give a little gift of a piece or two of silver to a poor carline, who loveth all fair ladies and bright warriors, and who needeth a little livelihood?'

"Now the woman seemed nought lovely unto us, and to me forsooth she seemed hateful; but we looked on each other, and we found that we were utterly weary of going up and down on the meadow, and lying about in the pavilion, and it seemed as if this would give us a little rest; withal we saw not that the woman could do us any hurt, whereas we were three, and strong enough as women go; nor were we mariners so evil but that we might sail or steer a boat at a

71

pinch. So we stepped into the boat straightway, and the woman sat aft and paddled deftly with the steering-oar, and we glided away from the land.

"Soon we were come so far that we could but just see our pavilion through the haze, which had somewhat thickened, and we said to the woman that she should go about and make for the shore, and that then we would go to and fro a while along by our stead. She nodded yeasay, and began by seeming to dight the craft for return. But therewith the haze was grown suddenly into a low cloud, which came down upon us from the south-west in the arms of a cold breeze, that grew stronger every minute, so no wonder it was though the steerer might not keep head to wind; and then who was afraid and ashamed save ourselves?

"But the woman said, and there seemed to be a mock in her voice: 'Ill luck, pretty ladies! Now is there nought for it but to drive, if we would not drown. But belike this duskiness will clear presently, and then at least we shall know whither we be going; and we may either turn back, or seek some other shelter, for I know the lake well; I know, I know.'

"We were too terror-stricken to speak, for we felt that still the wind grew stronger, and the lake began to rise into waves, and the craft to wallow; but well-nigh therewith was the dusk and the mist gone; the sky was bright blue overhead, and the westering sun shone cloudless; but on no land it shone, or on aught save the blue waters and the white wave-crests.

"Then wept Aurea, and this Viridis here, but as to me, I grew wroth and cried out to the steerer: 'Accursed carline! thou hast betrayed us; never now may we get back to our pavilion till the fight is foughten, and our lovers will deem that we have forsaken them, and we are shamed for ever.' 'Well, well,' said the carline, 'what remedy save patience for the winds and waves?' And she laughed mockingly. Quoth I: 'There is this remedy, that we three arise and lay hands on thee, and cast thee outboard, save thou straight-

72

way turn the boat's head and back to the main. Forsooth I doubt not but that as thou hast raised this foul wind against us, thou canst raise a fair wind for us.'

"'Hearken to the lovely lady!' quoth the carline, 'how she deemeth me to be none other than the great God himself, to hold the winds in the hollow of my hand, and still the waves with a word! What! am I wrought somewhat after his image, kind ladies?' And she grinned horribly therewith. Then she said again: 'As to thy remedy, sweetling, meseemeth it nought. For how shall ye sail this stormy water when your captain is gone, and ye but holiday sailors belike?'

"As she spake, a great wave came up from the windward, and brake over us, and half filled the craft, and lifted her bows up towering, and then down we went into the trough; and I sat cowed and quaking, and spake never another word.

"Now began the sun to sink, and the wind abated, and the sea went down, but the boat sped on as swift as ever over the landless waters.

"Now the sun was down, and dusk was at hand, and the carline spake, and drew a bright-gleaming sax from under her raiment: 'Damsels, I warn you that now it were best that ye obey me in all things; for though ye be three and I one, yet whereas I have here an edge-friend, I may take the life of any one of you, or of all three, as simply as I could cut a lamb's throat. Moreover it will serve you better in the house whereto ye are wending, that I make a good tale of you rather than a bad. For the mistress of that house is of all might; and I must say it of her, though she is my very sister, yet she is not so sweet-tempered and kind of heart as I am, but somewhat rough and unyielding of mood, so that it is best to please her. Wherefore, maidens, I rede you be sage.'

"Our unhappy hearts were now so sunken in wanhope, that we had no word wherewith to answer her, and she spake: 'Now obey ye my bidding and eat and drink, that ye may come hale and sound to your journey's end, for I

73

would not give starvelings to my dear sister.' Therewith she brought forth victual for us, and that nought evil, of flesh and bread, and cheese and cakes, and good wine withal; and we were hunger-weary as well as sorrow-weary; and hunger did at that moment overcome sorrow, so we ate and drank, and, would we, would we not, something of heart came back to us thereby.

"Then again spake the carline: 'Now my will is that ye sleep; and ye have cushions and cloths enough to dight you a fair bed; and this bidding is easy for you to obey.' Forsooth, so weary were we with sorrow, and our hunger was now quenched, that we laid us down and slept at once, and forgat our troubles.

"When we awoke it was after the first dawn, and we were come aland even where thou didst this morning, guest. And thou mayst deem it wondrous, but so it was, that close to where our boat took land lay the ferry which brought thee hither.

"Now the carline bade us get ashore, and we did so, and found the land wondrous fair, little as that solaced us then. But she said unto us: 'Hearken! now are ye come home; and long shall ye dwell here, for never shall ye depart hence save by the will of my sister and me, wherefore, once more, I rede you be good, for it will be better for you. Go forth now unto yonder house, and on the way ye shall meet the Queen of this land, and ye have nought to do but to say to her that ye are the Gift; and then shall she see to your matter.'

"Therewith she gat into her own craft, the Sending Boat, and therein did the deed and spake the words ye wot of, and was gone north-away; and when we turned to seek for our boat wherein we had come hither, it was gone.

"We stood miserably for a while on the lip of the land, and then I said that we might as well go meet our fate as die there of grief and hunger. So we went, and came into those fair gardens, and as we went slowly up toward the house came on us a woman clad in red scarlet and grandly dight. A big woman she was, and like to her that beguiled us, but far younger and fairer of favour, foolish and proud of visage. She stared on us, and seemed half afeard of us at first, but asked us what we were, and I answered that we were the Gift. 'The Gift?' said she, 'what meaneth that? Will ye obey me in all things? If ye gainsay it, ye will perish, unless ye can eat grass; for on this isle everything cometh from my hand.'

"What might we do? We all knelt down before her, and swore to do her will. Then she said, after she had stared on us awhile: 'Now I know: ye are they of whom my sister spake, that she would fetch me a gift of a leash of damsels for my service. Now I take the Gift and thank her good heart. But if ye would do my will, then—' But she broke off here and stared at us a long while, and then she said: 'Now I know; she bade me treat you well, and hold my hand from you, or evil would come of it, belike at last my bane. So go ye home to the House, and I will give you meat and drink, and show you my stores and the Wonder-coffer, and ye shall serve me in honour.'

"Even so did we; and we ate and drank and rested, and nought we lacked, save leave to depart home to our lovers, and some mistress better than this stupid and proud lump of flesh. But the next morning when we came before the lady, she knew nought of what we were; and again we had to tell her that we were the Gift, and again she glared at us balefully, and again she called to mind her sister and her rede concerning us. And this went on for many days, till at last she got to know what we were; and she followed her sister's rede in that she never mishandled us, though we could see that it irked her to forbear, nor did she speak to us more roughly than her fool's wont was; and we had in our hands all that was needed for our sustenance, and lived easily enough.

"Now our coming hither betid three years ago, and a month thereafter comes thy witch hither in her ferry, and she greeted us when we met, and asked us, grinning, had she not been kind to win us such good days? 'Yea, and over kind,' said she, 'ye would deem me, knew ye what would have betid you save for my good word.' Forsooth we deemed it no kind deed to steal us from our lovers; but we kept good tongues in our heads, for thralls must needs kiss the rod.

"She went away in two days, but came again many times thereafter, till we won the secret of the Sending Boat, and her spell therewith; but we knew not that was banned against us. Wherefore on a day in the grey of the morning, when we had been on this isle somewhat less than a year, we went down to it and stepped in, and reddened stem and stern and said the spell-words. But straightway arose an hideous braying and clatter, and thunder came therewith, and trembling of the earth, and the waters of the lake arose in huge waves; nor might we move from our seats in the boat till the two witches came running down to us, and haled us out ashore, and had us up into the house, and into this very prison-chamber, wherein we are now sitting so merry. And here we bore what was laid upon us, whereof, dear guest, we shall tell thee nought. But this came of it, that never thereafter durst we try the adventure of the Sending Boat, but have lived on in lazy sorrow and shameful ease, till thou, dear guest and sister, wert sent hither by heaven for our helping.

"Now what became of the king's court, and the hazelled field of our Champions, we wot not, or whether they be yet alive we cannot tell thee; but if they be alive, it is to them that we would have thee do our errand, and thereof will we tell thee closely to-morrow. And so, sweetling, an end of my tale."

CHAPTER VII. THE THREE DAMSELS TAKE BIRDALONE OUT OF THE WITCH'S PRISON.

BIRDALONE thanked Atra much for her tale, and strange it was to her to hear of such new things and the deeds of folk; but the dealing of the witches with those three was familiar to her and was of her world.

Now they talked merrily, till there came a footstep to the door and one without knocked. Viridis paled thereat, and a pang of fear smote Birdalone, and she swiftly got from out the chair and sat down on a stool; but when Atra opened, it was but Aurea come from her service to bid Atra take her place. So she went, and again was there pleasant converse betwixt Aurea and the other twain; and certain matters did Aurea tell Birdalone which had been left untold by Atra. And chiefly, when Birdalone asked if any other folk had come into the isle while they dwelt there, she said yea; once had come a knight with a lady, his love, fleeing from war and mishap, and these had the witch overcome by wizardry, and destroyed them miserably: and that again another had strayed thither, and him also the witch undid, because he would not do her will and lie in her bed. Withal had come drifting there a young damsel, a castaway of the winds and waves; her the witch kept as a thrall, and after a while took to mishandling her so sorely, that at last, what for shame and what for weariness of life, she cast herself into the water and was drowned. None of these folk might the damsels help so as to do them any good, though they tried it, and went nigh to suffer therefor themselves.

Now the day wore, and in a while Atra came back, and Viridis must serve. At last the dusk and the dark was come. Then said Atra: "Now must we twain begone to wait upon our lady, as the wont is: and that is now for our good hap, for if we be with her all three, and especially, to say sooth, if I be with her, we may well keep her from visiting thee here; since belike she shall yet dimly remember that thou art in her prison. Therefore thou must forgive it if I shackle thy wrists again. And now if thou wilt follow my rede, thou shalt try to sleep some deal, and it were well if thou might'st sleep till we come for thee in the grey dawn."

Therewith they left her there, and she nestled in the corner once more, and there did verily fall asleep, and slept till the key in the lock and the opening door awakened her, and Atra came stealing soft-footed into the prison. Eager she was and panting, and she kneeled before Birdalone and unlocked her leg-shackles, and then stood up and did the like by the irons on her wrists. Then she said: "Look up, dear friend, to thy prison windows, and behold the dawn beginning to break on the day of thy deliverance, and ours maybe. But come now at once: and again, wilt thou pardon me, that we clothe thee not here for thy journey? For from our own bodies must we clothe thee, and if by any hap our Lady were to see any one of us more or less unclad, it might draw her on to see what was toward, and we might yet be found out, for our undoing."

Therewith she took her hand, and led her forth of the prison, and locked the door behind her; and then downstairs they went, and out-a-doors by a little wicket at the stair-end. The dawn drew on apace now, and Birdalone saw at once the other twain lurking in the wall-nook hard by. No word was spoken between them, and with noiseless feet they went forth into the orchard, where the blackbirds and thrushes were beginning their first morning song, and ere they came out on to the meadow the full choir of them was a-singing.

CHAPTER VIII. IN WHAT WISE BIRDALONE WAS CLAD, AND HOW SHE WENT HER WAYS FROM THE ISLE OF INCREASE UNSOUGHT.

WHEN they were all clear of the orchard trees the three damsels kept Birdalone between them closely, so that her white body should not be seen if the lady were awake and looking forth. Thus they brought her to where a few thorn-bushes made a cover for them close to

78

the water's edge, some twenty yards from the Sending Boat.
There they stood together, and Atra said: "Now, dear guest, and dearest messenger, it is our matter to clothe thee from our very bodies; and do thou, Viridis, begin."

Viridis came forward blushing, as her wont was, and took off her green gown and laid it on the grass; then she set her hand to her smock, and did it off, and stood naked, knee set to knee, and swaying like the willow branch; and then was seen all the dainty fashion of her body, and how lovely of hue and sweet of flesh she was.

But she said: "Dear sister Birdalone, here is my smock, which I lend thee, but as to my love, I give it thee therewith; therefore grudge it not, though thou give me back the linen, for happy will be the day to me when I have it again; for now none may do it on me save the Green Knight, my own love." Therewith she gave her the smock, and kissed her, and Birdalone did it on, and felt the valianter and mightier when she had a garment upon her.

Then Aurea did off her golden gown, and stood in smock alone, so that her naked arms shone more precious than the golden sleeves that had covered them. And she spake: "Birdalone, dear messenger, take now my golden gown, and send it back to me when thou hast found the man unto whom it is due; and think meanwhile that, when thou wearest it, thou wearest my love, and that when thou pullest it off, thou art clad with my love instead of it."

So Birdalone did on the gown, and became to look on as the daintiest of the queens of the earth; and she turned her head about to look on her gold-clad flanks, and wondered.

Thereafter Atra knit up her skirts into her girdle, and then did off her shoon, so that her slim feet shone like pearls on the green grass; and she said: "Birdalone, sweet friend! wilt thou be my messenger to bear these shoon to my Black Squire, and meanwhile put my love for thee under thy feet, to speed thee and to bear thee up? Wherefore be good to me."

Birdalone then shod herself, and though pity it were to

79

hide her feet from the eyes of Earth, yet felt she the stouter-hearted thereby, and her cheeks flushed and her eyes brightened.

Thereafter Aurea gave her withal a golden collar for the neck, and Viridis a girdle of silver well-wrought, and Atra a gold finger-ring set with a sapphire stone; and all these she did on her; but yet she knew that they were tokens to be delivered to the three lovers according as was due.

Then spake Atra: "Lo, sister, we pray thee to bear these lendings on thy body in such wise that when thou comest to the mainland they may be seen by knights seeking adventures, and that thou mayst answer to any who may challenge thee thereof, and say that thou bearest this raiment and these jewels from Aurea and Viridis and Atra to Baudoin the Golden Knight, and to Hugh the Green Knight, and to Arthur the Black Squire. And if thou deem that thou hast found these, then shall they tell thee a token, such as we shall tell thee, that they be truly these and none other; and thereafter, when thou art made sure, they shall take of thee the raiment, the gems, and the Sending Boat, and come hither if they may. And God look to the rest! But as for the token to be told aforesaid, we have determined that each of us shall tell thee privily what question thou shalt ask for her, and what answer thou must look for."

When she had done speaking, each came up to Birdalone and spake something into her ear amidst blushes enough forsooth. And what they said will be seen hereafter. Then again said Atra: "Now by this errand shall we be well paid for the care we have had of thee. It may be, forsooth, that thou shalt not find our speech-friends; for they may be dead, or they may deem us untrue, and may have forsaken us and their land; and in any such case thou art free of our errand; but whatsoever may betide us, God speed thee!"

Then Viridis drew forth a basket from under a bush, and said: "We know not how long thy voyage may be, but some little provision for the way we may at least give thee: now wilt thou bear this aboard thyself, for we dare not touch thy

craft, nay, nor come nigh it, no one of us." And she set down
the basket and cast her arms about her, and kissed her and
wept over her; and the other twain, they also kissed her
lovingly. Birdalone wept even as Viridis, and said: "May
ye do well, who have been so kind to me; but now am I both
so glad and so sorry, that the voice of me will not make due
words for me. O farewell!"

Therewith she took up her basket, and turned and went
speedily to the Sending Boat; and they beheld her how she
stepped aboard and bared her arm, and drew blood from it
with the pin of her girdle-buckle, and therewith reddened
stem and stern; and a pang of fear smote into their hearts
lest their lady had banned it for Birdalone as for them. But
Birdalone sat down on the thwart, and turned her face south,
and spake:

> The red raven-wine now
> Hast thou drunk, stern and bow;
> Awake then, awake!
> And the southward way take:
> The way of the Wender forth over the flood,
> For the will of the Sender is blent with the blood.

No cloud barred the gateway of the sun as she spoke; no
wave rose upon the bosom of the lake; no clatter nor tumult
was there; but the Sending Boat stirred, and then shot out
swiftly into the wide water; and the sun arose as they looked, and his path of light flashed on Birdalone's golden
gown for a moment, and then it grew grey again, and presently she was gone from before their eyes.

So they turned up into the orchard: and now was Viridis
of good cheer, and Aurea no less; but Atra lagged behind,
and as she went, some passion took her, she knew not
wherefore; her bosom swelled, her shoulders heaved therewith, and she wept.

CHAPTER IX. HOW BIRDALONE CAME TO THE ISLE OF THE YOUNG AND THE OLD.

ALL went well with Birdalone when she had left the voyage, save that now she was both clad and victualled, much as it had on her first Isle of Increase Unsought, much as it had on her first led, and her heart, if yet it harboured fear, was also full of new and strange hope; and oft, even as she sat there amidst the waste of waters, she wondered what new longing this was which wrought so sweet a pain in her, that it made her cheeks burn, and her eyes dim, and her hands and her limbs restless. And then would she set her mind to her friends and their errand, and would hope and pray for them; but again would she fall to picture to herself what manner of men they were who were so sore longed for by those three beauteous women; and she deemed that since they were thus desired, they must be fairer even than her friends of the Isle; and again the nameless longing overtook her, and held her till it wearied her into sleep.

When she awoke again the boat had stayed, and she was come aland; but the dawn was not yet come, and the night was moonless, yet was there light enough to see, from the water and the stars, that the bows of the boat were lying safe on a little sandy beach. So she stepped out and looked around, and deemed she could see great trees before her, and imagined dark masses of she knew not what. So she walked warily up the said strand till she came on to soft grass, and smelled the scent of the clover as her foot-soles crushed it. There she sat down, and presently lay along and went to sleep.

After a while she awoke, and felt happy and well at ease, and had no will to move: the sun was shining brightly, but had not been up long: the song of birds was all about her, but amidst it she deemed she heard some speech of man, though it were not like to what she had heard in her life before. So she raised herself on her elbow, and looked up and saw a new thing, and sat up now, and beheld and wondered.

82

For there stood before her, gazing wide-eyed on her, two little children, some three winters of age, a man and a woman as it seemed: the man-child with light and fine whitegolden hair, falling straight down and square over his brow, and blue-grey eyes which were both kind and merry, and shyly seeking as it were. Plump and rosy he was, sturdy and stout-limbed. No less fair was the woman; her hair goldenbrown, as oft it is with children who grow up dark-haired, and curling in fair little rings all over her head; her eyes were big and dark grey; she was thinner than the lad, and somewhat taller.

These two babes had between them a milk-white shegoat, and had been playing with her, and now she turned her head to this and that one of them, bleating, as if to crave more of the game; but they had no eyes for her, but stood staring with might and main on the new-comer and her shining golden gown.

Birdalone laughed with joy when she saw the little ones, and a dim memory of the days of Utterhay passed before her: she stretched out a hand to them, and spake softly and caressingly, and the little lad came forward smiling, and took her hand, and made as if he would help her up for courtesy's sake. She laughed on him, and arose; and when she stood up, tall and golden, he seemed somewhat afeard of so big a creature, but stood his ground valiantly. Then she stooped down to him and kissed him, and he naysaid her not, but seemed rather glad when it was over; but when Birdalone went to the little maid and kissed her, the child clung to her as if she were her mother, and babbled to her.

Then comes the lad to her, and takes her hand, and would draw her away, and speaks to her in his prattle, and she understood him to mean that she should come with him to see the father. So she went, wondering what should next betide; and the little maiden went on the other side of her, holding by a fold of her skirt. Forsooth the goat followed bleating, not well pleased to be forgotten.

Now had Birdalone time to look about her, though the

two babes fell to prattling with her in their way, and she
thought it sweet to look down on the two little faces that
looked up to her so pleased and merry.

She was in a grassy plain, somewhat over rough and
broken to be called a meadow, and not enough be-timbered
to be called a wood; it rose up a little and slowly as they left
the water, but scarce so much as one might call it a hill.
Straight before her on the way that they were going went up
into the air great masses of grey stone builded by man's
hand, but looking, even from this way off, ragged and ruinous. It may well be thought that Birdalone wondered what
things might lie betwixt the trees and the towers.

Now as they went they came on other goats, who seemed
tame, and these joined them to their fellow, and suffered the
younglings to play with them. Moreover there were rabbits
great plenty scuttling in and out of the brakes and the rough
ground upon the way, and the younglings beheld them, and
the little lad said, after his fashion: "Why do the rabbits run
away from us, and the goats follow us?"

Now, sooth to say, Birdalone scarce knew why, and had
no word ready for the child; but she said at last: "Mayhappen they will come to me; so it was once when I dwelt away
from here. Shall I go fetch thee one?" The little ones yeasaid that, though somewhat shyly and doubtfully. Then
said Birdalone: "Do ye, sweetlings, abide me here, and go
not away." They nodded their heads thereat, and Birdalone
kilted her skirts and went her ways to some broken bushed
ground, where was a many rabbits playing about; but she
went not out of eye-shot of the babes. Before she was well
nigh to the little beasts, she fell to talking to them in a low
sweet voice, as had been her wont when she was little; and
when they heard it, those who had not scuttled away at first
glance of her, fell to creeping little short creeps one to the
other, as their manner is when they be alone together and
merry; and they suffered her to come quite amongst them,
and crept about her feet while she stood, still talking unto
them. Then she stooped down and took up one in her arms

84

and caressed it, and then laid him down and took up another,
and so with three or four of them; and she fell to pushing
them, and rolling them over with her foot; then she turned
a little away from them toward the children, and then a little
more, and the rabbits fell to following her, and she turned
and took up one in her arms, and went straight on toward
the children, but turning and talking to the rabbits now and
again.

As to the babes, she saw the goats, of whom were now a
dozen, or thereabouts, standing together in a kind of ring,
and the little ones going from one to the other playing with
them happily. But presently the lad turned and saw her
coming with her tail of little beasts, and he cried out a great
Oh! and ran toward her straightway, and the maiden after
him; and he held out his arms to have the rabbit she bore,
and she gave it to him smiling and said: "Lo now! here be
pretty playmates; but look to it that ye be soft and kind with
them, for they are but feeble people." So the younglings fell
to sporting with their new friends, and for a little forgat both
goats and golden lady; but the goats drew nigh, and stood
about them bleating, nor durst they run at the rabbits to
butt them, because of Birdalone and the little ones.

There then stood the slim maiden, tall and gleaming
above her little flock; and her heart was full of mirth and
rest, and the fear was all forgotten. But as she looked up toward the grey walls, lo, new tidings to hand! For she saw an
old man with a long white beard slowly coming toward them:
she started not, but abode his coming quietly, and as he
drew nigh she could see of him that he was big and stark,
and, old as he was, not yet bowed with his many years. He
stood looking on this Queen and her court silently a while,
and then he spake: "Such a sight I looked not to see on
this Isle of the Young and the Old." She said: "But meseemeth it is full meet that these younglings should sport
with the creatures." He smiled and said: "Such a voice I
looked not to hear on the Isle of the Young and the Old."

Birdalone became somewhat troubled, and said: " Am I

welcome here? for if I be not, I will pray thy leave to depart."

He said: "Thou art as welcome as the very spring, my child; and if thou have a mind to abide here, who shall naysay thee? For surely thou art young; nay, in regard to me thou art scarce older than babes. All blessings be with thee. But though thou art true and kind, as is clear to be seen by thy playing with these children and the landward beasts in peace and love, yet it may be so that thou hast brought hither somewhat less than peace." And he smiled upon her strangely.

She looked somewhat scared at his last words, and said: " But how so? If I might I would bear nought but peace and happiness to any place." The old carle laughed outright now, and said: "How so, dear child? because ladies so sweet and lovesome as thou be sent by love, and love rendeth apart that which was joined together."

She wondered at his word, and was bewildered by it, but she held her peace; and he said: "Now we may talk hereof later on; but the matter to hand now is the quenching of thine hunger; for I will not ask thee whereby thou camest, since by water thou needs must have come. Wherefore now I bid thee to our house, and these little ones shall go with us, and the three of these horned folk whom we are wont to tether amidst the wrack and ruin of what once was fair; the rest have our leave to depart, and these nibblers also; for we have a potherb garden by our house, and are fain to keep the increase of the same for ourselves."

Birdalone laughed, and shook her skirts at the coneys, and they all scuttled away after the manner of their kind. Thereat the little lad looked downcast and well-nigh tearful, but the maid stamped her foot, and roared well-favouredly.

Birdalone did her best to solace her, and plucked a bough from a hawthorn bush far above the little one's reach whereon was yet some belated blossom, and gave it to her and stilled her. But the old man picked out his milch-goats from

the flock (whereof was the white), and drave them before PART II
him, while the two babes went on still beside Birdalone, the Chap. 9
little carle holding her hand and playing with the fingers
thereof, the maiden sometimes hanging on to her gown,
sometimes going loose and sporting about beside her.

So came they to where the ground became smoother, and
there was a fair piece of greensward in a nook made by those
great walls and towers, which sheltered it from the north.
The said walls seemed to be the remnant of what had once
been a great house and castle; and up aloft, where was now
no stair to come at them, were chimneys and hearths here
and there, and windows with fair seats in them, and arched
doors and carven pillars, and many things beautiful; but
now was all ruined and broken, and the house was roofless
and floorless: withal it was overgrown with ash-trees and
quicken-beam, and other berry-trees and key-trees, which
had many years ago seeded in the rent walls, and now grew
there great and flourishing. But in the innermost nook of
this mighty remnant, and using for its lowly walls two sides
of the ancient ashlar ones, stood a cot builded not over
trimly of small wood, and now much overgrown with roses
and woodbine. In front of it was a piece of garden ground,
wherein waxed potherbs, and a little deal of wheat; and
therein was a goodly row of bee-skeps; and all without it
was the pleasant greensward aforesaid, wherein stood three
great ancient oaks, and divers thorns, which also were ancient after their kind.

The elder led his guest into the cot, which had but simple
plenishing of stools and benches, and a table unartful, and
then went to tether his goats in the ruined hall of the house,
and the children must needs with him, though Birdalone had
been glad of one of them at least; but there was no nay, but
that they must go see their dear white goat in her stall.
Howsoever all three came back again presently, the old
carle with a courteous word in his mouth; and he took
Birdalone's hand, and kissed it and bade her welcome to his
house, as though he had been a great lord at home in his

own castle. Therewith must the little ones also kiss her hand and be courteous; and Birdalone suffered it, laughing, and then caught them up in her arms, and clipped and kissed them well-favouredly; wherewith belike they were not over-well pleased, though the boy endured it kindly. Thereafter the elder set forth his banquet, which was simple enough: upland cheer of cream and honey, and rough bread; but sweet it was to Birdalone to eat it with good welcome, and the courtesy of the old man.

When they were done, they went out-a-doors, and Bird-alone and the old man laid them down under an oak-tree, and the children sported about anigh them. Then spake Birdalone: "Old man, thou hast been kind unto me; but now wouldest thou tell me about thee, what thou art, and what are these walls about us here?" Said he: "I doubt if I may do so, this day at least. But belike thou shalt abide with us, and then some day the word may come into my mouth."

She held her peace, and into her mind it came that it would be sweet to dwell there, and watch those fair children waxing, and the lad growing up and loving her; yea, even she fell to telling up the years which would make him a man, and tried to see herself, how she would look, when the years were worn thereto. Then she reddened at the untold thought, and looked down and was silent.

But the elder looked on her anxiously, and said: "It will be no such hard life for thee, for I have still some work in me, and thou mayst do something in spite of thy slender and delicate fashion."

She laughed merrily, and said: "Forsooth, good sire, I might do somewhat more than something; for I am deft in all such work as here ye need; so fear not but I should earn my livelihood, and that with joy." "Merry days shall we have then," said he.

But therewith her eye caught the gleam of her golden sleeve, and she thought of Aurea, and her heart smote her for her errand; then she laid her hand on her girdle and call-ed to mind little Viridis, and the glitter of the ring on her

88

finger brought the image of Atra before her; then she rose up and said: "Thou art kind, father, but I may not; I have an errand; this day must I depart from thee." He said: "Thou hast broken my heart; if I were not so old I would weep." And he hung adown his head.

She stood before him abashed, as if she had done him a wrong. At last he looked up and said: "Must it be to-day? Wilt thou not abide with us night-long, and go thy ways in the early morning?"

Now she scarce knew how to gainsay him, so wretched as the old carle looked; so it came to this, that she yeasaid the abiding till to-morrow. Then suddenly he became gay and merry, and he kissed her hand, and fell to much speaking, telling tales of little import concerning his earlier days. But when she asked him again of how he came there, and what meant the great ruined house, then he became foolish and wandering, and might scarce answer her; whereas otherwise he was a well-spoken old carle of many words, and those of the grandest.

Then changed his mood again, and he fell to bewailing her departure, and how that henceforth he should have none to speak to him with understanding. Then she smiled on him and said: "But yonder babes will grow up; month by month they will be better fellows unto thee."

"Fair child," he said, "thou dost not know. My days to come are but few, so that I should see but little of their waxing in any case. But furthermore, wax they will not; such as they be now, such shall they be till I at least see the last of them and the earth."

Birdalone wondered at this word, and the place seemed changed to her, yea, was grown somewhat dreary; but she said to the carle: "And thou, dost thou change in any wise, since these change not?"

He laughed somewhat grimly, and said: "The old that be here change from old to dead; how could I change to better? Yea, the first thing I had to do here was to bury an old man."

Quoth she: "And were there any children here then?"
"Yea," said he; "these same, or I can see no difference in
them." Said Birdalone: "And how long ago is that? And how
camest thou hither?" His face became foolish, and he gib-
bered rather than spake: "No, I wot not; no, no, no, not a
whit, a whit." But presently after was he himself again, and
telling her a tale of a great lady of the earl-folk, a baron's
dame, and how dear he was unto her.

He lay yet on the grass, and she stood before him, and
presently he put forth a hand to her gown-hem and drew her
to him thereby, and fell to caressing her feet; and Birdalone
was ashamed thereat, and a little angry. He was nought
abashed, but sat up and said: "Well, since thou must needs
depart to-morrow, be we merry to-day. And I pray thee talk
much with me, fair child, for sweet and sweet is thy voice to
hearken." Then he arose and said: "Now will I fetch thee
somewhat to eke the joy of us both." And he turned therewith and went into the house.

Birdalone stood there, and was now perplexed and downhearted; for now the look of the elder scarce liked her, and
the children began to seem to her as images, or at the best
not more to her than the rabbits or the goats; and she rued
her word that she would abide there the night through. For
she said to herself: I fear some trap or guile; is the witch behind this also? for the old man is yet stark, and though he be
foolish at whiles, yet may wizardry have learned him some
guile.

With that cometh out the carle again, bearing a little keg
and a mazer roughly wrought; and he came to Birdalone,
and sat down, and bade her sit by him, and said to her:
"Maybe I shall hear more of thy sweet voice when thy
sweet lips have been in the cup." Therewith he poured forth
into the mazer, and handed it to Birdalone, and lo! it was
clear and good mead. She sipped thereof daintily, and, to
say sooth, was well-pleased therewith, and it stirred the heart
in her. But then she gave back the cup to the elder, and
would no more of it. As for him, he drank what was left in

the cup, looking over the rim thereof meanwhile; and then filled himself another, and another, and yet more. But whereas it might have been looked for that his tongue should be loosened by the good mead into foolishness and gibbering, he became rather few-spoken, and more courteous and stately even than he had been at the first. But in the end, forsooth, he was forgetting Birdalone, what she was, and he fell a-talking, always with much pomp and state, as if to barons and earls, and great ladies; till suddenly his head fell back, he turned over on his face, and all wit was gone from him.

At first, then, Birdalone was afraid that he was dead, or nigh unto death, and she knelt down and raised his head, and fetched water and cast it over his face. But when she saw that he was breathing not so ill, and that the colour was little changed in his lips and cheeks, she knew that it was but the might of the mead that had overcome him. Wherefore she laid him so that he was easy, and then stood up and looked about her, and saw the children playing together a little way off, and nought else anigh her, save the birds in the brake, or flying on their errands eagerly from place to place. Then, as it were, without her will being told them, her limbs and her feet turned her about to the shore where lay the Sending Boat, and she went speedily but quietly thitherward, her heart beating quick, for fear lest something should yet stay her, and her eyes glancing from brake to bush, as if she looked to see some enemy, old or new, come out thence.

So now her will was clear enough to her feet, and they brought her down to the water-side and the long strand, past which the wide water lay windless and gleaming in the hot afternoon. Then lightly she stepped aboard, and awoke the Sending Boat with blood-offering, and it obeyed her, and sped swiftly on the way to the southward.

CHAPTER X. BIRDALONE COMES TO THE ISLE OF THE QUEENS.

BIRDALONE awoke the next morning while the boat was yet speeding over the water, and the sun was up: but she was hard on the land, which sat low and green, like a meadow exceeding fair, on the bosom of the water, and many goodly trees were sprinkled about the green land. But from amidst the trees, no great way from the water's edge, rose a great house, white and fair, as if it were new-builded, and all glorious with pinnacles, and tabernacles set with imagery.

Presently the boat's bows ran into the reed and rush at the brim of the water, and Birdalone stepped ashore without more ado, and the scent of the meadow-sweet amongst which she landed brought back unto her the image of Green Eyot that while agone.

But now when she was ashore the dread took hold of her again, and her knees trembled under her, so that she might scarce stand, so fearful was she of walking into some trap; especially when she beheld that goodly house, lest therein awaited her some proud and cruel lady, and no kind damsels to deliver her.

She looked about her, and saw in all the fair meadow neither man nor woman, nor draught-beast nor milch-beast, nought but the little creatures of the brake and the bent-grass, which were but as the blossoms thereof, and the birds running in the herbage or singing amidst the tree-boughs.

Then she thought that she must needs go forward, or be-like her errand would not speed; that the Sending Boat might not obey her, unless she saw through the adventure to the end; so she went on toward the house quaking.

Soon was she at the porch of the white palace, and had seen no man nor heard any voice of men; much she marvel-led, despite her dread, at the beauty of the said house, and the newness thereof; for it was as one flower arisen out of the earth, and every part of it made the beauty of the other parts

92

more excellent; and so new it was, that it would have seemed as if the masons thereof had but struck their scaffold
yesterday, save that under the very feet of the walls the
sweet garden flowers grew all uncrushed.

Now comes Birdalone through the porch unto the screens
of the great hall; and she stopped a little to recover her
breath, that she might be the quieter and calmer amongst
the great folk and mighty whom she looked to find therein.
So she gathered heart; but one thing daunted her, to wit,
that she heard no sound come from that great and goodly
hall, so that she doubted if it were perchance left desert by
them who had been its lords.

She raised her hand to the door of the screen, and it opened easily before her, and she entered, and there indeed she
saw new tidings. For the boards endlong and overthwart
were set, and thereat were sitting a many folk, and their
hands were reached out to knife and to dish, and to platter
and cup; but such a hush there was within, that the song of
the garden birds without sounded to her as loud as if they
were the voices of the children of Adam.

·Next she saw that all that company, from the great folk
on the dais down to those who stood about the hall to do the
service, were women, one and all; not one carle might she
see from where she stood: lovely were they many of them,
and none less than comely; their cheeks were bright, and
their eyes gleamed, and their hair flowed down fair of fashion. And she stood, and durst not move a long while, but
expected when someone would speak a word, and all should
turn their heads toward the new-comer. But none moved
nor spake. And the fear increased in her amidst that hush,
and weighed so heavy on her heart, that at last she might endure it no longer, but fell swooning to the floor.

When she came to herself, and the swoon-dreams had
left her, she saw by the changing of the sun through the
hall-windows, that she had lain there long, more nearly two
hours than one; and at first she covered her face with her
hands as she crouched there, that she might not see the sight

93

of the silent hall, for yet was it as hushed as before. Then
slowly she arose, and the sound of her raiment and her stirring feet was loud in her ears. But when she was upright on
her feet, she hardened her heart, and went forth into the
hall, and no less was her wonder than erst. For when she
came close to those ladies as they sat at table, and her raiment
brushed the raiment of the serving-women as she passed by,
then saw she how no breath came from any of these, and that
they neither spake nor moved, because they were dead.

At first, then, she thought to flee away at once, but again
she had mind of her errand, and so went up the hall, and so
forth on to the dais; and there again, close by the high-table,
she saw new tidings. For there was set a bier, covered with
gold and pall, and on it was laid a tall man, a king, belted and
crowned; and beside the said bier, by the head of the king,
knelt a queen of exceeding goodly body, clad all in raiment of
pearl and bawdekin; and her hands were clasped together,
and her mouth was drawn, and her brow knit with the anguish of her grief. But athwart the king's breast lay a naked
sword all bloody; and this Birdalone noted, that whereas the
lady was of skin and hue as if she were alive, the king was
yellow as wax, and his cheeks were shrunken, and his eyes
had been closed by the wakers of the dead.

Long Birdalone looked and wondered; and now if her fear
were less, her sorrow was more for all that folk sitting there
dead in their ancient state and pomp. And was not the
thought clean out of her head, that yet they might awake
and challenge her, and that she might be made one of that
silent company. Withal she felt her head beginning to fail
her, and she feared that she might swoon again and never
waken more, but lie for ever beside that image of the dead
king.

So then she refrained her both of fear and sorrow, and
walked speedily down the hall, looking neither to the right
nor left: and she came forth into the pleasance, but stayed
there nought, so nigh it seemed to that hushed company.
Thence came she forth into the open meadow, and sweet

and dear seemed its hot sunshine and noisy birds and rust- PART II
ling leaves. Nevertheless, so great was the tumult of her Chap. 10
spirits, that once more she grew faint, and felt that she might
scarce go further. So she dragged herself into the shade of a
thorn-tree, and let her body sink unto the ground, and lay
there long unwitting.

CHAPTER XI. AND NOW SHE COMES TO THE ISLE OF THE KINGS.

WHEN Birdalone came to herself it was drawing
toward the glooming, and she rose up hastily, and
went down to the Sending Boat, for she would not
for aught abide the night in that fearful Isle, lest the flock of
the hall should come alive and walk in the dusk and the dark.
She stepped aboard lightly, and yielded her blood to the
pride of that ferry, and it awoke and bore her forth, and she
went through the night till she fell asleep.

When she awoke it was broad day and the sun just aris-
ing, and lo! before her, some half mile off, an isle rugged
and rocky, and going up steep from the shore; and then,
held as it were by the fangs of the rocks and pikes of the
higher land, was a castle, white, high, and hugely builded,
though, because of the rock-land belike, it spread not much
abroad. Like to the lovely house of yesterday, it seemed
new-builded; and, little as Birdalone knew of such matters,
her heart told her that this new house was fashioned for
battle.

She was downcast when she saw the isle so rugged and
forbidding, but when the boat came aland in a stony bight,
whence the ground went up somewhat steeply toward the
heights, she went ashore straightway, and toiled up toward
the white battlement. Presently she found herself in a strait
and rugged path betwixt two walls of rock, so that she lost
sight of the castle a while, till she came out on to a level
place which looked down from aloft on to the blue water,
but all over against her close at hand were the great towers

95

and walls. She was worn by the rough road, and over helpless she felt her, and all too little to deal with that huge morsel of the world; and her valiancy gave way, and her trust in
her errand. She sat down on a stone and wept abundantly.

After a while she was amended, and she looked up and
saw the huge hold, and said: Yea, but if it were less by the
half than it is, it would still be big enough to cow me. Yet she
stood not up. Then she put forth a foot of her, and said
aloud: "Sorely hath this rough road tried Atra's shoon and
their goodly window-work; if they are to be known I must
be speedy on my journey or go barefoot."

As she spoke she stood up, and the sound of her own
voice frighted her, though nought noiseless was the place;
for the wind was there, and beat to and fro the castle and the
rock, and ran baffled into every corner of that market-place
of nothing. For in that garth was neither knight nor squire
nor sergeant; no spear-head glittered from the wall, no gleam
of helm showed from the war-swales; no porter was at the
gate; the drawbridge over the deep ghyll was down, the portcullis was up, and the great door cast wide open.

Birdalone steeled her heart and went forward swiftly, and
over the bridge, and entered the base-court, and came without more ado to the door of the great hall, and opened it
easily, as with the door of yesterday, looking to find another
show like unto that one; and even so it fell out.

Forsooth the hall was nought light and lovely, and gay
with gold and bright colours, as that other, but beset with
huge round pillars that bore aloft a wide vault of stone, and
of stone were the tables; and the hallings that hung on the
wall were terrible pictures of battle and death, and the fall of
cities, and towers a-tumbling and houses a-flaming.

None the less there also were the shapes of folk that
moved not nor spake, though not so thronged was that hall
as the other one; and it seemed as if men were sitting there
at a council rather than a feast. Close by Birdalone's right
hand as she entered were standing in a row along the screen

big men-at-arms all-weaponed, and their faces hidden by their sallets; and down below the dais on either side of the high-table was again a throng of all-armed men; and at the high-table itself, and looking down the hall, sat three crown-ed kings, each with his drawn sword lying across his knees, and three long-hoary wise-men stood before them at the nether side of the board.

Birdalone looked on it all, striving with her fear: but yet more there was, for she deemed that needs must she go through the hall up to the dais, lest the Sending Boat deny its obedience. Up toward the dais she went then, passing by weaponed men who sat as if abiding the council's end at the endlong tables. And now, though no shape of man there spake or breathed, yet sound lacked not; for within the hall went the wind as without, and beat about from wall to wall, and drave clang and clash from the weapons hung up, and waved the arras, and fared moaning in the nooks, and hummed in the vault above.

Came she up to the dais then, and stood beside one of the wise-men, and looked on the kings, and saw the mightiness which had been in them, and quaked before them. Then she turned from them and looked down to the floor, and lo! there, just below the dais, lay a woman on a golden bier; exceeding fair had she been, with long yellow hair stream-ing down from her head; but now waxen white she was, with ashen lips and sunken cheeks. Clad was she in raiment of purple and pall, but the bosom of her was bared on one side, and therein was the road whereby the steel had fared which had been her bane.

Now when Birdalone had gazed thereon a while, she deemed that if she tarried there long amidst those fierce men by the dead woman, she should lose her wit full soon, so sore the fear, held back, beset her now. Wherefore she turned and went hastily down the hall, and out-a-doors, and over the bridge, and ran fleet-foot down the rocky way whereby she had come, till she could run no further, and lay down

under a great stone breathless and fordone; yet her heart
upheld her and suffered her not to swoon, belike because she
had given her limbs such hard work to do.

There she lay awake and troubled for an hour or more,
and then she fell asleep, and slept till the day was worn toward sunset, and nought meddled with her. She arose and
went to her ship somewhat downhearted, wondering how
many such terrors should befall her; nay, whether the Sending Boat would so lead her that henceforth she should happen on no children of Adam but such as were dead images of
the living. Had all the world died since she left the Isle of
the Young and the Old?

Howsoever, she had nought to do save to board her ferry,
and content its greedy soul with her blood, and drive it with
the spell-words. And thereafter, when it was speeding on,
and the twilight dusking apace, she looked aback, and
seemed to see the far-off woodland in the northern ort, and
the oak-clad ridge, where she had met her wood-mother;
and then it was as if Habundia were saying to her: Meet
again we shall. And therewith straightway became life
sweeter unto her.

Deepened then the dusk, and became night, and she
floated on through it, and was asleep alone on the bosom of
the Water.

CHAPTER XII. OF BIRDALONE, HOW SHE CAME UNTO THE ISLE OF NOTHING.

LONG before sunrise, in the very morn-dusk, she awoke
and found that her ferry had taken land again. Little
might she see what the said land was like; so she sat
patiently and abode the day in the boat; but when day was
come, little more was to see than erst. For flat was the isle,
and scarce raised above the wash of the leeward ripple on a
fair day; nor was it either timbered or bushed or grassed, and,
so far as Birdalone might see, no one foot of it differed in
aught from another. Natheless she deemed that she was

98

bound to go ashore and seek out the adventure, or spoil
her errand else.

Out of the boat she stepped then, and found the earth all
paved of a middling gravel, and nought at all growing there,
not even the smallest of herbs; and she stooped down and
searched the gravel, and found neither worm nor beetle
therein, nay nor any one of the sharp and slimy creatures
which are wont in such ground.

A little further she went, and yet a little further, and no
change there was in the land; and yet she went on and found
nothing; and she wended her ways southward by the sun,
and the day was windless.

At last she had gone a long way and had no sight of water
south of the isle, nor had she seen any hill, nay, not so much
as an ant-heap, whence she might look further around; and it
seemed to her that she might go on for ever, and reach the
heart of Nowhither at last. Wherefore she thought she
would turn back and depart this ugly isle, and that no other
adventure abided her therein. And by now it was high noon;
and she turned about and took a few steps on the backward
road.

But even therewith it seemed as if the sun, which heretofore had been shining brightly in the heavens, went out as a
burnt-down candle, and all was become dull grey over head,
as all under foot was a dull dun. But Birdalone deemed she
could follow a straight course back again, and so walked on
sturdily. Hour after hour she went and stayed not, but saw
before her no glimpse of the northern shore, and no change
in the aspect of the ground about her.

It had so happened that a little before she had turned to
go back, she had eaten her dinner of a piece of bread and a
morsel of cheese, and now as she stooped and peered on the
ground, looking for some sign of the way, as her foot-prints
going south, and had her eyes low anigh the earth, she saw
something white at her feet in the gathering dusk (for the
day was wearing), and she put her hand to it and lifted it, and
found it a crumb of bread, and knew that it must have come

H2   99 from her dinner of seven hours ago, whereas till that time her bread had lain unbroken in her scrip. Fear and anguish smote her therewith, for she saw that in that dull land, every piece whereof was like every other piece, she must have gone about in a ring, and come back again to where she first turned to make for the northern shore.

Yet would she not cast aside all hope, but clad herself in her valiancy. Forsooth she knew it availed nought to try to move on in the twilight; so she laid herself down on that waste, and made up her mind to sleep if she might, and abide the new day there, and then to strive with the way once more, for belike, she thought, it may be fair to-morrow, and the sun shining. And as she was very weary with tramping the waste all day, she fell asleep at once, and slept the short night through.

But when she awoke, and saw what the new day was, her heart fell indeed, for now was she encompassed and shut in with a thick dark mist (though it seemed to be broad day), so that had there been aught to see she would not have seen it her own length away from her. So there she stood, hanging her head, and striving to think; but the master-thought of death drawing nigh scattered all other thoughts, or made them dim and feeble.

Long she stood there; but suddenly something came into her mind. She set her hand to the fair-broidered pouch which hung from Viridis' loin-girdle, and drew out thence flint and steel and tinder, which matters, forsooth, had served her before in the boat to make fire withal. Then she set her hand to her head, and drew forth the tress of hair which Habundia had given her, and which was coiled up in the crown of her own abundant locks which decked her so gloriously; she drew two hairs from the said tress, and held them between her lips while she did up the tress in its place again, and then, pale and trembling, fell to striking a light, and when she had the tinder burning, she cried out: "O Woodmother, Woodmother! How then may we meet again as thou didst promise me, if I die here in this empty waste?

O Woodmother, if thou mightest but come hither for my
deliverance!"

Then she burned the hairs one after another, and stood waiting, but nought befell a great while, and her heart sickened, and there she stood like a stone.

But in a while, lo! there came as it were a shadow amidst the mist, or rather lying thereon, faint and colourless, and it was of the shape of the Woodmother, with girt-up gown and bow in hand. Birdalone cried aloud with joy, and hastened towards the semblance, but came to it no nigher, and still she went, and the semblance still escaped her, and she followed on and on. And this lasted long, and faster and faster must she follow lest it vanish, and she gathered her skirts into her girdle, and fell to running fleet-foot after the fleeing shadow, which she loved dearly even amidst the jaws of death; and all her fleetness of foot had Birdalone to put forth in following up the chase; but even to die in the pain would she not miss that dear shadow.

But suddenly, as she ran, the mist was all gone from before her, the sun shone hot and cloudless; there was no shadow or shape of Habundia there, nought but the blue lake and the ugly lip of that hideous desert, with the Sending Boat lying a half score yards from her feet; and behind her stood up, as it were a wall, the mist from out of which she had come.

Forsooth Birdalone was too breathless to cry out her joy, but her heart went nigh to breaking therewith, and lovely indeed to her was the rippled water and the blue sky; and she knew that her Woodmother had sped a sending to her help, and she fell a-weeping where she stood, for love of her wise mother, and for longing to behold her: she stretched out her arms to the north quarter, and said blessings on her in a voice faint for weariness. Then she laid her down on the desert, and rested her with sleep, despite the hot sun, and when she awoke, some three hours thereafter, all was as before, save that the sky had now some light-flying clouds, and still was the wall of mist behind her. Wherefore she deemed she had yet time, and the blue rippling water wooed her much-besweated limbs; so she did off her raiment and took the water, and became happy and unweary therein. Then she landed and stood in the sun to dry her, and so, strengthened with that refreshing, clad her, and went a-board and did the due rites, and sped over the waters, and had soon lost sight of that ugly blotch on the fair face of the Great Water.

HERE ENDS THE SECOND PART OF THE WATER OF THE WONDROUS ISLES, WHICH IS CALLED OF THE WONDROUS ISLES, AND BEGINS THE THIRD PART OF THE SAID TALE, WHICH IS CALLED OF THE CASTLE OF THE QUEST.

THE WATER OF THE WONDROUS ISLES. THE THIRD PART: OF THE CASTLE OF THE QUEST.

CHAPTER I. BIRDALONE COMES TO THE CASTLE OF THE QUEST.

EMPTY was the day to Birdalone save for her thoughts, and she slept not a good while of the night. When she awoke in the morning there was no land before her, and she began to fear somewhat that so it might be many days, and that she might have to fare the water landless, and perchance till she starved for hunger; for now was there but little victual left of that which the kind Viridis had given her. So she wore the day somewhat uneasily, and by then night fell had eaten but little; yet was that little the last crumb and gobbet of her store. Wherefore it is no wonder though she were dismayed when she awoke early on the morrow, and beheld nought before her save the landless water.

But about noon she deemed she saw a little cloud in the offing that moved not as the other clouds, and she watched it closely at first, and it changed not any the more, and she grew weary of watching it and strove to sleep, turning her head to the after part of her ferry; and thus betwixt sleeping and waking she wore away three hours: then she stood up and looked ahead, and lo, the white cloud had taken shape, and was a white castle far away (for the day was exceeding clear), sitting, as it seemed, on the very face of the water. The boat sped on swiftly thitherward, so that it was not right long ere Birdalone beheld the green shore on either side of the said castle, and at last, three hours before sunset, she was drawing nigh thereto, and beheld it all clearly, what it was.

It was brand-new, and was fair enough, builded part of stone and lime, part of framed work, but was but middling big. As she drew nigher yet, she saw that there were folk on

winded from the battlement, and folk were running together to somewhither. And now was Birdalone come so
near, that she saw the water-gate of the castle, and folk
coming out thereby on to the landing-place; and she saw
presently, that a very tall man with grizzled hair stood foremost of them, and he waved his hand to her, and spake
something, but the wind bore the words away from her; yet
she seemed to know that this folk would do her to wit that
they would have none of her; and her heart died within her,
so faint and hungry as she was.

Howsoever the ferry sped on its way swiftly, and in a
minute or two had stayed itself at the landing-stair, whereabout were gathered a score of men, some armed some unarmed, and they seemed for the more part to be grey-headed
and past middle-age.

Birdalone stood up in her craft, and the aforesaid tall grey
man, who was unarmed, but clad in knightly raiment, stood
on the stair and spake unto her, and said: "Lady, this is an
house where women enter never since first the roof was
done thereon, which forsooth was but a year ago. We will
pray thee therefore to turn thy boat's head away, and seek
some other lodging by the water, either eastward or westward."

Little knew Birdalone of worldly courtesy, or she had
made him a sharp answer belike; but she only looked on
him ruefully, and said: "Good warrior, I am come a long
way, and may not turn back from mine errand; and I am
now lacking victual and hungry, and if ye help me not, it is
like that I shall die. Much lieth on mine errand, if ye knew
it." She was weeping-ripe, but refrained her tears, though
her lip quivered.

She stretched out her hands to the greybeard, and he
looked on her and found her exceeding fair; and he deemed
her to be guileless, both because of her simple speech and
sweet voice, and the goodliness of her face and eyes. But

he said: "Lady, thine errand hath nought to do with it, it PART III
is thy womanhood that bars our door. For all we are bound Chap. 1
by oath not to suffer a woman to abide in this castle till our
lords take the bann off, and bid us open to women."

She smiled faintly, and said: "If I might but see thy lords
then, since thou art not master here." He said: "They are
away, and will not be back till to-morrow morning; and
I wot not the hour of their return. And yet," said he, "I
would we might help thee somewhat."

"O I pray thee, I pray thee!" she said, "or mine errand
will come to nought after all."

Therewith came another man down the stair, and stood by
the old knight and plucked his sleeve, and fell to talk with
him softly. This man was by his habit a religious, and was a
younger man than the others, it might be of five and thirty
winters, and he was fair of favour. While they spake together Birdalone sat her down again, and was well-nigh
spent.

At last the old man spake: "Damsel," he said, "we deem
we may suffer thee to enter the castle since thy need is so
great, and have a meal's meat at our hands, and yet save our
oath, if thou depart thence by the landward gate before sunset. Will this serve thee?"

"Fair sir," said Birdalone, "it will save my life and mine
errand; I may say no more words for my faintness, else
would I thank thee."

She stood up on her feet, and the old man-at-arms reached out his hand to her, and she took it and came her ways up
the stair, but found herself but feeble. But the priest (forsooth he was chaplain of the castle) helped her on the other
side. But when she stood on the level stones by the water-
gate, she turned to the old man and said: "One thing I will
ask of thee, Is this place one of the Wondrous Isles?" The
elder shook his head. "We know not the Wondrous Isles,"
said he; "this castle is builded on the mainland."

Her face flushed for joy at the word, and she said: "One

thing I will crave of thee, to wit, that thou wilt leave my
barge lying here untouched till thy masters come back, and
wilt give command that none meddle therewith."

He would have answered, but the priest brake in, and
said: "This will he do, lady, and he is the castellan, and
moreover he will swear to obey thee herein." And therewith
he drew forth a cross with God nailed thereon, and the castellan swore on it with a good will.

Then the priest drew Birdalone on, and between them
they brought her into the great hall, and set her down in a
chair and propped her with cushions. And when she was
thus at rest, she began to weep somewhat, and the castellan
and the priest stood by and comforted her; for themseemed,
despite her grief, that she had brought the sun into their
house.

Next were victual brought unto her of broth and venison,
and good wine and cates and strawberries; and she was not
so famished but she might eat and drink with a good will.
But when she was done, and had rested a little, the castellan
stood up and said: "Lady, the sun is gone off the western
windows now, and I must save mine oath; but ere thou depart, I were fain to hear thy voice giving me pardon for my
evil cheer and the thrusting of thee forth." And therewith he
put one knee to the ground, and took her hand and kissed it.

But Birdalone was grown merry again, and she laughed
and said: "What pardon thou canst have of me, kind knight,
thou hast; but now methinks thou makest overmuch of me,
because I am the only woman who hath come into thy
castle. I am but a simple maiden, though mine errand be not
little."

Forsooth she wondered that the stark and gruff old man
was so changed to her in little space; for nought she knew as
yet how the sight of her cast a hot gleed of love into the
hearts of them who beheld her.

Now Birdalone arose; but the castellan knelt at her feet,
and kissed her hand again, and again, and yet again. Then

he said: "Thou art gracious indeed. But methinks the father here will lead thee out-a-gates; for he may show thee a lair, wherein thou shalt be safe enough to-night; and to-morrow may bring new tidings."

So the priest made obeisance to her and led her down the hall, and the castellan's eyes were following them till the screen hid them. The priest left her in the hall-porch a while, and went into the buttery, and came back with a basket of meat and drink, and they went forth at the great gate together, and there was the last of the sun before them.

CHAPTER II. OF BIRDALONE, AND HOW SHE RESTED THE NIGHT THROUGH IN A BOWER WITHOUT THE CASTLE OF THE QUEST.

ON a fair smooth road went they amidst of a goodly meadow-land, wherein were little copses here and there. When they were fairly out of the gate, the priest reached for Birdalone's hand, and she let him take it and lead her along thereby, thinking no evil; but he might scarce speak for a while, so great was the stir in his heart at the touch of her bare flesh. But Birdalone spake and said: "Thou art kind, father, to lead me on my way thus."

He answered in a husky voice with his eyes cast down and forsooth set on the feet of her: "It is not far that I am leading thee; there is a broken cot by the copse at the turn of the road yonder, where thou mayst abide to-night; it is better lodging than none, evil as it is for such an one as thou."

Birdalone laughed: "Worse have I had," said she, "than would be the copse without the cot." And she thought withal of the prison in the Isle of Increase Unsought.

Her voice seemed so cheery and friendly to the priest, that he shook off somewhat the moodiness of his desire, and looked up and said: "I shall tell thee, lady, that I suppose thou hast more errand with my lords than to crave lodging of them despite the custom of the castle. Nay, I

have an inkling of what thine errand may be, whereof more
anon; but now shall I tell thee what is best for thee to do so
as to have speech of them the soonest. They have gone forth
with some of our lads to gather venison, or it may be beeves
and muttons for our victualling, and somewhat of battle
may they have had on the way, for ill neighbours have we.
But if they come back unfoughten they will be wending this
road, and must needs pass by thy copse-side; and if thou be
sleeping the noise of them will full surely awaken thee. Then
all thou hast to do is to come forth and stand in the way before them, that they may see thee; and when once they have
seen thee, how may they pass thee by unspoken with?"

"I thank thee heartily for thy rede," said Birdalone;
"but I would ask thee two things: first, what is the name of
the castle behind us? and second, why have ye the custom
of shutting the door upon women?"

Said the priest: "The castle is called in this country-side,
the White Ward by the Water; but within there we call it
the Castle of the Quest; and thus is it called because my
lords are seeking their loves whom they have lost; and they
have sworn an oath that no woman shall enter therein till
their own loves have trodden its floors."

Rose the heart of Birdalone at that word, and she deemed
indeed that she was come thither whereas her she-friends
would have had her. The priest beheld her and saw how her
beauty was eked by that gladness, and he scarce knew how
to contain himself, and might speak no word awhile; then
he said: "Hearken further concerning thy matter; if my
lords be tarried, and come not by matin-song, then I doubt
not but the castellan will send folk to see to thee." He
looked down therewith and said: "I will come to thee
myself, and will bring thee men-at-arms, if need be. But
sometime to-morrow morning my lords will come, save
mischief hath betid, which God forbid." And he crossed
himself; then he looked up and full in her face, and said:
"But keep thine heart up; for whatsoever may betide, thou
shalt not be left uncared for."

Said Birdalone: "I see of thee that thou art become my
good friend, and it rejoiceth my heart; I shall be well at ease
to-night in thy cot, and to-morrow morn I shall be valiant
to do thy bidding."

The sweetness of her speech so overcame him, that he but
looked confusedly on her, as if he scarce heard her; and they
went on together without more words, till he said: "Here
are we at the cot, and I will show thee thy chamber." So he
led her to a little thatched bower, built with walls of wattle-
work daubed with clay, which stood without the remnant of
the cot: it was clean and dry, for the roof was weather-
tight; but there was nought in it at all save a heap of brack-
en in a corner.

There stood the priest, still holding Birdalone's hand,
and spake not, but looked about, yet always covertly on
Birdalone; but in a while he let go her hand, and seemed to
wake up, and said: "This it is; a sorry place enough, were
it even for a gangrel body."

"Even so am I," quoth she laughing; "and thou mayest
look to it, that herein I shall rest full happily."

Then he gave her a horn, drawing it from out of the basket of victual, which he now set down on the ground; and
he said: "If thou shouldst deem thee hard bestead, then
wind this horn, and we shall know its voice up there and
come to help thee. Now I give thee good-night."

She thanked him sweetly, and he went slowly out of the
bower, but was scarce gone ere he came back again, and
said: "One thing I may perchance tell thee without drawing thine anger on my head; to wit, that I it was who said to
the castellan that he should take thee in. Wilt thou say
aught to this?" She said: "I will thank thee again and again;
for it was the saving of my life and mine errand. And clearer
is it now than ever that thou art a good friend unto me."

As she looked on him and caressed him with kind eyes,
she saw that his brow was knit, and his face troubled, and
she said to him: "What ails thee? art thou wroth with me
in any wise?"

"O no," said he; "how should I be wroth with thee! But there is a thing I would ask of thee." "Yea, and what?" said she. He said: "Nay, I may not, I may not. It shall be for to-morrow, or another day." He spake it looking down, and in a broken voice; and she wondered somewhat at him, but not much, deeming that he was troubled by something which had nought to do with her, and which he might not refrain from thinking of, even before a stranger.

But presently he caught her hand and kissed it, and bade her good-night again, and then went hastily out of the bower; and when he was well without, he muttered, but not so as she might hear him: "Durst I have asked her, she would have suffered me to kiss her cheek. Alas! fool that I was!"

Birdalone turned then to her bracken bed, and found it sweet and clean; and she was at rest and peace in her mind, albeit her body was exceeding weary. She felt happy in the little lonely cot, and her heart had gone out to the sweet meadow-land, and she loved it after all the trouble of the water; and herseemed that even now, in the dusk a-growing into dark, it loved and caressed her. So she laid her down, nor unclad herself at all, lest she should have to arise on a sudden, and show those tokens of the three damsels on her body.

A little while she lay there happily, hearkening the voices of the nightingales in the brake, and then she fell into a dreamless sleep, unbroken till the short night passed into day.

CHAPTER III. HOW BIRDALONE DIGHT HER FOR MEETING THE CHAMPIONS OF THE QUEST.

IT was the birds beginning their first song once more that awakened Birdalone before the sun was up; but she had no will to stir a while, whereas she felt so happy and restful; and that all the more when she remembered where

she was, and told herself that her errand was now like to be
accomplished; and she thought of her friends whom she had
left on the Isle of Increase Unsought, and blessed them for
their kindness, and the love of them was sweet to her heart,
and amidst such thoughts she fell asleep again.

When she awoke thereafter there was a flood of sunshine
lying on the meadows, and she sprang up in haste lest she
had overslept herself, but when she was come out of the
bower, she soon saw that the sunbeams lay low on the land,
and that it was yet the first hour of the sun; so she turned
about, and went through the copse to the other side, and lo!
a little clear stream running before her. So she spake to herself softly and said: Fie on it! I was weary with the boat and
my hunger last night, and I went to bed unwashen; and this
morn I am weary for the foulness of my unwashen body.
Unseemly it were to me to show myself sluttish before
these lords; let me find time for a bath at least.

Therewith she went swiftly down to the water, undoing
her girdle and laces by the way. She came to the stream and
found it running between blue-flowering mouse-ear and
rushes, into a pool which deepened from a sandy shallow:
so anon her borrowed raiment was lying on the grassy lip of
the water, and she was swimming and disporting her in the
pool, with her hair loose and wavering over her white back
like some tress of the water-weed. Therein she durst not
tarry long, but came hurrying out on to the grass, and clad
herself in haste. But she covered not her shoulders with the
golden gown, nor laced it over her bosom, so that Viridis'
smock might be the plainer to see: which smock was note-
worthy, for the breast thereof was broidered with green
boughs, whence brake forth little flames of fire, and all so
dainty-wrought as if the Faery had done it.

Withal she gathered up the gown into her girdle, and let
the skirt-hem clear her ancles, so that Atra's shoon might
be seen at once; and they were daintily dight with window-
work and broidery of gold and green stones and blue. And
forsooth it was little likely that any man should stand before

111

her a minute ere his eyes would seek to her feet and ancles, so clean and kindly as they were fashioned.

Therewith she set her hands to her head, and trussed up her hair, and bound it closely to her head, so that it might hide no whit of her borrowed attire.

There she stood, with Aurea's collar lying on her dear neck, and Viridis' girdle about her shapen loins, and Atra's ring on her lovesome finger. And she hearkened awhile and heard no sound of coming men; and there came into her heart a gentle fear, which grieved her not. Over the water before her hung an eglantine bush, with its many roses either budding or but just out. Birdalone stole thither softly and said, smiling: Nay, if I have nothing that is mine on my body, I will take this of the maiden's bath and make it mine. And therewith she plucked a spray of the bush and turned it into a garland for her head; and then when she had stood shyly a while in that same place, she turned and went swiftly to her place beside her night-harbour, and stood there hearkening with that sweet fear growing upon her, her colour coming and going and her heart beating fast.

Now the thought of that kind priest who had led her to the bower last night came into her mind, and she wondered why he had been so troubled. And she thought, would those others be so kind to her, or would they deem her an impudent wench or a foolish, or pass her by?

Forsooth if any had passed her by, it had been not that he should miss seeing her beauty, but that he should fear it, and deem her some goddess of the Gentiles of old time come before him for his ensnaring.

CHAPTER IV. AND NOW SHE MEETS THE CHAMPIONS.

NOW, as she stood hearkening, she deemed she heard something that was not so loud as the song of the blackbird in the brake, but further off and longer voiced: and again she hearkened heedfully, and the sound came again, and she deemed now that it was the voice of an horn. But the third time of her hearing it she knew that it was nought less; and at last it grew nigher, and there was mingled with it the sound of men shouting and the lowing of neat.

Then she stepped down to the very edge of the way, and now she saw the riding-reek go up into the clear air, and she said: Now are they coming without fail, and I must pluck up a heart; for surely these dear friends of my friends shall neither harm a poor maiden nor scorn her.

Soon came the leading beasts from out of the dust-cloud, and behind them was the glitter of spear-heads; and then presently was a herd of neat shambling and jostling along the road, and after them a score or so of spearmen in jack and sallet, who forsooth turned to look on Birdalone as they passed by, and spake here and there a word or two, laughing and pointing to her, but stayed not; and all went on straight to the castle.

Thereafter was a void, and then came riding leisurely another score of weaponed men, whereof some in white armour; and amongst them were five sumpter horses laden with carcasses of venison. And all these also went by and stayed not, though the most of them gazed on Birdalone hard enough.

Last of all came three knights riding, one with a gold surcoat over his armour, and thereon a cleft heart of red; the second with a green surcoat, and on the same a chief of silver with green boughs thereon, their ends a-flaming; but the third bore a black surcoat besprinkled with silver tears.

And all these three rode bare-headed, save that the Black
Knight bore an oak-wreath on the head.

Now did Birdalone take to her valiancy, and she stepped
out into the road till she was but a ten paces from those men,
who reined up when they beheld her; and she said in a clear
voice: "Abide, warriors! for if ye be what I deem you, I
have an errand unto you."

Scarce were the words out of her mouth, ere all three had
leapt off their horses, and the Golden Knight came up to
her, and laid his hand upon her side, and spake eagerly and
said: "Where is she, whence thou gattest this gown of good
web?"

"And thou," said she, "art thou Baudoin the Golden
Knight?" But he set his hand to the collar on her neck, and
touched her skin withal, and said: "This, was she alive
when thou camest by it?"

She said: "If thou be Baudoin the Golden Knight, I have
an errand to thee." "I am he," said the knight; "O tell me,
tell me, is she dead?" Said Birdalone: "Aurea was alive
when last I saw her, and mine errand is from her to thee, if
thou be verily her lover. Now with this word I pray thee to
be content a while," said she, smiling kindly upon him,
"for needs must I do mine errand in such wise as I was bidden. And thou seest also that thy friends would have a word
of me."

Forsooth, they were thrusting in on her, and the Green
Knight gat a hold of her left wrist in his left hand, and his
right was on her shoulder, and his bright face close to her
bosom whereon lay Viridis' smock; and thereat she shrank
aback somewhat, but said: "Sir, it is sooth that the smock
is for thee when thou hast answered me a question or two.
Meanwhile I pray thee forbear a little; for, as I trow, all is
well, and thou shalt see my dear friend Viridis again."

He withdrew him a little, flushed and shamefaced. He
was a young man exceeding beauteous, clear-skinned and
grey-eyed, with curly golden hair, and he bore his armour
as though it were silken cloth. Birdalone looked upon him

kindly though shyly, and was glad to the heart's root that PART III
Viridis had so lovely a man to her darling. As for the Golden Chap. 4
Knight, as Birdalone might see now he stood a little aloof,
he was a very goodly man of some five and thirty winters,
tall he was, broad-shouldered and thin-flanked, black-haired, with somewhat heavy eyebrows, and fierce hawk-eyes;
a man terrible of aspect, when one first beheld him.

Now when the Black Squire had hearkened Birdalone's
word concerning Viridis, he threw himself down on the
ground before her, and fell to kissing her feet; or, if you
will, Atra's shoon which covered them. When she drew
back a little, he rose on one knee and looked up at her with
an eager face, and she said: "To thee also I have an errand
from Atra, thy speech-friend, if thou be Arthur the Black
Squire."

He spake not, but still gazed on her till she reddened.
She knew not whether to deem him less goodly than the
other twain. He also was a young man of not over five and
twenty years, slim and lithe, with much brown hair; his face
tanned so dark that his eyes gleamed light from amidst it;
his chin was round and cloven, his mouth and nose excellently fashioned; little hair he had upon his face, his cheeks
were somewhat more hollow than round. Birdalone noted of
his bare hands, which were as brown as his face, that they
were very trim and shapely.

Now he rose to his feet, and the three stood together and
gazed on her; as how might they do otherwise? Birdalone
hung her head, and knew not what next to do or say. But she
thought within herself, would these three men have been as
kind to her as her three friends of the Isle, had she happened
on them in like case as she was that time? And she settled
with herself that they would have been no less kind.

Now spake the Golden Knight, and said: "Will the kind
maiden do her errand to us here and now? for we be eager
and worn with trouble." Birdalone looked adown and was
somewhat confused. "Fair sirs," said she, "I will do your
will herein."

PART III
Chap. 4

But the Black Squire looked on her and saw that she was troubled, and he said: "Your pardon, fair fellows, but is it not so that we have an house somewhat anigh, not ill purveyed of many things? By your leave I would entreat this kind and dear lady to honour us so much as to enter the Castle of the Quest with us, and abide there so long as she will; and therein may she tell us all her errand at her leisure; and already we may see and know, that it may not be aught save a joyous one."

Then spake the Golden Knight, and said: "I will ask the lady to pardon me, and will now join my prayer to thine, brother, that she come home with us. Lady," he said, "wilt thou not pardon me, that in the eager desire to hear tidings of my speech-friend I forgat all else?"

And therewithal he knelt before her, and took her hand and kissed it; and for all his fierce eyes and his warrior's mien, she deemed him kind and friendly. Then needs must the Green Knight kneel and kiss also, though he had no pardon to crave; but a fair sweet lad she thought him, and again her heart swelled with joy to think that her friend Viridis had so dear a speech-friend to long for her.

Then came the turn of the Black Squire, and by then were the two others turned away a little toward their horses; and he knelt down on both knees before Birdalone and took her right arm above the wrist, and looked at the hand and kissed it as if it were a relic, but stood not up; and she stood bending over him, and a new sweetness entered into her, the like of which she had never felt. But as for the Black Squire, it seemed that one hand would not suffice him, and he took her left hand and fell to kissing it, and then both the hands together all over the backs of them, and then the palms thereof, and he buried his face in the two palms, and held them to his cheeks; and the dear hands suffered it all, and consented to the embracing of his cheeks. But Birdalone deemed that this was the kindest and sweetest of the three kind warriors, and sorry she was when he let go her hands and stood up.

His face was flushed, but his speech calm, as he spake so

116

that the other knights might hear him: "Now will we
straight to the castle, lady, and we will ask thee which of us
three thou wilt honour by riding his horse there; shall it be
Baudoin's bright bay, or Hugh's dapple-grey, or my red
roan?" And therewith he took her by the hand and led her
toward the horses. But she laughed, and turning a little,
pointed to the castle, and said: "Nay, sweet lords, but I will
fare afoot, such a little way as it is, and I all unwont to the
saddle."

Spake the Green Knight: "If that be so, lady, then shall
we three walk afoot with thee."

"Nay, nay," she said; "I have nought to carry but myself, but ye have your byrnies and your other armour, which
were heavy for you to drag on afoot, even a little way.
Moreover, I were fain to see you mount your horses, and
ride and run about the meadow with tossing manes and
flashing swords, while I trudge quietly toward the gate; for
such things, and so beauteous, are all new unto me, as ye
shall learn presently when I tell you my story. Do so much
to pleasure me, kind knights."

The tall Baudoin nodded to her, smiling kindly, as much
as to say that he thought well of her desire. But the Green
Knight ran to his horse with a glad shout, and anon was
in the saddle with his bright sword in his fist; then he
spurred, and went a-gallop hither and thither over the
mead, making his horse turn short and bound, and playing
many tricks of the tilt-yard, and crying, A Hugh, A Hugh,
for the Green Gown! The Golden Knight was slower and
more staid, but in manywise he showed his war-deftness,
riding after Hugh as if he would fall on him, and staying his
way just as it became perilous; and he cried, Baudoin, Baudoin, for Gold-sleeves! And all this seemed to Birdalone
both terrible and lovely.

But for the Black Squire, he was slow to let loose Birdalone's hand; but thereafter he was speedy to vault into his
saddle, and he made courses over the meadow, but ever
came back to Birdalone as she went her ways, riding round

and round her, and tossing his sword into the air the while and catching it as it fell. And no less lovely did this seem to Birdalone, and she smiled on him and waved her hand to him.

Going slowly in this wise, she came at last to the castle gate; and now had all those three out-gone her and stood afoot in the wicket to welcome her, and the Golden Knight, who was the oldest of the three, was the speaker of the welcome.

Over the threshold of the Castle of the Quest went Birdalone's feet then, and she was grown so happy as she had never deemed she should be all her life long.

CHAPTER V. BIRDALONE HAS TRUE TOKENS FROM THE CHAMPIONS OF THE QUEST.

NOW they brought Birdalone into a very fair chamber, where was presently everything she might need, save a tiring-woman, which, forsooth, was no lack unto her, since never had she had any to help her array her body. So she did what she might to make herself the trimmer; and in a while came two fair swains of service, who brought her in all honour into the great hall, where were the three lords abiding her. There were they served well and plenteously, and fair was the converse between them; and in especial was the talk of Arthur the Black Squire goodly and wise and cheery, and well-measured; and the Green Knight's speech merry and kind, as of an happy child; and the Golden Knight spake ever free and kindly, though not of many words was he. And who was happy if Birdalone were not?

But when they had eaten and washed their hands, then spake the Golden Knight: "Dear maiden, now are we ready to hear the innermost of thine errand, all we together, if thou wilt."

Birdalone smiled and reddened withal, as she said: "Fair
118

lords, I doubt not but ye are even they unto whom I was
sent, but they who sent me, and who saved me from death
and worse, bade me do mine errand in such a way, that I
should speak with each one of you privily, and that for a
token each should tell me a thing known but to him and his
love, and to me unto whom she hath told it. Now am I all
ready to do mine errand thus, and no other wise."

Laughed they now, and were merry, and the Green
Knight blushed like a maiden; forsooth like to his very
speech-friend Viridis. But the Black Squire said: "Fair fellows, get we all into the pleasance this fair morn, and sit
there on the grass, and our sweet lady shall take us one after
other into the plashed alley, and have the tokens of us."

Even so they did, and went into the pleasance, which was
a goodly little garth south of the castle, grassed, and set
thick with roses and lilies and gilliflowers, and other fragrant flowers. There then they sat on the daisied greensward, the three lords together, and Birdalone over against
them, and they three watched her beauty and loveliness and
wondered thereat.

But she said: "Now it comes to the very point of mine
errand; wherefore I bid thee, Baudoin the Golden Knight,
to come apart with me and answer to my questions, so that
I may know surely that I am doing mine errand aright."

Therewith she arose to her feet, and he also, and he led her
into the plashed alley, out of earshot of the other twain, who
lay upon the grass biding their turn with but little patience.

But when those two were in the deep shade of the alley,
Birdalone said: "Thou must know, Sir Golden Knight,
that the three lovers of you three were good to me in my
need, and clad my nakedness from their very bodies, but
this raiment they lent me, and gave it not; for they bade me
give it up piece by piece each unto the one who had given it
to his love, whom I should know by the token that he should
tell truly the tale of its giving. Now, fair sir, I know well,
for I have been told, what was the tale of thy giving this

golden gown to Aurea, and that same tale shalt thou now tell me, and if thou tell it aright, then is the gown thine. Begin, then, without more tarrying."

"Lady," said the knight, "thus it was: Aurea, my sweetling, abode with an ancient dame, a kinswoman of hers, who was but scantly kind to her; and on a day when we had met privily, and were talking together, my love lamented the niggard ways of her said kinswoman, and told how she had no goodly gown to make her fair when feasts were toward; but I laughed at her, and told her that so clad as she was (and her attire was verily but simple) she was fairer than any other; and then, as ye may wot, there was kissing and clipping between us. But at last, as from the first I meant it, I promised her I would purvey her such a gown as no lady should go with a better in all the country-side; but I said that in return I must have the gown she went in then, which had so long embraced her body and been strained so close to her body and her sides, and was as it were a part of her. That she promised me with kisses, and I went away as merry as a bird. Straightway thereafter I did do make this very gown, which thou bearest, dear maiden, and on the appointed day she came out to me unto the same place clad as she was before; but the new gown I had with me. Hard by our trysting-place was a hazel-copse thick enow, for it was midsummer, and she said she would go thereinto and shift gowns, and bear me out thence the gift of the old clout (so she called it, laughing merrily). But I said: Nay, I would go into the copse with her to guard her from evil things, beasts or men; and withal to see her do off the old gown, that I might know before I wedded her whatlike stuffing and padding went to make the grace of her flanks and her hips. And again was she merry, and she said: 'Come, then, thou Thomas unbelieving, and see the side of me.' So we went into that cover together, and she did off her gown before mine eyes, and stood there in her white coat with her arms bare, and her shoulders and bosom little covered, and she was as lovely as a woman of the Faery.

Then I made no prayer unto her for leave, but took my arms about her, and kissed her arms and shoulders and bosom all she would suffer me, for I was mad with love of her naked flesh. Then she did on this golden gown, and departed when she had given me the old clout aforesaid, and I went away with it, scarce feeling the ground beneath my feet; and I set the dear gown in a fair little coffer, and here in this castle I have it now, and many times I take it forth and kiss it and lay my head upon it. Now this is a simple tale, lady, and I am ashamed that I have made it so long for thee. And yet I know not; for thou seemest to me so kind and loving and true, that I am fain that thou shouldest know how sorely I love thy friend and mine."

Birdalone deemed Baudoin a good man indeed, and the tears came into her eyes as she answered and said: "True is thy tale, dear friend, and I have deemed it rather short than long. I see well that thou art Aurea's very lover; and it joys me to think that thou, O terrible champion, art yet so tender and true. Now is the golden gown thine, but I will pray thee to lend it me a little longer. But this jewel shalt thou have from my neck here and now; and thou knowest whence it came, thine Aurea's neck forsooth."

Therewith she betook it him, and he held it in his hand doubtfully a while, and then he said: "Dear maiden, I thank thee, but I will take this collar, and lay it in my casket, and be glad thereof; and that the more, as, now I look on thee, I see nought missing from the loveliness of thine own neck."

"Go to thy fellows now," said Birdalone, "and send me the Green Knight, the goodly lad." So went he, and presently came Hugh thither merry and smiling, and said: "Thou hast been long about the first token, sweet mistress; I fear me I shall make no such goodly story as hath Baudoin."

"And yet," said she, "Viridis' tale was the longest of all. I doubt thou mayst fail in the token." And she laughed; and he no less, and took her by the shoulders, and kissed her cheek frankly, and in such wise that she feared him nought, and said: "Now that is to pay thee for thy gibe; what wouldst thou have of me?" Said Birdalone: "I would have thee tell me how it was that Viridis came by the smock with the green boughs aflame, which now I bear upon me."

"Hearken, darling lady," said he: "On a day Viridis and I were alone in the meadow, and so happy, that we might find nought to do save to fall into strife together; and I said it to her, that she loved me not as well as I loved her; which, by the way, was no less than a lie, for of all things living she is the most loving, and when we be together she knoweth not how to make enough of me. Well, we fell to wrangling after the manner of lovers, till I, having nothing else to say, bade her remember that since we had first come to love each other, I had given her many things, and she had given me nothing. Lo, then! my dear, what an ill-conditioned lad was I. But, little as I meant it, she took it all amiss, and leapt up, and fell to running back home over the meadow; thou mayst think how easily I caught up with her, and how little loth she was to be dragged back by the shoulders. So when we were sitting again under the thorn-bush, we had well-nigh done our wrangle; but she unlaced her gown and drew down a corner thereof, to show me her shoulder, how I had hurt it e'en now; and forsooth some little mark there was on the rose-leaf skin; and that made good time for kissing again, as ye may well wot. Then she said unto me: 'And how may I, a poor damsel, give thee gifts, and my kindred all greedy about me? Yet would I give thee a gift, such as I may, if I but knew what thou wouldst take.' Now my heart was afire with that kissing of her shoulder, and I said that I would have that very same smock from her body, which then she bore, and that thereof I should deem that I had a rich gift indeed. 'What!' said she, 'and wouldst thou have it here and now?' And indeed I think she would have done it off her that minute had I pressed her, but I lacked the boldness thereto; and I said: Nay, but would she bring it unto me the next time we met; and forsooth she brought it folded in a piece of green silk, and dearly have I loved it

122

and kissed it sithence. But as for thy smock, I had it fairly
wrought and embroidered with the flaming green branches,
as thou seest it, and I gave it to her; but not on the day
when she gave me the gift; for the new one was long about
doing. Now this is all the tale, and how Viridis might eke it
into a long one, I wot not. But let it be, and tell me, have I
won thy smock, or lost it?"

Birdalone laughed on him and said: "Well, at least thou
shalt have it as a gift; and thou mayst call it given either by
Viridis or me, which thou wilt. But with it goes another gift,
which thou mayst have at once since thou must lend me the
smock a little longer." And therewith she betook him her
girdle, and he kissed it, but said: "Nay, fair lady, this befitteth well the loveliness of thy body that thou shouldst wear
it; and well it befitteth the truth and love of thy soul to ward
it for me; I pray thee to keep it."

"Nevertheless," she said, "I will not have it, for it goeth
with mine errand that thou take it of me. Now I bid thee
depart, and send hither thy fellow, the Black Squire."

Went he then, and anon comes the Black Squire, and
now that he was alone with Birdalone this first time, he
seemed moody and downcast, all unlike the two others.
He stood a little aloof from Birdalone, and said: "What
wouldst thou ask of me?"

Her heart was somewhat chilled by his moodiness, for
erst had she deemed him the kindest of the three; but she
said: "It is of mine errand to ask of thee concerning this
foot-gear which Atra lent me until I give it unto thee, if
thou be verily her lover." Said he: "I was verily her lover."
Birdalone said: "Then canst thou tell me the manner of
thy giving these fair shoon unto Atra?"

He said: "Even so; we were walking together in this
country-side and came to a ford of the river, and it was
somewhat deep and took me to over the knee, so I bore her
over in my arms; then we went on a little further till we
must cross the river back again in another place, and there
the ford was shallower, and, the day being hot, Atra must

123

needs wade it on her own feet. So she did off hosen and
shoon, and I led her by the hand, and it took her but up to
mid-leg. But when we came up out of the water and were on
the grass again, I craved the gift of her foot-gear for the love
of her, and she gave it straightway, and fared home barefoot,
for it was over the meads we were wending in early summer, and the grass was thick and soft. But thereafter I did
do make the fair shoon which thou hast on thy feet, and gave
them to her. And, for a further token that my tale is true, I
shall tell thee that the name of the first ford we waded
that day is the Grey-nag's Wade, and the second is called
Goat Ford. This is all my tale, lady; is the token true?"

"True it is, squire," said Birdalone, and was silent awhile,
and he also. Then she looked on him friendly, and said:
"Thou art out of heart as now, my friend. Fear not, for
thou shalt without doubt see thy speech-friend again. Moreover here is a ring which she set upon my finger, bidding
me give it thee." And she held it out unto him.

He took the ring, and said: "Yea, it is best that I have it
of thee, lest unluck come thereof." She saw trouble in his
face, but knew not what to say to cheer him, and they stood
silently facing one another for awhile. Then he said: "Let us
back to our fellows, and talk it over, what is now to be
done."

So they went their ways to where lay the other two upon
the green grass, and the Black Squire lay down beside them;
but Birdalone stood before them and spake unto the three.

CHAPTER VI. HOW THE CHAMPIONS WOULD DO BIRDALONE TO BE CLAD ANEW IN THE CASTLE OF THE QUEST.

LORDS," she said, "now is it clear by the tokens that
mine errand is to you and none other; now therefore
am I to tell you what to do to come unto your speech-
friends and deliver them and bring them back hither.
For this is their case, that they are in captivity in a wonder-

isle of this Great Water, and it is called the Isle of Increase
Unsought."

Spake the Golden Knight: "Fair lady, we have heard before that our friends fared hence, or rather were taken hence over the water. And that is the cause why we builded this castle on the water's edge, on the very stead where was raised the pavilion, the house made for the ladies to abide therein the battle of the Champions. Since that time, moreover, many a barge and keel have we thrust out into the water, that we might accomplish the Quest whereunto we were vowed; but ever one way went our seafaring, that when we were come so far out into the water as to lose sight of land, came upon us mist, rose against us dusk and darkness; and then a fierce driving wind that drave us back to this shore. It is but six days ago since we tried this adventure for the last time, and belike the same shall befall us the next time we try it. Wherefore I must ask thee, lady, dost thou know any way whereby we may come to the said Isle? For if thou dost, full surely we will try it, whatsoever may be the risk thereby to our bodies or our souls."

"Full surely I do," said Birdalone; "else how had I come from thence hither mine own self?" And therewith she told them of the Sending Boat, what it was, and how she had come all the way by means thereof from the Isle of Increase Unsought; and they all hearkened her heedfully, and wondered both at the sorcery, and the valiant heart of her who had driven it as she would in despite of the evil. But in the end she spake and said: "Lords, ye have now heard some deal of my story, even that which concerns you thereof, and which must needs be told at once: wherefore doubtless ye shall fare unto your speech-friends by this ferry in the very wise that I shall show you; unless perchance ye deem that I have been lying and making light tales to you, as, sooth to say, I deem ye think it not."

Spake the Golden Knight: "Damsel, in all wise we trow in thee and thy tale. And God forbid that we should tarry! Go we hence this very day."

"Yea, but hearken," said the Black Squire: "Is it not a part of this damsel's errand that she should deliver to us the raiment of our friends, which now she beareth on her own body, that we may bear it back unto them?"

"Sooth is that," said Birdalone, "and ye may well wot that this may be nought but needful, whereas the said ladies be all beset by sorceries."

"See ye then, fellows," said the Black Squire, "it may not be to-day nor yet to-morrow that we may take the road. For ye wot that there is no woman's gear in all the castle, and we must needs send otherwhere to seek it."

"Look thou, maiden," said the Golden Knight, laughing, "how duly this young knight thinketh of thee; whereas I, who am his elder, and should be wiser than he, am but heedless of thee. I pray thy pardon."

"Moreover," said the Black Squire, "there may well be wisdom in abiding; for it is to be thought that our dear loves considered this, and knew what the time of tarrying should be, and have so dight their matter as to fit in therewith; and I may not deem it of them that they would have us array this our dear sister and theirs in unseemly wise. Nay, for that would be an ill beginning of this deal of the Quest."

Now all yeasaid this gladly; and the Green Knight said: "It were not so ill done that we should see more of our sister here ere we depart, and hear more of her tale; for meseemeth she began it erewhile but half-way." And he turned to Birdalone, and took her hand and caressed it.

Birdalone smiled on them somewhat shyly, and thanked them; but bade them spend as little time as might be on her arrayal. "For," said she, "though those ladies may well have reckoned on the time of the arrayal of my body, yet surely also they shall have reckoned with the eager fire of love in the hearts of you, and the haste it shall breed therein."

Well pleased were they with that word of hers, but none the less sent two sergeants and a squire with led horses unto the cheaping-town, a goodly and great town hight Greenford, which was some twenty miles thence, with the errand to bring back with them a good shaper and embroideress, and sewing-women, and cloth and silk and linen, and all things needful.

As for jewels, each one of them was fain to give her something which he prized, and fair and rich were the gifts, though they had not been made for women. As a fair SS collar of gold, which the Golden Knight gave her, and a girdle of broad golden plates, wrought beauteously, which was the gift of the Black Squire. Albeit he did not offer to clasp it round her loins, as she deemed he would; for when the Green Knight brought his gift, a great gold ring, very ancient of fashion, he would have her turn back the sleeve from her fore-arm, that he might set his dwarf-wrought gold upon the bare flesh; neither did he refrain him from kissing it withal.

But the messengers came back with their work-women & stuffs early on the morrow; and now was changed all the manner of the womanless castle, and men were full merry therein.

CHAPTER VII. OF BIRDALONE, AND HOW SHE TOLD THE CHAMPIONS ALL HER TALE.

IT was a matter of eight days, the making of all Birdalone's raiment, and meanwhile she was ever with the three Champions, either all three together, or one or other of them. And as to their manners with her, ever was the Golden Knight of somewhat sober demeanour, as if he were an older man than he verily was. The Green Knight was for ever praising Birdalone's beauty to her face, and seemed to find it no easy matter to keep his eyes off her, and somewhat he wearied her with kisses and caresses; but a gay and sportive lad he was; and when she rebuked him for his overmuch fondness, as now and again she did, he would laugh at himself along with her; and in sooth she deemed him heart-whole, and of all truth to Viridis, and oft he would talk of her to Birdalone, and praise her darling beauty to her, and tell of his longing for his love aloof. "Only," quoth he, "here art thou, my sister, dwelling amongst us, and shedding thy fragrance on us, and showing to us, wilt thou, wilt thou not, as do the flowers, all the grace and loveliness of thee; and thou so tender of heart withal, that thou must not blame me overmuch if whiles I forget that thou art my sister, and that my love is, woe's me! far away. So thou wilt pardon me, wilt thou not?"

"Yea, verily," said she, "with a whole heart. Yet thou needest not reach out for my hand; thou hast had enough of it this morning." And she hid it, laughing, in the folds of her gown; and he laughed also and said: "Of a truth thou art good in all wise, and a young fool am I; but Viridis shall make me wiser, when we come together again. Sawest thou ever so fair a damsel?"

"Never," she said, "and surely there is none fairer in all the world. So hold thee aloof now for a while, and think of her."

As for the Black Squire, hight Arthur, Birdalone was troubled for him, and he made her somewhat sad. True it is that he came not before her again so moody and downcast as when he was giving her the token; yet she deemed that he enforced himself to seem of good cheer. Furthermore, though he sought her company ever, and that lonely with him, and would talk with her almost as one man with another, though with a certain tenderness in his voice, and looking earnestly on her the while, yet never would he take her hand, or touch her in any wise. And true it is that she longed for the touch of his hand.

On the third day of her sojourn in the Castle of the Quest, Birdalone took heart at the much egging of her friends, as they sat all together in the meadow without the castle, to tell them all the story of her; she hid none, save concerning the Woodmother, for she deemed that her sweet friend would love her the better if she babbled not of her.

So the Champions hearkened her telling the tale in her clear lovely voice, and great was their love and pity for the

poor lonely maiden. And in especial clear it was to see that
they were sore moved when she told how she first came on
the Sending Boat, and how the witch-wife tormented her
innocent body for that guilt. Then Baudoin laid his hand
upon her head, and spake: "Poor child, much indeed hast
thou suffered! and now I will say it, that it was for us and
our loves that thou hast borne all this anguish of captivity
and toil and stripes."

But Hugh leaned over to her, as she sat with her head
hanging down, and kissed her cheek, and said: "Yea! and I
was not there to smite the head off that accursed one; and
I knew nought of thee and thine anguish, as I took my light
pleasure about these free meadows." And he turned very
red, and went nigh to weep.

Arthur sat still with his eyes bent down on the ground,
and he said nothing; and Birdalone glanced on him wistfully
ere she went on with her tale. And she went on and told
closely all that had happened unto her in the crossing of the
water and on the Isle of Increase Unsought, and the other
Wonder Isles; and she deemed it not too much that she
should tell it twice over, nor they that twice over they
should hearken it.

That same evening as Birdalone walked by herself in the
castle pleasance, she saw Arthur peering about as if he were
seeking someone; so she stood forth, and asked him was he
seeking aught; and he said: "Thee was I seeking." But she
durst not ask him what he would, but stood silent and
trembling before him, till he took her hand, and spake not
loud but eagerly.

"After what thou hast told us to-day, I seem to know thee
what thou art; and I tell thee that it is a pain and grief to me
to leave thee—yea to leave thee were it but for a minute. O
I pray thee pity me for the sundering." And therewith he
turned about and hastened into the castle. But Birdalone
stood there with her heart beating fast and her flesh quivering, and a strange sweetness of joy took hold of her. But she
said to herself that it was no wonder though she felt so hap-

py, seeing that she had found out that, despite her fears, this one of her friends loved her no less well than the others. And then she spake it in a soft voice that she would indeed pity him for the sundering, yea, and herself also.

Nevertheless, when they met thereafter, his demeanour to her was none otherwise than it had been; but she no longer heeded this since now she trowed in him.

CHAPTER VIII. IN THE MEANWHILE OF THE DEPARTURE OF THE CHAMPIONS THEY WOULD PLEASURE BIRDALONE WITH FEATS OF ARMS AND GAMES OF PROWESS.

PASSED the days now speedily, and the three Champions did what they might for the solace of Birdalone. For they and their household showed her of arms, and they tilted together courteously; and the sergeants stood forth, and shot in the bow before her, till she herself by their bidding took the bow in hand, and shot straighter and well-nigh as hard as the best man there, whereat they marvelled, and praised her much.

Then the young men ran afoot before her for the prize of a belt and knife, and forsooth she wotted well that were she to run against them with trussed-up skirts she would bear off the prize; but she had no heart thereto, for amidst them all, and her new friendships, she had grown shamefast, and might play the wood-maiden no longer.

Yet twice the Champions fared further afield with her to show her some woodcraft; yet were not very free to go far, because of the ill neighbours whereof the chaplain had told her that first night of her coming.

And in all these pastimes, whatso they were, Birdalone bore herself well and merrily, and put from her the sorrow of the sundering, and the peril of her dear friends which grew now so near at hand.

The chaplain aforesaid, who hight Leonard, she fell in with not seldom; and he was ever meek and humble before

her; and ever withal was sorrow easy to be seen in his countenance, and trouble withal; and she knew not how to help
him, save by being courteous and kind with him whenso
they met; but none the more might he pluck up cheerful
countenance in answer to her kindness.

With Sir Aymeris, the grizzle-haired castellan, she fore-
gathered also oft enough, and could not forbear some
merry gibes with him concerning their first meeting, and
how that she had been a burden and a terror to him; and
these mocks she made him because she saw it liked him
not ill to be mocked in friendly fashion; though forsooth
betwixt the laughter he looked on her somewhat ruefully.
And ever, ere he parted from her, he made occasion to kiss
her hands; and she suffered it smiling, and was debonnaire to
him; whereas she saw that he was of good will to her. In
such wise then wore the hours and the days.

CHAPTER IX. BIRDALONE COMETH BEFORE THE CHAMPIONS IN HER NEW ARRAY.

NOW the time was come when Birdalone had all her
gear ready, and the women were to abide in the
castle as her serving-damsels while the Champions
were away.

So now in the summer eve, an hour before sunset, Birdalone did on the richest of her new raiment, and came into
the hall where sat the Three together, and Sir Aymeris with
them. She was so clad, that she had on a green gown with
broidered sleeves, and thereover a white cote-hardie welted
with gold, and gold-embroidered; on her feet were gold
shoon of window-work, pearled and gemmed; and on
her head a rose garland; on her neck she bore the Golden
Knight's collar; her loins were girt with the Black Squire's
girdle; and on her wrist was the Green Knight's ancient gold
ring; and she carried in her arms Aurea's gown and Viridis'
shift and Atra's shoon.

Rather sunrise than sunset it seemed, as verily birdalone

she came into the hall with bright eager eyes, and flushed cheeks, and countenance smiling with love. The men stood up all, and would come down from the dais to meet her; but she bade them go back, and sit each in his place till she stood before them.

Up the hall then she walked, and every step of hers seemed lovelier than the last, till she came to them and gave unto each his keepsake, and said: "Champions, now is mine errand all done, save that to-morrow I must show you the manner of the Sending Boat. Now there is nought save the darkness of the coming night to hinder you from this last deal of your Quest; and it is I that have brought you to this, and have done this good unto you, if no more good I do in the world. Wherefore I pray you to love me ever, and bear me ever in your minds."

They gazed on her, and were overcome by her loveliness and grace, and by the kindness and valiancy of her heart. Next arose the Golden Knight, Baudoin to wit, and took a cross from his breast, and held it up, and spake: " Maiden, thou sayest well, and never shall we forget thee, or cease to love thee; and here I swear by God upon the Tree, that it shall be a light thing for me to die for thee, if in any need I find thee. Brethren, will ye not swear the same? And this is but thy due, maiden, for I declare unto thee, that when thou didst enter the hall e'en now, it was as if the very sun of heaven was coming in unto us."

Thereon the other two took the Rood and swore upon it: and Hugh was hushed and meek and sad-faced after he had sworn; but Arthur the Black Squire bowed down his head and wept, and his fellows marvelled nought thereat, neither did Birdalone; and all her body yearned toward him to solace him.

Now turned Sir Baudoin to the castellan and said: "Sir Aymeris, I will now swear thee to guard this lady as the apple of thine eye whiles we three be away, and therein to spare neither thyself nor others. For thou seest well what grief it would be to us if she came to any harm."

132

"And to me also," said the castellan. And therewith he swore upon the Rood, and then came round the table, and knelt before Birdalone, and kissed her hands.

Thereafter were they all silent a space; and then came Birdalone to the inner side of the table and sat betwixt Baudoin and Hugh. But the Black Squire took up the word and spake: "Birdalone, sweet child, one thing is to be said, to wit, that it were well that thou keep within walls while we be away; or at least that thou go but a little beyond the castle, and never but within a half bowshot, save thou be well accompanied. For there be men of violence dwelling no great way off, reivers and rovers, who would be well pleased to take from us anything which we deem dear; besides others who would think the lifting of such a jewel good hap indeed. Sir Aymeris, have a care of the Red Knight; and if thou mightest come by a few more stout lads, to wage them, it were well."

Birdalone heeded not what the castellan answered, such a shaft of joy went to her heart when she heard that friend speak her own name in such wise as he had never done erst, and that before them all. She but murmured some yeasay to that which Arthur had spoken unto her, and then she held her peace for the sweetness of that moment.

So there they sat and talked a while in dear and pleasant converse; and Hugh fell to asking her of her life in the House under the Wood, and she answered all frankly and simply, and the more she told the dearer she seemed to them.

Thus drew night in, till folk came flockmeal into the hall; for needs must be feast and banquet for triumph of the furtherance of the Quest; and the most of men were merry; but somewhat sober were all the three Champions, so that whoso ran might read it in their faces. As for Birdalone, she showed cheerful to all that folk which loved her and praised her; but inwardly sorrow had come home to her heart.

CHAPTER X. THE CHAMPIONS GO THEIR WAYS IN THE SENDING BOAT.

WHEN the sun was arisen on the morrow the three Champions went down to the landing-place, and there was none with them; for they had given command that no man should pry into their doings. Thither to them cometh Birdalone, clad no more in her gay attire, but in a strait black coat and with unshod feet; and she looked no sorrier than she was.

By Birdalone's rede the Champions bore down in their own hands the victual and weapons and armour that they needed for the voyage; for she knew not but that the Sending Boat might take it amiss that any should touch her save the Senders. And when they had done lading her, then all four stood together by the water's edge, and Birdalone spake to her friends, and again bade them beware of the wiles of the Isle of Nothing; and again she told them of the woful images of the Isle of Kings and the Isle of Queens, and the strange folk of the Isle of the Young and the Old. Then she said: "Now when ye come to the Isle of Increase Unsought, what think ye to do?"

Said the Green Knight: "If I might rule, we should go straight up to the witch sitting in her hall, as thou toldest us, my dear, and then and there smite the head from off her." His eyes flashed and his brow knitted, and so fierce he looked that Birdalone shrank back from him; but the Black Squire smiled and said: "It may come to the smiting off of heads in the end; yet must we so fashion our carving, that it avail us for the freeing of our friends; else may the witch die, and the secret of the prison-house die with her. How sayest thou, dear Birdalone?"

She reddened at the caress of his voice, and answered: "By my rede ye shall seek and find your speech-friends ere ye make open war upon the witch; else may her malice destroy them ere ye undo her." Her face flushed yet more as she spake again: "But concerning all things, I deem that

134

Atra may give you the best rede, when ye have met the loves; for that she knoweth more of the Isle and its guiles than the others."

Quoth Baudoin: "Herein is wisdom, sweet maiden, for as guileless as thou mayst be; and so far as we may we shall follow thy rede; but all lieth in the fathom of the coming time. And now this moment is the moment of sundering and farewell."

Came he then to Birdalone and took his two hands about her head, and lifted her face unto him, and kissed it kindly, as a father might kiss a daughter, and said: "Farewell, dear child, and take heed to the word that Arthur spake yesterday, and go not from the castle even a little way save with good and sure company."

Then came Hugh to her, and took her hand somewhat timidly; but she put up her face to him in simple wise, and he kissed either cheek of her, and said no more than: "Farewell, Birdalone!"

Lastly came Arthur, and stood before her a little; and then he knelt down on the stones before her and kissed her feet many times, and she shuddered and caught her breath as they felt his kisses; but neither he nor she spake a word, and he stood up and turned away at once toward the Sending Boat, and boarded her first of the three; and the others followed straightway.

Thereafter the Champions bared each an arm, and let blood flow thence into a bowl, and reddened stem and stern of their barge, and then all three spake the spell together thus, as Birdalone had taught them:

The red raven-wine now
Hast thou drunk, stern and bow:
Wake then, and awake,
And the northern way take:
The way of the Wenders forth over the flood,
For the will of the Senders is blent with the blood.

Went all as before thereafter, that the Sending Boat stirred under them, and then turned about and pointed her bows to the northward, and sped swiftly over the waters. It was a fair sunny day, with no cloud, nought save the summer haze lying on the lake far away. Birdalone stood watching the speeding of the boat, till she could see it no longer, not even as a fleck on the face of the waters. Then she turned away and went toward her chamber, saying to herself that the sundering was easier to bear than she had deemed it would be, and that she had a many things to do that day. But when she came into her chamber, and shut the door, she looked about her on the things which had grown so familiar to her in these few latter days, and she stood watching the bright sunshine that streamed across the floor and lay warm upon her feet; then she took three steps toward the window, and saw the lake lying all a-glitter under the sun, and her heart failed her withal, and she had no might so much as to think about her sorrow and caress it, but fell down where she was swooning on to the floor, and lay there while all the house began to stir about her.

HERE ENDS THE THIRD PART OF THE WATER OF THE WONDROUS ISLES, WHICH IS CALLED OF THE CASTLE OF THE QUEST, AND BEGINS THE FOURTH PART OF THE SAID TALE, WHICH IS CALLED OF THE DAYS OF ABIDING.

THE WATER OF THE WONDROUS ISLES. THE FOURTH PART: OF THE DAYS OF ABIDING.

CHAPTER I. OF BIRDALONE'S GRIEF: AND OF LEONARD THE CHAPLAIN.

NOW came Birdalone to herself, and that was but little joy unto her, and she yet lay still on the floor for a while, for she loathed the hour that was to come. Then the life stirred in her, and whereas she would not that her women should find her there, she stood up, and clad herself somewhat more seemly; yet she did on her black raiment; and determined in her mind that nought would she wear save black unadorned while her friends were away.

She betook her now to the chamber where her women were gathered together, and watched them working a while, but spake nought. Then she went her ways into the pleasance, and paced the plashed alley up and down, letting the tears run down from her as they would. Then she turned back into the castle, and went out-a-gates and walked over the meadow a little, and might well have gone further than wisdom would. But the castellan espied her from a window, and came hurrying out after her, and with many prayers for pardon, brought her back again, babbling to her by the way; but not a word might he get from her; and when he came into the hall with her, and, after his wont, knelt down to kiss her hands, she caught them away from him peevishly, and was sorry for it thereafter.

Long she sat in the hall, scarce moving, till she heard one entering from the screen, and lo it was Leonard the chaplain. He came her way, and showed her rueful countenance; and pity of him smote her, and she remembered therewith how they first went out of gates together; and at the thought thereof her tears brake forth again, but she made him a sign with her hand to sit down beside her, and he did so; and when she might for her weeping, she looked kindly on him, and he fell to talk, making as if he noted not her tears and sorrow; but she answered him little, for she had shame to begin the talk concerning the Champions and their Quest, and their departure; yet might she not bring her tongue to make any speech else. But presently he took up the word, and asked her how long a while she deemed they would be away, and she answered, smiling on him for thanks, and having reckoned the days on her fingers: "If all go better than well, they may be back in ten days' time."

Said the chaplain: "There be longer whiles of waiting in most men's lives."

"Yea," she said, "but this is the delay at the best; it may be far longer; for how may we tell what haps may be?"

"Yea," said Leonard, "shall we then call it twenty days, or thirty? Forsooth, that may be long for thee; though there be some who must needs endure hope deferred a deal longer. But it may run out longer than even thirty days, thy waiting-tide."

She answered not, and he said: "Whenso the time hangs heavy on hand with thee, if thou hast will to fare abroad out of the castle, I shall be ever at hand to guide thee. Indeed, I wot that the castellan will be loth to let thee go; but he is old and straitlaced: and yet withal he wotteth, as do we all, that there is now little peril or none were we to fare a five miles or more, whereas we are as good as at peace for the last five days with all save the Red Knight, and of him we wot that he is gone into another land with as many of his folk as be not needed for the warding of his hold."

"I thank thee," said Birdalone, "but it is like to be my will not to fare out-a-gates till the Champions come back home. I was glad e'en now when the castellan fetched me in again: to say sooth, fear of peril had just entered my heart when he came up with me."

The priest seemed somewhat chapfallen at her answer. He spake little more, and presently he stood up, made his obeisance, and departed.

138

CHAPTER II. BIRDALONE LEARNETH LORE OF THE PRIEST. TEN DAYS OF WAITING WEAR.

WORE that day and the next, and Birdalone fell to talking with her women, whereof were five now left; and four of them were young, the eldest scarce of thirty summers, and the fifth was a woman of sixty, both wise and kind. All these told her somewhat of their own lives when she asked them; and some withal told of folk whom they had known or heard tell of. And well pleased was Birdalone to hear thereof, and learn more of the ways of the world, and quick-witted she was at the lesson, so that she needed not to ask many questions.

Furthermore, she took to her broidering again, and fell to doing a goodly pair of shoon for Atra, since she had worn those borrowed ones somewhat hardly. And the women wondered at her needlework, so marvellous fine as it was, and how that in little space of time were come flowers and trees, and birds and beasts, all lovely; and they said that the Faery must have learned her that craft. But she laughed and reddened, and thought of the Woodmother; and, sitting there within the four walls, she longed for the oak-glades, and the wood-lawns, and for the sight of the beasts that dwelt therein.

Again she fell in with Leonard the priest, and he asked her could she read in a book, and when she said nay, he offered to teach her that lore, and she yeasaid that joyously; and thenceforth would she have him with her every day a good while; and an apt scholar she was, and he no ill master, and she learned her A B C speedily.

Now it was the ninth day since the Champions were gone, and all that time she had not been out-a-gates; and after the first two days, had enforced herself to fill up her time with her work as aforesaid: but this last day she might do but little, for she could not but take it for sure that the morrow would be the day of return; nay, even she deemed that they might come in the night-tide; so that when she went to bed, though she was weary, she would wake if she might, so that it was nigh dawn ere she fell asleep.

Some three hours after she woke up, and heard a sound of folk stirring in the house, and the clashing of weapons; and the heart leapt in her, and she said: They are come, they are come! Nevertheless she durst not get out of bed, lest her hope had beguiled her; and she lay awake another hour, and no tidings came to her; and then she wept herself to sleep; and when she awoke once more, she found that she must have wept sleeping, for the pillow beside her face was all wet with the tears.

The sun was high now, and his beams were cast back from the ripple of the lake, and shone wavering on the wall of the chamber, the window whereof gave on to the water. Then came a hand on the latch of the door, and she started, and her heart grieved her; but it was one of the women who opened, and came in, and Birdalone rose up sitting in her bed, and said faintly, for she could scarce speak: "Is any tiding toward, Catherine?"

The maid said: "Yes, my lady; for early after sunrise came weaponed men to the gate, and would sell us beeves; and my lord, Sir Aymeris, must needs go forth and chaffer with them, though belike they had been lifting what was neither ours, nor theirs, nor the neighbours'. Maybe Sir Aymeris looked to buy tidings from them as well as beef. Anyhow they departed when they had gotten their money and drunk a cup. And now it is said that the Red Knight hath been hurt in some fray, and keepeth his bed; wherefore the land shall have peace of him awhile." Said Birdalone: "I thank thee, good Catherine; I shall lie a little longer; depart now."

The woman went her ways; and when she was gone, Birdalone wept and sobbed, and writhed upon her bed, and found no solace to her grief. But she arose and paced the chamber, and sithence looked out of the window over the empty water, and wept again. Then she said: Yet they may come ere noon, or it may be ere evening, or perchance to-

morrow morning. And she stayed her weeping, and was
calmer. But still she walked the floor, and whiles looked out
of window, and whiles she looked on her limbs, and felt the
sleekness of her sides, and she said: O my body! how thou
longest!

But at last she clad herself in haste, and went stealthily
from the chamber, as if she feared to meet anyone; and she
stole up to the tower-top that was nighest, and looked
through the door on to the leads, and saw no one there; so
she went out, and stood by the battlement, and gazed long
over the water, but saw neither boat nor burning mountain
coming towards her.

CHAPTER III. NOW WOULD BIRDALONE RIDE ABROAD.

AFTER a while she came down again, and went to the
women, and sat working with them a while, and so
wore away two hours. Then she sent for the priest
and had her lesson of him; and when she had been at it another two hours, she bade him begin and learn her writing;
and nought loth he was thereto; forsooth he had been longing to pray her to suffer him learn her, but durst not. For in
such teaching needs must he sit full nigh to her, and watch
her hands, and her fingers striving to shape the letters; nay,
whiles must he touch her hand with his, and hold it. Wherefore now he promised himself a taste of Paradise. Withal he
was full meet to learn her, whereas he was one of the best
of scribes, and a fair-writer full handy.

So they fell to the lesson, and she became eager thereover, and learned fast, and clave to the work, while his soul
was tormented with longing for her. And thus wore a three
hours, and then suddenly she looked up wearily from her
work, and her trouble was awake, and the longing for her
speech-friend, and she gave the priest leave for that day, but
suffered him to kiss her hand for wages.

Then she hurried up to the tower-top, when the afternoon

was wearing into evening; and abode there a long while looking over the waters, till it began to dusk, and then came down miserably and went to her women.

The next day was like unto this; nought betid, and she wore the hours whiles going up to the tower-top and looking over the lake, whiles broidering amidst her maids, whiles learning her clerk's work with Sir Leonard, but ever eating her heart out with her longing.

On the third of these days she called the castellan to her for a talk, and asked him what he thought of it, this delay of his lords' return. Quoth the greyhead: "My lady, we may not wonder if they be tarried for a few days; for this is an adventure on which they have gone, and many haps betide in such tales. Now I beseech thee torment not thyself; for the time is not yet come for thee even to doubt that they have miscarried."

His words solaced her much for that time, whereas she saw that he spake but the sooth; so she thanked him, and smiled upon him kindly; and he was ravished thereat, and was for kneeling before her at once and kissing her hands after his wont; but she smiled again and refrained him, and said: "Nay, not yet, fair friend; that is for the departure, and I have yet a word to say unto thee: to wit, that I long to go out-a-gates, and it will solace me and give me patience to abide the coming of my friends. For thou must know, Sir Aymeris, that I was reared amidst the woods and the meadows, with the burning of the sun, and the buffets of the wind; and now for lack of some deal of that am I waxing white and faint. And thou wouldst not have me falling sick on thine hands now, wouldst thou?"

"Nay, surely, lady," said Sir Aymeris; "this very day I will ride out with thee; and two score or more of weaponed men shall ride with us for fear of mishaps." Said Birdalone, knitting her brows: "Nay, knight, I need not thy men-at-arms; I would fain go free and alone. For hast thou not heard how that the Red Knight is hurt and keepeth his bed? So what peril is there?"

Said Sir Aymeris: "Yea, lady; but the Red Knight is not
the only foe, though he be the worst: but it may well be
that the story is but feigned, for the said enemy hath many
wiles. And look you, kind lady, it is most like that by now
he hath heard how in my poor castle is kept a jewel, a pearl
of great price, that hath not its like in the world, and will
encompass the stealing of it if he may."

Laughed Birdalone, and said: "But how if the said jewel
hath a will, and legs and feet thereto, and is ready to take the
peril on her, and will wend out-a-gates if she will? What
wilt thou do then, lord?"

"Then," said the castellan, "I shall fetch thee back, and,
though it be a grief to me, shall have thee borne back perforce if nought else may do. For so the oath sworn to my
lords compelleth me."

Again laughed Birdalone, and said: "Hearken, whereto
cometh all this kneeling and hand-kissing! But bear in mind,
fair lord, how once on a time thou wouldst have me out-a-
gates, would I, would I not, and now, will I, will I not, thou
wouldst keep me within; so have times changed, and mayhappen they may change yet again. But tell me, am I mistress
over my women to bid them what I will?"

"Certes," said he, "and over all of us." Said she: "If then
I bade them, some two or three, come with me into the meadows and woods a half day's journey for our disport, how
then?"

"For that once," said Sir Aymeris, "I should bid them
disobey their lady." Said Birdalone: "And how if they dis-
obeyed thee, and obeyed me?" Quoth Sir Aymeris: "If they
bring thee back safe, they may chance to sing to the twiggen
fiddle-bow, that they may be warned from such folly; but if
they come back without thee, by All Hallows the wind of
wrath shall sweep their heads off them!"

Birdalone flushed red at his word, and was silent a while;
then she said, making cheerful countenance again: "Thou
art a hard master, lord castellan; but I must needs obey
thee. Therefore I will take thy bidding, and ride abroad in

such wise that I shall scare the land with an army, since no
otherwise may I look on the summer land. But to-day I will
not go, nor to-morrow belike; but some day soon. And in
good sooth I thank thee for thy heedful care of me, and wish
I were better worth it. Nay, nay, thou shalt not kneel to me,
but I to thee: for thou art verily the master."

Therewith she rose from beside him, and knelt down before him and took his hand and kissed it, and went her ways,
leaving him ravished with love of her. But now she had no
scorn of him, but deemed, as was true, that he was both
valiant and trusty and kind, and she thanked him in her
heart as well as in words.

CHAPTER IV. OF BIRDALONE'S FARING ABROAD.

INDEED Birdalone longed on any terms to be out-a-
gates and to have some joy of the summer; for now she
began to see that she might have to abide some while ere
her friends should come to her in the Castle of the Quest;
and she was angry with herself that her longing was thus
wasting her, and she rebuked herself and said: Where is now
that Birdalone who let but few days go by without some
joyance of the earth and its creatures? she who bore lightly
the toil of a thrall, and gibes and mocking and stripes? Surely
this is grievous folly, that I should be worsened since I have
come to be the friend of gentle ladies, and noble champions,
and mighty warriors. Had it not been better to have abided
under the witch-wife's hand? For not every day nor most
days did she torment me. But now for many days there has
been pain and grief and heart-sickness hour by hour; and
every hour have I dreaded the coming of the next hour, till
I know not how to bear it.

So she strove with herself, and became of better heart, and
set herself strongly to the learning of the clerkly lore; she
gathered her wits together, and no longer looked for every
day and every hour to bring about the return of the Cham-

144

pions, nor blamed the day and the hour because they failed
therein, and in all wise she strove to get through the day
unworn by vain longing.

Wherefore, on a day when three whole weeks were gone
since the day of Departure, she was glad when the castellan
came to her and said: "Lady, these two days I have had men
out to spy the land, and their word goes that nought is stirring which a score of us well-armed might have cause to
fear; wherefore to-morrow, if it be thy will, we shall bring
thee out-a-gates, and so please thee, shall be in no haste to
come back, but may lie out in the wild-wood one night, and
come back at our leisure on the morrow of to-morrow. How
sayest thou of thy pleasure herein?"

She thanked him, and yeasaid it eagerly, and next morning they set forth; and Birdalone had with her three of the
women, and they had sumpter-beasts with them, and tents
for Birdalone and her maids.

So they rode by pleasant ways and fair meadows, and the
weather was good, for it was now the first days of July, and
all was as lovely as might be; and for that while Birdalone
cast off all her cares, and was merry, and of many words and
sweet; and all the folk rejoiced thereat, for all loved her in
the Castle of the Quest, besides those one or two that loved
her overmuch.

Rode they thus a twelve miles or more, and then they
came, as their purpose was, to the beginning of a woodland
plenteous of venison, and they hunted here, and Birdalone
took her part therein, and all praised her woodcraft; albeit
because of her went a head or two free that had fallen else,
whereas of the carle hunters were some who deemed the
body of her better worth looking on than the quarry.

Howsoever, they slew of hind and roe and other wood-
cattle what they would, some deal for their supper in the
wilderness, some to bear home to the castle. But when night
was nigh at hand they made stay in a fair wood-lawn about
which ran a clear stream, whereby they pitched the ladies'
tent; and Birdalone and hers went down into the water and

washed the weariness off them; and her ladies wondered at
the deftness of Birdalone's swimming; for they bathed in a
pool somewhat great into which the stream widened, so that
there was space enough for her therein.

By then they were washen and clad goodly in raiment
which they had brought on the sumpters, the men had
lighted fires and were cooking the venison, and anon there
was supper and banquet in the wild-wood, with drinking of
wine and pleasant talk and the telling of tales and singing of
minstrelsy; and so at last, when night was well worn, and out
in the open meadows the eastern sky was waxing grey, then
Birdalone and her ladies went to bed in their fair tents, and
the men-at-arms lay down on the greensward under the bare
heaven.

CHAPTER V. SIR AYMERIS SHOWETH BIRD-ALONE THE MOUNTAINS AFAR OFF.

WHEN it was morning and they arose, the day was
as fair as yesterday, and folk were even as joyous
as they had been then, all but Birdalone, and she
was silent and downcast, even when she came forth from
the fresh water into the sweetness of the midsummer wood.
She had dreamed in the night that she was all alone in the
Castle of the Quest, and that her old mistress came to her
from out of the Sending Boat to fetch her away, and brought
her aboard, and stripped her of her rich garments and sat
facing her, drawing ugsome grimaces at her; and she thought
she knew that her friends were all dead and gone, and she
had none to pity or defend her. Then somehow were they
two, the witch and she, amidmost of the Isle of Nothing, and
the witch drew close anigh her, and was just going to whisper into her ear something of measureless horror, when she
awoke; and the sun was bright outside the shaded whiteness
of her tent; the shadows of the leaves were dancing on the
ground of it; the morning wind was rustling the tree-
boughs, and the ripple of the stream was tinkling hard by.

146

At first was Birdalone joyous that what she had awakened
from was but a dream; but presently she felt the burden of
her longing, and she said to herself that when they came
back to the castle they should find tidings, and that she
should know either that her friends were indeed dead, or
that they were come back again alive and well. And then she
thought within herself, suppose the three Champions and
their loves were dead and gone, how would she do with
those that were left her, as Sir Aymeris, and Leonard the
priest, and her women? and her soul turned with loathing
from a life so empty as that would be; and yet she blamed
herself that she was so little friendly to these lesser friends,
whom forsooth she loved because of her love for the greater
ones. So, as abovesaid, she was troubled and silent amongst
the joy of the others.

That saw Sir Aymeris the castellan; and when they had
broken fast and were getting to horse, he came to her and
said: "Lady, the day is yet young, and if we fetch a compass
by a way that I wot of, we shall see places new to thee, and
mayhappen somewhat wonderful, and yet come home timely
to the castle. Wilt thou?"

Birdalone was still somewhat distraught, but she knew
not how to naysay him, though at heart she would liefer
have gone back to the castle by the shortest way. So folk
brought her her palfrey, and they rode their ways, the castellan ever by her side. And by fair ways indeed they went,
and so joyous was all about them, that little by little Birdalone's gladness came back to her, and she made the most of
it to be as merry of seeming as she might be.

Now they rode fair and softly by thicket and copse and
glade of the woodland, following up the stream aforesaid
for the more part, till at last the trees failed them suddenly,
and they came forth on to a wide green plain, all unbuilded,
so far as their eyes could see, and beyond it the ridges of the
hills and blue mountains rising high beyond them.

When Birdalone's eyes beheld this new thing, of a sudden
all care left her, and she dropped her rein, and smote her

palms together, and cried out: "Oh! but thou art beautiful, O earth, thou art beautiful!" Then she sat gazing on it, while the greyhead turned and smiled on her, well pleased of her pleasure.

After a while she said: "And might we go nigher?" "Yea, certes," said he, "yet I doubt if thou wilt like it the better, the nigher thou art." "Ah!" she said, "but if I were only amidst it, and a part of it, as once I was of the woodland!"

So thitherward they rode over the unharvested mead, and saw hart and hind thereon, and wild kine, and of smaller deer great plenty, but of tame beasts none; and the hills were before them like a wall. But as they grew nigher, they saw where the said wall of the hills was cloven by a valley narrow and steep-sided, that went right athwart the lie of the hills; the said valley was but little grassed, and the bare rocks were crow-black. When they had gone a little further, they could see that the ground near the foot of the hills rose in little knolls and ridges, but these were lower and fewer about the entry into that valley. Also presently they came upon a stream which ran out of the said valley, and Sir Aymeris said that this was the water whereby they had lain last night; albeit here it was little indeed.

Now when they had ridden some five miles over the plain, they came amongst those knolls at the mouth of the valley, and Sir Aymeris led Birdalone up to the top of one of the highest of them, and thence they could look into that dale and see how it winded away up toward the mountains, like to a dismal street; for not only was it but little grassed, but withal there was neither tree nor bush therein. Moreover, scattered all about the bottom of the dale were great stones, which looked as if they had once been set in some kind of order; and that the more whereas they were not black like the rocks of the dale-side, but pale grey of hue, so that they looked even as huge sheep of the giants feeding down the dale.

Then spake Birdalone: "Verily, Sir Knight, thou saidst but sooth that I should see things new and strange. But shall we go a little way into this valley to-day?"

148

"Nay, lady," said Sir Aymeris, "nor to-morrow, nor any day uncompelled; neither shall we go nigher unto it than now we be."

"Wherefore not?" said Birdalone, "for meseemeth it is as the gate of the mountains; and fain were I in the mountains."

"Lady," said the castellan, "overmuch perilous it were to ride the valley, which, as thou sayest, is the very gate of the mountains. For the said dale, which hight the Black Valley of the Greywethers, hath a bad name for the haunting of unmanlike wights, against which even our men-at-arms might make no defence. And if any might escape them, and win through the gates and up into the mountains, I wot not if suchlike devils and things unkent be there in the mountain-land, but of a sooth there be fierce and wild men, like enough to devils, who know no peace, and slay whatsoever cometh unto them, but if they themselves be slain of them."

"Well," said Birdalone, "then to-day, at least, we go not into the dale; but knowest thou any tales of these wild places?"

"Many have I heard," said he, "but I am an ill minstrel and should spoil them in the telling. Ask them of Sir Leonard our priest, he knoweth of them better than others, and hath a tongue duly shapen for telling them."

Birdalone answered nought thereto; she but turned her horse's head and rode down the knoll; and so they came unto their company, and all went their ways toward the Castle of the Quest.

Nought befell them on their way home; but the nigher they came to the castle the more pensive waxed Birdalone, and, though she hid it, when they were come to the gate she scarce had her wit; for it was as if she thought to have one rushing out and crying: Tidings, tidings! they are come.

Nowise it so befell; they were no more come than was the Day of Doom. And a little after they were within gates, it was night; and Birdalone crept wearily up to her chamber,

and gat to bed, and so tired was she that she fell asleep at
once and dreamed not.

CHAPTER VI. BIRDALONE HEARETH TELL TALES OF THE BLACK VALLEY OF THE GREY-WETHERS.

ON the morrow was Birdalone heavier of heart than
ever yet, and wearier for tidings; and she wondered
how she could have been so joyous that day in the
wild-wood. Yet she thought much of the Valley of the
Greywethers, and that solaced her somewhat after a while,
so sore she longed to go thither; and, as 'tis said, one nail
knocks out the other. So that morning, when she had had
her lesson of priest Leonard, she spake thereof to him, and
told him what Sir Aymeris had said concerning his knowledge thereof; and she asked him what he knew.

"I have been there," said he. She started at that word and
said: "Did aught of evil befall thee?"

"Nay," said he, "but a great fear and dread hung about
me; and 'tis said that they try their luck overmuch who go
thither twice."

Birdalone said: "Tell me now of the tales that be told of
that valley." Quoth Leonard: "They be many; but the
main of them is this: that those Greywethers be giants of
yore agone, or landwights, carles and queans, who have been
turned into stone by I wot not what deed; but that whiles
they come alive again, and can walk and talk as erst they
did; and that if any man may be so bold as to abide the time
of their awakening, and in the first moment of their change
may frame words that crave the fulfilment of his desire, and
if therewith he be both wise and constant, then shall he have
his desire fulfilled of these wights, and bear his life back
again from out the dale. And thus must he speak and no
otherwise: 'O Earth, thou and thy first children, I crave of
you such and such a thing, whatsoever it may be.' And if he
speak more than this, then is he undone. He shall answer no

question of them; and if they threaten him he shall not pray PART IV
them mercy, nor quail before their uplifted weapons; nor, Chap. 6
to be short, shall he heed them more than if they still were
stones unchanged. Moreover, when he hath said his say,
then shall these wights throng about him and offer him gold
and gems, and all the wealth of the earth; and if that be not
enough, they shall bring him the goodliest of women, with
nought lacking in her shape, but lacking all raiment, so that
he shall see her as she is verily shapen. But whoso shall take
any one of all these gifts is lost for ever, and shall become
one of that Stony People; and whoso naysayeth them all
until the cock crow, and abideth steady by his one craving,
shall win fulfilment thereof, and, as some say, all those gifts
aforesaid; for that the Stony People may not abide the day
to take them back again."

He was silent therewith, and nought spake Birdalone,
but looked down on the ground, and longing encompassed
her soul. Then the priest spake again: "This were a fair
adventure, lady, for a hapless one, but for the happy it were
a fool's errand." She answered not, and they parted for that
time.

But the next week, there being yet no tidings come to
hand, Birdalone prayed the castellan to take her out-a-gates
again, that she might once more behold the mountains, and
the gates thereof; and he yeasaid her asking, and went with
her, well accompanied, as before; but this time, by Birdalone's will, they rode straight to the plain aforesaid, and
again she looked into that dale of the Greywethers from the
knoll. Somewhat belated they were, so that they might not
get back to the castle before dusk, wherefore again they lay
out in the wild-wood, but there lacked somewhat of the triumph and joyance which they had had that other day. They
came back to the castle on the morrow somewhat after
noon, and found no news there; nor, to say sooth, did Birdalone look for any; and her heart was heavy.

CHAPTER VII. BIRDALONE BEGUILETH THE PRIEST TO HELP HER TO OUTGOING.

NOW had the time so worn that the season was in the first days of August, and weariness and heartsickness increased on Birdalone again, and she began to look pined and pale. Yet when she spake of the tarrying of the Champions both to the castellan and Sir Leonard the priest (who was the wiser man of the two), each said the same thing, to wit, that it was no marvel if they were not yet come, seeing what-like the adventure was; and neither of those two seemed in anywise to have lost hope.

Thrice in these last days did Birdalone go out-a-gates with Sir Aymeris and his company; and the last of the three times the journey was to the knoll that looked into the Black Valley; but now was Birdalone's pleasure of the sight of it afar off marred by her longing to be amidst thereof; yet she did not show that she was irked by the refraining of her desire to enter therein, and they turned, and came home safely to the castle.

On the morrow she sat with Sir Leonard the priest over the writing-lesson, and she let it be long, and oft he touched her hand, so that the sweetness of unfulfilled desire went deep to his heart.

At last Birdalone looked up and said: "Friend, I would ask thee if thou seest any peril in my entering the Black Valley of the Greywethers by daylight if I leave it by daylight?" "Alone?" quoth he. "Yea," she said, "alone."

He pondered a little, and then said: "Sooth to say I deem the peril little in the valley itself, if thou be not overcome by terror there. Yea, for my part I am not all so sure that thou shalt see the wonder of the Stony Folk coming alive; for 'tis not said that they quicken save on certain nights, and chiefly on Midsummer Night; unless it be that the trier of the adventure is some one fated above others thereto; as forsooth thou mayst be. And as for peril of evil men, there are few who be like to be as venturesome as

152

thou or I. They durst not enter that black street, save sore need compel them. But forsooth, going thither, and coming back again, some peril there may be therein. And yet for weeks past there has been no word of any unpeace; and the Red Knight it is said for certain is not riding."

Birdalone was silent awhile; then she said: "Fair and kind friend, I am eating my heart out in longing for the coming back of my friends, and it is like, that unless I take to some remedy, I shall fall sick thereby, and then when they come back there shall be in me but sorry cheer for them. Now the remedy I know, and it is that I betake me alone to this adventure of the Black Valley; for meseemeth that I shall gain health and strength by my going thither. Wherefore, to be short, if thou wilt help me, I will go to-morrow. What sayest thou, wilt thou help me?"

He turned very red and spake: "Lady, why shouldest thou go, as thy name is, birdalone? Thou hast called me just now thy kind friend, so kind as it was of thee; now therefore why should not thy friend go with thee?"

Kindly indeed she smiled on him, but shook her head: "I call thee trusty and dear friend again," said she; "but what I would do I must do myself. Moreover to what end shouldst thou go? If I fall in with ghosts, a score of men would help me nought; and if I happen on weaponed men who would do me scathe, of what avail were one man against them? And look thou, Sir Leonard, there is this avail in thine abiding behind; if I come not back in two days' space, or three at the most, thou wilt wot that I have fared amiss, and then mayst thou let it be known whither I went, and men will seek me and deliver me maybe."

Therewith she stayed her words suddenly, and turned very pale, and laid her hand on her bosom, and said faintly: "But O my heart, my heart! If they should come while I am away!" And she seemed like to swoon.

Leonard was afraid thereat, and knew not what to do; but presently the colour came into her face again, and in a little while she smiled, and said: "Seest thou not, friend,

153

how weak I am gotten to be, and that I must now beyond doubt have the remedy? Wilt thou not help me to it?"

"Yea verily," said he; "but in what wise wilt thou have it?" He spake as a man distraught and redeless; but she smiled on him pleasantly, and said: "Now by this time shouldst thou have devised what was to do, and spared me the pain thereof. Two things I need of thee: the first and most, to be put out of the castle privily betimes in the morning when nought is stirring; the second, to have my palfrey awaiting me somewhat anigh the gate, so that I may not have to go afoot: for I am become soft and feeble with all this house-life."

Leonard seemed to wake up with that word, and said: "I have the key of the priest's door of the chapel, and the postern beyond it; that shall be thine out-gate, lady. I will come and scratch at thy chamber-door much betimes, and I will see to it that thy palfrey is bestowed in the bower wherein thou didst rest the first night thou camest amongst us."

She said: "I trust thee, friend." And she thanked him sweetly, and then rose up and fell to pacing the hall up and down. Leonard hung about watching her a while, she nought forbidding him, for her thoughts were elsewhere, and she had forgotten him; and at last he went his ways to set about doing what she would.

CHAPTER VIII. BIRDALONE FARES ON HER ADVENTURE.

DAWN was but just beginning when Birdalone awoke, and though she had not heard Leonard at the door, she sprang out of bed and clad herself, doing on her black gown; and she had a scrip with some bread therein, and a sharp knife at her girdle. Then even as she had done she heard the priest's nail on the door, and she turned thereto; but as she went, her eye caught her bow and quiver of arrows where they hung on the wall, so she took the bow in her hand and slung the quiver over her shoulder ere she

opened the door and found Leonard standing there. Neither
of them spake aught, but they stole downstairs, and so to
the chapel and out by the priest's door and the postern in
the wall-nook, and were presently out in the fresh morning
air; and Birdalone was joyous and lightfoot, and scarce felt
the earth beneath her soles for pleasure of her hope, whereas
she deemed she had a thing to crave of the Stony Folk, if
they should come alive before her. Fain were she, if she
might withal, to give a joy to some other; so that when they
were gone but a little way from the castle she reached out her
hand to Leonard and took his, and said: "Hand in hand we
walked when first I went this way, and I deemed thee kind
and friendly then, and even so hast thou been sithence."

He was dumbfoundered at first for joy of the touch of her
hand and the sweetness of her words; but presently he
spake to her confused and stammering, and praised her that
she had thought to take her bow and arrows; for, said he,
that they might stand her in stead for defence or for getting
of food, or for an excuse for wending the woods. She nodded yeasay unto him, and bade him again to bide three
days for her, and if she came not again in that time, to make
a clean breast of it to Sir Aymeris.

"Yea," said the priest, "and then— Why, what then?
He can but shove me out by the shoulders, and then I can
seek to the little house of canons that is at Gate Cross on the
road to Greenford."

"Ah, my friend!" said Birdalone, "how we women think
of nothing at all but ourselves! And wilt thou be thrust out
of thine home for helping me herein? Why did I not look
to my palfrey myself? And the keys I might have stolen
from thee, always with thy good will. But now I see that I
have done thee a hurt."

Said Sir Leonard: "Lady, a priest hath a home wheresoever is an house of religion. There is no harm done, save
Sir Aymeris bethink him of hanging me over the battlements; as I doubt he will not with a priest. Moreover, I
pray thee believe, that wert thou gone from the castle, house

and home were none for me there." And he looked upon her piteously, as if he were beseeching.

But she knew not what to say, and hung her head adown; and presently they were come to the bower in the copse, which this time was a stable for Birdalone's palfrey instead of a chamber for herself. So Leonard went in and fetched out the comely beast; and Birdalone stood with him just in the cover of the copse waiting to put her foot in the stirrup; but she might not but abide to look upon the priest, who stood there as if he were striving with his words.

So she said: "Now is need of haste to be gone. Yet one word, my friend: Is there aught betwixt us wherein I have done thee wrong? If so it be, I pray thee to say out what it is; for it may be (though I think it not) thou shalt not see me again from henceforth."

He caught his breath, as if he had much ado to refrain the sobbing; but he mastered it, and said: "Lady and dear friend, if I see thee not again, I heed not what shall befall me. Thou hast done me no wrong. There is this only betwixt us, that I love thee, and thou lovest not me."

She looked on him sweetly and pitifully, and said: "I may not choose but understand thy word, to wit, that thy love for me is the desire of a man toward a woman; and that is unhappy; for I love thee indeed, but not as a woman loveth a man. It is best to say thus much to thee downright. But I feel in my heart that when I have said it, it is as much as to say that I cannot help thee, and therefore am I sorry indeed."

He stood before her abashed, but he said at last: "Now art thou so sweet, and so kind, and so true, that I must perforce love thee yet more; and this maketh me bold to say that thou mayst help me a little, or so meseemeth."

"How so?" said Birdalone. Quoth he: "If thou wouldst suffer me to kiss thy face this once." She shook her head, and spake: "How may it avail thee, when it is for once, and once only, as forsooth it must be? Yet it is thy choice, not mine, and I will not naysay thee."

156

And therewith she put up her face to him, and he kissed her cheek without touching her otherwise, and then he kiss- ed her mouth; and she knew that he was both timorous and sad, and she was ashamed to look on him, or to speak to him any more, lest she should behold him ashamed; so she but said: "Farewell, friend, till to-morrow at least."

And therewith her foot was in the stirrup, and anon she sat in the saddle, and her palfrey was ambling briskly on the way she would.

CHAPTER IX. BIRDALONE COMES TO THE BLACK VALLEY.

LITTLE is to tell of Birdalone's journey unto the knoll above the Black Valley of the Greywethers. It was about noon when she came there, and had met but few folk on the way, and those few were husbandmen, or car-lines, or maidens wending afield betimes not far from the Castle of the Quest.

Now she sat on her horse and looked down into the dale and its stony people once more, and saw nought stirring save three ravens who, not far off, were flapping about from stone to stone of the Greywethers, and croaking loud to each other as if some tidings were toward. She watched their play for a little, and then gat off her horse, and sat down on the grass of the knoll, and drew forth her victual, and ate and drank; for she deemed it happier to eat and drink there than in the very jaws of the Black Valley.

Soon was her dinner done, and then she got to her saddle again, and rode slowly down to the little stream, and along it toward the valley and the gates of the mountains, which she had been fain to pass through; but now, as had happed with her that morning when she was boun for the Sending Boat, somewhat she hung back from the adventure, and when she lacked but some five score yards from the very dale itself, she lighted down again, and let her way-beast bite the grass, while she sat down and watched the rippling water.

In a while she drew off shoon and hosen, and stood in the
shallow ripple, and bathed her hands and face withal, and
stooped up-stream and drank from the hollow of her hands,
and so stepped ashore and was waxen hardier; then she
strung her bow and looked to the shafts in her quiver, and
did on her foot-gear, and mounted once more, and so rode
a brisk amble right on into the dale, and was soon come
amongst the Greywethers; and she saw that they were a
many, and that all the bottom of the dale was besprinkled
with them on either side of the stream, and some stood in the
very stream itself, the ground whereof was black even as
the rest of the valley, although the water ran over it as clear
as glass.

As for the dale, now she was fairly within it, she could see
but a little way up it, for it winded much, and at first away
from her left hand, and the sides of it went up in somewhat
steep screes on either side, which were topped with mere
upright staves and burgs of black rock; and these were
specially big and out-thrusting on the right hand of her; and
but a furlong ahead of where she was, one of these burgs
thrust out past the scree and came down sheer into the dale,
and straitened it so much that there was but little way save
by the stream itself, which ran swift indeed, but not deep,
even there where it was straitened by the sheer rocks.

But up the dale would she go, whatever was before her;
and now she told herself her very purpose, as forsooth she
scarce had heretofore; to wit, that she would abide in the
dale the night over and see what should betide, and if those
wights should chance to come alive, then she looked to have
valiance enough to face them and crave the fulfilment of her
desire.

So she took the water and rode the stream till she was past
the said sheer rock, and then the valley widened again, and
presently was wider than it was in the beginning; and here
again were the Greywethers grown many more and closer
together, and, as she deemed, were set in rings round about
one very big one, which, forsooth, was somewhat in the
158

shape of a man sitting down with his hands laid on his knees.

Birdalone reined up for a minute, and looked about her, and then went up on to the grass, and rode straight to the said big stone, and there lighted down from off her horse again, and stood by the stone and pondered. Presently she deemed that she saw something dark moving just beyond the stone, but if it were so, it was gone in a twinkling; nevertheless she stood affrighted, and stared before her long, and saw no more, but yet for a while durst not move hand nor foot.

At last her courage came again, and she thought: Yet how if this great chieftain be inwardly stirring and will come awake? Shall I say the word now, lest hereafter it be of no avail? Therewith she stretched out her right hand and laid it on the stone, and spake aloud: "O Earth, thou and thy first children, I crave of you that he may come back now at once and loving me." And her voice sounded strange and unkent to her in that solitude, and she rued it that she had spoken.

CHAP. X. HOW BIRDALONE FELL IN WITH A MAN IN THE BLACK VALLEY OF THE GREY-WETHERS.

CAME new tidings therewithal; for the moment after she had spoken, a tall man drew out from behind the big stone, and stood before her; and at first it was in her mind that this was the very chieftain come alive for her, and for terror she was like to swoon this time; but he spake nought a while, but looked on her eagerly and curiously.

She came to herself presently, so much that she could see him clearly, and was now growing more shamefast than afraid, when she saw beyond doubt that the man was of the sons of Adam; but what with her shame that was now, and her fear that had been, she yet had no might to move, but stood there pale and trembling like a leaf, and might scarce keep her feet.

159

Now the new-comer bowed before her smiling, and said: "I ask thy pardon, fair damsel (or indeed I should say fairest damsel), that I have scared thee. But sooth to say I beheld thee coming riding, and even from a little aloof I could see that nought which might befall could ever make it up to me for not seeing thee close at hand and hearing thee speak. Wherefore I hid myself behind the King's Stone here; and no harm is done thereby I trow; for now I see that the colour is coming into thy cheeks again, and thy fear is gone. And as for me, thou hast not fled away from me, as thou wouldst have done had I not hidden and come on thee suddenly; and then thou being horsed and I unhorsed, thou wouldst have escaped me, whereas now thou art within reach of my hand." Then he smiled, and said: "Furthermore, thou hast told so little of thy secret to this stony king here, that I am little the wiser for thy word, and thou the little more betrayed. Only this I will say, that if He loveth thee not, He is more of a fool than I be."

He reached out his hand to hers, but she drew it aback, and grew yet more ashamed, and could find no word for him. His voice was soft and full, and he spake deftly, but she was not content with it for its kindness, as she had been with all the other men whom she had met since she left the House under the Wood, and she durst not trust her hand to him.

As for his aspect, she saw that he was tall and well-knit, and goodly of fashion; dark-haired, with long hazel eyes, smooth-cheeked and bright-skinned; his nose long, and a little bent over at the end, and coming down close to his lips, which were full and red; his face was hairless save for a little lip-beard. He was so clad, that he had no helm on his head, but a little hat with a broad gold piece in the front thereof; he was girt to a long sword, and had an anlace also in his belt, and Birdalone saw the rings of a fine hauberk at his collar and knees; otherwise he was not armed. Over his hauberk he wore a black surcoat, without device of any kind, and his foot and leg gear were of the same hue; wherefore may we

160

call him the Black Knight. Sooth to say, for all his soft
speech, she feared him and rued the meeting of him.

Now he spake to her again: "I see that thou art wroth
with me, lady; but mayhappen it is not so ill that I have
happened on thee; for this dale hath a bad name for more
than one thing, and is scarce meet for damsels to wander in.
But now since thou hast a weaponed man with thee, and
thou, by All hallows! not utterly unarmed, thou mayst well
go up the valley and see something more thereof. So come
now, mount thine horse again, and I will lead him for thee."

Now Birdalone found speech and said: "Knight, for such
thou seemest to me, I deem now that I have no need to fare
further in this dale, but I will get me into the saddle and
turn my horse's head outward again, giving thee good day
first and thanking thee for thy courtesy." And therewith
she turned to get to her palfrey, but sore trembling the
while; but he followed her and said, with brow somewhat
knitted: "Nay, lady, I have left my horse somewhat further
up, and I must go back to fetch him, that we may wend out
of the dale together. For I will not suffer thee to flee from
me and fall into the hands of evil wights, be they ghosts or
living men, and that the less since I have heard the speech
in thy mouth, as of honey and cream and roses. Therefore if
thou go out of the dale, I shall go with thee afoot, leading
thine horse. And look to it if it be courteous to unhorse a
knight, who is ready to be thy servant. Moreover, since thou
hast come to this dale of wonder, and mayst leave it safely,
pity it were that thou shouldst see nought thereof, for strange
is it forsooth, and belike thou shalt never seek thither again.
Wherefore I crave of thee, once more, to mount thine horse
and let me lead thee up the dale."

He spake these last words rather as one giving a command than making a prayer, and Birdalone feared him now
sorely. Forsooth she had her bended bow in hand; but let
alone that the knight was over near to her that she might get
a shaft out of her quiver and nock it, ere he should run in on
her, and let alone also that he was byrnied, she scarce deem-

ed that it behoved her to slay or wound the man because she would be quit of him. Wherefore angrily, and with a flushed face, she answered him: "So shall it be then, Sir Knight; or rather so must it be, since thou compellest me."

He laughed and said: "Nay, now thou art angry. I compel thee not, I but say that it will not do for thee to compel me to leave thee. Go which way thou wilt, up the dale, or down it and out of it; it is all one unto me, so long as I am with thee. Forsooth, damsel, I have said harder words to ladies who have done my pleasure and not deemed themselves compelled."

She paled but answered nought; then she mounted her palfrey, and the knight went to her bridle-rein without more words, and so led her on up the valley by the easiest way amongst the Greywethers.

CHAPTER XI. BIRDALONE IS LED UP THE BLACK VALLEY.

AS they went, the knight fell a-talking to Birdalone, and that without any of the covert jeering which he had used erewhile; and he showed her places in the dale, as caverns under the burgs, and little eyots in the stream, and certain stones amongst the Greywethers whereof stories ran; and how this and the other one had fared in dealings with the land-wights, and how one had perished, and another had been made happy, and so forth. Withal he told of the Mountain-folk, and in especial how they of the Plains, when he was scarce more than a boy, had met them in battle in that same dale, and how fierce the fight was; whereas the mountain-men were fighting for a life of desires accomplished, which hitherto had been but a dream unto them; and the men of the plain fought for dear life itself, and for all that made it aught save death in life. Wherefore up and down the dale they fought, at first in ordered ranks and then in knots, and lastly sword to sword and man to man, till there was no foot of grass or black sand there which had

not its shower of blood; and the stream was choked with
the dead, and ran red out of the dale; till at last well-
nigh all the host of the mountain-men was fallen, and scarce
less of the folk of the plains, but these men held the field
and had the victory.

All this he told her deftly and well, and though he said
not so right out, yet let her wot that, youth as he was, he was
of the battle; and his voice was clear and good, and Birdalone's wrath ran off her, and she hearkened his tale, and
even asked him a question here and there; and so courteous
was this Black Knight now become, that Birdalone began to
think that she had fallen short of courtesy to him, because of
her fear and the weariness of the waiting which so oppressed
her; and that shamed and irked her, for she would fain be
of all courtesy. Wherefore now she deemed that perchance
she had erred in deeming him an evil man; and she looked
on him from time to time, and deemed him goodly of
fashion; she thought his eyes were deep, and his face sober
and fair of aspect, but that his nose turned down at the end,
and was over thin at the bridge, and moreover his lips
looked over-sweet and licorous.

Now when the knight was silent of his tales, Birdalone
fell to asking him questions sweetly concerning this Stony
People which was all about them; and he told her all he
knew, soberly enough at first, yet indeed ended by mocking
them somewhat, but mocked not at her any more. At last he
said: "Fair lady, that thou hast not come here all for nought
I partly know by those words which I heard come from thy
mouth at the King's Stone; wherefore I marvelled indeed
when I heard thee say that thou wouldst go straight out of the
dale; for I had deemed thee desirous of trying the adventure
of waking this Stony People a-night-tide. Forsooth was this
thy mind when thou soughtest hither to the dale?"

She reddened at his word, and yeasaid him shortly. Then
said he: "Is it not thy mind still?" "Sir," said she, "as
now I have got to fear it."

"Yea? and that is strange," said he, "for thou wouldst have waked the dale alone; and now thou art no longer alone, but hast me to watch and ward thy waking, thou art more afeard."

She looked on his face steadily, to wot if there were no half-hidden smile therein; but herseemed that he spake in all soberness; and she had nought to say to him save this: "Sir, I am now become afraid of the waking." And he said no more thereof.

Now they went thus, and Birdalone not without pleasure, since her fear of the knight was minished, some three hours up the dale, and still were the Greywethers everywhere about them, so that there were well-nigh as many hours as miles in their wending.

At last they seemed to be drawing nigh to the head of the dale, and the burgs and the rocks were before them all round it as a wall, though yet about a mile aloof at the further end; and this end it was wider than elsewhere.

Came they then to a level space of greensward clear of the grey stones, which were drawn all around it in ordered rings, so that it was as some doom-ring of an ancient people; and within the said space Birdalone beheld a great black horse tethered and cropping the grass. The knight led her into the ring, and said: "Now are we come home for the present, my lady, and if it please thee to light down we shall presently eat and drink, and sithence talk a little." And he drew nigh to help her off her horse, but she suffered him not, and lighted down of herself; but if she suffered not his hand, his eyes she must needs suffer, as he gazed greedily on the trimness of her feet and legs in her sliding from her horse.

Howsoever, he took her hand, and led her to a little mound on the other side of the ring, and bade her sit down there, and so did she, and from under the nighest of the stones he drew forth a pair of saddle-bags, and took victual and wine thence, and they ate and drank together like old

164

companions. And now Birdalone told herself that the knight was frank and friendly; yet forsooth she wotted that her heart scarce trowed what it feigned, and that she yet feared him.

CHAPTER. XII. HOW THOSE TWAIN GET THEM FROM OUT OF THE BLACK VALLEY OF THE GREYWETHERS.

WHEN they had dined, and had sat a while talking, the knight said: "I will ask thee once more wherefore thou must needs depart from this dale leaving the Greywethers unwaked? Yet this must I tell thee first, that this ring at the dale's end is the only one due place where the Greywethers can be rightly waked, and that there be few who wot this. Wilt thou not tell me then what is in thy mind?"

Birdalone gazed down on the ground a while; then she lifted up her head and looked on the Black Knight, and said: "Sir Knight, we have been brought so close together to-day, and as meseemeth I am so wholly in thy power, that I will tell thee the very truth as it is. My mind it was to wake the dale here to-night, and take what might befall me. And well indeed might I fear the adventure, which few, meseemeth, would not fear. But so strong is my longing for that which I would crave of these wights, that it overmastered my fear, and my purpose held when I entered the dale. Then I met thee; and here again is the truth, take it how thou wilt, that presently I feared thee, and yet I fear thee; for I have noted thee closely all this while, and have seen of thee, that thou art over heedful of my poor body, and wouldst have it for thine own if thou mightest. And there is this in thee also, as I deem, though thou thyself mayst not know it, that thou wouldst have thy pleasure of me whether it pleasure me or grieve me; and this thy pleasure must I needs gainsay; for though thou mayest hereafter become my

165

friend, yet are there other friends of mine, who be such, that
my grief would mar any pleasure they might have. Hast
thou heard and understood?"

She looked on his face steadily as she spake, and saw that
it flushed, and darkened, and scowled, and that his hands
were clenched, and his teeth set hard together. And again
she spake: "Sir, thou shalt know that beside these shot-
weapons, I have a thing here in my girdle that may serve
either against thee or against me, if need drive me thereto;
wherefore I will pray thee to forbear. Forsooth, thou shalt
presently happen on other women, who shall be better unto
thee than I can be."

By then Birdalone had spoken the word, the knight's
face had cleared, and he laughed aloud and said: "As to thy
last words, therein at least thou liest, my lady. But for the
rest, I see that it must all be as thou willest. Yea, if such be thy
will, we shall presently to horse and ride down the dale
again, and at the end thereof I shall leave thee to go home
alone at thy will." She said: "For that I can thee thanks with
all my heart. But why hast thou not asked me of whence I
am, and whither I would go home?"

Again he laughed and said: "Because I know already. I
have had more than two or three tales from them who have
seen thee, or spoken unto others who have seen thee, how
the gay Champions of the Castle of the Quest had fished up
a wondrous pearl of price from out of the Great Water; and
when I set eyes on thy beauty, I knew that the said pearl
could be nowhere else than under mine eyes."

"Let that pass," she said, and blushed not; "but now tell
me the truth as I have told thee, why thou art so instant with
me to wake the Greywethers to-night?"

He kept silence a while, and, as she looked on him, she
thought she saw confusion in his face; but at last he said:
"Thou wert wrong in saying that I heeded not thy pleasure,
and solace, and welfare. Meseemed, and yet doth, that it
might be to thine avail to wake the Greywethers to-night;
and never again mayst thou have a chance of the waking, as

166

erst I said. I say I wish thee to have fulfilment of thy craving.
Nor hast thou aught to fear of them, seeing that it is but
dastards and fools that they undo."

He broke off his speech, and Birdalone yet looked on
him, and after a little he said: "Thou drawest the truth out
of me; for moreover I would have thee with me longer than
thou wouldst be if we but rode together down the water and
out of the dale, and thou to fare away alone."

Birdalone spake in a while, and that while he gazed upon
her eagerly; she said: "I shall now tell thee that I shall
abide the adventure of the waking to-night, whatever befall."

"And I," said he, "will so do that thou mayst fear me the
less; for I will unarm me when the night cometh, and thou
thyself shalt keep mine hawberk and sword and anlace." She
said: "It is well; I will take that, lest desire overmaster
thee."

They spake no more of it at that time, and it was now five
hours after noon. Birdalone arose, for she found it hard to
sit still and abide nightfall: she went without the two first
rings of the Greywethers, which were set in more open order
beyond that, and she looked all about her, to the black rocks
on either side, and to the great black wall at the dale's ending, and the blue mountains aloof beyond it; then down
toward the plain of the dale came her eyes, and she looked
through the tangle of the grey stones. Now she seemed to
be looking more intently upon some one thing; with that
she called to her the Black Knight, who was hanging about
watching her, and she said to him: "Fair sir, art thou clear-
seeing and far-seeing?"

"I am not thought to be purblind," quoth he. Then
Birdalone reached out her hand and pointed and said:
"Canst thou see aught which thou didst not look to see,
there, up the dale as I point?" Said he: "All too clear I see
the hand and the wrist of thee, and that blinds me to aught
else."

"I pray thee fool not," she said, "but look heedfully,

167

and thou mayst see what I see, and then tell me what it
means. Though forsooth I am exceeding in far sight."

He looked under the sharp of his hand heedfully, then he
turned unto her and said: "By Allhallows! there is in thee
every excellency! Thou art right; I see a bay horse up there
feeding on the bites of grass amongst the Greywethers."

"Look again!" she said; "what else canst thou see? Is
there aught anigh to the bay horse which is like to the gleam
and glitter of metal." "Christ!" said he, "once more thou
art right. There be weaponed men in the dale. Tarry not, I
beseech thee, but get to horse forthright, and I will do no
less."

"There goeth the Waking of the Dale for this time," said
Birdalone, laughing. "But art thou not in haste, fair sir?
may not these be friends?"

The knight laid his hand upon her shoulder, and thrust
her on toward her palfrey, and spake fiercely, but not loud:
"Thee I pray not to fool now! there is not a minute to spare.
If thou deemest me evil, as I think thou dost, there are
worser than I, I tell thee, there are worser. But we will talk
of it when we be in the saddle, and clear of this accursed
dale."

Birdalone knew not what to do save obey him, so she
lightly gat into her saddle, and followed him, for he was
mounted in a twinkling, and riding on. He led out of the
ring, and fell to threading the maze of the Greywethers,
keeping ever toward the steep side of the dale, which was on
that hand that looked toward the Castle of the Quest, that is
to say, the eastern bent. Birdalone wondered at this leading,
and when she was come up with the knight she spake to him
breathlessly, and said: "But, fair sir, why wend we not
down the dale?" He answered: "First, lady, because we
must hide us from them straightway; and next because they
be more than we, many more, and their horses be fresh,
while thine at least is somewhat spent; and if they were to
spur down the dale in chase, they would soon be upon us;
for think not that I would escape and leave thee behind."

168

Said Birdalone: "But thou knowest them, then, what they be? since thou wottest of their numbers and their riding. Hearken now! Upon thy soul and thy salvation, be they more friends unto thee than unto me?"

He said, as he rode on a little slower than erst: "Upon my soul and my salvation I swear it, that the men yonder be of the worst unfriends to thee that may be in the world. And now, lady, I promise thee that I will unravel thee the riddle, and tell thee the whole truth of these haps, whatsoever may come of my words, when we be in a safer place than this; and meantime I beseech thee to trust in me thus far, as to believe that I am leading thee out of the very worst peril that might befall thee. Nay, thou must needs trust me; for I tell thee, that though I now love thee better than all the world and all that is in it, I would slay thee here in this dale rather than suffer thee to fall into the hands of these men."

Birdalone heard him with a sick heart; but such passion went with his words that she believed what he said; and she spake softly: "Sir, I will trust thee thus far; but I beseech thee to have pity upon a poor maiden who hath had but little pity shown unto her until these latter days; and then—O woe's me, to have fallen out of the kindness and love once more!"

The Black Knight spake to her in a little while, and said: "What pity I can to thee, that I will. Once more I tell thee, that if thou but knew it thou wouldst thank me indeed for what I have done for thee in this hour; and henceforth I will do and forbear with thee to the uttermost that love will suffer me. But lo thou! here are we safe for this present; but we must nowise tarry."

Birdalone looked and saw that they were come to the wall of the dale, and that there it went down sheer to the plain thereof, and that before them was a cleft that narrowed speedily, and over which the rocks well-nigh met, so that it was indeed almost a cave. They rode into it straightway, and when that they had gone but a little, and because it had winded somewhat, they could but see the main valley as a

PART IV
Chap. 12
star of light behind them, then it narrowed no more, but was
as a dismal street of the straitest, whiles lighter and whiles
darker, according as the rocks roofed it in overhead or drew
away from it. Long they rode, and whiles came trickles of
water from out the rocks on one hand or the other; and now
and again they met a stream which covered all the ground of
the pass from side to side for the depth of a foot or more.
Great rocks also were strewn over their path every here and
there, so that whiles must they needs dismount and toil afoot
over the rugged stones; and in most places the way was toilsome and difficult. The knight spake little to Birdalone, save
to tell her of the way, and warn her where it was perilous;
and she, for her part, was silent, partly for fear of the strange
man, or, it might be, even for hatred of him, who had thus
brought her into such sore trouble, and partly for grief. For,
with all torment of sorrow, she kept turning over and over
in her mind whether her friends had yet come home to the
Castle of the Quest, and whether they would go seek her to
deliver her. And such shame took hold of her when she
thought of their grief and confusion of soul when they
should come home and find her gone, that she set her mind
to asking if it had not been better had she never met them.
Yet in good sooth her mind would not shape the thought,
howsoever she bade it.

CHAPTER XIII. NOW THEY REST FOR THE NIGHT IN THE STRAIT PASS.

AT last, when they had been going a long while, it
might be some six hours, and it had long been night
in the world without, but moon-lit, and they had
rested but seldom, and then but for short whiles, the knight
drew rein and spake to Birdalone, and asked her was she not
weary. "O yea," she said; "I was at point to pray thee suffer
me to get off and lie down on the bare rock. To say sooth, I
am now too weary to think of any peril, or what thou art, or
whither we be going."
170

He said: "By my deeming we be now half through this
mountain highway, and belike there is little peril in our
resting; for I think not that any one of them knoweth of
this pass, or would dare it if he did; and they doubtless came
into the dale by the upper pass, which is strait enough, but
light and open."

As he spoke, Birdalone bowed forward on her horse's
neck, and would have fallen but that he stayed her. Then he
lifted her off her horse, and laid her down in the seemliest
place he might find; and the pass there was much widened,
and such light as there was in the outer world came down
freely into it, though it were but of the moon and the stars;
and the ground was rather sandy than rocky. So he dight Birdalone's bed as well as he might, and did off his surcoat and
laid it over her; and then stood aloof, and gazed on her; and
he muttered: "It is an evil chance; yet the pleasure of it, the
pleasure of it! Yea," said he again, "she might well be
wearied; I myself am ready to drop, and I am not the least
tough of the band." And therewith he laid him down on the
further side of the pass, and fell asleep straightway.

CHAPTER XIV. THE BLACK KNIGHT TELLS THE TRUTH OF HIMSELF.

WHEN the morning was come down into the strait-
ness of their secret road, Birdalone opened her eyes
and saw the Black Knight busy over dighting their
horses: so she arose and thrust her grief back into her heart,
and gave her fellow-farer the sele of the day, and he brought
her victual, and they ate a morsel, and gat to horse thereafter and departed; and the way became smoother, and it
was lighter overhead everywhere now, and the rocks never
again met overhead athwart the way; and it seemed to
Birdalone that now they were wending somewhat down-
ward.

The knight was courteous unto Birdalone, and no longer
for the present thrust his love upon her, so that now she had

some solace of his fellowship, though he was but few-spoken
to her.

It was betimes when they arose, and they rode all the
morning till it was noon, which they might well wot of, because the way was much wider, and the cliff-walls of the pass
much lower, so that the sun shone in upon them and cheered
them.

Now the Black Knight drew rein and said: "Shall we rest,
lady, and eat? And thereafter, if thou wilt, I shall tell thee
my tale. Or rather, if thou wilt suffer me, I shall speak first
and eat afterwards, or else the morsel might stick in my
throat." "Knight," said Birdalone, smiling, "I hope thou
hast no lie to swallow down before the meat." "Nay, lady,"
said he; "no lie that is of moment at least."

So they lighted down, and Birdalone sat on the wayside
under a birch-bush that came thrusting out from the rock,
and the knight stood before her, hanging his head, as though
he were one accused who would plead his cause; and he began:

"Lady, I must tell thee first of all, that to-day I have done
as an unfaithful servant and a traitor to my lord." Said Birdalone simply: "Shall I tell thee the truth, and say that from
the first I seemed to see in thee that thou wert scarce trusty?"
He said: "Well, that mind I saw in thee, and it went to my
heart that thou shouldest think it, and that it should be no
less than true. But now I must tell thee, that it is for thy sake
that I have been untrusty to my lord." "How so?" said she.
Quoth he: "Heardest thou ever of the Red Knight?" "Yea,"
said Birdalone, "I have heard of him ever as a tyrant and
oppressor." Then she grew pale, and said: "Art thou he?"

"Nay," said the knight, "I am but a kinsman of his, and
his best-trusted man; nor have I failed him ever till yesterday."

He kept silence a while, and then said: "This is the true
tale: that we have had tidings of thee and of thy ridings a-
broad with that old fool, Sir Aymeris, and how thou hadst

172

been twice to look into the Black Valley. This I say hath the Red One heard, and the heart of him was touched by the mere hearsay of thee; and moreover 'tis blessed bread to him the doing of any grief to the knights of Quest Castle; wherefore he hath sent me to hang about the dale, to lay hands on thee if I might; for he knew, being wise, that thou wouldst hanker after it; and moreover he let one of his wise women sit out in spells on thee. So I espied, and happened on thee all alone; and mine errand it was, since I came upon thee thus, to draw thee till I had thee safe at home in the Red Hold. Forsooth I began mine errand duly, and fell to beguiling thee, so that thou mayst well have seen the traitor in me. But then—and then my heart failed me, because I fell, not to desiring thee as coveting my master's chattel, but to loving thee and longing for thee as my fellow and speechfriend. And I said to myself: Into the Red Hold she shall not go if I may hinder it."

Birdalone was very pale, but she refrained her from grief and fear, and said: "But those horsed and weaponed men up the dale, who were they?"

He said: "I will not lie now, not even a little; they came into the dale by that upper pass whereof I told thee; they were of our men; I brought them. I was never all alone in the dale; I was to have fetched thee to them, so that thou mightest not see a rout of folk and flee away; and then would we all have gone home together by the upper pass. But we two must have gone on unto them in the dale's head, whereas for all that I could say I might not bring them down into that doom-ring where we ate and talked yesterday. We two have been valianter than thou mayst have deemed, to have done the deed of dining there; for all men fear it. But as for me, I have been there more than twice or thrice, and thence have I wandered, and found this pass wherein now we be; concerning which I have held my tongue, deeming that it might one day serve my turn; as it hath done now abundantly, since it hath been a refuge unto thee."

"Yea, but whither are we going now?" said Birdalone;
"is it perchance to the Red Hold?" "Nay, never," said the
knight, "so help me God and Allhallows!"

"Whither then?" said Birdalone; "tell me, that I may at
least trust thee, even though I owe thee for all the pain and
grief which thou hast wrought me." He reddened and said:
"Wait a while; I bring thee to no ill place; there shall no
harm befall thee." And he fretted and fumed, and was confused of speech and look, and then he said: "When we come
there I shall belike crave a boon of thee."

"O, but I crave a boon of thee here and now," said Birdalone. "Wipe away thine offence to me and take me back to
my friends and the Castle of the Quest! So mayst thou yet
be dear unto me, though maybe not wholly as thou wouldst
have it." And she reached out her two hands toward him.

His breast heaved, and he seemed nigh to weeping; but
he said: "Nay, lady, ask me not here and now, but there and
to-morrow. But again I swear to thee by thine hands that to
the Red Hold I will not bring thee, nor suffer thee to be
brought, if I may hinder it; nay, not though I give my life
therefor."

Birdalone was silent a while; then she said: "And what
shall befall me if I come to the Red Hold? What is the
Red Knight, and what would he do with me?" Said he:
"The Red Knight is terrible and fierce and wise; and I fear
him, I." He held his peace, and said: "I must needs say it,
that to thee he would have been as Death and the Devil. He
would have bedded thee first—" She broke in: "Nay,
never!" and flushed very red. But the knight went on:
"And after, I wot not; that were according to his mood.
And as to thy never, lady, thou wottest not the like of him
or of the folk he hath about him."

"Such as thou?" she said angrily. "Nay," he said, "far
worse than me; men who fare little afield, and are not sweet-
ened by adventures and war-perils; and women worser yet;
and far worser were they dealing with a woman."

She was silent again awhile, and paled once more; then

her colour came back to her, and she held out her hand to him and said kindly: "Thou being what thou art, I thank thee for thy dealings with me; and now until to-morrow, when I shall ask thee of that again, I am friends with thee; so come now, and let us eat and drink together."

He took her hand and kissed it, and then came and sat down meekly beside her, and they ate and drank in that wild place as though they had been friends of long acquaintance.

CHAPTER XV. THE BLACK KNIGHT BRINGS BIRDALONE TO THE BOWER IN THE DALE.

WHEN they had made an end of their meal, they gat to horse again and rode on their ways; and every mile now was their road the easier, the pass wider, and its walls lower and now also more broken; till at last they began to go down hill swiftly, and after a little their road seemed to be swallowed in a great thicket of hornbeam and holly; but the knight rode on and entered the said thicket, and ever found some way amidst the branches, though they were presently in the very thick of the trees, and saw no daylight between the trunks for well-nigh an hour, whereas the wood was thick and tangled, and they had to thread their way betwixt its mazes.

At last the wood began to grow thinner before them, and the white light to show between the trunks; and Birdalone deemed that she heard the sound of falling water, and presently was sure thereof; and the knight spake to her: "Patience, my lady; now are we near home for to-day." She nodded kindly to him, and therewith they rode on to open ground, and were on the side of a steep bent, broken on their right hands into a sheer cliff, as Birdalone saw when the knight led her to the edge and bade her look over. Then she saw down into a fair dale lying far below them, through the which ran a little river, clear and swift, but not riotous, after it had fallen over a force at the upper end of the dale, and made

the sound of water which she had heard. The said dale was
so, that whatsoever was on the other side thereof was hidden
by tall and great trees, that stood close together some twenty
yards aloof from the stream, and betwixt them and it was fair
greensward with a few bushes and thorn-trees thereon.

Quoth the knight: "Down there shall we rest till to-morrow, if it please thee, lady; and since the sun will set in an
hour, we were best on our way at once." "It pleases me
well," said Birdalone, "and I long to tread the turf by the
river-side, for I am weary as weary may be of the saddle
and the pass."

So down the bent they rode, and it was but a little ere they
had ridden it to an end, and had met the river as it swept
round the cliff-wall of the valley; and they rode through it,
and came on to the pleasant greensward aforesaid under the
trees; and in a bight of the wood was a bower builded of turf
and thatched with reed; and there, by the bidding of the
knight, they alighted; and the knight said: "This is thine
house for to-night, my lady; and thou mayest lie there in
all safety after thou hast supped, and mayst have my weapons by thy side if thou wilt, while I lie under the trees
yonder. And if thou wilt bathe thee in the cool water, to
comfort thee after the long ride and the weariness, I swear
by thy hand that I will take myself out of eye-shot and abide
aloof till thou call me."

Said Birdalone, smiling somewhat: "Fair sir, I will not
have my watch and ward unarmed; keep thou thy weapons;
and thou wilt not forget, perchance, that I am not wholly
unarmed, whereas I have my bow and arrows and my knife
here. And as to my bathing, I will take thee at thy word, and
bid thee go aloof a while now at once; for I will go down to
the water; and if thou spy upon me, then will it be thy shame
and not mine."

The knight went his ways therewith, and Birdalone went
down to the water and unclad her; but ere she stepped into
the river, she laid her bow and three shafts on the lip thereof.
Then she took the water, and desported her merrily therein;

176

and now, forsooth, she was nowise downcast, for she said to
herself, This man is not all evil and he loveth me well, and I
look for it that to-morrow he will bring me on my way toward the Castle of the Quest, for mere love of me; and then
shall he be a dear friend to me, and I will comfort him what
I can for as long as we both live.

So she came out of the water and clad her, and then called
aloud for the knight, and he came speedily unto her, as if he
had been not exceeding far away, though he swore with a
great oath that he had nowise espied her. She answered him
nought, and they went side by side to the bower; and there
the knight dight the victual, and they sat together and ate
their meat like old friends; and Birdalone asked the knight
concerning this valley and the bower, if he had known it
for long, and he answered: "Yea, lady, I was but a stripling
when I first happened on the dale; and I deem that few
know thereof save me; at least none of our flock knoweth
thereof; and I am fain thereof, and keep them unknowing,
for if my lord were to hear of my having a haunt privy unto
me he would like it but ill."

Birdalone turned pale when she heard him speak of his
lord; for fear of the Red Knight had entered into her soul, so
that now the flesh crept upon her bones. But she enforced
her to smile, and said: "Yea, and what would he do to thee
were he ill-content with thy ways?"

"Forsooth, lady," said he, "if he could spare me he would
make an end of me in some miserable way; nay, if he were
exceeding ill-content, he would do as much for me whether
he could spare me or not; otherwise he would watch his occasion, and so grieve me that what he did would go to my
very heart."

"Woe's me!" said Birdalone, "thou servest an evil master." The knight answered not, and Birdalone went on
speaking earnestly: "It is a shame to thee to follow this fiend;
why dost thou not sunder thee from him, and become
wholly an honest man?" Said he gruffly: "It is of no use
talking of this, I may not; to boot, I fear him." Then did

Birdalone hold her peace, and the knight said: "Thou dost
not know; when I part from thee I must needs go straight to
him, and then must that befall which will befall. Speak we no
more of these matters."

Birdalone flushed with hope and joy as he spake thus, for
she took him to mean that he would lead her, on the morrow, on her way to the Castle of the Quest. But the knight
spake in a voice grown cheerful again: "As to this bower,
lady, the tale thereof is soon told; for with mine own hands
I builded it some fifteen years ago; and I have come to this
place time and again when my heart was overmuch oppressed with black burdens of evil and turmoil, and have whiles
prevailed against the evil, and whiles not."

"Mayst thou prevail this time, then!" said she. He answered her not, but presently fell to talking with her of
other matters, and the two were frank and friendly together,
till the August night grew dark about them; and then spake
Birdalone: "Now would I rest, for I can no longer keep
mine eyes open. Abide aloof from me to-morrow morning
till I call to thee, as thou didst this evening; and then, before
we eat together again, thou shalt tell me what thou wilt do
with me."

He stood up to depart, and she reached out her hand to
him in the glimmer, and he saw it, but said: "Nay, if I take
thine hand, I shall take thine whole body."

And therewith he departed, and she laid her down in her
smock alone, and slept anon, and was dreamless and forgetting everything till the sun was up in the morning.

CHAPTER XVI. YET A DAY AND A NIGHT THEY TARRY IN THE DALE.

BIRDALONE awoke when the sun came into the
bower to her, and stood up at once, and went down
to the river and washed the night off her; and then,
when she was clad, called on the knight to come to her; and

178

he came, looking downcast and troubled; so that Birdalone
thought within herself: It is well, he will do my will.

She stood before him, and gave him the sele of the day, and he looked on her sorrowfully. Then she said: "Now is come the time when I am to ask thee to take me back to the Castle of the Quest and my own people." He was not hasty to answer her, and she spake again: "This must thou do, or else take me to the Red Hold and deliver me to the tyrant there; and I have heard it from thine own mouth that will be nought else than casting me into shame and torment and death. And I deem thou canst not do it. Nay," she said, staying the words that were coming from his mouth, "I wot that thou canst do it if thine heart can suffer it; for thou art stronger than I, and thou mayst break my bow, and wrest this knife out of mine hand; and thou canst bind me and make me fast to the saddle, and so lead my helpless body into thraldom and death. But thou hast said that thou lovest me, and I believe thee herein. Therefore I know that thou canst not will to do this."

He answered in his surly voice: "Thou art right, lady, I cannot. Nay, hearken thou this time. I have been turning over night-long what thou didst say about leaving my lord, that is, betraying him, for it comes to that; and now I have made up my mind to do it, and I will betray him for thy sake. Wherefore there is a third way to take which thou hast not seen; we will ride out of this dale in an hour's time, and I will bring thee to them who are only less the mortal foes of the Red Knight than are thy fellows of the Quest, to wit, to the captain and burgesses of the good town of Greenford by the Water; and I will do them to wit that I have rescued thee from the hands of the Red Knight, and am become his foe; and will show them all his incomings and outgoings, and every whit of rede, and entrap him, so that he fall into their hands. Now, though were I to be taken in battle by them, I should be speedily brought to the halter, or may be to the bale-fire (for we be wizards all in the Red Hold); yet with

N2

this word in my mouth, if they trow in it, I shall be made
their captain, and presently their master. Trow in my tale
they will, if thou bear me out therein, and they will honour
thee, and suffer thee to give thyself to me in marriage; and
then I know thee, and myself also, and that ere long we
shall be both mighty and wealthy and beloved, and fair will
be the days before us."

His voice had grown softer as he spake, and toward the
end of his words he faltered, and at last brake out a-weeping, and cast himself wordless on the grass before her.

She was pale, and her brow was knitted, and her face
quivered; but she spake coldly to him and said: "This way
I cannot take; and I wonder at thee that thou hast shown it
unto me, for thyself thou knowest that I cannot go with
thee. I will go nowhere hence save to the Castle of the
Quest. If thou wilt not lead me thereto, or put me on the
road, I ask thee straight, Wilt thou stay me if I go seek the
way thither myself?"

He rose up from the ground with a pale face full of anger
as well as grief, and caught her by the wrists and said, scowling
the while: "Tell me now which of them it is; is it the stupid
oaf Baudoin, or the light fool Hugh, or the dull pedant
Arthur? But it matters not; for I know, and all the country-
side knows, that they be vowed, each man of them, to his own
woman; and if they find not the women themselves, such
dolts they are, that they will ever be worshipping the mere
shadows of them, and turn away from flesh and blood, were
it the fairest in the world, as thou art, as thou art."

She shrank away from him what she might, but he still
held her wrists; then she spake in a quivering voice, her very
lips pale with fear and wrath: "It is well seen that thou art a
man of the Red Knight; and belike thou wouldst do with me
as he would. But one thing I crave of thee, if there is any
grain of mercy in thee, that thou wilt draw thy sword and
thrust me through; thou mayst leave thine hold of me to get
at the blade, I will not stir from where I stand. O! to think
that I deemed thee well-nigh a true man."

180

He dropped her hands now and stood aloof from her, staring at her, and presently cast himself on the ground, rolling about and tearing at the grass. She looked on him a moment or two, and then stepped forward and stooped to him, and touched his shoulder and said: "Rise up, I bid thee, and be a man and not a wild beast."

So in a while he arose, and stood before her hangdog-like; then she looked on him pitifully, and said: "Fair sir and valiant knight, thou hast gone out of thy mind for a while, and thus hast thou shamed both me and thyself; and now thou wert best forget it, and therewithal my last words to thee."

Therewith she held out her hand to him, and he went on his knees and took it, sobbing, and kissed it. But she said, and smiled on him: "Now I see that thou wilt do what I prayed of thee, and lead me hence and put me on the road to the Castle of the Quest." He said: "I will lead thee to the Castle of the Quest."

Said Birdalone: "Then shall it be as I promised, that I will be thy dear friend while both we live. And now, if thou canst, be a little merrier, and come and sit with me, and let us eat our meat, for I hunger."

He smiled, but woefully, and presently they sat down to their meat; and he strove to be somewhat merry of mood, and to eat as one at a feast; but whiles his heart failed him, and he set his teeth and tore at the grass, and his face was fierce and terrible to look on; but Birdalone made as if she heeded it nought, and was blithe and debonaire with him. And when they had done their meat he sat looking at her a while, and at last he said: "Lady, dost thou deem that, when all is said, I have done somewhat for thee since first we met the day before yesterday at the lower end of the Black Valley?"

"Yea," she said, "as erst I spake, all things considered I deem that thou hast done much."

"And now," said he, "I am to do more yet; for I am to lead thee to where henceforth I shall have no more part or lot in thee than if thou wert in Heaven and I in Hell." "I pray thee say not so," said Birdalone; "have I not said that I will be thy friend?"

"Lady," said the knight, "I wot well that according to the sweetness of thine heart wilt thou do what thou canst do." And therewith he was silent a while and she also.

Then he said: "I would ask thee a grace if I durst." "Ask it," said she, "and I will grant it if I may; I have gainsaid thee enough meseemeth."

"Lady," he said, "I will ask this as a reward of the way-leader, to wit, that thou abide with me here in this dale, in all honour holden, till to-morrow morning; and let this place, which has helped me aforetime, be hallowed by thy dwelling here; and I, I shall have had one happy day at least, if never another. Canst thou grant me this? If thou canst not, we will depart in an hour."

Her countenance fell at his word, and she was silent a while; for sore she longed to be speedily whereas her friends should find her if they came back to the castle. But she thought within herself how wild and fierce the man was, and doubted if he might not go stark mad on her hands and destroy her if she thwarted overmuch; and, moreover, frankly she pitied him, and would do what she might to ease his pain and solace his grief of heart. Wherefore she cleared her face of its trouble and let it be vexed no longer, but smiled upon the knight and said: "Fair sir, this meseemeth but a little thing for me to do, and I grant it thee with a good will, and this shall now be the first day of the friendship if so thou wilt take it; and may it solace thee."

Who then was gleeful but the knight, and strange it was to see all his sorrow run off him; and he became glad and gamesome as a youth, and yet withal exceeding courteous and kind with her, as though he were serving a mighty queen.

So then they wore the day together in all good fellowship; and first they went up the dale together and right to the foot

of that great force, where the stream came thundering down
from the sheer rocks; and long Birdalone stood to look
thereon, and much she marvelled at it, for no such thing had
she seen before.

Thereafter they went afoot into the wood behind the
green bower, and when they had gone some way therein for
their pleasure, they fell to seeking venison for their dinner;
and the knight took Birdalone's bow and shafts to strike the
quarry withal, but he would have her gird his sword to her,
that she might not be weaponless. So they gat them a roe and
came back therewith to the bower, and the knight dight it
and cooked it, and again they ate in fellowship and kindness;
and Birdalone had been to the river and fetched thence store
of blue-flowered mouse-ear, and of meadow-sweet, whereof
was still some left from the early days of summer, and had
made her garlands for her head and her loins; and the knight
sat and worshipped her, yet he would not so much as touch
her hand, sorely as he hungered for the beauty of her body.

Next, when dinner was done, and they lay in the shadow
of the trees, and hearkened the moor-hen crying from the
water, and the moaning of the wood-doves in the high trees,
she turned to him and bade him tell her somewhat of the tale
of his life and deeds; but he said: "Nay, lady, I pray thee
pardon me, for little have I to tell thee that is good, and I
would not have thee know of me aught worse than thou
knowest of me already. Rather be thou kind to me, and tell
me of thy days that have been, wherein I know full surely
shall be nought but good."

She smiled and blushed, but without more ado fell to telling him of her life in the House under the Wood, and spared
not even to tell him somewhat of the Woodmother. And he
said no word to her thereover, save thanks and praises for
the kindness of her story.

At last the day wore to its ending, and then the knight's
grief strode over him again, and he was moody and few-
spoken; and Birdalone was blithe with him still, and would

have solaced his grief; but he said: "Let it be; as for thee, thou shalt be happy to-morrow, but this happy day of mine is well-nigh worn, and it is as the wearing of my life."

And the dark night came, and he bade her good-night sorrowfully, and departed to his lair in the wood. Birdalone lay in the bower, and might not sleep a long while for her joy of the morrow, which should bring her back to the Castle of the Quest.

But when morning was, and the sun was but just risen, Birdalone awoke, and stood up and did on her raiment, and called her servant the knight, and he came at once leading the two horses, and said: "Now go we to the Castle of the Quest." And he was sober and sorrowful, but nought fierce or wild.

So Birdalone thanked him kindly and praised him, and he changed countenance no whit therefor.

Then they mounted and set forth, and the knight led straight into the wood, and by roads that he wotted of, so they went nowise slowly for wenders through the thick woodland. Thus went they on their way together, he sorry and she glad.

But now leaves the tale to tell of Birdalone and the knight on whom she happened in the Black Valley of the Greywethers, and turns to the Castle of the Quest and the folk thereof, and what they did in this while and thereafter.

HERE ENDS THE FOURTH PART OF THE WATER OF THE WONDROUS ISLES, WHICH IS CALLED OF THE DAYS OF ABIDING, AND THE FIFTH PART NOW BEGINS, WHICH IS CALLED THE TALE OF THE QUEST'S ENDING.

THE WATER OF THE WONDROUS ISLES. THE FIFTH PART: THE TALE OF THE QUEST'S ENDING.

CHAPTER I. OF SIR LEONARD'S TROUBLE AND THE COMING OF THE QUEST.

TELLS the tale that when the chaplain had departed from Birdalone at the bower in the copse, he went home to the castle sadly enough, because of his love and longing for her, which well he wotted might never be satisfied. Moreover when he was come into the castle again, there fell fear upon him for what might betide her, and he rued it that he had done her will in getting her forth of the castle; and in vain now he set before himself all the reasons for deeming that her peril herein was little or nothing, even as he had laid them before her, and which he then believed in utterly, whereas now himseemed there was an answer to every one of them. So he sighed heavily and went into the chapel, wherein was an altar of St. Leonard; and he knelt thereat, and prayed the saint, as he had erst delivered folk from captivity, now to deliver both him and Birdalone from peril and bonds. But though he was long a-praying and made many words, it lightened his heart little or nothing; so that when he rose up again, that if anything evil happened to this pearl of women, he wished heartily that some one might take his life and he be done with it.

Now was the house astir, and the chaplain came from out the chapel, and thinking all things over, he thought he would go straight to Sir Aymeris and make a clean breast of it, so that weaponed men might be sent at once to seek Birdalone. And he said to himself: What matter if he slay me or cast me into prison, if Birdalone be lost?

So he went his ways to the highest tower, which looked landward and hight the Open Eye, deeming to find Sir Aymeris; but when he got to the topmost, he found neither captain nor carle there: wherefore he stayed a little and looked forth betwixt the battlements, if perchance there were some wild chance of seeing Birdalone's coming home again; but his keen eyes beheld nothing more than he looked to see, as sheep and neat, and the fieldfolk of thereabouts. So he turned away and went by the swale toward the next tallest tower, which looked lakewards, and was called Heart's Hope; and as he went he fell to framing in his mind the words which he should say to the castellan.

Thus came he, haggard and hapless, on the leads of the tower, which were nought small; and there gathered together in a knot, and all gazing eagerly out over the lake, he found a dozen of men-at-arms and the castellan amongst them. They took no heed of him as he came up, though he stumbled as he crossed the threshold and came clattering over the lead floor, and he saw at once that there was something unwonted toward; but he had but one thought in his mind, to wit, the rescuing of Birdalone.

He went up now behind where the castellan was leaning over the battlement, and pulled his skirt, and when Sir Aymeris turned round, he said: "Lord, I have a word for thine ear." But the old knight did but half turn round, and then spake peevishly: "Tush, man! another time! seest thou not I have got no eyes for aught save what we see on the lake?"

"Yea, but what then?" said the priest. "There cometh a boat," said Sir Aymeris, not looking back at him, "and our thought is that therein be our lords."

When the priest heard that word, it was to him as if Hell had opened underneath his feet; and he had no might to speak for a minute; then he cried out: "Sir Aymeris, hearken, I pray thee."

But the old knight but thrust him back with his hand, and even therewith one of the men-at-arms cried out: "I hear the voice of their horn!" Then shouted Sir Aymeris: "Where art thou, Noise? Blow, man, blow, if ever thou blewest in all

186

thy life!" And therewithal came the blare of the brass, and
Sir Aymeris nodded to the trumpeter, who blew blast after
blast with all his might, so that the priest might as well have
been dumb for any hearing he might get; and all the while to
Leonard the minutes seemed hours, and he was well-nigh
distraught.

And then when the knight held up his hand for the Noise
to stay his blowing, and Leonard strove to speak, the castellan
turned on him and said: "Peace, Sir Leonard; dost thou not
know that now we would listen with our ears to heed if they
answer us? Not a word any one man of you, learned or lewd,
or ye shall rue it!"

Even therewith came clearly the sound of the horn from
the water, and again and yet again; and no man spake but the
chaplain, who cried out: "Hearken, knight, it is of Birdalone." But Sir Aymeris laid his hand on his shoulder and
said in an angry whisper: "Thou shalt be put downstairs,
priest, if thou hold not thy peace."

Leonard drew aback scowling, and went out of the door,
and so slowly down the stair, and withdrew him into the
cover of the door of the first chamber down from the tower-
top, with the mind to waylay Sir Aymeris as he came down;
and meanwhile he cursed him for a fool and a dull-wit—and
himself yet more, as was but right, for a fool and a licorous
traitor.

But he had not tarried there more than a score of minutes,
ere he heard a great shout from those up above: "They are
come! they are come!" And next thereafter came all the men
clattering down the stair past him, scarce refraining them
from shoving each his neighbour on to the next one; Leonard
followed on them, and presently arose great shouting and
tumult through all the house, and all folk, men and women,
hurried flock-meal toward the water-gate, and with them
went Leonard perforce; and sick of heart he was, calling to
mind the first coming thither of Birdalone.

But now when they came to the water-gate, there verily was

the Sending Boat just coming to hand; and in the stern stood the three knights together, all clad in their armour, and before them sat three lovely ladies, clad one in gold, one in green, and one in black: and lo, there was the Quest come home.

CHAPTER II. NOW ASK THEY OF BIRDALONE, AND SIR LEONARD SPEAKS.

NOW the prow touched the stones of the stair, and folk were busy to lay hold of it that the wayfarers might land, but Sir Baudoin cried out in a great voice: "Let none be so hardy as to touch this ferry, either now or hereafter; for there is peril therein." And therewith he took Aurea by the hand, and led her out of the boat and up the stair, and she all joyous and wondering; and thereafter came Hugh and his darling, and last of all Arthur and Atra, and she alone of the three women looked downcast, and her eyes wandered about the throng that was before them there, as though she sought something, yet feared to see it.

But when they were all standing together on the landing-plain, and the folk were all about them in a ring, Sir Baudoin spake to the castellan and said: "Sir Aymeris, thee and other folk I see here, the sight of whom doth me great joy; but where, I pray thee, is the lady, our friend Birdalone, by whom it is that all we are thus come happily hither?" And he looked around with an anxious face; but Arthur was as pale as ashes, yet he spake nought, and Atra let her hand fall away from his.

Then spake the castellan, and said: "No harm hath befallen the Lady Birdalone; but whiles she hath been somewhat ailing of late, and it is like that she wotteth not what is toward, and keepeth her chamber now, for it is yet betimes in the morning."

As he spake, came thrusting a man through the throng, eager and pale-faced; who but the chaplain; and he said: "He would not let me speak, this fool; I cannot choose my time. Lords, I bear evil tidings and an ugly welcome home.

188

The Lady Birdalone is in peril, and she is not in the castle; I wot not where she is. Ye must send armed men to seek her out."

Thereat fell the silence of woe upon the throng; but Arthur ran forward on the priest with drawn sword, and cried out: "I misdoubt me that thou art a traitor; speak! or I will slay thee here and now."

"If I be a traitor," quoth Leonard, "I shall tell thee in little while what ye must do to undo my treason, if there be yet time thereto; so slay me not till ye have heard, and then do what ye will with me."

But Baudoin put Arthur aside, and said: "Refrain thee a little, fair brother, else shall words tumble over each other and we shall know nothing clear. Sir Aymeris, bring our dear ladies to the fairest chambers, and do all honour and courtesy to them. And ye, sweetlings, ye will not begrudge us that we go to seek your friend. Thou priest, come with us a little apart, and tell thy tale as shortly as thou mayst, and fear nought; we be not God's dastards, as the Red Knight and his men."

Viridis wept and kissed her love before all folk, and bade him go and do his best to find her friend, or never come back to her else. Much moved, even to tears, was Aurea withal, and reached her hand to Baudoin, and said: "If any man on earth can help us it is thou. Go thou." But Atra wept not, and but said to Arthur: "Go thou, it is meet."

Therewith were the ladies brought to fair chambers; but the three knights went with the priest and Sir Aymeris into the solar, and set a guard at the door that their talk should be privy.

CHAPTER III. HOW THEY FOLLOW THE SLOT OF BIRDALONE AND THE BLACK KNIGHT.

IT was but five minutes ere the priest had told them all that need was; so they let him abide alone there, though sooth to say there was none of them but had good will to break his neck; and the same rede had all three, that there

was nought for it but to go their ways with all speed to the
Black Valley of the Greywethers, and follow up the slot of
Birdalone if it might yet be found; wherefore they bade saddle their horses straightway; and while that was a-doing
they ate a morsel, and bade farewell to their lovelings. And
they dight them to go, they three together, with but one
squire and a sergeant, who were both of them keen trackers
and fell woodsmen. But ere they went, by the rede of Arthur
they bade Sir Aymeris to arm a two score of men and ride
toward the Red Hold, and beset the ways 'twixt that and the
Castle of the Quest; for one and all they deemed that if any
harm befell Birdalone, the Red Knight would be at the bottom of it.

So rode those fellows, and came unto the dale but some
four hours after Birdalone had happened on the stranger
knight; and they took up the slot of her, but not easily,
whereas the ground was hard and stony; howbeit, they
found tokens of the knight also, finding here and there what
they deemed the footprints of a tall man. And this was grievous to those fellows, since now they could not but deem
that somewhat untoward had befallen Birdalone. But they
went on making out the slot, and they followed it with much
toil until they came to the doom-ring in the head of the dale,
whereas Birdalone and the stranger had sat down to meat;
but by that time, so toilsome had been their going, it was
somewhat more than dusk, and there was nought for it but
to abide there night-long. So a while they sat talking, all of
them, and the squire and the sergeant aforesaid were not a
little timorous of the adventure of making that stead unkenned their sleeping chamber; and to while away the time,
their lords made them tell tales such as they knew concerning that place; and both they said that they had never erst
come into the dale but a very little way, and said that they
had done so then but trusting in their lords' bidding and the
luck of the Quest. Thereafter turned the talk as to what had
befallen Birdalone, and the chances of coming on her; and,

as folk will in such a plight, they talked the matter over and
over again till they were weary and could say no more.

PART V
Chap. 3

Then they went to sleep, and nought befell them till they
awoke in the broad daylight; but they had little inkling of
what hour it was, for all the dale was full of thick white mist
that came rolling down from the mountains, so that they
could scarce see their hands before them, and there they had
to tarry still, would they, would they not; and the sergeant
fell to telling tales of folk who had been lost in that stony
maze; and all of them deemed, more or less, that this was the
work either of evil wights, or it might be of the wizardry of
the Red Knight; and, to be short, they all deemed that he it
was who had wielded it, save the sergeant, who said that the
mountain wights were the masters and not the servants of
him of the Red Hold.

Thus, then, it betided; but when the said mist had been
hanging upon them for some six hours, it rolled up like a
curtain, and lo the blue sky and the sun, and the mountains
as clear blue as in a picture; and they saw by the sun that it
was but a little after high noon.

But as they rejoiced herein, and betook them once more to
tracking out the slot of Birdalone and the other, the sky became suddenly overcast, and down from the jaws of the
mountain came a storm of wind and rain, and thunder and
lightning, so great that they might scarce see each other's
faces, and when it cleared off, in about an hour and a half, and
went down the wind to the south-east, the stream was waxen
great, and ran brown and furious down the dale, so that it
was fordable only here and there; and as for tracking the
slot of those twain, there was no need to talk thereof, for
the fury of the driving rain had washed all away.

Then they talked together as to what was best to do;
and the sergeant aforesaid spake: "Lords," said he, "meseemeth I am more at home in the Black Valley than
ye be; heed ye not wherefore. Now so it is that if we
tarry here till night come we wot not what of evil may

191

betide us, or at the least we do nought. Or if we turn back and go southward out of the dale we shall be safe indeed; but safe should we have been at your house, lords, and should have done no less. But now I shall tell you that, if ye will, lords, I shall guide you to a pass that goeth out of the head of the dale to our right hands, and so turneth the flank of the mountains, and cometh out into the country which lieth about the Red Hold; and meseemeth it is thitherward that we must seek if we would hear any tidings of the lady; for there may we lay in ambush and beset the ways that lead up to the Hold, by which she must have been brought, if she hath not been carried through the air. How say ye, lords? Soothly there is peril therein; yet meseemeth peril no more than in our abiding another night in the Black Valley."

Said Arthur: "We heed not the peril if there be aught to be done; wherefore let us be stirring straightway." And so said they all. Wherefore they gat to horse, and rode up to the very head of the valley, and the weather was now calm and bright.

But the sergeant brought them to the pass whereof the stranger knight had spoken to Birdalone, which led into the Red Knight's country, and without more ado they entered it when it was now about three hours after noon. But the way was both steep and rough, so that they had much toil, and went not very far ere night fell upon them, and the moon was not yet up. So when they had stumbled on another two hours, and their horses were much spent and they themselves not a little weary, they laid them down to sleep, after they had eaten such meat as they had with them, in a place where was a little grass for the horses to bite; for all the road hitherto had been mere grim stones and big rocks, walled on either side by stony screes, above which rose steep and beetling crags.

In the dawn they arose again, and made no ado till they were in the saddle, and rode till they came to the crest of the

192

pass, and came out thence after a while on to the swelling
flank of a huge mountain (as it might be the side of the
mountain of Plinlimmon in Wales), which was grassed and
nought craggy, but utterly treeless.

Now the sergeant led them somewhat athwart the said
mountain till they began to go down, and saw below them a
country of little hills much covered with wood, and in a
while, and ere it was noon, they were among the said woods,
which were grown mostly with big trees, as oak here and
beech there, and the going was good for them.

CHAPTER IV. OF THE SLAYING OF FRIEND AND FOE.

SO came they, three hours after noon, to where was a
clearing in the woodland, and a long narrow plain some
furlong over lay before them, with a river running
along it, and the wood rose on the other side high and thick,
so that the said plain looked even as a wide green highway
leading from somewhence to somewhither.

At the edge hereof their wayleader, the sergeant, bade
draw rein, and said: "Lords, we are now in the lands of the
Red Hold, and therein is mickle peril and dread to any save
stout hearts as ye be; but meseems we are so steaded, that
whatever may come out of the Black Valley of the Greywethers to the Red Hold, ye now may scarce miss. Yonder
along this plain to the north lies the way to the said Hold, and
any man coming from the head of the valley is sure to come
by the way we have come, and will pass us not many yards at
the worst from where we now be. On the other hand, if any
come to the Hold from the mouth of the Black Valley, then
along this green road must they needs pass under your very
eyes. Lastly, if we do what we are come to do, to wit, to deliver the lady from the Red Knight, then, the deed done,
we have to take the green road southward, and ride it for
a league and then turn east, and we shall have our heads

turned toward the Castle of the Quest, and shall speedily fall
in with Sir Aymeris and our men who be guarding the out-
gates of the Red Knight's country toward our house. So
now, by my rede, ye shall lay in covert here and abide a while
what may befall; if nought come hereby ere two hours be
lacking of sunset, then may we seek further."

They all yeasaid this, and gat off their horses, and lay quiet
on the grass, not even speaking save softly. And when they
had abided thus scarce an hour's space, the squire, who was
a man of very fine ear, held up his hand as though to bid utter silence, and all hearkened eagerly. Presently he said:
"Hear ye not?" Said Arthur: "Meseemeth I hear a faint
tinkle as of a sheep-bell." Said the squire: "'Tis the clashing
of swords down the plain to the south, and meseemeth 'tis
but of two: ride we thither?"

Quoth Baudoin: "Nay, not by my rede; for if we can hear
them they can hear us; let us quietly edge along afoot somewhat nigher their way, ever keeping the cover of the wood
betwixt us and the open plain. Now then to it; and let each
man keep his weapons ready."

Even so did they, and spread out in a line as they went, in
such wise that there was some six paces betwixt each man of
them, and they went softly forward; Baudoin went first,
Hugh second, then Arthur; then the squire and the sergeant
last of all.

Now when they had gone but a quarter of an hour, the
squire caught up with Arthur, and spake to him softly, and
said: "The voice of the swords has been silent now a while,
and I heard a voice crying out e'en now, a woman's voice.
And now again I could well-nigh deem that I hear horse-
hoofs."

Arthur nodded to him, and they went but a little further
ere he said: "Lo, lo! 'tis the time of the eyes now! Here
come folk." And therewithal they stayed them. For the
wood turned somewhat here, so as to hide all but a little of
the plain, and round the wood-neb the new-comers hove in
sight, and were close on them at once, so that they might see

194

them clearly, to wit, a knight weaponed, clad all in red,
a very big man, riding on a great bay horse, and behind him
a woman going afoot in very piteous plight; for she was
tethered to the horse's crupper by a thong that bound her
wrists together, so that she had but just room left 'twixt her
and the horse that she might walk, and round about her
neck was hung a man's head newly hewn off.

This sight they all saw at once, and were out of the wood
in a trice with weapons aloft, for they knew both the man
and the woman, that they were the Red Knight and Birdalone.

So swift and sudden had they been, that he had no time
either to spur or even to draw his sword; but he had a heavy
steel axe in his hand as the first man came up to him, which
was the tall Baudoin; and therewith he smote down on Baudoin so fierce and huge a stroke, that came on him betwixt
neck and shoulder, that all gave way before it, and the
Golden Knight fell to earth all carven and stark dead: but
even therewith fell Hugh, the squire, and the sergeant on
the Red Knight; for Arthur had run to Birdalone and
sheared her loose from her tether. The sergeant smote him
on the right arm with a maul, so that the axe fell to the
ground; the squire's sword came on the side of his head, and,
as it was cast back beneath the stroke, Hugh thrust his
sword through the throat of him, and down he fell unto the
earth and was dead in less than a minute.

Then gathered the others round about Baudoin, and saw
at once that he was dead; and Birdalone came thrusting
through the press of them, and knelt down beside him, and
when she saw her friend so piteously dight, she wept and
wailed over him as one who might not be comforted; and
Hugh stood over her and let his tears fall down upon the
dead man; and withal the squire and the sergeant did not
refrain their lamentations, for sore beloved was Sir Baudoin
the Golden Knight.

But Arthur spake dry-eyed, though there was grief in his
countenance, and he said: "Fellows, and thou, lady, let us

lament afterwards, but now is time for us to get us gone
hence as speedily as may be. Yet I will ask, doth any know
whose is this head that the slain tyrant here had hung about
the lady's neck? May the fiends curse him therefor!"

Said the sergeant: "Yea, lords, that wot I; this is the head
of the Red Knight's captain and head man, Sir Thomas of
Estcliffe; one of the hardiest of knights he was while he was
alive, as ye surely wot, lords; neither, as I have heard say,
was he as cruel a tyrant as his lord that lieth there ready for
the ravens."

Now had Birdalone arisen and was standing facing Arthur; her face was pale and full of anguish, and she was
dabbled with blood from the dead man's neck; but there
was nought of shame in her face as she stood there and
spoke: "O my living friends, who have but now saved me,
ye and my dead friends, from what shame and death I know
not, the tale of this woful hap is over long to tell if there be
peril at hand, and I scarce alive from dread and sorrow; but
shortly thus it is: This man, whose head here lieth, entrapped me as I foolishly wandered in the Black Valley, and afterwards delivered me, and was leading me to your castle, my
friends, when this other one, his master, the tyrant of the
Red Hold, came upon him, and fell upon him and slew him
as a traitor, and dighted me as ye saw. And woe's me! I am
the fool whose folly has slain your friend and mine. Wherefore I am not worthy of your fellowship, and ye shall cast
me forth of it; or to slay me were better."

So she spake, gazing earnestly on Arthur; and so troubled
and grieved, that she might well have died but for her woodland breeding, and the toil of the days she had won through
in the House under the Wood.

But Hugh spake gently to her and said: "Keep up thine
heart yet, maiden; for the hand of Fate it is that led thee, and
none doeth grievously amiss but if he mean wrong-doing in
his heart; and we know thee for true; and thou hast been our
helper, and brought our lovelings unto us to make us
happy."

196

But she brake out weeping afresh, and said: "O no, no! it is but woe and weariness I have brought unto my friends; and to myself woe and weariness yet more."

And she looked piteously into Arthur's face, and hard and stern it seemed unto her; and she writhed and wrung her hands for anguish. But he spake and said: "This will we look into when we be safe behind our walls, and see what she hath done amiss and what not amiss. But now is there but one thing to do, and that is to get us speedily on our way to the Castle of the Quest, and bind our fellow's body on his horse that he also may ride with us, and the lady shall ride the horse of the accursed thief."

Then they turned to go toward their horses; but therewith Birdalone smote her foot against the slain knight's head, and shrank aback from it, and pointed down toward it and spake no word; and Hugh said: "Friends, the lady is right, this at least we will cover with earth. Do ye go fetch hither our horses, since we be on the road, and I will do here what need is meanwhile."

So they went on that errand, and then Hugh and Birdalone between them dug a hole with the swords and laid the head of the captain of the Red Knight therein. And forsooth, somewhat would Birdalone have wept for him had she had a tear to spare.

Then they fell to and bound the dead Baudoin on the Red Knight's mighty bay steed, so that no time might be wasted; and when that was done, and the others had not come back with their horses, Hugh took Birdalone's hand and led her down to the stream and washed the gore off her bosom, and she washed her face and her hands and let him lead her back again in such wise that now she could hearken to the words of comfort he spake to her, and piteous kind he seemed unto her; so that at last she plucked up heart, and asked him how Viridis did. Quoth he: "They be all safe at home in the castle, and Viridis is well and loveth thee well. And Aurea was well—woe worth the while for her now! As for Atra, she has not been so glad as the other twain, I wot not wherefore."

Even as he spake were the others come up with the horses,
and Arthur nodded yeasay when he saw what had been done
with Baudoin dead; and so they gat to horse, and Birdalone
it was that rode Baudoin's steed. Then they went their ways,
crossing the river into the wood; and the sergeant was ever
way-leader, but the squire led the horse which bore the sorrowful burden of the dead Knight of the Quest.

CHAPTER V. THEY COME HOME TO THE CASTLE OF THE QUEST.

NOW they had gone but some three hours, riding
dreary and nigh speechless all of them, ere they began to know the land they were in, and that they
were coming to the place where they might look presently
to fall in with Sir Aymeris and his company; and even so
the meeting betid, that they saw men standing and going
about their horses beside a little wood, and knew them
presently for their folk, who mounted at once and spurred forward to meet them, spears aloft. Speedily then was
the joy of those abiders turned into sorrow, nor may the
grief of Sir Aymeris be told, so great it was; and Birdalone
looked on and saw the mourning and lamentation of the
warriors, and eked was her anguish of mind; and she beheld
Arthur the Black Squire, how he sat still upon his horse
with a hard and dreary countenance, and looked on those
mourners almost as if he contemned them. But Sir Aymeris
came up to Birdalone, and knelt before her and kissed her
hand, and said: "If my heart might rejoice in aught, as some
day it will, it would rejoice in seeing thee safe and sound,
lady; here at least is gain to set beside the loss."

She thanked him, but looked askance toward Arthur,
who said: "If that be gain: yet is there more, for the Red
Knight lieth in the green plain for a supper to the wolf and
the crow. Vengeance there hath been, and belike more yet
may come. But now, if ye have lamented as much as ye deem
befitteth warriors, let us tarry here no longer: for even yet

198

meseemeth shall we be safer behind walls, now that our chief and captain is slain, I scarce know in what quarrel."

None naysaid it, so they all rode forth together, and the sergeant and the squire and Sir Hugh told of their tale what they might to Sir Aymeris and the others; but Arthur held his peace, and rode aloof from Birdalone, whereas Sir Aymeris and Hugh rode on either side of her, and did not spare to comfort her, what they might.

They rode straight on, and made no stay for nightfall, and thus came home to the Castle of the Quest before the day was full; and woful was their entry as they went in the dawn underneath the gate of the said castle, and soon was the whole house astir and lamenting.

As for Birdalone, when she got down from her horse in the gateway, and was stiff and weary of body, and all dazed and confused of mind, there was but little life in her; nor could she so much as think of the new day and Aurea's a-wakening, but crept up unto her own chamber, so long as it seemed since she had left it, though it was but a little while; and she cast herself upon the bed and fell asleep whether she would or not, and so forgat her much sorrow and her little hope.

CHAPTER VI. OF THE TALK BETWIXT BIRD-ALONE AND VIRIDIS.

WHEN she woke again, she had slept the night away, and it was broad day, and for a moment she lay wondering what was the burden upon her; but presently she called it all to mind, and deemed it were well might she forget it all again. Anon she became aware of someone moving about the chamber, and she looked about unhappily; and lo! a woman, fair and dainty, clad all in green, and it was Viridis that had come there. But when she saw Birdalone stirring, she came up to her and kissed her sweetly and kindly, and wept over her, so that Birdalone might nowise refrain her tears.

But when she might cease weeping, she said to Viridis:
"Tell me, art thou weeping for thy friend who is lost, and
who shall be thy friend no more; or thy friend whom thou
hast found?" Said Viridis: "Forsooth I have wept for Baudoin plenteously, and he is worthy of it, for he was valiant
and true and kind." Said Birdalone: "True is that; but I
meant not my question so; but rather I would ask thee if
thou weepest because thine heart must needs cast me away,
or because thou hast found me again?"

Quoth Viridis: "Whoso may be dead, or whoso alive,
but if it were Hugh, my loveling, I were rejoiced beyond
measure to find thee, my friend." And again she kissed her
as one who was glad and kind. But for new rest of soul and
for joy, Birdalone fell a-weeping afresh.

Again she spake: "And what mind have the others about
me? For thou art but one, though the dearest—save— And
would they punish me for my fault and folly that has slain
the best man in the world? If the punishment be short of
putting me forth of their fellowship, I were fain thereof."

Viridis laughed: "Forsooth," she said, "they have much
to punish thee for! whereas it was by thy doing and thy valiance that we all came together again and the Quest was accomplished."

"Nay, but tell me," said Birdalone, "what do they say of
me, each one of them?"

Viridis reddened; she said: "Hugh, my mate, saith all
good of thee; though no one of carle-folk may be sorrier of
the loss of his fellow. Aurea layeth not the death of her man
upon thee; and she saith: 'When the fountain of tears is
dried up in me, I will see her and comfort her, as she me.'
Atra saith—she saith but little, yet she saith: 'So is it fated.
I had done belike no better, but worse than she.'"

Now turned Birdalone red and then pale again, and she
said, but in a quavering voice: "And the Black Squire—and
Arthur, what sayeth he?" Said Viridis: "He sayeth nought
of thee, but that he would hear all the tale of what befell
thee in the Black Valley."

"Sweet friend," said Birdalone, "I pray thee of thy kindness and sweetness that thou go unto him presently and bring him in hither, and then I will tell him all; and he and thou and I together."

Viridis said: "There is this to be said, that when a man loveth a woman he coveteth her, to have her all wholly to himself, and hard and evil he groweth for the time that he misdoubteth her whom he loveth. And I will tell thee that this man is jealous lest thou wert never so little kind to the slain stranger knight whose head the tyrant hung about thee. Furthermore, I fear there is no help for it that thou wilt undo the happiness of one of us, that is Atra; yet were it better that that befell later than sooner. And if Sir Arthur come in here to thee, and hath thy tale with none beside save me, meseems the poor Atra will feel a bitter smart because of it. Were it not better that we all meet presently in the solar, and that there thou tell thy tale to us all? and thereafter shall we tell the tale of our deliverance and our coming hither. And thus doing, it will seem less like to the breaking up of our fellowship."

Said Birdalone: "It will be hard for me to tell my tale before Atra and before him. Might it not be that thou hearken to it here and now, and tell it to the others hereafter?"

"Nay, nay," said Viridis, "I am not a proper minstrel to take the word out of thy mouth. Never shall I be able to tell it so that they shall trow it as if they had seen it all. Besides, when all is told, then shall we be more bound together again. I pray thee, and I pray thee, sweet, do so much for me as to tell thy tale to the fellowship of us. And if it be hard to thee, look upon it as my share of the punishment which is due to thee for falling into that mishap."

Smiled Birdalone ruefully, and said: "So be it; and may the share of the others be as light as thine, sister. Yet soothly were I liefer that my body and my skin should pay the forfeit. But now, since I must needs do this, the sooner is the better meseemeth."

"In a little half hour," said Viridis, "will I bring what is left of our fellowship into the solar to hearken thee. So come thou there unto us when thou art clad. And hear thou! be not too meek and humble, and bow thyself to us in fear of our sorrow. For whereas thou didst speak of our punishing thee, there will be one there whom thou mayst easily punish to thy pleasure. Forsooth, friend, I rue that so it is; but since it will not better be, what may I do but wish thee happy and him also."

Therewith she turned and went out of the chamber, and Birdalone, left to herself, felt a secret joy in her soul that she might not master despite all the sorrow of her friends, whatever it might be.

CHAPTER VII. BIRDALONE TELLETH THE TALE OF HER WANDERING.

NOW Viridis did as she said, and brought them all into the solar; there was none lacking save Baudoin, and they sat silently in a half ring, till the door opened and Birdalone came in to them, clad all simply in but a black coat; and she made obeisance to them, and stood there with her head bent down as if they were her judges, for so in sooth she deemed them. Then Hugh bade her sit down amongst them; but she said: "Nay, I will not sit amongst you till ye have heard my story, and ye have told me that I am yet of your fellowship." None said aught; Atra looked straight before her, and her eyes met not Birdalone's eyes; Arthur looked down on the ground; but Hugh and Viridis looked kindly on Birdalone, and to Viridis' eyes the tears were come.

Then spake Birdalone and said: "I am here as one that hath done amiss; but I will tell you, so that ye may not think worse of me than ye should, that when ye were gone, ye Champions, and the time wore long that ye came not again, it lay heavy on my heart, and hope waned and fear waxed, and my soul so grieved my body that I thought to fall sick thereof, and I knew that it would be ill for you to come home hither and find me sick; so that I longed sore to do somewhat

which should make me whole again. Then Weird would
that I should hear all the tale of the Black Valley of the Greywethers, and of how therein is whiles granted fulfilment of
desire; and methought how well it were if I might seek the
adventure there and accomplish it. Thereof, doubtless, hath
the chaplain, Sir Leonard, told you; but this furthermore
would I say, that his doing herein was nought; all was done
by my doing and by my bidding, and he might not choose
but do it. Wherefore I do pray you all earnestly that ye keep
no grudge against him, but pardon him all. Tell me, then,
will ye do thus much?"

Said Hugh: "Let him be pardoned, if he can take pardon."
But Arthur spake not, and Birdalone looked on him
anxiously, and her face was moved, and it was with her
throat as if she had swallowed something down. Then she
spake again, and fell to tell them all that had betid to her
when she went to the Black Valley, even as is here afore-writ,
hiding nought that had been done and said; and freely she
told it, without fear or shame, and with such clearness and
sweetness of words that no one of them doubted her aught;
and Arthur lifted up his head, and once and again his eyes
met hers, and there was nought of hardness in them, though
they turned away at once.

So at last fell Birdalone to telling what betid after they
two, the stranger knight and she, left the valley of the force
and fell to riding the wildwood with their heads turned toward the Castle of the Quest; and she said:

"When we turned into the wood away from the said valley it lacked some four hours of noon; and we rode till noon
was, and rested by a stream-side and ate, for we knew no
cause wherefore we should hasten overmuch; but my fellow
the strange knight was downcast and heavy, and some might
have called him sullen. But I strove to make him of better
cheer, and spake to him kindly, as to one who of an enemy
had become a friend; but he answered me: 'Lady, it availeth
not; I grieve that I am no better company than thou seest
me, and I have striven to be merrier; but apart from all that

203

I wot and that thou wottest which should make me of evil cheer, there is now a weight upon my heart which I cannot lift, such as never have I felt erst. So by thy leave we will to horse at once, that we may the speedier come to the Castle of the Quest and Sir Aymeris' prison.'

"So I arose, but smiled on him and said: 'Hold up thine heart, friend! for thee shall be no prison at the Castle of the Quest, but the fair welcome of friends.' He said nought, and mended not his cheer; and in this plight we gat to horse and rode on for some three hours more, till we came out of the thick forest into a long clearing, which went like a wide highway of greensward between the thicket, and it seemed as if the hand of man had cleared that said green road. Thereto we had come, following a little river which came out on to the clearing with us, and then, turning, ran well-nigh amidst it toward the north.

"Now when we were come thither, and were betwixt the thicket and the water's edge, we drew rein, and it seemed to me as fair a stead as might be in the woodland, and I looked thereon well pleased and with a happy heart. But the knight said: 'Lady, art thou not exceeding weary?' 'Nay,' said I, 'not in any wise.' Said he: 'It is strange then, for so weary am I, that I must in any case get off my horse and lay me down on the grass here, or I shall drop from the saddle.' And therewith he lighted down and stood by me a little, as to help me off my horse; but I said to him: 'Knight, I pray thee, even if ye be weary, to struggle forward a little, lest we be in peril here.' 'In peril?' quoth he; 'yea, that might be if the Red Knight knew of our whereabouts; but how should that be?' He spoke this heavily, as one scarce awake; and then he said: 'I pray thee pardon me, lady, but for nought may I hold my head up; suffer me to sleep but a little, and then will I arise and lead thee straight to thy journey's end.' Therewithal he laid him down on the grass and was presently asleep, and I sat down by him all dismayed. At first, indeed, I doubted some treachery in him, for how might I trust him

204

wholly after all that had come and gone? but when I saw that
there was no feigning in his sleep, I set that doubt aside, and
knew not what to make of it.

"Thus passed an hour, and from time to time I shook
him and strove to waken him, but it was all in vain; so I knew
none other rede than to abide his awakening; for I knew not
the way to take toward this castle; and, moreover, though
he were a knight, and armed, yet might it be perilous for
him if he were left there alone and unguarded; so I abode.

"But now came new tidings. Methought I heard the sound
of the tinkling of weapons and armour; the green highway so
turned that a wood-neb about an hundred yards to the north
hid it from my sight, so that a man might have drawn somewhat near to us without being seen, came he on the hither
side of the river. So I stood up hastily, and strung my bow,
and took a shaft in my fingers, and no sooner was it done
than there came a rider round about the aforesaid wood-neb.
He was all-armed and had a red surcoat, and rode a great
shining bay horse. I kept my eye upon him while I stirred
the sleeping knight with my foot, and cried to him to wake,
but he scarce moved, and but uttered words without sense.

"Now the new-comer drew rein for a moment when he
saw us, and then moved on a little toward me, but I nocked
a shaft and pointed it at him, and cried out to him to stay.
Then I heard a great rattling laugh come from him, and he
shouted: 'Nay, do thou stay, fair wood-wife, and I will risk
thy shafts to come at thee. But why doth not the sluggard at
thy feet rise up and stand before me, if he be thy loveling?
Or is he dead?' His voice was harsh and big, and I feared
him sore; and it was as much because of fear as of hardihood,
that I drew and loosed straightway; and doubtless it was because of fear that I saw my shaft fly an inch or so over his
right shoulder. I heard his rattling laugh again, and saw him
bend forward as he spurred; I knew that time lacked for
drawing another shaft, so I caught up my skirts and ran
all I might; but swift-foot as I be, it availed me nought, for

I was cumbered with my gown, and moreover I was confused with not knowing whither to run, since I wotted that
in the water the horse would do better than I.

"So he was up with me in a twinkling, and reached out
his hand and caught hold of me by the hair, and tugged me
to him as he reined back his horse. Then he laughed again
and said: 'Forsooth she will look better when she is no
longer reddened and roughened with fleeing; and, by Red
Peter! what limbs she hath.' Then he let me loose and got off
his horse, and shoved me on before him till we came to where
the Black One lay still sleeping heavily. Then the Red Knight
stood over against me, and looked hard into my face; and I
saw how huge a man he was, and how a lock of bright red
hair came out from under his sallet. His eyes were green and
fierce underneath shaggy red eyebrows; terrible he was to
look on.

"Now he spake fiercely and roughly, and as though he
had something against me: 'Tell me, thou, who thou art and
who this is?' I answered nought, for fear had frozen my
speech. He stamped his foot on the ground and cried:
'Hah! art thou gone dumb? Speak! thou wert best!' I said,
all quaking: 'My name is Birdalone; I belong to no one; I
have no kindred: as for this man, I know not his name.' He
said: 'Comest thou from the Castle of the Quest? Art thou
the whore of those lily-and-rose champions there?' My
heart was hot with anger in spite of my dread, but I spake:
'I came from the Castle of the Quest.' He said: 'And this
man' (therewith he turned about and spurned him in the
side), 'where didst thou happen upon him?' Again I was
silent, and he roared out at me: 'So thou wilt not answer!
Beware, or I may see how to compel the speech of thee. Now
answer me this: Was it in the Black Valley of the Greywethers that ye two came together?' Again I knew not how
to answer, lest I might do a wrong to him who had repented
him of the wrong he had done me.

"But the Red Knight burst out a-laughing and said: 'It
shall be remembered against thee, first, that thou didst let
206

fly a shaft at me; second, that thou didst run from me; and
thirdly, that thou hast been slack in answering my questions.
But all this scathes me nought; first, because thy shaft missed me; second, because thy legs failed thee (though they
were fair to look on, running); and third, because all thou
canst tell me I know without thine answering. Now thee will
I tell that this is Friday, and that ye two first met in the Black
Valley on Tuesday; now I will ask this last question, and
thou mayst answer it or not as thou wilt; for presently I
shall wake this brisk and stirring knight, and I deem that he
will tell me the truth of this if of nought else. Tell me, thou
whore of the Questing Champions, where and how many
times thou hast lain in this good knight's arms since last
Tuesday?'

"'Nowhere and never,' quoth I. 'Thou liest, I doubt
me,' said the Red Knight; 'howsoever, let us see what this
doughty one will say. Hah? thou deemest he shall be hard
to wake up, dost thou not? Well, I shall see to that. He who
giveth sleep may take it away again.'

"Therewith he went up to the Black One and stooped a-
down over his head, and spake some words over him, but so
softly that I heard not their import; and straightway the
sleeper rose up so suddenly that he wellnigh smote against
the Red Knight. He stood awhile staggering, and blinking at
the other one, but somehow got his sword drawn forth, and
the Red Knight hindered him nought therein, but spake
anon when the other was come to himself somewhat: 'The
sele of the day to thee, Sir Thomas, True Thomas! Fair is
thy bed, and most fair thy bedfellow.'

"The Black Knight drew aback from him and was now
come awake, wherefore he stood on his guard, but said
nought. Then said the Red Knight: 'Sir Thomas, I have
been asking this fair lady a question, but her memory faileth
her and she may not answer it; perchance thou mayst do
better. Tell me where and how many times hast thou bedded her betwixt last Tuesday and this?' 'Nowhere and
never,' cried Sir Thomas, knitting his brows and handling

207

his sword. 'Hah,' said the Red Knight, 'an echo of her speech is this. Lo, the tale ye have made up betwixt you. But at least, having done mine errand, though meseemeth somewhat leisurely, and having gotten the woman for me, thou art now bringing her on to the Red Hold, whatever thou hast done with her on the road?' 'I am not,' said my fellow, 'I am leading her away from the Red Hold.' 'Pity of thee,' quoth the other, 'that thou hast fallen in with me, and thou but half-armed.' And he raised aloft his sword; but presently sank it again, and let the point rest on the earth.

"Then he spoke again, not mockingly as erst: 'A word before we end it, Thomas: thou hast hitherto done well by me, as I by thee. I say thou hast gotten this woman, and I doubt not that at first thou hadst the mind to bring her to me unminished; but then thou wert overcome by her beauty, as forsooth I know thee woman-mad, and thou hadst meant to keep her for thyself, as forsooth I marvel not. But in thy lovemaking thou hast not bethought thee that keep her to thyself thou mayst not while I am above ground, save thou bewray me, and join thee to my foemen and thine. Because I am such a man, that what I desire that will I have. For this reason, when I misdoubted me of thee for thy much tarrying, I cast the sleep over thee, and have caught thee. For what wilt thou do? Doubt it not, that if our swords meet, I shall pay thee for trying to take my bed-thrall from me by taking from thee no more than thy life. But now will I forgive thee all if thou wilt ride home quietly with me and this damsel-errant to the Red Hold, and let her be mine and not thine so long as I will; and then afterwards, if thou wilt, she shall be thine as long as thou wilt. Now behold, both this chance and thy life is a mere gift of me to thee, for otherwise thou shalt have neither damsel nor life.'

"'Yea, yea,' said my friend, 'I know what thou wouldest: I have been no unhandy devil to thee this long while, and thou wouldst fain keep me still; but now I will be devil no longer, on this earth at least, but will die and take my luck of
208

it. And do thou, God, see to the saving of this damsel, since thou hast taken the matter out of my hands. Farewell, dear maiden!'

"Scarce was the word out of his mouth ere his sword was in the air, and he smote so fierce and straight that he beat down the huge man's blade, and ere he could master it again, smote the Red Knight so heavily on the crest that he fell to his knees; and the heart rose in me, for I deemed that he might yet prevail; and in as 'twere a flash I bethought me of the knife at my girdlestead, and drew it and ran to the Red Knight, and tore aside his mail hood with one hand and thrust the knife into his shoulder with the other; but so mighty was he that he heeded nought the hurt, but swept his sword back-handed at the Black Knight's unarmed leg, and smote him so sore a wound that down he fell clattering. Then arose the Red Knight, and thrust me from him with the left hand, and strode over my fellow-farer and thrust his sword through his throat. Then he turned to me, and spake in a braying voice as if a harsh horn were blown: 'Abide thou; if thou takest one step I will slay thee at once.' So he went and sat down on a bank a little way from the dead man, and wiped his sword on the grass and laid it beside him, and so sat pondering a while. Thereafter he called me to him, and bade me stand in face of him with my hands clasped before me. Then he spake to me: 'Thou art my thrall and my having, since I had thus doomed it no few days ago; and thou art now in my hands for me to do with as I will. Now instead of being meek and obedient to me thou hast rebelled against me, shot an arrow at me, run from me, denied answer to my questions, and thrust a knife into me. To be short, thou hast made thyself my foe. Furthermore, it is by thy doing that I have lost a right good servant and a trusty fellow, and one that I loved; it is thou that hast slain him. Now have I been pondering what I shall do with thee.' I said: 'If I have deserved the death, then make an end and slay me presently; but bring me not to thine house, I pray thee. I pray by the mother that bore thee!'

"Quoth he: 'Hold thy peace, it is not what thou deservest that I am looking to, but what shall pleasure me. Now hearken; I say that thou hast made thee my foe, and I have overcome thee; thou art my runaway thrall, and I have caught thee. As my foe I might slay thee in any evil way it might like me; as my thrall I might well chastise thee as sharply and as bitterly as I would. But it is not my pleasure to slay thee, rather I will bring thee to the Red Hold, and there see what we may make of thee; whereas I cannot but deem that in thee is the making of somewhat more than a thrall; and if not, then a thrall must thou needs be. Again as to the chastising of thee, that also I forgive thee since I have gotten the hope aforesaid. Yet forsooth some shame must I do thee to pay thee back for the love that was betwixt thee and the slain man. I will ponder what it shall be; but take heed that whatsoever it shall be, it will not avail thee to pray me to forego it, though thy speech be as fair and sweet as thy body.'

"Therewith he was silent a while, and I stood there not daring to move, and my heart was so downcast that all the sweetness of life seemed departed. Yet I withheld lamentations or prayers, thinking within myself, who knows what occasion may be between this and the Red Hold for my escaping; let me keep myself alive for that if it may be.

"Presently he arose and took his sword, and went up to the slain man's body and smote the head from off it. Then he went to the two horses of Sir Thomas and of me, and took from them such gear of girths and thongs as he would, and therewith he dight me as ye saw, doing a girth about my middle and making me fast to a line wherewith to hold me in tow. And then he did that other thing which sickens my very soul to tell of, to wit, that he took the slain man's head and tied a lace thereto, and hung it about my neck; and as he did so, he said: 'This jewel shalt thou thyself bear to mine house; and there belike shall we lay it in earth, since the man was my trusty fellow. Lo now, this is all the ill I shall do thee

210

till it be tried of what avail thou art. This is a shaming to
thee and not a torment, for I will ride a foot's pace, and the
green way is both soft and smooth; wherefore fear not that I
shall throw thee down or drag thee along. And to-morrow
thy shame shall be gone and we shall see what is to betide.'

"Lo, friends, this is the last word he spake ere he was
slain, and the ending of my tale; for we had gone thus but a
little way ere ye brake out of the wood upon us; and then
befell the death of one friend, and the doubt, maybe, of the
others, and all the grief and sorrow that I shall never be quit
of unless ye forgive me where I have done amiss, and help
me in the days to come." And she spread out her hands before them, and bowed her head, and the tears fell from her
eyes on to the floor.

Viridis wept at Birdalone's weeping, and Aurea for her
own sorrow, which this other sorrow stirred. Atra wept not,
but her face was sadder than weeping.

But Arthur spake and said: "Herein hath been the hand
of Weird, and hath been heavy on us; but no blame have we
to lay on our sister Birdalone, nor hath she done light-
mindedly by us; though maybe she erred in not trusting to
the good-hap of the Quest to bring us back in due time: and
all that she saith do we trow as if it were written in the Holy
Gospel." They all yeasaid this, and called on her to come
amongst them; but she thought of little at first save the joy
of hearing the sweetness of those words as Arthur spake
them; wherefore she hung back a little, and thought shame
of it that she might not give more heed to the others of them.
Then came Viridis and took her by the hand and led her to
Sir Hugh, and Birdalone knelt down before him and took
his hand to kiss it, but he put both hands about her face and
kissed her kindly and merrily on the lips. Then she knelt
before Aurea, and was hapless before her; but Aurea kissed
her, and bade her be of better cheer, albeit the words came
coldly from her mouth. Next she came to Arthur, and knelt
before him and took his hand and kissed it, and thanked him

kindly for his kind words, looking into his face meanwhile; and she saw that it was pale and troubled now, and she longed to be alone with him that she might ask him wherefore.

As for Atra, she arose as Birdalone came before her, and cast her arms about her neck, and wept and sobbed upon her bosom, and then went hurrying from out the solar and into the hall, and walked to and fro there awhile until the passion that tore her was lulled somewhat, and she might show her face to them calm and friendly once more. And as she entered Arthur was speaking, and he said:

"To you ladies I tell, what we of the castle wot better than well, that our dear friend hath escaped so heavy a fate in escaping the Red Hold, that it were unmeet for us to murmur at our loss in our fellow; for a warrior's life, which is ever in peril of death, is nought over heavy a ransom for such a friend, and so dear and lovely, from such a long and evil death. Whereas ye must wot that the said Hold hath this long while been a very treasure-house of woes and a coffer of lamentations; for merciless was the tyrant thereof, and merciless all his folk. Now another time, when ye are stronger in heart than now ye be, I may tell you tales thereof closer and more nicely of those who did his will; as of his innermost band of men-at-arms, called the Millers; and of his fellow-worker in wizardry and venoms, called the Apothecary; and the three hags, called the Furies; and the three young women, called the Graces; and his hounds that love man's flesh; and the like tales, as evil as nightmares turned into deeds of the day. But now and here will I say this, that when we have done the obsequies of our dear fellow, it were good that we follow up the battle so valiantly begun by him. I mean that, the Quest of our ladies being now accomplished, we should turn what is left of the fellowship into a war against the Red Hold and its evil things; and that so soon as the relics of Baudoin are laid in earth, we gather force and go thither in arms to live or die in the quarrel, and so sweeten the earth, as did the men of ancient days when they slew the dragons and the giants, and the children of Hell, and the Sons of Cain."

His cheek flushed as he spoke, and he looked around till his eyes fell on Birdalone, and he saw that her face also glowed and her eyes gleamed; but Viridis, her heart sank so that she paled, and her lips trembled.

But Aurea spake and said: "I thank thee for thy word, Black Squire, and I know that my man shall rejoice in Paradise when he knoweth of it, and thereof shall I tell him to-morrow when the mass is said for him."

And Atra said: "Good is the word, and we look to it that the deed shall be better yet. Thus hath the evil arisen that shall destroy the evil, as oft hath been when the valiant have been grieved, and the joy of the true-hearted hath been stolen from them; then the hand doth the doughty deed and the heart hath ease, and solaced is sorrow."

They looked on her and wondered, for she spake with her head upraised and her eyes glittering, as she had been one of the wise women of yore agone. And Birdalone feared her, though she loved her.

Lastly spake Hugh, and said: "Brother, this is well thought of indeed, and I marvel that I did not prevent thee; and I am thine to live and die with thee. And the adventure is nought unlikely; for if we have lost a captain they have lost their head devil, and their head little devil; moreover, the good men of Greenford shall join them to us, and that shall make us strong, whereas they have men enough, and those stout men-at-arms; and artificers they have to make us engines, and do other wisdom; and therewithal money to buy or to wage what they will. Wherefore, to my mind, we were best to make no tarrying, but send out the messengers for the hosting straightway."

"Straightway," said the Black Squire; "and let us go now and find Sir Aymeris." So they arose both and went their ways, and left the women there alone, and were gone a good while.

CHAPTER VIII. ATRA AND BIRDALONE TALK TOGETHER WHILE THE LORDS SIT AT THE WAR-COUNCIL.

MEANWHILE of their absence, Viridis sat sad and silent and downcast, though she wept not, for her gladness, which erst had been so great, seemed now reft from her; and no merrier was Aurea, as might have been looked for. But Atra came quietly unto Birdalone, and said softly: "I have a word for thee if thou wilt come forth with me into the hall." Birdalone's heart failed her somewhat, but she suffered Atra to take her hand, and they went into the hall together, and Atra brought her into a shot-window, and they sat down together side by side and were silent awhile. Spake Atra then, trembling and reddening: "Birdalone, knowest thou what thought, what hope, was in my heart when I spake so proudly and rashly e'en now?" Birdalone kept silence, and trembled as the other did. "This it was," said Atra: "He will go to this battle valiantly, he may fall there, and that were better; for then is life to begin anew: and what is there to do with these dregs of life?"

Said Birdalone, with flushed face: "If he die he shall die goodly, and if he live he shall live goodly."

"Yea, yea," said Atra; "forsooth thou art a happy woman!"

"Dost thou hate me?" said Birdalone.

Said Atra: "Proud is thy word, but I hate thee not. Nay, e'en now, when I spake thus boastfully, I thought: When he hath died as a doughty knight should, then, when life begins again, Birdalone and I shall be friends and sisters, and we two we will talk together oft and call him to mind, and the kindness of him, and how he loved us. Woe's me! that was when he was there sitting beside me and I could see him and his kindness; and then it was as if I could give him away; but now he is gone and I may not see him, it is clear to me that I have no part or lot in him, and I call back my thought and

214

my word, and now it is: O that he may live! O thou happy woman, that shall be glad whether he liveth or dieth!"

Said Birdalone:"And now thou hatest me, dost thou not, and we are foes?" Atra answered not, nor spake for a while; then she said: "Hard and bitter is it, and I know not what to turn to. I have seen once and again, on the wall of the Minorites' church at Greenford, a fair picture of the Blessed, and they walking in the meads of Paradise, clad in like raiment, men and women; their heads flower-crowned, their feet naked in the harmless blossomed grass; hand in hand they walk, with all wrath passed for ever, all desire changed into loving-kindness, all the anguish of forgiveness forgotten. And underneath the picture is it writ:

Bitter winter, burning summer, never more shall waste and wear;
Blossom of the rose undying brings undying springtide there

O for the hope of it, that I might hope it! O for the days to be and the assuaging of sorrow: I speak the word, and the hope springeth; the word is spoken, and there abideth desire barren of hope!" And she bowed down her head and wept bitterly; and Birdalone called to mind her kindness of the past and wept for her, she also.

After a while Atra lifted up her head, and thus she spake: "I hate thee not, Birdalone; nor doth one say such things to a foe. Yea, furthermore, I will crave somewhat of thee. If ever there come a time when thou mayst do something for me, thou wilt know it belike without my telling thee. In that day and in that hour I bid thee remember how we stood together erst at the stair-foot of the Wailing Tower in the Isle of Increase Unsought, and thou naked and fearful and quaking, and what I did to thee that tide to comfort thee and help and save thee. And then when thou hast called it to mind, do thou for me what thou canst do. Wilt thou promise this?"

"Yea, yea," said Birdalone; "and with all the better will, that oft and over again have I called it to mind. Wherefore I

215

behight thee to let me serve thee if I may whenso the occasion
cometh, even if it be to my own pain and grief—for this I
know thou meanest."

"See thou to this then," said Atra coldly; "and thou shalt
be the better for it in the long run belike: for thou art a
happy woman."

She arose as she spake, and said: "Hist! here come the
lords from the murder-council; and lo, now that he cometh,
my heart groweth evil toward thee again, and well-nigh biddeth me wish that thou wert naked and helpless before me
again. Lo my unhap! that he should mark my face that it
shows as if I were fain to do thee a mischief. And nought of
that would I do; for how should it avail me, and thou my
fellow and the faithful messenger of the Quest?"

Now little of her last words did Birdalone meet, as into
the hall came Hugh and Arthur; and though she strove to
sober her mind and think of her she-friend and her unhappi-
ness, yet she could not choose but to be full of joy in her
inmost heart now she knew without doubt that she was so
well-beloved of her beloved: and she deemed that Atra was
in the right indeed to call her a happy woman.

So now they all went into the solar together, and sat them
down with the two others; and Hugh did them to wit, how
they had ordered all the matter of the messengers who were
to summon the knights and chiefs of thereabouts, and the
aldermen of Greenford, to meet at the Castle of the Quest, that
they might set afoot the hosting to go against the Red Hold.

CHAPTER IX. HUGH TELLS THE STORY OF THE QUEST'S ENDING.

WHEN this was said, and there had been silence a
while, Birdalone took up the word, and spake
meekly and sweetly, saying: "Dear friends, how
it fared with you on the Isle from the time of my leaving
you, and how with you, true knights, from the time of your
departure, I both were fain to know for the tale's sake, and

also I would take the telling thereof as a sign of your for- giveness of my transgression; so I would crave the same of you but if it weary you overmuch."

All they yeasaid her kindly, and Hugh spake and said: "By your leave, fellows, I will tell in few words what betid us on our way to the Isle of Increase Unsought, and then shall Viridis take up the tale from the time that Birdalone left the said Isle in the witch's ferry." None said aught against it, and Hugh went on: "Short is my tale of the jour- ney: We came to the Isle of Nothing on the morrow's morn of our departure, and being warned of thee, Birdalone, we abode there but a little while to rest us from the boat, and went nowhither from the strand, and so went on our way in a three hours' space.

"Thence again we took the water, and came to the Isle of Kings, and that was in the middle of the night: we beheld the dead long and heedfully when the morning came, and departed again before noon, and came to the Isle of Queens a little after nightfall. The next morning we deemed we needs must go see the images of those ladies, lest aught might have befell since thou wert there which might be of import to the Quest, but all was unchanged, and we came away while the day was yet young.

"We made the Isle of the Young and the Old about sun- set that day, and the boy and the girl came down to the strand to behold us and wonder at us, and we sported with them merrily a while; and then they brought us to the house of the old man, who received us courteously and gave us to eat and drink. Forsooth, when the night was somewhat spent, he brought out strong drink to us, and took it somewhat amiss that we drank not overmuch thereof, as forsooth he did, and so fell asleep. Before he was drunk we asked him many questions about the isle and its customs, but he knew nought to tell us of them. Of thee also we asked, sister, but he had no memory of thee.

"On the morrow he fared down with us to our ferry, and made many prayers to us to take him along with us. 'For

217

here,' said he, 'is neither lordship nor fair ladies; and if here I abide, soon shall I come to mine ending day, and sore I yearn for joyance and a long term to my years.' Now we durst not take him aboard lest we should fare amiss with the wight of the Sending Boat; so we naysaid him courteously, thanked him for his guesting, and gave him gifts, to wit, a finger gold-ring and an ouch of gold, so he turned away from us somewhat downcast as we deemed; but ere we had given the word to the Sending Boat we heard him singing merrily in a high cracked voice as he went on his way.

"Now on this last day betid somewhat of new tidings; for scarce was this isle out of sight behind, ere we saw a boat come sailing toward us from the north-east, and it came on swiftly with a blue ripple of the lake behind it. Thereat we marvelled, and yet more when we saw that its sail was striped of gold and green and black; next then were we betwixt fear and joy when, as it drew nigher, we saw three women in the said boat, clad in gold, green, and black; and it came so nigh unto us at last, that we could see their faces that they were verily those of our lovelings; and each reached our her arms to us and called on us for help, each by our name: and there we were, oarless, sail-less, at the mercy of our unkenned ferry. Then would Baudoin and I have leapt overboard to swim to our loves at all adventure; but Sir Arthur here stayed us, and bade us think of it, that we were now nearing the Witch-land, and if we might not look to be beset with guiles and gins to keep us from winning to our journey's end; wherefore we forbore, though in all wretchedness, and the gay boat ran down the wind away from us, and the breeze and the ripple passed away with it, and the lake lay under the hot sun as smooth as glass; and on we went, weary-hearted.

"Came again another sail out of the north-east, when the sun was getting low, and speedily it drew nigh, but this time it was no small boat or barge, but a tall ship with great sails and goodly; towered she was and shield-hung, and the bas-nets gleamed and the spears glittered from her castle-tops
218

and bulwarks, and the sound of her horns came down the
wind as she neared us. We two handled our weapons and did
on our basnets, but Arthur there, he sat still, and said: 'Not
over-wise is the witch, that she lets loose on us two sendings
in one day so like unto each other.' 'Hah,' said Baudoin, 'be
we wary though; they are going to shoot.' And sure enough
we saw a line of bowmen in all the castles and even along, and
a horn blew, and then forth flew the shafts, but whither we
knew not, for none came anywhere anigh us; and Arthur
laughed and said: 'A fair shot into the clouds; but, by our
Lady! if none shot better in our country, I would bear no
armour for their shafts.' But we two were confused and
knew not what to think.

"The great ship flew past us on the wind as the barge had
done, but when she was about half a mile aloof we saw her
canvass fall to shivering and her yards swaying round, and
Arthur cried out: 'St. Nicholas! the play beginneth again!
she is coming about!'

"Even so it was, and presently she was bearing on us, and
was ere long so close aboard that we could see her, every spar
and rope, and her folk all gathered to the windward, knights,
sergeants, archers, and mariners, to gaze at us and mock us;
and huge and devilish laughter arose from amongst them as
she ploughed the water so close beside us, that one might
well-nigh have cast a morsel of bread aboard her; for clear it
was presently that she had no mind to run us down.

"Spake Arthur then: 'There will be a fresh play presently, my mates, but ye sit fast, for meseemeth this show is no
more perilous than the other, though it be bigger.'

"Scarce were the words out of his mouth, ere there was a
stir amongst the men gathered in the waist, and lo, amidst a
knot of big and fierce mariners, three women standing, pale,
with flying hair, and their hands bound behind them, and
one was clad in gold and another in green and the third in
black; and their faces were as the faces of Aurea and Viridis
and Atra.

"Then there came forth from that ship a huge cruel roar blent with mocking laughter that shamed our very hearts, and those evil things in the form of mariners took hold of each one of the ladies and cast them overboard into the gulf of the waters, first Aurea, next Viridis, and then Atra; and we two stood up with our useless swords brandished and would have leapt over into the deep, but that Arthur arose also and took hold of an arm of each of us and stayed us, and said: 'Nay then, if ye go, take me with you, and let all the Quest sink down into the deep, and let our lovelings pine in captivity, and Birdalone lose all her friends in one swoop, and we be known hereafter as the fools of lovers, the unstable.'

"So we sat us down, but huge shrieking laughter rose up unblended from the keel of the evil things, and then they let her go down the wind, and she went her way with flashing of arms, and streaming of banners and pennons, and blowing of horns, and the sun was setting over the wide water.

"But Arthur spake: 'Cheer up, brethren! see ye not how this proud witch is also but an eyeless fool to send us such a show, and the second time in one day to show us the images of our dearlings, who hours ago flitted past us in the stripe-sailed boat? Where then, did they of the ship meet with them? Nay, lords, let not the anguish of love steal all your wits.'

"We saw we had been fools to be so overcast by guile, and yet were we exceeding ill at ease, and over-long the time seemed unto us until we should be come to the Isle of Increase Unsought, and find our lovelings there.

"Now was the night come, and we fell asleep, but belike were not often all asleep at once; and at last it was, when we felt the dawn drawing near, though, the moon being down, it was the darkest of the summer night, that we were all three awake, when all of a sudden we heard just astern the rushing of the water, as though some keel were cleaving it, and dimly in the dark we saw a sail as of a boat overhauling us. Close at hand there rang out a lamentable cry: 'O, are ye

there, fellows of the Quest? O, help me, friends! save me and PART V
deliver me, who am snatched away to be cast into the hands Chap. 9
of my mistress that was. Help me, Baudoin, Hugh, Arthur!
Help! help!'

"Then all we knew the voice of Birdalone, and Arthur
leapt up, and would have been overboard in a trice had not
we two held him, and he fought and cursed us well-favouredly, there is no nay thereto; and meanwhile the wailing
voice of thee, my sister, died out in the distance, and the east
grew grey, and dawn was come.

"Then spake Baudoin: 'Arthur, my brother, dost thou not
mark that this also was of the same sort of show as those two
others, and thou who wert so wise before? It is but beguilings
to bring the Quest to nought; wherefore call to mind thy
manhood and thy much wisdom!'

"And we admonished him and rebuked him till he became
quiet and wise again, but was sad and downcast and silent.
But the Sending Boat sped on through the dawning, and
when it was light we saw that we had the Isle of Increase
close aboard, and we ran ashore there just as the sun was
rising. Fain were we then to get out of the boat and feel earth
under our feet. We took all our hardes out of the boat, and
hid away under the roots of an old thorn a little mail wherein
was your raiment, my ladies, which ye had lent to Birdalone;
then we did on our armour, and advised us of whereabout on
the Isle we were, and we saw the orchards and gardens before
us, and the great fair house above all, even as ye told us of
them, Birdalone.

"Next, then, without more ado, we went our ways up
through the orchard and the gardens, and when we were
well-nigh at end of them, and in face of those many steps
ye spake of, we saw at the foot of them a tall woman clad in
red scarlet, standing as if she abode our coming. When we
drew nigh we saw that she was strong-looking, well-knit,
white-skinned, yellow-haired, and blue-eyed, and might
have been called a fair woman, as to her shaping, save that
her face was heavy, yet hard-looking, with thin lips and

221

somewhat flagging cheeks, a face stupid, but proud and
cruel.

"She hailed us as we came up, and said: 'Men-at-arms, ye
be welcome to our house, and I bid you to eat and drink and
abide here.'

"Then we louted before her, and bade her Hail; and
Baudoin said: 'Lady, thy bidding will we take; yet have we
an errand to declare ere we break bread with thee, lest when
it is told we be not so welcome as ye tell us now.' 'What is
it?' said she. Said Baudoin: 'This man here is called the
Green Knight, and this the Black Squire, and I am the
Golden Knight; and now will we ask thee if this isle be called
the Isle of Increase Unsought?' 'Even so have I called it,'
quoth she, 'wherefore I deem none other will dare call it
otherwise.' 'It is well,' quoth Baudoin; 'but we have heard
say that hereto had strayed three dear friends of ours, three
maidens, who hight Viridis, the friend of the Green Knight,
and Atra, who is the Black Squire's, and Aurea, who is mine
own friend, so we have come to take them home with us,
since they have been so long away from their land and their
loves. Now if they be thy friends thou wilt perchance let
them go for love's sake and the eking of friendship; but if
they be thy captives, then are we well willing to pay thee
ransom, not according to their worth, for no treasure heaped
up might come nigh it, but according to thy desire, lady.'

"Laughed the proud lady scornfully and said: 'Big are
thy words, Sir Knight: if I had these maidens in my keeping
I would give them unto you for nothing, and deem that I had
the best of the bargain. But here are they not. True it is that
I had here three thralls who were hight as thou hast said;
but a while ago, not many days, they transgressed against
me till I chastised them; and then was I weary of them and
would be quit of them; for I need no servants here, whereas
I myself am enough for myself. Wherefore I sent them away
across the Water to my sister, who dwells in a fair place hight
the House under the Wood; for she needeth servants,
because the earth there yieldeth nought save to the tiller and

the herdsman and the hunter, while here all cometh unsought. With her may ye deal, for what I know, and buy the
maidens whom ye prize so high; though belike ye may have
to give her other servants in their place. For indeed, a while
ago her thrall fled from her and left her half undone, and it
is said that she came hither in her shamelessness: but I know
not; if she did, she slipped through my fingers, or else I
would have made her rue her impudence. Now meseemeth,
Sir Knights, here is enough of so small and foolish a matter;
and again I pray you to enter my poor house, and take meat
and drink along with me, for ye be none the less welcome
because of your errand, though it be a foolish one.'

"Now would Sir Baudoin have answered wrathfully, but
Arthur plucked at his skirt, & he yea said the Lady's bidding,
though somewhat ungraciously; but that she heeded nought;
she took Sir Baudoin by the hand and led him up the stately
perron, and thence came we into a pillared hall, as fair as
might be. And there on the dais was a table dight with dainty
meats and drinks, and the Lady bade us thereto, and we sat
to it.

"Thereat was the Lady buxom and merry: Baudoin
scowled across the board; I was wary and silent, but Arthur
was as blithe with the lady as she with him; nor did I altogether marvel thereat, since I knew him wise of wit.

"But when we were done with the meal, the Lady stood up
and said: 'Now, Sir Knights, I will give you leave; but this
house is as your own to roam through all its chambers and
pleasure you with its wonders and goodliness; and when ye
are weary of the house, then is the orchard and the garden
free to you, and all the Isle wheresoever ye will go. And here
in this hall is meat and drink for you whenso ye will; but if
ye would see me again to-day, then shall ye meet me where
ye first happened on me e'en now, at the foot of the great
perron.'

"Then she laid her hand on Arthur's shoulder, and said:
'Thy big friend may search out every nook in this house,
and every bush in the whole island, and if he find there the

223

maidens he spake of, one or all of them, then are they a gift from me unto him.'

"Therewith she turned, and went out of the hall by a door in the side thereof; and now already meseemed that though the woman was hateful and thick-hearted and cruel, yet she was become fairer, or seemed so, than when we first came on her; and for my part I pondered on what it might grow to, and fear of her came into my soul.

"Now spake Baudoin: 'Fellows, let us get out into the garden at least; for this place is evil, and meseems it smells and tastes of tears and blood, and that evil wights that hate the life of men are lurking in the nooks thereof. And lo, our very she-friend that was so kind and simple and dainty with us, there is, as it were, the image of the dear maiden standing trembling and naked before the stupid malice of this lump of flesh.' So spake he, Birdalone.

"But I said to Arthur in a soft voice: 'And when shall we slay her?' Said he: 'Not until we have gotten from her all that may be gotten; and that is the living bodies of our friends. But come we forth.'

"So did we, and came down to the orchard and did off our helms, and lay down under a big apple-tree which was clear of cover all round about, and so fell to our redes; and I asked Arthur what he deemed of the story of our loves having been carried to the House under the Wood, and if it might not be tried seeking thither; but he laughed and said: 'Never would she have told us thereof had it been sooth: doubtless our friends are here on this isle, but, as I deem, not in the house, else had not the witch left all the house free for us to search into.' 'Yea,' said I, 'but how if they be in her prison?' Said he: 'It is not hard to find out which is the prison of so dainty a house as is yonder; and when we had found it, soon should we have hit upon a way to break it, since we be three, and stout fellows enough. Nay, I deem that the lovelings be stowed away in some corner of the Isle without the house, and that mayhappen we shall find them there; and yet I trow not before we have made guile meet guile, and overcome the

224

sorceress. But come now, let us be doing, and begin to quarter this little land as the kestrel doth the water-meadow; and
leave we our armour, lest we weary us, for we shall have no
need for hard strokes.'

"We hung up there on the tree helm and shield and hauberk, and all our defences, and went our ways quartering the
Isle; and the work was toilsome, but we rested not till the
time was come to keep tryst with the Lady; and all that while
we found no sign of the darling ones: and the isle was everywhere a meadow as fair as a garden, with little copses of
sweet-growing trees here and there, and goodly brooks of
water, but no tillage anywhere: wild things, as hart and buck
and roe, we came upon, and smaller deer withal, but all un-
hurtful to man; but of herding was no token.

"Came we then back to that lordly perron, and there, at
the foot thereof, stood the witch-wife, and received us joyously; clad was she all gloriously in red scarlet broidered and
begemmed; her arms bare and her feet sandalled, and her yellow hair hanging down from under its garland; and certainly
it was so that she had grown fairer, and was sleek and white
and well-shapen, and well-haired; yet by all that, the visage
of her was little bettered, and unto me she was loathsome.

"Now the feast went much as the earlier meal had done;
and Baudoin was surly and Arthur blithe and buxom; and
nought befell to tell of, save that dishes and meats, and flasks
and cups, and all things came upon the board as if they were
borne thereon by folk unseen; and thereat we wondered not
much, considering in what wonder-house we were. But the
lady-witch looked on us and smiled, and said: 'Knights, ye
marvel at the manner of our service, but call to mind that we
told you this morning that we were enough for Ourselves,
and we have so dight our days here that whoso is our friend
on this Isle of Increase shall lack nothing. Fear not, therefore, to see aught ugly in our servants as now unseen, if their
shapes were made manifest unto you.'

"All things were we heedful to note at this banquet; but
when it was over, then came music into the hall from folk un-

seen, but not as if the musicians were a many, only belike
some three or four. And thereat the Lady spake, saying:
'Knights, ye may deem our minstrels but few, but such is
our mind that we love not our music overloud, and for the
most part only three sing or play unto us at one time.'

"Thereafter the Lady brought us to fair chambers, and we
slept there in all ease, and we arose on the morrow and found
the Lady still blithe with us; yet I noted this, that she seemed
to deal with Arthur as if she saw him now for the first time,
and much he seemed to be to her liking.

"Again we fared forth, and were no less diligent in search-
ing the Isle than erst, and found nought; and all went that
day as before.

"On the morrow (that is, the third day) the witch seemed
to have somewhat more memory of Arthur than erst, and
even yet more liking of him, so that she reached out her
hand for him to kiss, which needs must he do, despite his
loathing of her.

"When we had lain under the apple-tree a little while,
Baudoin spake and said: 'Yesterday and the day before we
searched the open land and found nought; now to-day let us
search the house, and if we find nought, then at least it shall
lie behind us.' We yeasaid it, and presently went back, and
from chamber to chamber, and all was fair and goodly as
might be, and we marvelled what would betide to it when
the witch was undone and her sorcery come to an end.

"To the Wailing Tower we came, and up the stairs, and
found the door open of the prison-chamber, and all there as
thou hast told us, Birdalone; only we opened the great coffer, whence thou didst refrain thee, and found it full of
hideous gear truly, as fetters and chains, and whips and rods,
and evil tools of the tormentors, and cursed it all and came
away; and Arthur said: 'Lo you, this stupid one! How eager
is she to bid us what to do, and to tell us that our ladies are
not in this evil house, since she leaveth all open to us.' Yet
we went about the house without, and counted the windows
heedfully to see that we had missed no chamber, and found

nought amiss; and then we went in again and sought as low down as we might, to see if perchance some dungeon there were underground, but found nought save a very goodly undercroft below the great hall, which was little less fair than that which was above it. So came the evening and the banquet, and the end of that day; but the witch-wife led Arthur by the hand to the board, and afterwards to the chamber ere we slept.

"On the fourth day and the fifth it was no otherwise than erst; and when I fared to bed I felt confused in my head and sick of heart.

"The night of the next day (the sixth), as we went to our chambers, and the witch-wife and Arthur hand-in-hand, she stayed him a while, and spake eagerly to him in a soft voice; and as he came up to me afterwards he said: 'To-night I have escaped it, but there will not be escape for long.' 'From what?' said I. He said: 'From bedding her: for now it has come to this, that presently we must slay her at once and have no knowledge of our sweetlings, or I must do her will.'

"In such wise passed four more days, and it was the twelfth morning of our sojourn there, and we went forth on our search of every mead and every covert of the Isle, and all day we found nought to our purpose; but as it grew toward sunset, and there grew great clouds in the eastern ort, piled up and copper-coloured, we came over a bent on to a little green dale watered by a clear brook, and as we looked down into it we saw something shine amongst its trees; so we hastened toward that gleam, and lo, amidst the dale, with the brook running through it, a strange garth we saw. For there was a pavilion done of timber and board, and gaily painted and gilded, and out from that house was, as it were, a great cage of thin gilded bars, both walls and roof, just so wide apart as no one full-grown, carle or quean, could thrust through.

"Thitherward then ran we, shouting, for we saw at once that in the said cage were three women whose aspect was that of our sweetlings, and presently we were standing by the said herse, reaching our hands out to them to come to us and tell us their tale, and that we would deliver them. But they stood together in the midst of the said cage, and though they gazed piteously on us thence, and reached out their hands to us, they neither spake nor came to the herse to us; so we deemed that they were bewitched, and our joy was dashed.

"Then we went all about the cage and the pavilion to find ingate, and found it not; and then the three of us together strove with the bars of the herse, and shook and swayed them, but it was all to no purpose.

"Moreover, while we were at this work the sun seemed to go out, and there came a heavy black mist rolling into the dale, and wrapped us about so that we saw not each other's faces, and the bars of the herse were gone from our hands as we stood there. Then came rain and thunder and lightening on to the black night, and by the glare of the lightening we could see the leaves and grass of the dale, but neither herse nor house nor woman. So we abode there in the dark night and the storm, all bewildered, till the rain and clouds drew off and it was calm fair starlight again, but clean gone was the golden cage and they that stood therein; and we turned sadly, and went our ways toward the witch-house.

"On the way said Arthur: 'Brethren, this meseemeth is but a going on with the shows which were played us on the water as we came hither; but whether she doth this but for to mock and torment us, or that she would beguile us into deeming that our friends are verily here, I wot not; but to-morrow, meseemeth, I shall can to tell you.'

"Now came we to the perron of the house, and there stood the witch-wife under the stars to meet us. And when she saw us, she took hold of Arthur by the hand and the arm to caress him, and found that he and we were drenched with the rain and the storm, as might well be deemed; then she bade us up to our chambers to do on raiment which she had dight for us, and we went thither, and found our garments rich and dainty indeed; but when we came down into the

228

hall where the witch abode us, we saw that Arthur's raiment
was far the richest and daintiest. But the witch ran to him
and cast her arms about him, and clipped and kissed him
before the others, and he suffered it. So sped the feast again.

"But when they went to bed, the said witch took Arthur's
hand and spake a word unto him, and led him away, and he
went with her as one nought loth; but we twain were afraid
lest she should destroy him when she had had her will of
him. Wherefore we waked through the more part of the
night with our swords ready to hand.

"But when we were clad in the morn he came unto us, he
also clad, and was downcast and shamefaced indeed, but safe
and sound; and he said: 'Speak no word about our matter
till we be out in the open air, for I fear all things about us.'

"So when we had gone forth and were under the apple-
tree once more, spake Arthur: 'Now, lords, am I shamed
for ever, for I have become the leman of this evil creature;
but I pray ye not to mock me; and that the more as the same
lot may happen on you both, or either; for I can see for sure
that the wretch will weary of me and desire one of you two.
Let it pass. Somewhat have I found out from her, but not
much: first, that she has forgotten her first lie, to wit, how
she sent our ladies to the sister-witch; for I told her of the
Golden Cage, and how we had missed it in the storm; and she
said: "Though I deem it a folly that ye should seek these
thralls, yet would I help you if I might, since ye are now become my dear friends. Though, forsooth, when ye meet
them I deem that ye will find them sore changed to you.
For, as I told you, they fled away from me, after I had chastised them for a treason, into the hidden places of the Isle,
whereas they had no keel to sail away hence. And I cared not
to follow them, as I myself am Queen and Lady of all things
here, and am enough for myself, save when love constrain-
eth me, dear lord. Now, my rede is that ye seek the Golden
Cage again and yet again, because I deem that these thralls
have somehow learned some wisdom, and they have en-

229

chanted the said cage for a defence against me, from whom they might not hide as they did from you; for of me have they stolen their wizardry, and I am their mistress therein."

"'This, therefore, is the new lie of her, and my rede is that we heed it nought. For my mind is that she it is that hath made the appearance of the cage and the women therein, and that she hath our poor friends somewhere underneath her hand.'

"Now this we deemed most like; yet whereas we had nought to do with the time, which, now that we had searched the Isle throughly, hung heavy on hand, we deemed it good to go to the dale of the Golden Cage again, though we looked not to find the cage there any more. But this betid, that we found the little dale easily enough, and there stood the cage as we had seen it yesterday, but nought was there within its bright bars save the grass and the flowers, and the water of the brook a-running.

"We loitered about that place a while, and went back to the house in due time; and to shorten the tale, I shall tell that for many days it betid that we went every day to seek the Golden Cage, but after the first three days we saw it no more.

"Now began sadness and weariness to overcome us as the days and weeks wore, and belike the witch-wife noted it that we were worse company than heretofore.

"And now on a day Arthur bade us note that the said witch was growing weary of him, and he bade me look to it; 'for,' said he, 'she is turning her face toward thee, brother.' My heart burned with rage at that word; I said nought, but made up my mind that I would try to bring the matter to an end.

"That same night befell what Arthur had threatened; for the feast being done in the evening, the witch drew me aside while the music was a-playing, and caressed my hand and my shoulder, and said: 'I am yet wondering at you Champions, that ye must needs follow after those three wretched thralls, whom never will ye find, for they need ye

230

not, but will flee from you if ye have sight of them, as they did that other day. And therein they are scarce in the wrong, whereas they may well think that if ye find them they should fall into my hands; for easily may I take them any day that I will, and then I have a case against them, and may lawfully chastise them according to the law that has been given unto me; and then shall they be in grievous plight. Wherefore the rede We give unto you three now is the rede of friendliness that ye make yourselves happy in Our Island, and then will We do everything We may for your pleasure and delight; and if ye will that We make ourselves even fairer than now We be, that may be done, and shall be a reward unto you for your yielding and obedience. And if ye will women thralls for your pleasure, that also may be gotten for you; for We be not wholly without power in these waters, though We have no keel or ferry upon them. And now, thou fair lad, We give thee this last word: Ye Champions have been dwelling in Our house a long while, and that while have ever striven to thwart me. We now counsel you to make an end of it, and it shall be better for you.'

"She seemed to my eyes prouder and stupider than ever erst, despite her golden hair and white skin and lovely limbs; and I said to myself that now must we destroy the evil of that house even if we died for it, or else we were all undone; withal I saw somewhat of truth thrusting up through her much lying, and I deemed, even as Arthur did, that she had our friends under her hand somewhere.

"Nought else betid that night; but on the morrow we went forth and strayed on till we were come into the southernmost quarter of the Isle, and not very far from the water we came upon a wood or big thicket which was new to us. So we entered it, and as we went and noted the wild things of the wood going hither and thither, we espied afar off the shape of a man going amidst the thicket; wherefore we went warily towards him, lest he should see us and flee from us; and when we drew a little nigher we saw it was a woman, though she was clad as a hunter, with legs naked to above

231

the knee. She had a quiver at her back and a bow in her hand, and her coat was black of hue. Belike now she heard our going amongst the dry leaves, for she turned her face to us, and lo, it was the face of Atra.

"When she saw us, she gave a shrill cry, and fell to running at her swiftest away from us, and we followed all we might, but we could not over-run her, though we kept her in sight ever, till we had run all through the wood, and before us was the sheer side of a rocky hill and the mouth of a cave therein, and by the said mouth who should there be but Aurea and Viridis, as we thought, clad in gold and in green, but the fashion of their raiment not otherwise than Atra's. Their bows were bended and they had shafts in their hands, and as we came out of the thicket into the open lawn before the cave, Viridis nocked a shaft and aimed at us and drew, and the shaft flew over my head; therewith mocking laughter came from them, and they ran into the cave. Speedily we ran up to it, but when we came home thither, there was the sheer hill-side, but never a cave nor an opening.

"Dismayed were we thereat; but more dismayed had we been but that we deemed that all this was but a cheat and a painted show put upon us by the witch to back up her lying. Nevertheless we fared the next day to seek the wood and the cave in the sheer rock, but nowise might we find either wood or cave.

"Now it was the night of the day hereafter, that as we went to our chambers, the witch-wife took me by the hand and led me apart, and said me many soft things of her accursed lust, whereof I will not say one again. But the upshot of it all was that she would bring me to her chamber and her bed. And whereas I was determined what to do, and had my war-sword by my side, I naysaid her not, but made her good countenance. And when we came to her chamber, which was full gloriously dight, and fragrant as with the scent of the roses and lilies of mid-June, she bade me to lie in her bed of gold and ivory and she would be with me anon. So I unclad

232

myself and laid me down, but I drew forth my sword, and
laid the ancient naked blade betwixt my side and her place.

"Anon she cometh back again unclad, and would step into the bed; but she saw the sword and said: 'What is this, Champion?' Said I: 'These edges are the token of sundering between us, for there is a spell on me, that with no woman may I deal, save with mine only love, but I shall do her mortal scathe; so beware by the token of the grey edges of battle.' She drew aback, and was as a spiteful and angry cat, and there was no loveliness in her; and she said: 'Thou liest, and thou hatest me; see thou to it, both for thyself and thy loveling!' And she turned about and strode out of the chamber; but I arose and clad myself in haste, and took my naked sword in my hand. But before I went, I looked around, and espied an ambry fashioned in the wall of the bed-lane, and the door was half open; and the said ambry was wrought of the daintiest, all of gold and pearl and gems; and I said to myself: Herein is some treasure, and this is a tide of war. So I opened the ambry, and within it was even more gloriously wrought than without; and there was nought therein save a little flask of crystal done about with bands of gold set with great and goodly gems. So I took the said flask and went my ways hastily to my own chamber, and there I looked at the said flask and took out the stopple; and there was a liquor therein, white like to water, but of a spicy smell, sweet, fresh, and enheartening. So I yet thought this was some great treasure, and that much hung upon it, could I find out unto what use it might be put. And I said: To-morrow we will put it to the proof. Then I put the said flask under my pillow, and laid my sword by my side and slept, and was not ill-content so far.

"But on the morrow, when I met my fellows, they asked me how I had sped, and I told them, well, and that we would talk the matter over under our tree of counsel. So we went down into the hall, where we met the witch-lady; and I looked for it that she would be angry and fierce with me;

but it went far otherwise; for she was blithe and buxom, and abounding in endearments more than I could away with. But this I noted, that her eyes wandered, and her speech faltered at whiles, and ever she seemed to be seeking somewhat; and withal that her caressing hands were seeking if they could aught stowed away in the bosom of my coat. But all was nought, for as we came to the door of the hall I gave Baudoin the flask to guard until we should come to our apple-tree of rede. Wherefore the she-wolf went red and white by turns, and fumed, and fretted her bedizenments with unrestful hands, and when she should let us go our ways, she lingered and looked back oft, and was loth to depart ere she had gotten what she lacked, and that forsooth was the said flasket.

"But when we were without the house, I bade our fellows go with me to another place than the wonted apple-tree of rede, and they understood my word, and I led them to a little grassy plain without the orchard, where was no covert for a wide space about it, nought but the one linden-tree under which now we sat. There I told them all the tale of the last night and of the flasket, and put before them all that was in my mind to do that evening at the banquet, and they both of them yeasaid it. But what it was, that shall ye hear anon when we carried the matter through; but I bade Baudoin still carry the flasket till the evening.

"Thereafter we spake of other matters; but soon we had good cause to rejoice that we had not talked our talk under the apple-tree (whereas I doubted not that the witch would spy upon us there), for not long had we been at our talk ere, looking that way, we saw the evil creature by the hedge of the orchard and gazing over at us.

"We arose then, and came to her as if nought had happened; and she bade us walk the garden with her, and we yeasaid it, and went with her, and paced about amidst the flowers and lay on the blossomed grass. Forsooth, both to her and to us the time hung heavy on hand. And meseemed that the sleekness and fairness of her body was worsened

234

since yesterday, and she was pale and haggard, and her eyes were wandering and afraid.

"Now she bade us come a little further into the garden and eat a morsel at noon; and we arose, and she brought us to where were vines trellised all about and overhead, so that it was like a fair green cloister; and there was a board laid and spread with many dainties of meat and drink. And she bade us sit. Verily we had but little stomach to that dinner; and I said to myself, Poison! poison! and even so my fellows deemed, as afterwards they told me. And I saw Baudoin loosen his sword in the sheath, and I knew that his mind was to smite at once if he saw aught amiss. And I, who sat next to the witch, laid my hand on a little dagger which I wore at my girdle. She also saw this, and turned as pale as death, and sat trembling before us; and whatso we ate or drank at that board under the rustling vine-leaves, she gave unto us with her own hand; and then we wotted full surely that she had meant our deaths there and then, but was cowed by the fierce eyes of Baudoin and the threat of my hand.

"Withal it seemed that she might not bear it to sit there long amongst us. She rose up and smiled on us as ghastly as a corpse, and gave us leave, and went hurrying into the house. And right glad we were to be at rest from her. Yet as we ourselves durst not go far away from the house, lest some new thing might happen, neither could she leave us quite alone, but thrice again that afternoon at some turn of the garden, or orchard, or meadow, we came upon her wan face and eyes full of all hate and staring pride, and she enforced her to smile upon us, and turned away with some idle word.

"At last the sun began to sink, and we went to the perron of the house, and found her standing to meet us in her wonted way. But when we came up she gave no hand to any one of us, but went up the stairs before us, and we followed with no word spoken.

"There was the hall with the lordly service on the board, and the wax-candles lighted all about, and the great vault of stone fair and stately over it. We went to the dais and the

235

board and sat down, the witch-wife in her gold and ivory
chair at the board's end, and I at her right hand and looking
down the hall, my two fellows facing me, with their backs to
the clear of the hall.

"There we sat, and the meats and drinks were before us
as dainty as ever erst; but we put forth no hand to them, but
sat staring at each other for some two minutes it might be,
and the witch looked from one to the other of us, and quaked
that her hands shook like palsy.

"Then I rose up and put my hand to my bosom (for Baudoin had given me the flasket ere we came to the perron): I
spake in a loud voice, and it sounded wild and hard in the
goodly hall: 'My lady,' I said, 'thou art looking but pale now,
and sick and downcast. Drink now to me out of this precious
flasket, and thou shalt be whole and well.'

"And therewith I held the flasket aloft; but her face
changed horribly; she sprang up in her chair and reached
out her arm to clutch at the flasket, screaming like an eagle
therewith. But I thrust her back into the chair with my left
hand; and therewith arose Baudoin and Arthur, and caught
her by the shoulders, and bound her fast to the chair with
cords that they had gotten thereto. But when she got her
breath she yelled out: 'Ah, now shall all tumble together,
my proudful house and I under it! Loose me, traitors! loose
me, fools! and give me one draught of the Water of Might,
and then shall I tell you all, and ye shall go free with your
thralls if ye will. Ah! ye will not loose me? ye will not? Well
then, at least ye, the fools, shall be under it, and they also, the
she-traitors, the scourged and tormented fools that might
not save themselves from me. O loose me! loose me! thou in
whose arms I have lain so many a night, and give me to drink
of the proud Water of Might!'

"So she yelled; and now had all the fairness gone from
her body: flaggy and yellow were her limbs, and she looked
all over as her face, a lump of stupid and cruel pride, and her
words lost meaning and changed into mere bestial howling.
But for me, since she so desired that water, I knew that it

was good for us to drink, and I took out the stopple and
drank, and it was as if fire ran through all my veins, and I felt
my strength three-folded straightway, and most wondrous
clear was my sight grown therewith; and I raised my eyes
now and looked down the hall, and lo, there was Aurea,
chained by the ancle to the third pillar from the dais; and
over against her, Viridis; and next, to the fourth pillar, Atra.
Then I cried in a loud voice that rang through the witch's
hall: 'Lo what I see!' And I ran round the head of the board,
and thrust and dragged Baudoin and Arthur along with me,
crying out: 'Come, come! they are found! they are here!' And
I came to my sweetling, and found her clad but in her white
smock, which was flecked with blood all about, and her face
was wan and pined, and the tears began to run when she saw
me, but no word came from her lips though the kissing of
them was sweet.

"Then I turned about to my two fellows, and they stood
bewildered, not knowing what was toward; and I came to
them and made them drink of the flasket, and their eyes
were opened and the strength of giants came to them, and
they ran each to his sweetling; but Baudoin, before ever he
kissed Aurea, caught hold of the chain that bound her to the
pillar, and by main force dragged it out. Wise was that, meseemed, for words were again come into the witch's howls,
and I heard her: 'Ah, long may ye be playing with the chains,
long! for now the house rumbleth toward its fall. Ah, the
bitches are loose! Woe's me! to die alone!' And once more
she howled wordless, as both I and Arthur had our loves in
our arms, and fell to following Baudoin out on to the perron
and down into the fresh fragrant garden wherein now was
the moon beginning to cast shadows.

"Stood we then aloof from the house, and the rumbling
whereof the evil hag had howled waxed into a thunder, and
under our very eyes the great white walls and gold-adorned
roofs fell together, and a great cloud of dust rose under the
clear moonlit sky.

"We looked and wondered, and our loves also, but no

237

word they spake; but ere the other two had time to grieve thereat, I gave Viridis to drink of the Water of Might, and she fell to sweet speech straightway, of such sort and such wise as I will not tell you. Then I did the same by Aurea and Atra, and forthwith the speech flowed from them to their friends.

"Full happy were we then in the early night-season, for the Water of Might gave them strength also, as to us, and healed all the stripes and wounds their bodies had suffered of the foul witch, and made their eyes bright, and their cheeks full and firm, and their lips most sweet, and their hands strong and delicious.

"Now when we had stood gazing toward the melting of the beauteous palace for a little, we took our darlings in our arms again, whereas the chains would have hindered their walking, and went down to the lip of the water whereas lay the Sending Boat, so that we might be anigh our ferry in case of need; for we knew not what might betide the Isle now its mistress had perished. Then we fell to and sawed off the chains from the dear ancles with our swords, and took Birdalone's lendings from the mail. And Aurea had her gown again, and Viridis her smock, and my green surcoat over it, and Atra wore the battle-coat of the Black Squire. As for their bare feet (for Atra would not have hers dight prouder than her sisters'), we so clad them with kisses that they were not ill-covered belike.

"So gat we aboard our ferry, and did blood-offering to the wight thereof, and so sped merrily and lovingly over the wide lake back on our homeward road. And we said: 'This hath the dear Birdalone done for us.'

"And now, my Viridis, I will that thou fill up the tale by telling to Birdalone, as ye told us, how it fared with you three and the evil one from the time that ye sped Birdalone on her way till the moment when mine eyes first beheld you made fast to the pillars of the palace which has crumbled into dust."

238

CHAPTER X. HOW IT FARED WITH THE THREE LADIES AFTER THE ESCAPE OF BIRDALONE.

VIRIDIS took up the word without more ado, and said : "I will do my best herein, and ye, sisters, must set me right if I err. When we had seen the last of you, dear Birdalone, that early morning, we turned back again to the house as speedily and as covertly as we might, lest the witch might espy our disarray and question us thereover. Then we went to the Wonder-coffer, and gat thereout raiment for that which we had given away, which was easy for us to do, whereas the witch-mistress was so slothful that she had given to us the words of might wherewith to compel the coffer to yield, so that we might do all the service thereof, and she not to move hand or foot in the matter. So when we were clad, and the time was come, we went into the hall, by no means well assured of our mistress.

"When we came before her, she looked on us in surly wise, as her wont was, and said nought for a while; she stared on us and knit her brows, as if she strove to call to mind something that ran to and fro in her memory ; and I noted that, and for my part I trembled before her. But she spake at last: 'Meseemeth as if there is a woman in the Isle besides you three; some misdoer that I was minded to punish. Tell me, you! was there not a naked one who came into this hall a while ago, one whom I threatened with pining ?' Atra, who was the boldest of us, bowed the knee before her, and said : 'Nay, our lady, since when do stranger women come naked into thine hall, and dare thee there?'

"Said the witch : 'Yet have I an image of a naked woman standing down there before me; and if I have it in mine eye, so should ye. Tell me therefore, and beware, for We are not bidden to hold Our hand from you if We take you in misdeeds.'

"If I quaked before, now much more I quaked, till my legs well-nigh failed me for fear; but Atra said: 'Great lady,

239

this image will belike be of that one whom a while ago ye had stripped and tied to a pillar here, and tormented while ye feasted.'

"The Lady looked on her hard, and again seemed striving to gather up the thrums of some memory, and then her face became smooth again, and she spake lightly : 'All that may well be ; so do ye go about your due service, and trouble Our rest here no longer; for We love not to look on folk who be not wholly our own to pine or to spare, to slay or let live, as We will; and We would that the winds and the waves would send us some such now ; for it is like to living all alone to have but such as you with us, and none to cower before us and entreat us of mercy. So begone, I bid you.'

"Thus for that time were we saved from the witch's cruelty; but our time came before long. For three days thereafter as we stood on the steps of the perron and served my lady with dainties, of a hot afternoon, came two great white doves a-flying, who pitched down right before our mistress' feet ; and each had a gold ring about his neck, and a scroll tied thereto, and the witch bade us take the doves and take off the scrolls and give them unto her; and she looked on the gold rings which the doves bore, and for a moment on the scrolls, and then she said: 'Take ye the doves and cherish them, lest We have need of them; take also the two scrolls and keep them till to-morrow morning, and then give them into our hands. And look ye to this, that if ye give them not unto Us it will be treason against Us, and We shall have a case against you, and your bodies will be ours.'

"Then she rose up slowly, and bade me to her that she might lean upon my shoulder and be helped upstairs, so slothful a beast as she was; and as we went up I heard her say softly to herself: 'Weary on it, now must I drink a sup of the Water of Might, that I may remember and do and desire. But dear is my sister, and without doubt she hath matters of import to tell me by these doves.'

"So when we were together alone I told the others here-
240

of, and we talked it over; and they deemed the tidings ill, even as I did; for we might not doubt but that the doves were a sending from the witch-sister who dwelt at the House under the Wood; and sore we misdoubted that they were sped to our mistress to tell her of thee, Birdalone, and may-happen of the Quest, so wise as we knew she was. As to the two scrolls, forsooth they were open, and not sealed; but when we looked on them we could make nought of it; for though they were writ fairly in Latin script, so that we read them, yet of the words no whit might we understand, so we feared the worst. But what might we do? we had but two choices, either to cast ourselves into the water, or abide what should befall; and this last one we chose because of the hope of deliverance.

"Next morning, therefore, we came before our mistress in the hall, and we found her pacing up and down before the dais; though her wont was at that hour to be sitting in her throne of gold and ivory, lying back on the cushions half asleep.

"So Atra went up to her, and knelt before her and gave her the scrolls, and she looked on her grimly, and smiled evilly, and said: 'Kneel there yet; and ye others kneel also, till I see what befitteth you.' So did we, and indeed I was fain to kneel, for I might scarce stand up for terror; and all of us, our hearts died within us.

"But the witch read those scrolls to herself, sitting in her throne, and spake not a long while; then she said: 'Come hither, and grovel before Us, and hearken!' Even so we did; and she said again: 'Our sister, who hath been so kind unto you, and saved you from so many pains, here telleth Us, by the message of the two doves, that ye have betrayed Us and her, and have stolen her thrall and her Sending Boat, and sent her an errand for Our destruction; and therewith she delivereth you into Our hands, and ye are Ours hence-forward; nor is it to be thought that ye may escape Us. Now, for your treason, some would slay you outright here and now. But We will be merciful, and let you live, and do no more than chastise you sharply now; and thereafter shall ye be Our very thralls to do as We will with: thereafter, that is to say, when they whom ye have sent Our sister's thrall to fetch have come hither (as belike I may scarce stay them), and I have foiled them and used them, and sent them away empty. Now I tell you, that meanwhile of their coming shall ye suffer such things as We will; and when they be here We will not forbid you to be anigh them; but We shall see that there will be little joy to you in that nighness. Yea, ye shall know now to what market ye have brought your wares, and what the price of treason is therein.'

"Verily then we suffered at her hand what she would, whereof it would shame me to tell more as at this present; and thereafter did she chain us to those three pillars of the hall whereas ye found us chained; and we were fed as dogs be, and served as dogs, but we endured all for the sake of hope; and when we durst, and deemed the witch would not hear us, we spake together and enheartened each other.

"But on the fourth day of our torment came the witch to us, and gave us to drink a certain red water from out of a leaden flasket; and when I drank I deemed it was poison, and was glad, if gladness might be in me at such a tide; and when I had drunk I felt an icy chill go through all my body, and all things swam before my eyes, and deadly sickness came over me. But that passed away from me presently, and I felt helpless and yet not feeble; all sounds heard I clearer than ever yet in my life; also I saw the hall, every arch and pillar and fret, and the gleam on the pavement from the bright sun that might not enter; and the witch I saw walking up and down the hall by the dais; but my sisters I saw not when I looked across to their pillars. Moreover, I might not see myself when I reached out my hand or my foot, though I saw the chain which made my ancle fast to the pillar; and withal, when I set my hand on my face, or any other part of my body, or what else I might touch, I felt there what I

242

looked to feel, were it flesh or linen, or the cold iron of my fetter, or the polished face of the marble pillar.

"Now I knew scarce if I were alive or dead, or if I were but beginning to be dead; but there came upon me the desire of life, and I strove to cry out to the sisters, but though I formed the words in my mouth, and did with my throat as when one cries out aloud, yet no sound of a voice came from me, and more helpless did I feel than erst.

"But even therewith I saw the witch come toward me, and therewith all my body felt such fear of her that I knew I was not dead. Then she came before me and said: 'O shadow of a thrall, whom none can see but them unto whom wisdom hath given eyes to see wonders withal, now have I tidings for thee and thy sisters, to wit, that your lovers and seekers are at hand; and presently I shall bring them into this hall, and they shall be so nigh unto you that ye might touch them if I did not forbid it; but they shall not see you, but shall wonder where I have hidden you, and shall go seeking you to-day and many days, and shall find you not at all. So make ye the most of the sight of them, for in them henceforward ye have no other part or lot.'

"Therewith she spat out at me, and went over to my sisters, and said words of like import to those which she had said unto me. And presently she went out of the hall; and not long afterwards I heard voices speaking on the perron, and knew one for the voice of the witch, and the other for the voice of my lord Baudoin; and then again wore a little while, and I saw the witch come through the great door of the hall leading Sir Arthur by the hand, as if she were his dear friend, and Baudoin and Hugh, my man, following them. And the said witch was clad full fair, and had laid by her sloth and stupid pride, as meseemed; and her limbs were grown rounder and sleeker, and her skin fairer, so that to them that knew her not she might well seem to be a goodly woman.

"Now they sat to meat as my man hath told you, and then

R2   243

departed from the hall, and the witch also. But after a while
she came back again and loosed us, and grimly bade us go
with her, and needs must we, though we could not so much
as see our own feet upon the floor. And she set us to tasks
about the house, and stood by while we toiled for her, and
mocked us not without stripes, and in all ways was as rough
and cruel and hard with us as she had been smooth and
debonaire to our lords; but after noon she brought us back
and chained us to our pillars again. And when the evening
came and the banquet was, it was we who were the unseen
players of the string-play; and we might play no other
melody than what the witch bade us; else belike, could we
have held converse, we might have played such tunes as
would have smitten the hearts of our loves, and told them
that we were anigh. To make a short story of it, thus did she
day by day, and no comfort or converse might we sisters have
of each other, or of aught else save the sight of our beloved
ones, and a glimmer of hope therewith. And, forsooth, for as
grievously as my heart was wrung by the yearning of me for
my love, yet was it a joy unto me to think that he went there
desiring me, and that I whom he desired was not the poor
wretched creature chained there in her nakedness, with her
body spoiled by torment and misery, but the glad maiden
whom he had so often called fair and lovesome.

" So passed the days, and at last hope had grown so pale
and wan, that she was no more to be seen by us than we were
by our lords; and now it seemed to me that death was coming,
so feeble and wretched as I grew. But the witch would not
let us die, but sustained us from time to time with some
little draughts of a witch-drink that revived us.

" So wore the time till that evening, when came hope together with the fulfilment of hope, so that one minute we
durst hope for deliverance, and the next we were delivered.

" Nor is there more to tell, Birdalone, my dear, save that
we came safely to the Isle of the Young and the Old in the
full morning-tide; and as our ferry drew nigh the green
shore, there were the two younglings whereof thou didst tell

us awaiting our landing, and when we stepped ashore they came to us bearing cakes and fruit in a fair basket, and they made much of us and we of them. And so we came to the old man, who was exceeding fain of us, and grand and courteous, till he became a little drunk, and then he was somewhat over kind to us women. Nevertheless, there in that pleasant isle we rested us for three days, that we might somewhat calm and refresh our spirits with what was small and of little account. And when we departed, the old man followed us down to the strand, and lamented our departure, as he had done with our lords erewhile; only this time yet greater was his lamentation, and needs must we kiss him, each one of us, or never had he been done. So he turned up landward, bewailing the miss of us, but presently, before we had seen the last of him, was cheerful again and singing.

"So we went on our way; and we also, we maidens, in our turn, saw those woeful images of the Isle of Queens and the Isle of Kings; and we came to the Isle of Nothing, and abode warily by our ferry, and so came away safe, and thus, as thou wottest, home to the castle to hear evil tidings of thee. Now is this all my tale."

Birdalone sat shyly and hushed when all was done; and then all they did somewhat to comfort her, each after their own fashion; and now sorrow for the slain man was made softer and sweeter for them, whereas they had to lose not two fellows, but one only. Yet, despite of all, trouble and care was on Birdalone's soul betwixt the joy of loving and being beloved, and the pain and fear of robbing a friend of her love. For Atra's face, which she might not hate, and scarce might love, was a threat to her day by day.

CHAPTER XI. BIRDALONE AND THE BLACK SQUIRE TALK TOGETHER IN THE HALL OF THE CASTLE.

NOW within a few days was the body of Baudoin laid in earth in the chapel of the castle; and in the solemnest of fashions was the burial done. When it was over, the two knights and Sir Aymeris turned them heartily to dighting the war against the Red Hold, and less than a month thereafter was the hosting at the Castle of the Quest, and if the host were not very many (for it went not above sixteen hundreds of men all told), yet the men were of the choicest, both of knights and sergeants and archers. There then they held a mote without the castle, whereas Arthur the Black Squire was chosen for captain, and in three days they were to depart for the Red Hold.

Now this while Birdalone had seen but little of Arthur, who was ever busy about many matters, and never had she had any privy talk with him, though sore she longed for it; yet indeed it was more by her will than his that so it was. But when it was come to the very last day before the departure, she said that she must needs see him before he went, and he perchance never to come back again. So when men were quiet after dinner she went into the hall and found him there, pacing up and down the floor. For indeed she had sent a word to him by Leonard the priest that he should be there.

So she went up to him, and all simply she took him by the hand and led him into a shot-window and set him down by her; and he, all trembling for love and fear of her, might not forbear, but kissed her face and her mouth many times; and she grew as hot as fire, and somewhat she wept.

Then she spake after a while: "Dear friend, I had it in my mind to say to thee many things that meseems were sage, but now neither will the thought of them come into my mind, nor the words into my mouth. And this is a short hour." And therewith she fell to kissing him, till he was well nigh

beside himself betwixt desire and joy and the grief of departure, and the hardness of the case.

But at last she forbore and said: "Will it not be when thou art gone to-morrow as it was when ye were away upon the Quest, and I knew not how to bear myself, so heavy lay all the world and its doings and its fashion upon me?" "It will be hard to me," he said; "evil and grim will be the days."

She said: "And yet, even now in these last days, when I see thee oft every day, my soul is worn with grief, and I know not what to do with myself." "I shall come back," he said, "and bear my love with me, and then belike we shall seek some remedy."

She was silent a while, and then she said: "Meanwhile of thy coming, and I see thee not at all for many days, how will it be with my grief then?" Quoth he: "More than enough of grief no soul may bear; for either death comes, or else some dullness of the pain, and then by little and little the pain weareth."

Then she said: "And how would it be if thou come not back and I see thee never again, or if when thou come back thou find me not, for that I be either dead or gone away out of thy reach?" He said: "I know not how it would be. When thou sayest thou shalt die, dost thou wholly believe it in thy sense or thy body—otherwise than Holy Church would?"

"I will tell thee," she said, "that now I am sitting by thee and seeing thy face and hearing thy voice, it is that only which I believe in; for I may think of nought else of either grief or joy. Yea, when I wept e'en now, it was not for sorrow that I wept, but for I cannot rightly tell what." And she took his hand and looked fondly upon him.

But presently she looked on his hand, and said: "And now meseemeth that we twain are grown to be such close friends that I may ask thee what I will, and thou be neither angry, nor wonder thereat. I see on thy finger here the ring that I brought with me from the Isle of Increase, and which thereafter thou hadst of me when I gave thee back also the

247

shoon which were lent unto me. Tell me how thou hadst it
back from Atra, as I suppose thou gavest it unto her. But
how now! art thou angry? for I see the blood come up in thy
face."

"Nay, beloved," said he, "I am not angry, but whenso
I hear of Atra, or think of her closely, shame comes on me
and confusion, and maybe fear. But now will I answer thee.
For even in those hours which we wore on the Isle of the
Young and the Old, when all we should have been so happy
together, she divined somewhat of my case, or indeed, why
do I not say it out, all thereof. And she spake to me such
words (for she is both tender and wise and strong of heart)
that I cowered before her and her grief and pain; and she
gave me back the said ring, which forsooth I gave to her in
the Sending Boat in the first hour that the Isle of Increase
lay astern of us. And I wear it now as a token of my grief
for her grief. See now, love, since I have answered thee this
question without anger or amaze, thou needest not fear to
ask me any other. For this of all things lies closest to my
heart."

Birdalone drooped her head, and she spake in a low voice:
"Lo now! the shadow of parting and the shadow of death
could not come between our present joy; but this shadow
of the third one cometh between us and is present between
us. Woe's me! how little did I think of this when thou wert
away and I was sick of longing for the sight of thee, and
deemed that that would heal it all."

He spake not, but took her hand and held it; and presently she looked up again and said: "Thou art good, and
wilt not be angry if I ask thee something else; this it is:
Why wert thou so grim with me that other day when ye
found me in that evil plight in tow of the Red Tyrant, so
that I deemed that thou of all others hadst cast me off? That
was worse to me than the witch's stripes, and I kept thinking to myself: How simple was my trouble once, and now
how tangled and weary!"

Then he might not refrain him, but threw himself upon
248

her, and clipped her and kissed her all he might, and she felt
all the sweetness of love, and lacked nought of kindness and
love to him. And thereafter they sat still awhile, and he said,
as if her question had but that moment left her lips: "This,
forsooth, was the cause that I looked grim on thee: first, that
from the time I first saw thee and heard thy tale, and of thy
deeds, I had deemed thee wise above the wisdom of women.
But this going forth of thee to the Black Valley, whereof
came the slaying of Baudoin, seemed unto me a mere folly,
till again I had heard thy tale of that also ; and then the tale
and thy speech overcame me. But again, though I was
grieved and disappointed hereat, belike that had passed from
me speedily, but then there was this also which would not
let my soul rest, to wit, that I feared concerning that slain
knight whose head the Red One had hung about thy neck;
for how else, methought, might he have been so wroth with
him and thee; and meseemed, moreover, that thou wert kind
in thine heart to the dead man, even when we were come to
thee; and then, seest thou, my desire for thee and the trouble
of Baudoin's slaying, and the black trouble aforesaid. Lo
now, I have told thee this. When wilt thou cease to be angry
with me?"

She said: "I ceased to be grieved with thine anger when
thine anger died; yet strange, meseemeth, that thou shouldst
trust me so little when thou lovest me so much!"

And she leaned against him and caressed him gently, and
again was he at point to take her in his arms, when lo! the
sound of men coming unto the screen of the hall; so then
those two stood up and went to meet them, and there was the
speech of their sundering done. Yet belike for a little while
both those twain were happy.

CHAPTER XII. THE DEPARTURE OF THE KNIGHTS AND TIDINGS OF THEM.

ON the morrow, when the day was yet young, the knights were ready for departure, and in the very gate they bade farewell to the ladies, who kissed them kindly one and all, and Viridis wept sore, and Atra constrained herself to do even as the others did; but pale she was and quaking when she kissed Arthur and watched him get a-horseback.

But the knights bade their ladies be of good cheer, for that they would send them tidings of how they sped every seven days at least, whereas it was no long way thence to the Red Hold, save there were battle on the road, and they deemed their host which should beset the Hold would be enough to clear all the ways behind it. For that same cause withal they had Sir Aymeris with them, nor left a many men behind them, and they under the rule of three squires, whereof two were but young, and the third, who was made the captain of the castle, was an old and wise man of war, who had to name Geoffrey of Lea. There, withal, was the priest Sir Leonard, who went about now much hushed and abashed, and seemed to fear to give a word to Birdalone; albeit she deemed of him that his thoughts of her were the same as erst they had been.

So now when the knights were departed, and all the host was gone out of sight, it was heavy time indeed in the Castle of the Quest till they should hear tidings of them again. Both Aurea and Atra kept much to themselves, and did I know not what to wear away the time; for now it was not to be looked for that they should venture out-a-gates. But as for Viridis, she waxed of better cheer after a while, but whatever betid she would not sunder herself from Birdalone; nay, not for an hour; and Birdalone took all her kindness kindly, though forsooth it was somewhat of a pain unto her; it shall be told wherefore ere long.

Withal, as if to wear the time, Birdalone betook her diligently to her needlework, and fell to the cunningest of broidery; so that Viridis and the others wondered at her, for when they were done it seemed indeed that the flowers and creatures and knots had grown of themselves upon the cloth, such wondrous work it was.

Moreover, to his great joy, the very first day of the departure of the host she called Sir Leonard unto her, and prayed to go on again with the learning her fair scribe-craft; and therein also was she diligent hours of every day; and Viridis would sit beside her wondering at the deftness of her fingers, and crying out for joy as the page grew fair and well-learned under them.

Thus wore a week, and at the end thereof came a messenger from the host and told how they had come before the Red Hold and had summoned them thereof to yield, which they had utterly denied to do, but defied the host; wherefore the host had now beset the Hold, and more folk were daily flocking unto them; but that the said Hold would be hard to win by plain assault, whereas it was both strong and well-manned; but few of the host had been slain or hurt as yet, and of the chieftains not one.

Right glad were they of the Castle because of these tidings; though, forsooth, the men-at-arms knew well enough that the time would soon come when some fierce assault would be made, and then, forsooth, would be sore peril of life and limb unto the chieftains.

CHAPTER XIII. BIRDALONE BETHINKS HER TO FULFIL THE PROMISE MADE UNTO ATRA.

AGAIN wore a week, and once more came the messenger, and did them of the Castle to wit that there had been nought more done at the Red Hold, save skirmishing at the barriers, wherein few were hurt on either side; and also that the engines for battering the walls were

now well nigh all dight, and they would begin to play upon
the Hold, and in especial one which hight Wall-wolf, which
had been set up by the crafts of Greenford.

This tidings also was deemed good by all, save it might be
by Atra, who, as Birdalone deemed, pined and fretted herself at the delay, and would fain that, one way or other, all
were over. Atra spake but little to Birdalone, but watched
her closely now; oft would she gaze on her wistfully, as if
she would that Birdalone would speak unto her; and Birdalone noted that, but she might not pluck up heart thereto.

Wore a third week, and again came the messenger, and
told how three days ago, whenas Wall-wolf had sorely bat-
tered one of the great towers which hight the Poison-jar,
and overthrown a pan of the wall there beside, they had
tried an assault on the breach, and hard had been the battle
there, and in the end, after fierce give and take, they of the
Hold had done so valiantly that they had thrust back the
assailants, and that in the hottest brunt the Black Squire had
been hurt in the shoulder by a spear-thrust, but not very
grievously; but withal that he sent, in so many words, forbidding the ladies to make any account of so small a matter.
"And," quoth the sergeant, "most like my lord will wear
his armour in four days' time; also now we have reared another great slinger, which we call Stone-fretter, and soon,
without doubt, we shall be standing victorious within that
den of thieves."

Now though these tidings were not so altogether ill, yet
were those ladies sore troubled thereby, and especially Atra,
who swooned outright when she had heard the last word
thereof.

As for Birdalone, she made as little semblance of her
trouble as she might, but when all was quiet again she went
to find Viridis, and brought her to her chamber and spake to
her, saying: "Viridis, my sister, thou hast been piteous kind
unto me from the first minute that thou sawest me naked
and helpless and fleeing from evil unto worse evil; nowise
mightest thou have done better by me hadst thou been

verily my sister of blood; and I know it that thou wouldst
be loth to part from me."

Viridis wept and said: "Why dost thou speak of parting
from me, when thou knowest it would break my heart?"

Said Birdalone: "To say it as short as may be, because the
parting must now come to pass." Viridis waxed pale and
then red, and she stamped her foot and said: "It is unkind
of thee to grieve me thus, and thou doest wrong herein."

"Hearken, dear sister," said Birdalone: "thou knowest,
for thou thyself wast the first to tell me thereof, that I am the
supplanter in our fellowship, and that I have undone Atra's
hope. This I did not of mine own will, but it came unto me;
yet of mine own will I can do the best I may to amend it;
and this is the best, that I depart hence before the Red Hold
is taken and my lords come back; for if they come back and
I see my lord Arthur, so fair and beauteous as he is, before
me, never shall I be able to go away from him. And lo thou,
I have promised Atra by all the kindness she did me when
we were come to the Wailing Tower, and I naked and quaking and half-dead with terror, that if occasion served I would
do my utmost to help her, even if it were to my own grief.
Now behold this that now is, is the occasion, and there will
not be another. For when my love comes home hither and
beholdeth me, think thou how all the desire which has been
gathering in his heart this while will blossom and break
forth toward me; and mayhappen he will make but little
semblance of it before other folk, for proud and high of
heart is he; but he will seek occasion to find me alone, and
then shall I be with him as the lark in the talons of the spar-
row-hawk, and he will do his pleasure of me, and that with
all the good-will of my heart. And then shall I be forsworn
to Atra, and she will hate me, as now she doth not, and then
is all the fellowship riven, and that by my deed."

Yet was Viridis wrath, and she said: "Meseemeth this is
fool's talk. Will not the fellowship be all the more riven if
thou depart and we see thee no more?"

"O nay," said Birdalone; "for when I am gone thy love

shall be no less for me, though as now thou art angry; and
Atra will love me for that I shall have held to my promise to
mine own scathe; and thy man and Aurea will lay it to me that
I have done valiantly and knightly. And Arthur, how can
he choose but love me; and—and maybe we shall yet meet
again."

And therewithal she did at last bow down her head and
fall to weeping, and Viridis was moved by her tears and fell
to kissing and caressing her.

After a little Birdalone lifted up her head and spake again:
"Moreover, how can I dare to abide him? didst thou not see
how grim he was to me when they delivered me and brought
me back? and he with his own lips told me so much, that it
was because he doubted that I had done amiss; and now if I
do amiss again, even if it be at his bidding, will it not be so
that he will speedily weary of me, and curse me and cast me
off? What sayest thou, Viridis mine?"

"What is to say," said Viridis, "save that thou hast
broken my heart? But thou mayst heal it if thou wilt take
thy words back, and tell me that thou wilt not sunder thee
from us."

But Birdalone brake out weeping and lamenting aloud,
and she cried out: "Nay, nay, it may not be; I must depart,
and Atra hath smitten me amidst of my friends." And Viridis knew not what to say or to do.

At last came Birdalone to herself again, and she looked
sweetly on Viridis and smiled on her from out her tears, and
said: "Thou seest, sister, how little a loss thou wilt have of
me, a mere wild woman. And now nought availeth either
me or thee but I must begone, and that speedily. Let it be
to-morrow then. And when the messenger comes at the end
of this week, send word by him of what I have done; and
look thou to it but both our lords will praise me for the
deed."

Said Viridis: "But whither wilt thou, or what wilt thou
do?" "To Greenford first," said Birdalone, "and after

254

whither the Good Lord shall lead me; and as for what I will
do, I am now deft in two crafts, script and broidery to wit;
and wheresoever I be, folk shall pay me to work herein for
them, whereby I shall earn my bread. Hearken also, my
sister, canst thou give me any deal of money? for though I
wot little of such matters, yet I wot that I shall need the
same. And I ask this whereas, as e'en now I said, I deem our
lords shall praise my deed, and that therefore they would
not that I should depart hence as an outcast, wherefore they
shall not begrudge it to me. Moreover, for the same cause I
would have thee speak to the old squire Geoffrey of Lea, and
tell him that I have an errand to Greenford, and crave of
him that he lend me one of the two younglings, Arnold or
Anselm, and two or three men-at-arms to bring me safely
thither; since now forsooth I need no more adventures on
the road."

She smiled as she spake; and now all the passion of anguish seemed to have left her for that while; but Viridis cast
her arms about her neck and wept upon her bosom and said:
"Woe's me! for I see that thou wilt go whatsoever I may say
or do; I strove to be angry with thee, but I might not, and
now I see that thou constrainest me as thou dost all else. I
will go now straightway and do thine errand."

Thus then they parted for that time; but it was not till the
day after the morrow that Birdalone was alboun. Viridis told
of her departure both to Aurea and Atra; and Aurea lamented it, but would not do aught to stay her; for she was waxen
weary and listless since the death of her man. As for Atra,
she spake but little concerning it, but to Viridis praised
Birdalone's valiance and kindness. Yet unto herself she
said: Verily she understood my word that I spake to her
about the occasion of her helping. Yet woe's me! for she shall
carry his love with her whithersoever she wendeth; and a
happy woman is she.

But when Geoffrey the squire knew that the ladies, all
three, were at one with Birdalone as to her departure, he

doubted nothing, but bade Arnold, his mate, take four good
men with him, and bring the Lady Birdalone unto Greenford and do her bidding there. Albeit, he deemed no less
but they would bring her back again.

CHAPTER XIV. BIRDALONE LEAVES THE CASTLE OF THE QUEST.

ON the morrow morn, then, Birdalone spake farewell
both to Aurea and Atra; but as for Viridis, she sent
her word that she had no heart thereto, and yet she
sent her a word of comfort, to wit, that she deemed that they
would one day meet again. Aurea, in her parting words, part
praised her, part chid her; saying that she did well and kindly
and valiantly, as her wont was. "Yet," said she, "when all is
said, thou mightest have abided this tangle and trouble,
which at the worst had not been so evil as death between us."
"Yea, sister," said Birdalone, "but might not death have
come of my abiding?"

As she spake, in came Atra, with her head somewhat
drooped, meek and humble, her cheeks red, her hands
trembling; and she said: "Wilt thou take now my word of
farewell and blessing, and the kiss of peace betwixt us, and
bear away the memory of our kindness together?"

Birdalone stood up proud and straight, and was somewhat
pale as she suffered Atra to kiss her cheeks and mouth, and
said: "Now hast thou forgiven me that Weird dragged me
in betwixt thy love and thy goodhap; and I have forgiven
thee that I am led away by Weird into the waste and the
wilderness of love. Farewell." Therewith she went her way
to the gate, and the others followed her not.

Without abode her Arnold and the four men-at-arms, and
her palfrey and a sumpter-horse bearing two goodly coffers,
wherein Viridis had let load raiment and other havings for
her; and Arnold came up to her smiling, and said: "My lady
Viridis hath given me a pouch wherein is money to bear for
thee to Greenford and hand over to thee there when we be

256

safe; and she hath bidden me to be in all wise obedient unto thee, lady, which needed not: whereas now and from hence- forth am I by mine own will thy very servant to do thy pleasure always and everywhere."

She thanked him and smiled on him kindly, so that his heart beat fast for joy and love of her; and therewith she gat into the saddle and they rode their ways together, and Bird-alone looked back never till the Castle of the Quest was shut from their eyes by the nesses of the little hills.

HERE ENDS THE FIFTH PART OF THE WATER OF THE WONDROUS ISLES, WHICH IS CALLED THE TALE OF THE QUEST'S ENDING, AND BE-GINS THE SIXTH PART OF THE SAID TALE, WHICH IS CALLED THE DAYS OF ABSENCE.

THE WATER OF THE WONDROUS ISLES. THE SIXTH PART: THE DAYS OF ABSENCE.

CHAPTER I. BIRDALONE RIDETH TO GREENFORD.

NOUGHT there is to tell of tidings on the road to Greenford; they came thither when the sun was at point to set, for they had ridden diligently all day.

As they rode the streets of the good town, they noted of them, that though it was evening wherein folk do much disport them abroad, there were women and children enough in the streets or standing at their doors, but of carles very few, and they for the more part grey-heads.

Now did Arnold bring Birdalone to the town hall, wherein yet sat the deputy of the Burgreve, who himself was in the leaguer at the Red Hold; this man, who was old and wise and nothing feeble of body, made much of Birdalone and her folk, and was glad of them when he knew that they had the seal and let-pass of Geoffrey of Lea; wherefore he gave them to eat and drink, and lodged them in his own house, and made them the best of cheer.

But betimes on the morrow did Birdalone send back Arnold and the four men-at-arms, with no tale but that such was her will; and bidding farewell to the said Arnold, she suffered him to kiss her hands, and gave him a ring from off her finger, so that he went on his way rejoicing.

So soon as she saw him and his men well on the road, she went to the old man, the vice-ruler of the town, who was of the aldermen thereof, and did him to wit that she would wage two or three carles who could deal with horses and beasts, and withal handle weapons if need were, to be both as servants and guards for her, as she had errands in that country-side, and belike might well have to go from town to town thereabout. He took her asking kindly, but said it was none so easy to find men who for any wage would fare forth

of Greenford at that stour, whereas well-nigh all their fight-
ing-men were lying before the Red Hold as now. Howsoever, ere noontide he brought before her a man of over three
score, but yet wayworthy, and two stout young men, his
sons, and told her that these men were trusty and would go
with her to the world's end if need were.

She took these men readily, and agreed with them for a
good wage; and whereas each one had bow and arrows and
short sword, she had but to buy for them jacks, sallets, and
bucklers, and they were well armed as for their condition.
Withal she bought them three good horses and another
sumpter-horse; which last was loaded with sundry wares that
she deemed that she needed, and with victual. Then she took
leave of the alderman, thanking him much for his good will,
and so departed from Greenford at all adventure, when the
day was yet young.

The alderman had asked her whither away, and she had
told him that she was boun for Mostwyke first, and thereafter for Shifford on the Strand; whereas she had heard talk
of these two towns as being on one and the same highway,
and Mostwyke about a score of miles from Greenford; but
when she was well out-a-gates she came to a little road on the
right hand which turned clean away from Mostwyke, and
she took the said road; and when she had followed it some
three miles, she asked the old carle whither it led. He looked
on her and smiled somewhat, and she on him in turn; and
she said: "Wonder not, my friend, that I am not clear about
my ways, for I shall tell the sooth that I am a damsel adventurous, and am but seeking some place where I may dwell
and earn my livelihood till better days come; and this is the
whole truth, and thou shalt know it at once, to wit, that I
am indeed fleeing, and were fain to hide the footsteps of me,
and I bid you three to help me therein. But ye must know
that I am fleeing, not from my foes, but from my friends;
and if ye will, as we go by the way, I will tell you all the
story of me, and we will be friends while we are together,
yea and thereafter if it may be."

Now she said this because she had looked carefully on

s2   259

these men, and her seemed that they were good men and true, and not dull of wit. Forsooth the old man, who hight Gerard of the Clee, was no weakling, and was nought loathly to look on, and his two sons were goodly and great of fashion, clear-eyed, and well-carven of visage; they hight Robert and Giles.

Now spake old Gerard: "Lady, I thank thee heartily of thy much grace unto me; now would I get off my nag and kneel to thee in the highway therefor, but that I see that thou wert fain to make as much way as may be to-day; wherefore, by thy leave, I will tarry my homaging till we rest our horses by the wayside." She laughed and praised his wisdom, and the young men looked on her and worshipped her in their hearts. Forsooth, the fellowship of these good and true folk was soft and sweet to her, and soothed the trouble of her spirit. And she enforced herself to talk cheerfully with them, and asked them many things and learned much of them.

But now went on Gerard to say: "Lady, if thou wilt hide thy ways from whomsoever it may be, thou hast happened on no ill way; for though this road be good to ride, it is but a byway through the sheepwalks that folk may drive their wains hereby in the wet season of winter and spring; and for a great way we shall come to but little save the cots of the sheep-carles, scarce a hamlet or two for the space of two days' riding; and on the third day a little town hight Upham, where are but few folk save at the midsummer wool-fair, which is now gone by.

"Now there is a highway cometh into this road from out of the tilled country and Appleham, a good town, and goeth through it toward the tillage and the City of the Bridges and the Liberties thereof; and all that land is much builded and plentiful; but, if thou wilt, we will not take either high-way, but wend over the downland which lieth north-east of Upham, and though it be roadless, yet is it not ill going, and I know it well and its watering-places, little dales and waters therein all running north-east, wherein be certain little thorps here and there, which shall refresh us mightily. Over that downland we may wend a four days, and then the land will

260

swell up high, and from the end of that high land we shall behold below us a fair land of tillage, well watered and wooded,
and much builded; and in the midst thereof a great city with
walls and towers, and a great white castle and a minster, and
lovely houses a many. In that city mayest thou dwell and
earn thy livelihood if thou canst do aught of crafts. And if
thou mayst not, then may we find somewhat to swink at for
a wage, and so maintain thee and us. But the said city is called
the City of the Five Crafts, and the land round about it is the
Frank thereof; and oftenest, Frank and City and all, it is
called the Five Crafts all simply. Now what sayest thou hereof, my lady?"

She said: "I say that we will go thither, and that I thank
thee and thy sons of thy good-will, and so may God do to me
as I reward you well therefor. But tell me, good Gerard, how
it is that thou art so willing to leave kith and kin to follow a
gangrel wife along the ways?"

Said Gerard: "Dame, I think that the face and body of
thee might lead any man that yet had manhood in him to follow thee, even if he left house and all to go with thee. But as
for us, we have no longer a house or gear, whereas they of the
Red Hold lifted all my bestial, and burned my house and all
that was therein a month ago."

"Yea," said Birdalone, "and how befalleth it, then, that
ye are not before the Red Hold to avenge thee?"

"Dame," said he, "when the muster was I was deemed
somewhat over old, wherefore the sheriff took me not, but
suffered my sons also to abide behind to earn a living for me;
may God be good to him therefor, and St. Leonard! But as
to my kindred, I must tell thee that I am not kinned hereabout, but in a good town hight Utterhay, and that when our
alderman sent for me to bring me to thee, I was more than
half-minded to get me back thither. Now sooth it is that the
best way thither, though it may be indeed the safest rather
than the shortest, lies through the Five Crafts: for the road
goes thence to Utterhay a three score miles or so, making the
longer of it, as it skirteth ever some way off a perilous forest,

a place of sore dread and devilish, which hight Evilshaw, on the edge whereof lieth Utterhay, a merry cheaping-stead and a plenteous, and the home of my kindred. Wherefore now is the City of the Five Crafts handy to us; because when thou hast done with us, as I hope it may be long first, then are we others nigh home, and may all simply wend our way thither."

Birdalone thanked him again full heartily; but therewithal as they rode along there seemed to stir in her some memory of the earliest of her days in the witch's house, and she began to have a longing to betake her to Utterhay and the skirts of Evilshaw.

CHAPTER II. THEY FARE OVER THE DOWN-LAND.

THUS rode they along and loitered not, though they talked blithely together; and Birdalone wondered to herself that she might so much as hold up her head for bitter thoughts of the days and the longings but late passed away, but so it was, that it was only now and again that they stung her into despair and silence, and for the most part she hearkened to the talk of the old man and the lads about the days of Greenford and the alarms of lifting and unpeace, and the ways of the chapmen and the craftsmen.

An hour after noon they rested in a little dale of the downland where was a pool and three thorn-bushes thereby; and when they had lighted down, the old man knelt before Birdalone and took her hand, and swore himself her man to do her will, whatso it were; and then he stood up and bade his sons do likewise; so they two knelt before her in turn, somewhat shy and abashed, for all that they were such stout, bold fellows, and found it hard to take her hand, and then when they had it in theirs, hard to let it go again.

A score of miles and five they rode that day, and had no roof over them at night save the naked heaven, but to Birdalone that was but little scathe: they made a shift to have some fire by them, and the three men sat long about it that even

while Birdalone told them somewhat of her life; and as she
told of the House under the Wood and the Great Water,
Gerard had some inkling of whereabouts it was; but was
nought so sure, because, as above-said in this tale, seldom
did any from the world of men venture in Evilshaw, or know
of the Great Water from its banks that gave unto the Forest.

In like wise they rode the next day, and came at eventide
to a thorp in a fair little dale of the downland, and there they
guested with the shepherd-folk, who wondered much at the
beauty of Birdalone, so that at first they scarce durst venture
to draw nigh unto her until Gerard and his sons had had some
familiar converse with them. Then indeed they exceeded in
kindness toward them, in their rough upland fashion, but
ever found it hard to keep their eyes off Birdalone, and that
the more after they had heard the full sweetness of her voice;
whereas she sang to them certain songs which she had learned
in the Castle of the Quest, though it made her heart sore;
but she deemed she must needs pay that kindly folk for their
guestful and blithe ways. And thereafter they sang to the pipe
and the harp their own downland songs; and this she found
strange, that whereas her eyes were dry when she was singing the songs of love of the knighthood, the wildness of the
shepherd-music drew the tears from her, would she, would
she not. Homelike and dear seemed the green willowy dale
to her, and in the night ere she slept, and she lay quiet amidst
of the peaceful people, she could not choose but weep again,
for pity of the bitter-sweet of her own love, and for pity of
the wide world withal, and all the ways of its many folk that
lay so new before her.

CHAPTER III. THEY COME TO THE CITY OF THE FIVE CRAFTS, AND BIRDALONE MEETS WITH THE POOR-WIFE.

THEY made not so much way that they came to the Five Crafts on the fourth day, but lay under the bare heavens in a dale below the big swell of the downland, whereof Gerard spake. But betimes in the morning Birdalone arose and stirred up her men, and they gat to horse, and rode the hill before them till they came on to the crest thereof. Then Birdalone cried aloud with joy to see the lovely land before her, and the white walls and the towers of the great city, whereas Greenford was but small beside it.

So they rode down into the frank, and entered the gates of the city a little after noon, and again was Birdalone in all amaze at the going to and fro in the streets and the thronging of the markets, and the divers folk, as chapmen and men-at-arms, and craftsmen and lords, who used the said city; and to say sooth, somewhat her heart sank within her, and it seemed to her that it would be hard and troublous to have to deal with so much folk, and that they must needs go past her on the right hand and the left without heeding her life.

Howsoever, Gerard, who knew the city, brought her to a fair hostel, where she was well lodged, she and her men. Straightway, then, before she went out into the streets again, she fell to getting together what she had of fine broidered work and of fair script, and to finishing what she had unfinished. And she sent forth Gerard and his sons to find out where was the market for such goods, and if she would have leave to sell the same therein, or anywhere in the town; and Gerard found the hall of the Embroiderers, and therein the master of the craft, and he received the carle courteously when he heard that there was fine work come to town, and did him to wit that none in any such craft might have freedom of the market save by leave of the gild of the craft: but, said he, the gilds were open-handed and courteous, and were nowise wont to refuse the said leave, were the work good and true; and he bade Gerard withal tell his mistress that she were best to bring samplings of her work to the Gild-hall so soon as she might.

So the very next day went Birdalone thither, and found the Master a well-looked tall man of some five-and-forty winters, who looked on her from the first as if he deemed it were no ill way of wearing the time. To this man she showed her work, and though he found it not easy to take his eyes off Birdalone herself, yet when he looked at her handiwork, he found it better than very good, and he said to her: "Damsel, here is what will be sought for at a great price by the great lords and ladies of the land, and the rich burgesses, and especially by the high prelates; and so much of it as thou hast a mind to do is so much coined gold unto thee; and now I see thee what thou art, I were fain that thou gathered good to thee. But as diligent as thou mayst be, thou hast but one pair of hands, wonderful soothly, and yet but one pair."

He broke off at that word, for he was verily staring at her hands, and longing to see more of her arms than the wrists only, so that he scarce knew what he was saying. Then he turned red and said: "Soothly I wot that no other hands save thine may do such needlework, or make the draughts for them. But thou wilt need women-servants to help thee, both in dighting the house for thee (for this big old carle here will be scarce meet thereto) and as apprentices to help thee about the work itself; and if thou wilt, I shall seek the best ones out for thee. Moreover I must tell thee, that though I know for sure how that no woman in the world may work such needlework as thine, yet whiles there cometh hither a woman of middle age, a woman worn by troubles, pious, meek, and kind; and by St. Lucia! now I look on thee again, she might be somewhat like unto thee, were she young and fresh-looking and strong as thou art. Now this woman I say, and thereat I marvel, doeth needlework that is somewhat after the manner of thine, and which seemed to

265

us excellent till I had seen thine. Good livelihood she earneth thereby, and is diligent therein; but she hath no heart to get apprentices, or be made one of our gild, both of which were lawful to her as to thee, lovely damsel. But now I shall counsel her to be made of our gild along with thee, if thou wilt have it so, and then may ye both have three apprentices each, and may make in our city a goodly school, so that our gild shall be glorified thereby, for there will be none such work in the world. How sayest thou?"

She thanked him much, and yeasaid him, and thought in her heart that such work which would keep her hands and her head both busy, would solace the grief of her heart, and wear away the time, that she might live till hope might peradventure arise in her.

Then said the Master: "There is one thing else, that is, thy dwelling-place; and if thou wilt I shall hire thee a house in the street of the Broiderers, a goodly one: sooth to say, that same is mine own, so thou mayst deem that I tell thee hereof to mine own [gain]; and that may be" (and he reddened therewith), "but there is this in it, that if thou lackest money I shall let thee live therein without price till thou shalt have earned more than enough to pay me."

Birdalone thanked him well, but she did him to wit that she was nowise penniless; and presently she departed well pleased, though she deemed that the said Master was wellnigh more friendly than might be looked for. And the next day he came to her in the hostelry, and without more ado brought her to the house in the street of the Broiderers, and she found it fair and well plenished, and so she fell to work to get all things ready.

Now the next week was the day appointed when she should be received into the Broiderers' Gild, and the day before came the Master aforesaid to see Birdalone. Sooth to say, he had not failed to come see her every day, on one pretence or another, since the first day they had met, but ever he did to her with all honour and simply. But on this day he

266

brought with him the woman skilful of her hands, to show
her unto Birdalone, who received her gladly, and thereafter
Master Jacobus left them alone together.

The said woman looked worn and aged indeed, but was
not of more than five-and-forty winters even by seeming,
after the first look at her; she was somewhat tall and well-
knit, her face well shapen, and her hair yet goodly. There
was a kind look in the eyes of her, as if she might love anyone with whom she lived that would be kind to her. Meek,
or rather over-meek, of mien she was, and it seemed of her
that she had been sore scared and oppressed one while or
another.

So when Master Jacobus was gone, Birdalone set her
down on the settle beside her, and spake to her full sweetly
and kindly, and the woman spake little in turn save answering simply to her questions. Birdalone asked where she was
kinned, and she answered: "In Utterhay."

Then said Birdalone: "Within these last few days I have
heard that town named twice or thrice, and never before, as
meseemeth; and yet, hearing the name from thy mouth, it
seemeth to stir something in me, as if I had been there one
time and longed to be there again. Is there aught in the place
whereof folk tell wide about, so that I might have heard it
told of and not noted it at the time?"

"Nay, lady," said the dame, "save perchance that it is on
the verge of a very great and very evil wood, otherwise it
was once a merry town and of much resort from the country-
side."

Birdalone looked on her, and saw that the tears were
coming from her eyes and running down her cheeks as she
spake; so she said to her: "Why dost thou weep, mother? Is
there aught I may do to assuage thy grief?"

Said the dame: "Thou art so kind to me, and thy voice is
so dear and sweet, that I cannot choose but weep. Meseems
it is because love of thee hath taken mine heart, and therewith is blended memory of past sorrow of mine. Thou askest

267

me if thou mayest do aught to assuage my grief; dear lady, I am not grieved now, that has gone by; nay, now I am more than not grieved, I am made happy, because I am with thee. But since thou art so debonaire with me, I will ask thee to do somewhat for me; and that is, to tell me somewhat of thy life gone by; I mean, sweet young damsel, of thy life when thou wert a little child."

Then Birdalone kissed her and said: "It goes to my heart that thou lovest me; for soon as I set eyes on thee my heart went out to thee; and now belike we shall be dear friends; and that is a thing that shall avail me much, to have a friend who is so much older than I, so that nought can come between us, of the love of men and other griefs."

"Yea, now," said the dame, smiling somewhat sadly; "now do I see the water standing in thine eyes, and thy voice quavers. Is it so, thou lovely kind damsel, that thou hast been grieved by love of a man? Who then may prevail in love if thou prevail not?" And she fell to fondling Birdalone's hand; but Birdalone said: "It is over long to tell of all my life, mother, though I be so young; but now I will do as thou badest me, and tell thee somewhat of my days when I was little."

And therewith she fell to telling her of her days in the House under the Wood, and the witch and her surliness and grimness, and of her love of the wild things, and how she waxed there. And she spake a long while, for the memory of those days seemed to lead her along, as though she verily were alive now in them; and the woman sat before her, gazing on her lovingly, till Birdalone stayed her tale at last and said: "Now have I told thee more than enough of a simple matter, and a life that was as that of a wild creature of the woods. Now shalt thou, mother, tell me somewhat of thee, and what was thy grief of Utterhay: for thou shalt find that the telling thereof shall solace thee."

"Ah! so think young folk," said the woman sadly, "because there are many days left for them to hope in. But
268

though the telling of my sorrow be a fresh sorrow to me, yet PART VI
shalt thou hear it. It is but of the loss of my babe; but she Chap. 3
was of all babes the fairest and the sweetest."

Then she fell to telling Birdalone all that concerning the
witch at Utterhay and the poor-wife that ye have heard in
the beginning of this book, until the time when she left the
house to buy meat for the witch; for she herself was the said
poor-wife. And then she told how she came back again and
found her guest gone and the child withal; and though she
had wept for love of Birdalone, she wept not at telling of this
grief, but told it as a tale which had befallen some other one.
And she said: "And so when I had done running up and
down like a wild thing, and asking of the neighbours with
lack of breath and fierceness of speech, who had taken my
child away from me; and when I had gone up to the wood
and even some way into it, and when I had wandered up and
down again, and night was falling, I came back again to my
poor house so weary with my woe, that I scarce knew what
had befallen me. And there upon the board lay the victual and
drink which I had brought, and the money which the witch
had given unto me; and despite of grief, hunger flamed up
in me at the sight, and I threw myself on to it and ate and
drank, and so came to myself, that is, to my grief. But the
next day I ran about hither and thither, and wearied folk with
my asking and my woe; but it was all of none avail. The child
was gone away from me. There is little more to tell of me,
sweet lady. If I were to live, needs must I take the poor price
of my little one, to wit, the witch's money, and deal with folk
for my livelihood; wherefore I bought me cloth and silks,
having now the wherewithal, and set to work on broidery,
for even then was I a cunning needle-woman. So were God
and the Saints good to me, and inclined the folk to me, that
they were good and piteous, and I lacked not work nor due
livelihood; but after a while I wearied of Utterhay, where my
dear child should have been running about before my feet;
and having by this time gotten a little money together, and

269

being exceeding deft in my craft, I came on hither to live, and praise be to St. Ursula! I have found it easy to live: and praise be to Allhallows withal that I have found thee, who art so kind and lovely; and thou by seeming of the very age my child should be if she be living: or how old art thou, dear lady?"

Birdalone laid her hand on her breast, and she was turned pale, but she said in a low voice: "I deem that I am of twenty summers."

Then they both sat silent, till Birdalone might master the fluttering of her heart, and she said: "Now meseems I have a memory even earlier than those I told thee erst. A woman took me out of a basket and set me on the back of an ass, and I looked about, and I was in a grassy lawn of the woods; and I saw a squirrel run up a tree-trunk before me, and wind round the tree and hide him; and then I stretched out my hands and cried out to him; and then came the woman unto me, and gave me wood-strawberries to eat out of her hand."

Brake out the poor-wife thereat, pale and trembling: "Tell me now, my child, hast thou any memory of what the woman was who set thee on the ass and gave thee the straw-berries?" Birdalone looked on her, and scanned her face closely, and then shook her head, and said: "Nay, it was not thou, mother."

"Nay surely, nay surely," said the woman; "but think again." Said Birdalone, speaking slowly: "Was it my mistress then? She was a tall woman, somewhat thin and bony, with goodly red hair and white-skinned, but thin-lipped." Quoth the poor-wife: "No, no; it is of no use; nought such was she."

Then Birdalone looked up and said eagerly: "Yea, but it was her other shape belike: therein was she a tall woman, dark-haired, hook-nosed, and hawk-eyed, as if of thirty summers; a stark woman. Hast thou seen such? dost thou remember her?"

The woman sprang up and cried out, and was like to have

270

fallen, but Birdalone arose and held her in her arms and
comforted her, and set her in her seat again and knelt before
her; and presently the poor-wife came to herself and said:
"My child, thou sayest do I remember her; how shall I ever
forget her? she was the thief who stole my child."

Therewith she slid from off her seat, and knelt by Birdalone, and stooped low down on the floor as if the tall maiden
were but a little one, and she fell to kissing her and patting
her, her face and her hands, and all about; and said, sobbing
and yet smiling: "Suffer me a little, my child, mine own
lovely child! For in good sooth I am thy mother, and it is
long since I have seen thee: but hearken, when I come quite
to myself I shall pray thee not to leave me yet awhile, and I
shall pray thee to love me."

Birdalone clipped and kissed her, and said: "I love thee
dearly, and never, never shall I leave thee."

Then they stood up, and the mother took Birdalone by
the shoulders, and held her a little aloof, and devoured her
with her eyes; and she said: "Yea, thou hast grown tall, and
belike wilt grow no taller: and how fair and lovely thou hast
grown; and thou that wert born in a poor man's house! no
wonder that any should covet thee. And I, I wonder if ever
I was as fair as thou art; forsooth many called me fair for a
little while; and now behold me! Nay, child and darling, let
not thy face grow downcast, for now shall I know nought
more of fear and grief; and is it not like that I shall grow
fairer of flesh, and shapelier, in the happy days we shall dwell
together?" And therewith she took her to her arms, and it
seemed as if she might never have enough of clipping and
embracing her; and she would look at Birdalone's hands and
her feet and her arms, and stroke them and caress them; and
she wondered at her body, as if she had been a young mother
eaten up with the love of her first-born.

And as for Birdalone, she was as glad of her mother as
might be; and yet in her heart she wondered if perchance
one of the fellowship might stray that way, and be partaker
in her joy of this new-found dear friend; and she said, might

it be Viridis; but in her inmost heart, though she told it not
to herself, she longed that the Black Squire might find her
out at last.

CHAPTER IV. OF THE LOVE OF GERARD'S SONS AND OF JACOBUS FOR BIRDALONE.

NOW dwelt Birdalone in rest and peace when she had
been taken into the gild along with her mother, and
they had taken the due apprentices to them; and they
began to gather much of goods to them, for of fine broidery
there was little done in the Five Crafts, and none at all that
could be put beside their work, either for beauty of the draft
of it, or for skill of handiwork. She declared unto all folk
how that the poor-wife (who had to name Audrey) was her
very mother, from whom she had been stolen in her young-
est days; but she told none any tale of how she was stolen.
And the twain dwelt together in the greatest loving-kindness; and it was with Audrey as she had forecast, that now
her days were happy, and she living in all ease and content,
that the goodliness of her youth came back to her, and she
became a fair woman as for her years; and therewith it grew
to be clear that the two were so much alike one to the other,
that all might see that they were mother and daughter.

Gerard and his two sons she maintained yet as her men;
and not only were they of much use to her in fetching and
carrying, but also true it is that her beauty was so manifest,
that she whiles needed a stout lad weaponed at her back
when she was in the streets or amidst the throng of the market; and many were they, and whiles of the highest, who
craved love of her, some with honour, and some with lack
of it.

Of these, forsooth, were but two that anywise troubled
her; and the most trouble was this, that she might not fail to
see that the love of her had entered into the hearts of the two
Gerardsons, Robert and Giles; so that times were when she
deemed she must even send them away, but when it came to

272

the point she had not the heart thereto; though none other
remedy there seemed, so sorely as their souls were wounded
by longing for her. It is not to be said that they ever spake to
her thereof, or wittingly wearied her with signs of love; but
they could not so easily cover it up but that it was ever before
her eyes. But she suffered it all for friendship's sake and
for their true service, and in all friendliness did what she
might to solace their grief. Forsooth so good and true she
found that fatherkind, and the young men so goodly and
kind, that she said to herself, had she not another man lying
in her heart, she might well have chosen one of those twain
for her very speech-friend and true lover.

The second wooer that troubled her was the Master
Jacobus, who, when but three months were worn of her
dwelling in his house, did all openly crave her love and offer
her marriage, he being a man unwedded. Sore was her heart
that she must needs gainsay him, so kind and courteous as
he had been to her at their first coming together: though this
indeed is sooth, that straightway, so soon as he saw her, he
fell into the captivity of her love. Howsoever, gainsay him
she needs must, and he took the naysay so hardly that he was
scarce like a man before her, and wept and prayed and lamented many times over, till she wearied of it, and well-nigh
fell to loathing him. So that it came to this at last, that one
day she spake to him and said that she might no longer bear
it, but must seek another house and leave his. There then
was the to-do, for he fell on his knees before her, and kissed
her feet, would she, would she not, and cried out in his grief,
till at last for pure weariness of his folly she gave way unto
him, and said that she would still abide there; whereon he
rose up from her and went away with all the grief run off him
for that time, and as glad a man to look on as you might see
on a summer's day.

But the next morning he came unto her again, and she
thinking all was begun afresh, made him no glad countenance; but he stood up before her and spake friendly, and said
how that she was in the right of it, and that if they both dwelt

in one house together they were like to have but a weary
time of it, both she and he. "But," said he, "I will not that
thou shouldst depart out of this house, for a goodly one it is,
and full meet for thee: it is for me to depart, and not for thee.
I tell thee, forsooth, that I had from the first meant this house
as a gift from me to thee."

And therewith he drew from his pouch a scroll, which
was a deed of gift of the said house, duly sealed and attested,
and he gave it into her hands; but she was sore moved thereat, and at the demeanour of him that morning, and she let
the scroll fall to the floor and wept for pity of him, and
reached out both her hands, and he kissed them, and then
her lips also, and sithence he sat down beside her. But she
said: "Alas! that thou wilt give me what I may not take, and
wouldst have of me what I may not give."

But now he waxed hotter, and said: "This once I command thee to do my will, and take my gift. It will be nought
to my gain if thou take it not; for I may not live in this house
when thou art gone from it; and I swear by Allhallows that
I will not let any have it to hire, nor will I sell it since thou
hast made it holy by dwelling therein."

Yet was she sore moved by his generous fashion, and she
said: "I will take thy gift then, and live here in honour of
thee and thy friendship: for well I wot thou hadst no mind
to buy me with thy gift."

So she spake, and he stood up stark and stern, and so departed, and kissed her not again; though meseems she would
have suffered him had he offered it. Nay, belike had he at that
moment pressed his wooing somewhat masterfully, it is not
so sure but she might have yeasaid it, and suffered him to
wed her and lead her to bed; though it would have gone ill
both with him and with her thereafter.

Thenceforth dwelt Birdalone with her mother and her
maidens and her men in that house, and it became famous in
the Five Crafts because of her beauty and her wisdom, which
minished not, but waxed day by day; but therewithal as the
time wore, waxed her longing and sadness. But all this she

274

hid in her own heart, and was debonaire to all about her, and so good to poor folk that none had a word save of blessing on her beauty and her wisdom.

CHAPTER V. OF THE DEATH OF AUDREY. BIRDALONE IS MINDED TO LEAVE THE CITY.

THUS dwelt Birdalone in the Five Crafts in such rest and peace as her heart would let her; and dear and good friends she had about her; her mother first, whose love and desire for love of her made all things soft and dear unto her: Gerard and the Gerardsons were next, who were ever faithful and true unto her, and deft both of hand and of mind, so that they wrought many things for her avail. Then came the Master Jacobus, who held himself unwedded for her sake, and though he no longer dwelt in the same house with her, might scarce endure to miss the sight of her for two days running: a dear friend she deemed him, as forsooth he was, though whiles he tormented and wearied her; and belike had wearied her more, but for the sorrow which lay on her own heart, whereof it came that she might not think of any man as of one who might be a lover, and so felt safe even with so kind a friend and so stubborn in his love as was this one. Moreover he never again craved love of her in so many words, but only in his goings and comings so did, that it was clear how he had her, and the love of her, ever in his heart.

Wore thus a five years; and then came a sickness on the city, and many died thereof; and the said sickness entered into Birdalone's house, and slew Audrey her mother, but spared all else therein. Thereby at the first was Birdalone so overwhelmed that she might heed nought, neither her craft nor her friends, nor the days to come on the earth for her. And moreover when she came more to herself, which was not for many days, and asked why her friend Jacobus had not been to see her the last days, she was told that he also was dead of the pestilence; and she sorrowed for him sorely, for she loved him much, though not in the way he would.

And now did the city and land of the Five Crafts begin to look unfriendly to Birdalone, and she fell to thinking that she must needs depart thence, as she well might do, whereas she had foison of goods: and at first it was in her mind to go with Gerard and his sons unto Utterhay; but then she deemed the thought of her mother, and how she would be ever thinking of the loss and the gain and the loss once more stood in the way; and she turned one thing and another over in her mind, and might not face it.

On a night, as she slept, came to her dreams of her days in the House under the Wood (as very seldom betid), and the witch-wife was speaking to her in friendly fashion (as for her) and blaming her for fleeing away, and was taunting her with the failure of her love, and therewith telling her how fair a man and lovesome was the Black Squire, and what a loss she had of him; and Birdalone was hearkening and weeping for tenderness' sake, while the witch was unto her neither fearful nor irksome, and forsooth nought save a mouthpiece for words that both grieved Birdalone and yet were an eager pleasure unto her. But in the midst thereof, and ere the dream had time to change, Birdalone awoke, and it was an early morning of later spring, and the sky was clear blue and the sun shining bright, and the birds singing in the garden of the house, and in the street was the sound of the early market-folk passing through the street with their wares; and all was fresh and lovely.

She awoke sobbing, and the pillow wet with her tears, and yet she felt as if something strange and joyous were going to betide her, and for joy of the love of life the heart beat fast in her bosom.

She arose all darling naked as she was, and went to the window and looked out on the beauty of the spring, while the sound of the market-wains brought to her mind the thought of the meads, and the streams of the river, and the

276

woodsides beyond the city; and she fell a-longing for them, as a while she knelt on the window-seat, half dreaming and asleep again, till the sun came round that way, and its beams fell upon her bosom and her arms; and she stood up and looked on the fairness of her body, and a great desire took hold of her heart that it might be loved as it deserved by him whom she desired. And thus she stood there till she became ashamed, and hastened to do on her raiment; but even as she was about it, it came upon her that what she had will to do was to seek to the Castle of the Quest, and find out where was her love if there he were not, and so to seek him the world over till she found him. And such a flood of joy possessed her when she thought this, and so eager to begone she was, that she deemed every minute wasted till she were on the road.

Nevertheless, in a while, when her mind was steadied, she knew that she had somewhat to do ere she might be gone, and that here, as oft, it would be more haste less speed.

So she abode a little, and then came into her hall duly dight, and found Gerard and his sons there to serve her; and she brake her fast, and bade them sit by her at table, as oft she did; and she spake to them of this and that, and Gerard answered lightly again; but the two Gerardsons looked at one another, as though they would speak and ask a question from time to time, but forbore because they durst not. But Gerard looked on them, and deemed he wotted what was in their minds; so at last he spake: "Our lady, both I, and meseemeth my sons also, deem that there is some tidings toward which are great unto thee; for thine eyes sparkle, and the red burns in thy cheeks, and thine hands may not be quiet, nor thy feet abide in one place. Wherefore I see that thou hast something in thy mind which strives to be forth of it. Now thou wilt pardon us, our dear lady, that we ask concerning this, because it is in our love for thee that we speak, lest there be some change toward which shall be a grief to some of us."

"My men," said Birdalone, flushing red, "sooth it is that there is a change at hand, and I shall tell you straightway

277

what it is. Years ago I told you that I was fleeing from my friends; now the change hath betid, that I would seek them again; and needs must I leave the Five Crafts behind to do so. And moreover there is this ill word to be said, which I will say at once, to wit, that when I am but a little way gone from the Five Crafts, I must wend the other deal of my journey bird-alone, as my name is."

All those three sat silent and aghast at that word, and the young men grew pale; but after a while spake Gerard: "Our lady most well-beloved, this word which thou hast spoken, to wit, that thou needest us no longer, I have looked to hear any time this five years. And praise be to the Saints that it hath come late and not soon. Now there is no more to be said but that thou tell us what is thy will that we should do."

Birdalone hung her head awhile for sorrow of sundering from these men; then she looked up and said: "It seemeth, my friends, as if ye deem I have done you a wrong in sundering our fellowship. But all I may say hereon is to pray you to pardon me, that I needs must go alone on my quest. And now what I would have you do, is first of all to fetch hither a notary and scrivener, that he may draw up a deed of gift to you, Gerard and Gerardsons, of this house and all that is therein, saving what money I may need for my journey, and gifts such as I shall bid you, to be given to my workwomen. Ye must needs yeasay this, or ye are forsworn of your behest to do my will. But furthermore, I will have you to let the workwomen of mine (and the head one ruling) to hire the aforesaid house, if so they will; for now are they skilled, and may well earn good livelihood by the work. But the next work is simple; it is to furnish for me the array of a young man, with such armour as I may easily bear, to dight me for my road. Forsooth ye wot that not unseldom do women use the custom of going arrayed like men, when they would journey with hidden head; and ye may happen upon such gear as hath been made for such a woman rather than any man; but thou shalt get me also a short bow and a quiver of arrows, for verily these be my proper weapons that I can

278

deal with deftly. Now my last command is that, when all is
done, maybe to-morrow, or maybe the next day, ye bring me
out of the City and the Frank of the Five Crafts, and bring
me somewhat on my way over the downs; for loth am I to
part from you ere needs must."

Then they knelt before her and kissed her hands, and
they were full of grief; but they saw that so it had to be.

Thereafter Gerard spake with his sons apart, and in a
while came to Birdalone, and said: "Our lady, we will do
your will in all wise; but we shall tell thee that the Five
Crafts will look but strange to us when thou art gone, and
that we have a mind to betake us to Utterhay and the land of
our kindred. Wherefore we pray thee to give this house
that hath been so dear to us unto thy workwoman and her
mates; for we need it not, nor the hire thereof, but shall do
well enough with what money or good thou mayst give us.
Is this according to thy will, or have I spoken rashly?"

She said: "Ye are good and ungreedy, and I bless you for
it; be it as ye will: and this the more, as I were fain that ye
go to Utterhay; for whiles I have deemed that I myself am
drawn thitherward. Wherefore it may be that we shall meet
again in that place."

And when she had so spoken, she might not refrain her
tears; and the Gerardsons turned away; for they were a-
shamed, both that they should see her weep, and she them.
But at last she called to them and said: "Now make we the
speediest end we may of this, for sorry work is the tarrying
of farewell. So I pray you, my friends, to go about the work
I have bidden you."

So all was done as she would, and the day after the morrow was Birdalone abiding the coming of Gerard and his
sons with the horses; and despite of the sundering of friends
and the perils that belike lay before her, the world seemed
fair to her, and life beginning anew. And she made no doubt
that she would soon be at the Castle of the Quest, and there
find all things much as she had left them; and there at least
would be the welcome of her dear friend Viridis.

CHAPTER VI. BIRDALONE DEPARTETH.

PRESENTLY were the horses come with Gerard and
his sons, and Birdalone gat to horse amongst them.
She was armed in a light hawberk, and over it a long
and loose surcoat that came down beneath the knee of her;
and a sallet she had upon her head, wide but light, so that
not very much of her face was to be seen. She had made up
her mind to this tale upon the road, when she was among
folk, that she was under a vow not to do off her helm for a
seven days' space. Withal she had covered up the lovely
shapeliness of her legs with long boots of deer-leather, and
her surcoat was wide-sleeved; she was well hidden, and
whereas she was a tall and strong woman, she might well pass
for a young man, slender and fair-faced. She was girt with a
good sword, and Gerard had gotten her a strong horseman's
bow and a quiver full of arrows, wherewith, as aforesaid, she
knew well how to deal; wherefore she was by no means without defence.

So they went their ways through the streets and out-a-
gates; and it must be said, that were not Birdalone's thoughts
turned toward the Castle of the Quest, and what she should
meet there, her heart had been somewhat sore at leaving the
city which had cherished her so well these years past: nay, as
it was, the shadow of the Southern Gate, as she passed there-
under, smote somewhat cold upon her, and she silently bade
farewell to the City of the Five Crafts with some sorrow,
though with no fear.

Forth they rode then through the Frank and up on to the
shepherd country, and whereas their horses were of the best,
and they had no sumpter-beast with them till they came to
Upham, where they must needs have victual, they made but
five days of it to the place where the road turned aside from
the country of Mostwyke. There then they drew rein, and
Birdalone lighted down from her horse, and they all, and
they lay upon the grass and ate and drank together.

But when they were done, spake Birdalone and said:

" Dear friends, this is the hour and the place when we must needs part; for ye shall go back again to Five Crafts, and do what I have bidden of you, and do your will, and wend your ways with your livelihood unto Utterhay. But as for me, I must go my ways first unto Greenford, and thence to seek my friends from whom erst I was fleeing when ye first became my friends. Now perchance ye will say that I have taken you up in my need, and cast you aside at my pleasure. But I may only say that there be at present two deals of my life, and of one of them have ye been partakers, and of the other ye may not be. Forsooth that is a grief unto me, as I suppose unto you is it a greater one. But unto me also were it heavier but that my heart tells me it shall not ever be so; for as I said to you the day before yesterday, I have a hope that we shall yet meet again, be it in Utterhay or in some other place. And now I pray you to pardon me wherein I may have done amiss unto you, and begrudge it not that there be others, who indeed were first-comers in regard to you, and whom I love better than you; for of your truth and your goodwill and loving-kindness will I bear witness wheresoever I may be."

Then spake Gerard: "Do ye speak, my sons; for I have no grudge against her, nor aught to bewail me as to her, save, it may be, that I am now so well on in years that it may well befall that I shall not live till the time of the meeting in Utterhay. But I will pray thee this, dear lady, that if thou come to the place where I lie dead thou wilt kiss my burial-stone, and sing due masses for me."

"Nay," she said, "but this is the worst shall betide betwixt us."

Then spake Robert Gerardson: "I am not deft of speech, but this parting makes me bold to say this: that from the time when first I set eyes on thee I have loved thee in such wise that never mayst thou love me as much as I love thee, if thou hast anywhere, as I deem thou hast, a lover of thy body, whom thou lovest. Now I have seen that for a long while thou hast known this, and hast ever because of it been as meek and kind with me as thou mightest be. And this hath

281

partly grieved me the more, because it hath eked my longing for thee ; and yet it hath comforted me the more, because it hath made me deem better of thee, and deem thee worthier of worship and holier. Therefore have thou all my blessing for it. And now I know that thou sunderest from us that thou mayst go seek thy very bodily lover; and I say that if the sundering had been for any lighter cause, grieved at heart should I have been; but since it is even so, once more I bless thee, and ever shall I be happy in the thought of thee; and if ever we meet again, still shalt thou find me as now I am in heart and in soul."

She turned to him, not dry-eyed, and said: "I know that what thou sayest is sooth; and thou hast guessed right as to my goings; and I take thy blessing with love and joy."

Then were they silent; but Giles Gerardson was struggling with words, for he was slow to speech; at last he said: "I say much as saith my brother: but see thou, our lady, how ill it had gone if thou hadst loved one of us with an equal love. Woe worth the strife then! But now I will crave this of thee, that thou kiss me on the lips, now whenas we part; and again, that thou wilt do as much when first we meet again hereafter. And I tell thee right out, that if thou gainsay this, I shall deem it unfriendly in thee, and that those lovely words which thou didst speak e'en now were but words alone, and that thou art not as true as I have deemed thee."

She laughed amidst her tears, and said: "Dear lad, doom me not till I have been found guilty! I shall nowise naysay thee this; for I love thee, and now and ever shalt thou be unto me as a brother, thou and Robert also ; for even so have ye done by me. But thou wottest, dear lad, that whiles and again must sister sunder from brother, and even so it has to be now."

Then they sat silent all four; and thereafter Birdalone arose and did off her sallet, and kissed and embraced Gerard and his sons, and bade them farewell, and she and the young men wept. Then she armed herself and gat to horse, and went her ways towards Greenford, having nought with her but the

raiment and arms that her body bore, and her horse, and some
gold pieces and gems in a little pouch. So rode she; and the
others turned back sadly toward the Five Crafts.

CHAPTER VII. BIRDALONE COMETH TO GREENFORD AND HEARETH TIDINGS.

NOW came Birdalone riding into Greenford an hour before sunset on a day of the latter end of May; and she had no doubt but to go straight to the hostelry, and that the less as she had not abided there before, as hath been told. To them that served her she told the tale of her vow, that she might not do off her sallet that seven days; and some trowed her, and some deemed her a woman, but whereas she seemed by her raiment to be of condition none meddled with her. Moreover, as she told her intent to ride on betimes in the morning, it mattered the less unto them: withal she gave out that she came from foreign parts, as sooth it was.

In the evening she sat in the hall, and with her were three chapmen travelling with their wares, and two good men of the town sitting; and they were talking together, and were courteous and blithe, and amidst their talk they threw many a glance at the slim and fair young squire, as Birdalone seemed, and were fain to speak unto him, but refrained them for courtesy's sake. For her part, Birdalone longed sore to ask them somewhat of the Castle of the Quest, but the words clave to her throat for very fear; and she sat restless and ill at ease. However at last said a townsman to a chapman: "Art thou for the Red Hold, Master Peter, when thou art done here?"

Birdalone turned very pale at that word; and Master Peter spake: "Yea surely, neighbour, if the folk leave aught in my packs for others to buy."

He spake in a jovial voice, as if he were merry, and the others all laughed together, as though they were well pleased and in good contentment. And now deemed Birdalone would be her time to speak if she would learn aught; so she constrained herself at last, and spake, though in a quavering voice: "Meseems then, masters, this good town is thriving as now? This I ask because I am a stranger in these parts this long while, and now I am come back hither fain were I to find the land in good peace; for I may chance to take up my abode hereby."

The goodmen turned to her and smiled kindly when they heard the sweetness of her voice; and one of them said: "Sir of the Sallet, ye shall be content with the peace in this land, and the thriving of its folk; the very villeins hereabout live as well as franklins in most lands, and the yeomen & vavassours are clad as if they were knights of a good lord's household. Forsooth their houses are both goodly and easy to enter: and well is that, whereas there lacks never good meat and drink on the board therein. And moreover their women are for ever seeking whatso is fair and goodly, whatso is far-fetched and dear-bought, whereof we chapmen also thrive, as thou mayst well deem. Ah! it is a goodly land now!"

The others nodded and smiled. But Birdalone spake, hardening her heart thereto for very need:

"Belike then there is a change of days here, for when I last knew of the land there was little peace therein." "And that will not be so long agone," said a townsman, smiling, "for I doubt we should see no grey hair in thine head if thy sallet were off it." Birdalone reddened: "It will be some five years agone," said she. "Yea, yea," said the townsman, "we were beginning to end the unpeace then, and it was the darkest hour before the dawn; for five years agone we and the good knights of the Castle of the Quest were lying before the walls of the Red Hold. Forsooth we cleared out that Den of Devils then and there."

"What betid unto it after ye won it?" said Birdalone, and she trembled withal. Said the townsman: "Heard ye never of the Black Squire, a very valiant knight, since thou sayest that thou hast known this country-side?" She bowed a yea-say, for this time she found it hard to speak.

"Well," said the townsman, "we held garrison in the Red

284

Hold for some three months, and thereafter we craved of
him to come and be our captain therein; for, even after the
Hold was won, there was yet a sort of runagates that haunted
the country-side, men who had no craft save lifting and slaying. And forsooth we knew this Lord Arthur for the keenest
and deftest of men-at-arms; so he yeasaid our asking, and
did all he might herein, and forsooth that was all there was
to do; for he was ever in the saddle, and at the work. Forsooth he was not a merry man, save when he was at his
busiest; and little he spake in hall or chamber, else had he
been better beloved. But at least by no man better might the
land have been served."

There was silence a little, and Birdalone waxed deadly
pale; then she strove with herself and said: "Thou sayest he
was and he was; is he dead then?" Said the townsman: "Not
to our knowledge. When he had brought the land into good
peace, which is some three years and a half agone, he went his
ways from the Red Hold all alone, and we saw him no more.
But some folk deem that he hath entered into religion."

Birdalone's heart sickened, and she thought to herself that
now all was to begin again; yet she felt that the worst was
over since he was not dead, and she was able to think what
she should do. So she said: "Mayhappen he hath gone back
to the Castle of the Quest?"

"Nay, nay," said the townsman, " that may not be; for
waste is that house now; there is none dwelleth there, save
it may be now and again a wandering carle or carline abideth
there a day or two."

Said Birdalone: "How hath that befallen? or where is gone
Sir Hugh the Green Knight?"

Said the townsman: "We knew the Green Knight well;
frank and free and joyous was he; all men loved him; and his
lady and speech-friend, none ever saw a lovelier, and as kind
as was he. But we might not keep them with us; they are
gone into their own country. Sir Hugh left the Castle of the
Quest some three months after the Black Squire came to us
for captain, and he gave over the castle to Sir Geoffrey of Lea,

285

an old and wise man of war. But not many months thereafter
we heard that he also had departed, leaving it ungarnished
of men; and we deem that the cause thereof is that something
uncouth is seen and heard therein, which folk may not endure. Is it not so, my masters?"

They all yeasaid that, and the talk went on to other matters. As for Birdalone, though her hope to come amongst
friends was so utterly overthrown, yet she saw not what to
do save to go her ways to the Castle of the Quest, and see if
perchance she might find any tidings there. And she said to
herself, that if the worst came to the worst, she would herself
dwell there as an hermit of love; or maybe, to face those uncouth things and see if any tidings might be compelled out
of them.

CHAPTER VIII. SHE COMETH TO THE CASTLE OF THE QUEST, AND DEPARTETH THENCE.

SHE arose betimes on the morrow, and was out of
Greenford so soon as the gates were open, and at first
made all speed that she might toward the Castle of the
Quest; and nothing hindered her, for the land was verily in
good peace, and she might have come there if she would before sunset, for all whom she met furthered her. But as the
day waned her courage waned with it, so that at last she
stayed some six miles short of the house, and craved shelter
at a yeoman's stead there, which was granted her with all
kindness; and they made much of her, and she told them her
vow of the sallet, and they deemed nought save that she was
a young man.

She departed early in the morning with their God-speed,
and while the day was yet young came into the meadows before the castle, and saw the towers thereof rising up before
her: then she checked her horse, and rode on no faster than
a foot's pace; yet as slow as she might ride, needs must she
get to the gate while the day was yet young.

So came Birdalone by that bower wherein she had slept
286

that first night she came to the castle; and she reined up to
look on it; and as she sat there gazing, came a man out from
it clad as a man of religion; and her heart beat quick, and she
was like to fall from her horse, for there came into her mind
what the townsman had said, that the Black Squire had gone
into religion. But the hermit came towards her with a cup
of water in his hand, and he cast his hood aback from him,
and she saw at once that it was Leonard the priest, and
though it was not the friend whom she sought, yet was she
glad that it was a friend; but he came and stood by her, and
said: "Hail, wayfarer! wilt thou drink of our well and rest
thee a while?" So she took the cup and drank of the water,
looking kindly on him, while he wondered at the beauty of
her hand, and misdoubted him. Then she gave him back the
cup and lighted down off her horse, and took the sallet from
her head, and spake: "I may not pass by a friend without a
word; think if thou hast not seen me before?"

Then he knew her, and might not refrain him, but cast
his arms about her and kissed her, weeping; and she said:
"It is sweet to me to find a friend after what I have been
told of yonder house." "Yea," said he, "and art thou going
up thither?" "Certes," said she, "and why not?" Said he:
"They are gone and all gone!" "How and whither?" said
she. "But I must full certainly go thither at once; I will go
afoot with thee; do thou tether my horse till thou comest
back."

He said: "But wilt not thou come back?" "I know
not," she said: "I know nought save that I would go thither;
let it be enough that I suffer thee to go with me, and on the
way thou shalt tell me what thou canst of the tale."

Then went Leonard and tethered the horse, and they
went together afoot to the gate; and Birdalone told what
she had heard of Arthur and Hugh; and Leonard said:
"This is true, and there is not much else to be said. When
the Black Squire came back from the leaguer of the Red
Hold, and had heard before of thy departure, he was heavy
of mood and few-spoken, and wandered about as one who

287

might find no rest; yet was he not stern with Atra, who for her part was no less heavy-hearted: soothly a sad company we were, and it was somewhat better when my lord Arthur went his ways from us; and indeed eager he was to be gone; and it could be seen of him that he was fain of the toil and peril which they of Greenford offered him. Then in some four months spake my lord Hugh that he also would be gone to a place where were both a land and folk that would look friendly on him; so he went with my lady Viridis and my lady Aurea, and they had Atra also with them; and me also they would have had, but my heart failed me to leave the place where I had been so glad and so sorry with thee; death had been better: wherefore in yonder bower as in an hermitage I serve God and abide my time. But though I wot nought of where is gone the Black Squire, I know whereto those four are gone, and it is but a seven days' ride hence, and the land is goodly and peaceable, and if they be not dead, most like they be there yet. How sayest thou then, thou dearest and kindest, wilt thou thither to them? For if so, I may well lead thee thither."

Birdalone shook her head. "Nay," she said, "I deem that I am drawn elsewhither. But soon I shall tell thee. Lo now the gate. But ere we enter, tell me of Sir Geoffrey of Lea, and why it was that they might not abide the uncouth things, or if there were any such." Spake Leonard: "Things uncouth there were, and I was called upon to lay them; and I did as biddeth Holy Church in all wise, but prevailed not against them, and still were they seen and heard, till folk might endure it no longer."

"And what like were these things?" said Birdalone, "and are they yet seen and heard?" Said Leonard: "Strange it is, but last night I went into the great hall where they mostly betid, and laid me down there, as whiles I do, for I fear them not, and would see if they yet appear; but all night came nothing at all. As to the likeness of them—" Then he stopped, but said presently: "Hard it is to tell thee of them, but needs must I. There be two of these things; and one is

288

an image of a tall woman of middle-age, red-haired, white-
skinned, and meagre, and whiles she has a twiggen rod in
her hand, and whiles a naked short sword, and whiles nought
at all. But the voice of her is cursing and blaspheming and
ill-saying."

Said Birdalone: "This is then a fetch of my witch-mistress
of whom I told thee erst, and the image of her; what is the
other?" Said Leonard: "I were fain not to tell thee." "Yet
needs must thou," said Birdalone. "Dear lady," said Leonard, "the other is an image of thee, and even most like unto
thee; but whiles clad in a scanty grey coat and barefoot, and
whiles clad in a fair green gown goodly broidered, and
broidered shoon; and whiles all mother-naked."

"And what voice cometh from mine image?" said Birdalone, smiling, yet somewhat pale withal. Said Leonard:
"One while a voice of sweet singing, as of a bird in the brake,
and that is when thou art clad; and again, when thou art
naked, a voice of shrieking and wailing, as of one enduring
torments."

Spake Birdalone: "And when did these wonders begin?"
Said he: "Not till after Sir Hugh and thy she-friends were
gone hence."

Pondered Birdalone a little; then she said: "I see herein
the malice of my witch-mistress; she would not send these
fetches while Hugh was here, lest he should turn to seeking
me with all his might. But when they departed, she would
have the castle waste, and then she sent them, wotting that
thereby she would rid her of Sir Geoffrey of Lea; while, on
the other hand, I was nought so much unto him that he would
spend all his life seeking me. But now I deem I know so
much of her that I may bid thee to look on her as dead if
these fetches come not again within a little while. Then mayst
thou send and do Sir Geoffrey to wit thereof, and belike he
will come back again; and fain were I thereof, for it will be
merrier if the Castle of the Quest be dwelt in once more."

"Yea verily," said Leonard; "but far merrier yet wert
thou to dwell there." "Nay," she said; "but now I see that

it is not fated for me. Let us go in, for I would get to what I would do."

So therewith they passed under the shadow of the archway, and Birdalone stayed not but went straightway into the hall, and through it; and the priest, who lagged somewhat behind her speedy feet, cried out unto her: "Whither wilt thou? what chamber wilt thou visit first?" But she stayed not, and spake to him over her shoulder as she went: "Follow me if thou wilt; I have but one place only to come to ere I leave the Castle of the Quest, save I must needs turn back on my footsteps."

Then Leonard came up with her, and she went her ways out of the hall, and out on to the water-swale of the castle, and so to the little haven of the water-gate. There Birdalone looked about her eagerly; then she turned to Leonard and pointed with her finger and said: "Lo thou! there yet lieth my ferry of old time, the Sending Boat; now wot I wherefore I was drawn hither." And her eyes glittered and her body quivered as she spake.

"Yea forsooth," said Leonard, "there it lieth; who of all folk in the castle had durst to touch it? But what hath it to do with thee, O kindest lady?"

"Friend," she said, "if this day weareth, and I am yet within these walls, then meseemeth there must I abide for evermore; and there perchance shall I meet that seeming of myself, maybe for this night, maybe for ever, till I die here in this castle void of all that I love. And I over-young for it, friend, and I know now that there is hope within me; for I bethink me of a dear friend over yonder water of whom I have never told any, nor will tell thee now, save this, that she is the wisdom of my life. Wherefore now I will try this ferry and wot if the wight thereof will yet obey the voice of the speaker of the spell, who has shed of her blood to pay therefor. Put not forth a hand therefore nor speak a word to let me, but take this farewell of me, with my pity and such love as I may give thee, and let me go, and think kindly of me."

290

Then she went up to him, and laid her hands upon his
shoulders, and kissed him, and turned about without more
ado and stepped into the boat; then she sat down and stripped
her arm of its sleeve, and drew forth a knife and let blood of
her arm, and then arose and smeared stem and stern therewith, and then sat down with her face to the stern and sang:

> The red raven-wine now
> Hast thou drunk, stern and bow;
> Wake then and awake
> And the Northward way take:
> The way of the Wender forth over the flood,
> For the will of the Sender is blent with the blood.

Then she abode a little, while Leonard stood staring on
her speechless with grief and blinded with his bitter tears, till
the boat began to move under her, and presently glided out
of the little haven into the wide lake; then she turned her
face back unto him and waved her hand, and he knelt down
and blessed her, weeping. And so she vanished away from
before him.

CHAPTER IX. BIRDALONE FINDETH THE ISLE OF NOTHING GREATLY BETTERED, AND IS KINDLY ENTREATED THERE.

NOW it was scarce noon when she departed, and the
dark night came upon her in the midst of the water;
and she fell asleep in the boat ere the night had
grown very old, and woke up in the morning not exceeding
early, maybe about six o'clock; then she looked ahead and
thought presently to see the ill-favoured blotch of the Isle
of Nothing on the bosom of the blue waters, whereas it was
a fair and cloudless morning of latter May. Sure enough she
saw land ahead, and it lay low down on the water, but she
deemed from the first that it was green of hue, and as she
neared it she saw that it was verily as green as emerald.

Thereat she was a little troubled, because she thought that mayhappen the Sending Boat had gone astray, and that if the wight thereof were not wending the old road, maybe he was not making for the old haven. For now indeed she told herself right out that her will was to go back again to the House under the Wood, and see what might betide there, and if she and the Woodmother together might not overcome the witch.

But whatever might happen nought could she do but sit in her place and wend as the Sending Boat would; and in an hour's space she was right under the lee of the land, and she saw that it was shapen even as the Isle of Nothing had been aforetime. But this made her wonder, that now the grass grew thick down to the lip of the water, and all about from the water up were many little slim trees, and some of them with the May-tide blossom yet on them, as though it were a fair and great orchard that she was nearing; and moreover, beyond all that she saw the thatched roofs of houses rising up.

Presently then the Sending Boat had brought her to the land, and she stepped ashore, but was wary, and gat her bow bent and set an arrow thereto ere she began to go up from the water. Yet she thought within herself, it will be nought ill if I be come amongst folk, so long as they be peaceful, or else how might I live the journey out to all the isles and so home to the House under the Wood?

So she turned her face to where she had seen those roofs, which now she saw no longer because of the thick leaves of the little trees, and so went along a narrow path, which grew to be more and more closely beset with trees, and they were now no longer apple and pear and quince and medlar, but a young-grown thicket of woodland trees, as oak and hornbeam and beech and holly.

At last as she went she heard voices before her, so she stole warily to the edge of the copse, finger on shaft; and presently could see clear of the saplings and out on to a wide space of greensward, beyond which was a homestead of many houses

292

and bowers, like unto that of a good yeoman in peaceful
lands, save that the main building was longer, though it
were low. But amidst the said greensward was a goodly flock
of sheep that had been but of late washed for the shearing,
and along with the sheep four folk, two carles and two
queans, all of them in their first youth, not one by seeming
of over a score and two of summers. These folk were clad but
simply, man and woman, in short coats of white woollen
(but the women's coats a little longer than the men's), without shoon or hosen; they had garlands of green leaves on
their heads, and were wholly unarmed, save that one of the
men bore an ashen wand in his hand. As for their bodies,
they were goodly of fashion, tanned indeed by the sun's
burning, but all sweet of flesh were they, shapely and trim,
clean-made and light and slim.

Birdalone's heart yearned toward them, and she stepped
straightway from out of the cover of the coppice, and the sun
flamed from her sallet and glittered in the rings of her hawberk, so that the folk might not fail to see her; the sheep fled
bundling from her past their keepers, who stood firm, but
seemed somewhat scared, and moved not toward Birdalone.
She gave them the sele of the day and stood still herself; but
the man with the ash-wand said: "Hail, thou man; but we
would have thee come no nearer a while, though thy voice
be sweet: for we know what things they be which thou bearest, and that thou art a warrior. Wilt thou hurt us?"

Birdalone laughed as sweetly as the blackbird sings, and
she did off her sallet and shook the plenteous hair down over
her, and then drew forth her sword and dagger and cast them
to earth, and laid her bow and quiver of arrows upon them,
and said: "Now will I come to you, or ye shall come to me,
whereas I am unweaponed, and no warrior but a woman,
and ye are four to one, and two of you carles; wherefore now
ye may bind me or slay me if you will; but in any case I pray
you first to give me a mouthful of meat."

When she had done her speech, she went up to the fairest
of the women and kissed her; but the two carles made no

more ado but came to Birdalone and kissed her one after other, and that as men who needed nought to compel them therein, and each thereafter took a hand of her and held it and caressed it. But the other woman had run into the house as soon as Birdalone spoke, and came back again with a treen bowl full of milk, and a little loaf, not white but brown; and there blundered about her legs as she came a little lad of some three winters old, naked and brown, who was shy of the gleaming new-comer, and hid him behind the woman one while, and the other while came forth to see the new thing. But the woman said: "Dear woman, here is for thee some of the ewes' milk, and a bite of bread, and a little deal of cheese; the said milk is yet warm, so that it is not yet clottered; but if thou wilt come with us thou mayest speedily drink cows' milk, and we be now at point to go milk them."

Birdalone thanked her with a heart full of content, and was not ill-pleased to get her hands free from the two carles; so she sat down and ate her breakfast while they talked with her, and told her of diverse work of theirs; as to how their trees were waxing, and new tillage they had done the past spring, and how it befell to the kine and the goats; of their children also they spake, and how there were already four thereof, and one of the women, the meat-bringer, already quickened with child once more. "So that ere we die," quoth the carle who was speaking, "we look to see many grandchildren, and shall have some stout carles and queans here. And by that time will some of the trees be well grown, so that we may fell timber and make us some keel that will wend the lake, and help us a-fishing; or we may go to other lands; or whiles folk may come to us, even as thou hast, thou dear-handed, sweet-voiced woman. But wilt thou abide here ever?"

"Yea," said the other, "but that is looking forward a long while, that building of ships. What is nearer and well to think of is, that these apple and pear trees be so well fruited, small as they be, that this harvest we shall be able to make us cider

294

and perry; yea, and no little deal thereof. But art thou minded to abide with us ever? That were dear to us; and belike thou wouldest bear us children, thou also."

Then spake the meat-fetching woman and laughed withal: "Nay, thou also lookest aloof a pretty deal; whereas what is now to do is to go milk the kine, and to take this guest with us, so that she may drink somewhat better than ewes' milk though the cider be not ready to hand. But tell me, our dear guest, art thou verily going to abide with us a long while? That were sweet to us, and we will do all we may to pleasure thee."

"Nay," said Birdalone, "it will no better be but that I depart on the morrow; and all thanks do I give you for your kindness."

The woman kissed her, and she arose, and all they went together to the milking of the kine some half mile inland; and they passed through much of orchard, and some deal of tillage, wherein the wheat was already growing high; and so came they to a wide meadow through which ran a little stream, and therein was a goodly herd of kine. So they fell to the milking, and made Birdalone drink of the sweet cows' milk, and then went and lay down under the shade of the little, young trees, and talked and were merry together. But the men were both of them somewhat willing at first to kiss Birdalone and toy with her, but when she let them know that she desired it not they refrained them without grudging.

All this while of their talk they asked Birdalone nought of whence and whither, and she would not ask them, lest it might stir their asking, and then she would have to tell them some deal of her story; and telling it was now become unto her somewhat weary work.

In a while they arose all, and the men and one woman went their ways to deal with the acreland, but the meat-fetcher went back with Birdalone into the house; and she showed her all that was therein, which was for the more part, forsooth, the four babes aforesaid. The others came

295

back in the eventide, bearing with them foison of blue hare-
bells, and telling joyously how they had found them anigh
the coppice edge in such a place: and thereafter they were
merry, and sang and talked the evening away, and showed
Birdalone at last to a fair little chamber wherein was a bed
of dry grass, where she lay down and slept in all content.

CHAPTER X. OF BIRDALONE'S FLITTING FROM THE ISLE OF NOTHING.

ON the morrow Birdalone arose betimes, and would
not tarry despite all the kindness of that folk
and the change which had come over the Isle of
Nothing; so the friends saw her down to the boat all together, and bore down with them a deal of bread and cheese
and late apples of the last year, for her provision on the road,
and a pail of milk withal; and men and women they kissed
her at departure, and the meat-fetcher said: "If by any means
thou mayst find a keel which will carry thee hither, at some
time, I would thou wouldst come; for even if thou be old,
and we passed away, yet here shall be our children or our
grandchildren to welcome thee; and we will tell them the
tale of thee that they remember it and long for thee."

Then Birdalone kissed her again, and made much of her,
and so stepped into the boat, and fell to her sacrifice to the
wight thereof; and those others stared at her and wondered,
and spake nought unto her till she was gone gliding over
the face of the waters; but as they walked back to the house,
they spake amongst themselves that this must be some Goddess (for of Holy Church they knew nought) who had come
to visit them in her loveliness; and in after-times, when this
folk waxed a many, and tilled all the isle and made ships and
spread to other lands and became great, they yet had a
memory of Birdalone as their own very Lady and Goddess,
who had come from the fertile and wise lands to bless them,
when first they began to engender on that isle, and had

broken bread with them, and slept under their roof, and
then departed in a wonderful fashion, as might be looked for
of a goddess.

But as for Birdalone, she came not back ever, nor saw
that folk again, and now she sped over the Water toward the
Isle of Kings.

CHAPTER XI. COMING TO THE ISLE OF KINGS BIRDALONE FINDETH THERE A SCORE AND TWO OF FAIR DAMSELS WHO WOULD FAIN HAVE HER COMPANY.

BIRDALONE came ashore at the said isle at the day-
dawn, and saw but little change in the isle when it
grew light, and still the castle stood looking down
awfully on to the meadows. But when she had set foot on the
land, she handled her bow lest the worst might befall, and
looked about her, deeming that this time she would not go
her ways to the dread show that was arrayed in the castle, if
forsooth those dead folk yet abode there.

So now as she looked across the meadow, she saw one
with light and fluttering raiment come forth from the trees,
and look toward her whereas she stood flashing and gleaming in the sun like an image of the God of Love turned warrior. Now Birdalone deemed for sure that this was a woman;
she saw her come a little nigher to her, and then stand looking at her under the sharp of her hand; then she turned
about and ran back to the brake whence she came; and presently Birdalone heard the sound of voices coming thence,
and in a little while thereafter came forth from the said
brake a rout of women (one score and two as they were told
thereafter) and walked over the meadow straight unto her.
She stood where she was, so as to be nigh unto her ferry in
case they willed her unpeace; for though they were weaponless by seeming, they were a many.

When they were come near they stood about her in a half
ring, whispering and laughing each to each. Birdalone saw

that they were all young, and that none of them might be called ungoodly, and some were full fair. They were bright and fine of array, and most bore gold and gems on fingers and neck and arms; they were clad in light, or it may be said, wanton raiment of diverse colours, which had only this of their fashion in common, that they none of them hid over-much of their bare bodies; for either the silk slipped from the shoulder of her, or danced away from her flank; and she whose feet were shod, spared not to show knee and some deal of thigh; and she whose gown reached unsheared from neck to heel, wore it of a web so thin and fine that it hid but little betwixt heel and neck.

Birdalone stood gazing on them and wondering, and she had a mind to think that they were some show sent by her old mistress the witch for her undoing, and she loosened her sword in its sheath and nocked an arrow.

But then ran forward two of the damsels and knelt before her, and each took an hand of her and fell to kissing it, and she felt their hands that they were firm and their lips that they were soft and warm, and they were doubtless alive and real. Then spake one of them and said: "Hail our lord! How can words say how we rejoice in thy coming this happy morn! Now do all we give ourselves to thee as thy slaves to do as thou wilt with. Yet we pray thee be merciful to us and our longings."

Therewith all the sort of them knelt down on the grass before Birdalone and joined their hands as praying to her. And Birdalone was full ill at ease, and wotted not where she was. But she said: "Hail! and good days and fulfilment of wishes unto you, fair damsels! But tell me, is this the Isle of Kings, as I deemed; for strange it is for me to see ye womenfolk here?"

Said she who had spoken afore: "Yea verily this is the Isle of Kings; but long ago are the kings dead, and yet they sit dead in the great hall of the Castle yonder, as thou mayst see if thou, who art a man and a valiant warrior, durst follow up yon mountain path thereto: but we, weak women and little-hearted, durst not go anigh it; and we tremble when whiles

hearted, durst not go anigh it; and we tremble when whiles
a-nights cometh down thence the sound of clashing swords
and clattering shields, and the cries of men in battle. But
praise be to the God of Love, nought cometh down from
thence unto us. Therefore do we live peaceful lives and
pleasant here, lacking nought but thee, lord; and lo now
thou hast come unto us, and we are happy in our inmost
hearts."

Now was Birdalone perplexed and knew not what to do;
but at last she said: "Gentle maidens, I pray you pardon me,
but I must depart straightway; for I have an errand, and life
or death lieth on it. In all else than my abiding here may ye
have your will!"

Therewith did she move a little way toward her ferry; but
forthwith all they brake out weeping and wailing and lamenting, and some of them came up to Birdalone and cast themselves down before her, and clasped her knees, and took hold
of her skirts, and besought her piteously to abide with them.
But she put them aside as well as she might, and stepped
aboard the Sending Boat, and stood amidst it waiting on
their departure: but they went not, and stood along on the
lip of the land crying out and beseeching with much clamour.

Then Birdalone waxed somewhat wrath at their noise and
tumult, and she drew forth her knife and bared her arm
and let blood from it. But when they saw the whiteness and
roundness of it, and how fine and sleek it was, straightway
they changed their tune, and cried out: "A woman, a woman,
a fool of a woman!" and they laughed in scorn and mockery.
And the speaker of them said: "Now there is but one thing
for thee to do, and that is to come forth from thy boat and
strip off thy stolen raiment, and we shall make thee as fine
as ourselves, and thou shalt come with us, and with us abide
the coming of our lord. Nay, thou art so fair and lovely, that
thou shalt be the Lady and Queen of us, and we will do after
thy commands, and thou mayst chastise us if we fail therein.
But now if thou wilt not come forth of the boat uncompelled,
we shall pluck thee forth of it."

299

And therewith she set her foot on the gunwale of the boat, and two or three others did the like. But now had Birdalone her sword naked in her hand, and she waxed as red as blood, and cried out: "Forbear I bid you! Yea verily I am a woman: but I will not take this offer either, whereas I have an errand, as I told you. And so stern it is, that if ye now let my departure I will not spare to smite with this sword whoso first cometh aboard my ferry, and though I be not a man, yet shall ye find that in this matter I shall be little worse, whereas I am armed and ye be naked."

Then they drew back and stood gibing and jeering at her; but she heeded no whit, but reddened stem and stern of the Sending Boat, and sang her spell, and forth glided the ferry, while the damsels stood and stared astonished. As for Birdalone, as she sped on her way she might not refrain her laughter. Thus she wended the wet highway.

CHAPTER XII. BIRDALONE COMETH AGAIN TO THE ISLE OF QUEENS, AND FINDETH A PERILOUS ADVENTURE THEREIN.

IT was not yet daybreak when Birdalone came ashore again, and the moon was down, and it was dark; wherefore she durst not go up on the land, but lay down in the ferry and fell asleep there. When she woke again it was broad daylight, the sun was up, and a little ripple was running over the face of the water. She stepped ashore straightway, and looked up the land and to the right hand and the left, and saw at once that it was indeed the Isle of Queens, and the house stood trim and lovely as of old time; then she longed somewhat to tread the green meadow a little, for yet young was the day, and she saw nought stirring save the throstle and a few small beasts. However, she said to herself that she would go nowhere nigh to the goodly house wherein abode those images of death. Yet her body longed so sore for the springtide freshness of the grass, and was so bewooed of the flowery scent thereof, that though she durst not go unarmed, she did

off her footgear and went stealing softly barefoot and with
naked legs over the embroidered greensward, saying aloud
to herself: If run for the ferry I needs must, lighter shall I
run so dight.

Nonetheless, she had gone but a little way ere a terror
took hold of her, though she saw no child of Adam anigh,
and she turned and ran back swiftly to her old place and sat
down under a twisted oak-tree hard by the Sending Boat,
and abode there panting and quaking, and scarce daring to
look up from the grass for a while. Then her heart came back
to her, and she laughed, and said to herself: I am a fool, for I
need fear nought on this Isle of Queens save women like
myself.

Yet she sat there a little while longer without stirring;
then she stood up and looked keenly around, and, as aforesaid, exceeding far-sighted she was; but still she saw neither
man nor maid nor suckling child.

Then her eyes sought the lips of the lake, and rested on a
little bight some stone's throw ahead of the Sending Boat,
where, a little back from the water, slim willows made a veil
betwixt the water and the meadow; and she looked, and saw
how pleasant a place it were for a one to stand and look on
the ripple just left, while the water dripped from the clear
body on to the grass. And her bare feet fell to telling her clad
sides of the sweet coolness of the water, and waited for no
naysay, but lightly bore her toward the willowy bight. And
when she was there, she did off her sallet and ungirt her, and
laid her sword on the grass, and did off her surcoat and hawberk, and so was a woman again in one white coat above her
smock. Then she looked heedfully betwixt the willow-
boughs, and saw no more than before, nought but a little
whitethorn brake, now white indeed with blossom, some
fifty yards landward from where she stood. So she laughed,
and did off her other raiment, and slid swiftly into the water,
that embraced her body in all its fresh kindness; and as for
Birdalone, she rewarded it well for its past toil by sporting
and swimming to her full.

301

Then she came forth from the water, and clad herself in
no great haste, and did on her hawberk and sallet and sword,
and so went back to her place, and sat down and began to do
on her foot-gear.

But as she looked up from her work a moment, lo! a tall
man coming toward her, and just about the willows whereby
she had bathed. Her heart beat quick and her face changed,
yet she hastened, and was shod and stood up in knightly array
by then he stayed his steps some five paces from her, and gave
her the sele of the day in courteous wise; and she strove to
think that he had not seen her, or at least noted her otherwise
dight; yet her heart misgave her.

He was a grizzled-haired man of over fifty summers by
seeming, but goodly enough and well-knit; he was clad in a
green coat more than a little worn, but made after the fashion
of knighthood; he had nought on his head but an oak-chap-
let, and no weapons but a short sword by his side and a stout
staff in his hand.

She gave back his greeting in a quavering voice; and he
said: "Welcome again, young man. Art thou come to dwell
with us? Truly thou art trim now, but ere some few months
thine attire will be not so much fairer than ours, and thine
hawberk will be rusted; for here be no joyous tiltings nor
deeds of arms, and no kind ladies to give the award of honour. So that if we fight amongst ourselves it will be because
we have fallen out, and spitefully. Yet" (and he laughed,
mockingly, as she thought) "thou mayst bring us luck, and
draw some fair damsels unto us; for that is what we await in
this isle, which is barren of their fair bodies, despite of its
deceitful name."

Thereat Birdalone reddened, deeming that he divined her
womanhood, but she enforced her to speak hardily, and as
manly as she might, and said: "Yea, fair sir, and if I be the
God of Love, as thou deemest, and not merely a poor squire
(Louis Delahaye, at thy service), how many damsels shall I
send thee if there must needs be one to each man of you?"

Quoth he: "Thou must make up the tale to a score or

302

more, or some of us must lack. Sooth to say, at this time thou
needest not haste overmuch for all the tale, whereas there is
but one other of the company near at hand, a mere foolish
young man; the others are gone to the leeward side of the
isle, to fetch us venison and fish, both of which are more
plenty there than here; wherefore are we two somewhat lonesome in this stead, all the more as we be over nigh to the
sorcery in the great house, which we durst not enter: for
though nought cometh out thence down unto us, yet hear
we a night-tides, first songs, and then cries and shrieking,
come out therefrom."

Then he stayed his speech, and drew a little nigher to
Birdalone, and then grinned, and said: "Forsooth we can
spare him, we twain." And he looked on her hard, and the
colour came into her cheeks, and she laughed uneasily, as a
dainty lady when she heareth some unmeet tale.

But again the old carle drew nigher to her, and said:
"Thou seemest to have a good bow and store of arrows; if
thou wouldst lend them to me for a little and come with me
into the wood hard by, I might shoot thee some venison with
little toil to thee: whereas, forsooth, thou lookest scarce like
one who is meet for over-much toil." Again she reddened,
and spake nought this time; and he said: "Deem not there
be no deer this end of the isle because I said that the others
were gone to fetch home venison; only the deer be tamer
there and more, and we have but evil shooting-gear, whereas
thou art well found therein. Wilt thou not come? we shall
have merry feast after the hunt."

Now had Birdalone come to her wits again, and she answered like a merry youth, with a flavour of mockery in her
speech: "Fair sir, thou needest not deem that I need much
help in slaying the dun deer; for I do thee to wit that I shoot
not ill in the bow; neither am I heavy-footed. But I will not
hunt in your park to-day, for I have an errand which calleth
me away, so that I shall depart hence presently. Besides, wise
elder, there is thine errand to see to; and if I be the God of
Love, as thou sayest, I must not keep thee and thy valiant

303

fellows languishing mateless; so with thy leave I will now depart, that I may send you a score of fair damsels for your company."

And she turned about and made a step toward her boat; but the carle drew nearer, laughing; and he said: "Truly sayest thou that thou art not heavy-footed, for never saw I feet lighter or fairer than glided over the meadow e'en now; nor a fairer body than came like rosy-tinted pearl fresh out of the water while I lay hidden in yonder thorn-brake that while. Wherefore trouble not thyself to bring any more damsels than thyself, fairest Goddess of Love, for thou art enough for me."

And therewith he ran forward, and stretched out a hand to her; but in that nick of time had she her sword naked in her hand, and the carle drew back before the glitter thereof, and cried out: "Ho, ho! is it to be battle, my mistress? Deemest thou that thou wilt slay me as lightly as the dun deer, and thou with thy bow unstrung at thy back? Now shall I show thee a trick of fence; but fear not that I shall hurt thee to spoil thee."

He advanced on her with his staff aloft, and her heart failed her, and she quaked, and lightly he beat down her guard and did the sword out of her hand; and again he turned on her to take her, but she sprang aside and ran from him, but ran landward perforce, as he was betwixt her and the boat: and he followed heavily, and had nought to do in the race.

But she had not gone a two-score yards ere she heard a great shout, and another man came running over the meadow; a slim young man was this, and worse of attire than the old carle, for so tattered was his raiment that he was half naked; but he was goodly of fashion, fresh-coloured and black-haired. Birdalone stayed her feet when she saw him, for though she doubted not to outrun him, yet whither should she run, since her ferry was behind her?

So the young man came up to her, and the old carle met him all panting, and the young man said: "How now,
304

Antony! what battle is this? and wherefore art thou chasing this fair knight? And thou, fair sir, why fleest thou this grey dastard?"

Said Antony: "Thou art but a young fool, Otter; this is no man, but a woman, and I have taken her, and she is mine."

"Well," said Otter, "I say she is as much mine as thine; nay, more, if she will give herself unto me. But if she will not, she shall go whither she will in thy despite. Or art thou a woman?"

"Yea, yea," said Birdalone; "and I pray thee, by thy mother's head, suffer me to depart; for heavy and full of need is the errand that I am about."

"Go thou shalt then," said Otter; "lead back to thy place, and I will walk with thee." So did they: and Birdalone went beside the young man quaking; but he put out no hand unto her; and sooth to say, she deemed that she had seldom seen so fair a young man, but it were Arthur or Hugh.

Now he, as Antony, was girt with a short sword, but he let it be in its sheath; and as they went, Antony drew his blade again, and hove it up to smite Otter, but as it befell, Birdalone saw him, and turned round sharp upon him and gat hold of his wrist, and therewith Otter turned also, and caught the old carle by the nape as he turned away, and put a foot before his and shoved mightily, so that he went noseling to the earth.

Then turned Otter about again, laughing, and he said to Birdalone: "By Saint Giles! thou art wellnigh too valiant for a woman, and I would that we two might be together; and then between us we might achieve the adventure of the dead ladies up yonder." She hung her head, and said: "Fair sir, it may not anywise be; yet I thank thee, I thank thee."

So came they to the water-side and the Sending Boat, and Birdalone stayed her feet there, and the young man said: "What is this keel, that seemeth unto me as if it were a ferry for malefactors wending to a death of torment, so grey and

bleared and water-logged and sun-bleached as it is, and
smeared over with stains of I know not what?"

Said Birdalone: "Such as it is, it is my ferry over the
water to where I would be." "Strange!" said Otter; "to my
mind it is like to our fortunes on this Isle, we who were once
knights and merry squires and are now as gangrel men, and
of ill conditions, thinking of nought save our first desires,
even those which we share with the wolf and the kite."

She said: "But art thou of evil conditions, thou who hast
just delivered me from trouble?" He smiled grimly:
"Damsel," said he, "I have not delivered thee yet from
me, though I have from him. But tell me, art thou a sorceress?" "Not a black one," said Birdalone; "but I will tell
thee at once that I have been bred by a witch most mighty,
and some deal of lore have I learned." And therewith she
told him of the Sending Boat, and how she would have to
speed it on the way.

He looked on her a little and then turned away, and saw
her sword lying on the grass; so he went to it and picked it
up and brought it to her, and said: "Thou mayst yet need
this keen friend." So she took it and thrust it back into the
scabbard, quaking somewhat because of him; so feeble and
frail as she felt before him. Then he said: "If thou deemest
thou hast somewhat to reward me for, I have a boon to ask
of thee, and granting that, we shall be quits again." "Yea,"
she said faintly, "and what is the boon?" He said: "Art thou
pressed to depart now, this minute?" "Nay," said Birdalone,
"not for an hour if there be no peril here from other men,
and ... and ..." "And if I be true to thee and will let thee
go?" said he, laughing; "hah! is that not thy word? Fear not,
I swear by thine eyes that thou shalt depart whenso thou wilt.
Now then, the boon I crave is, that thou wilt sit down here
beside me and tell me the tale of thy life that has been." Said
she: "It wearies me to think thereof; yet hast thou a right to
crave somewhat of me, and this is not hard to grant."

And she sat down by him; but he said: "Do this also for
me, take off thine headpiece, since now that we know thee

for a woman it serveth thee nought." So did she, and began her tale straightway, and told him all thereof, save as to the wood-wife, and he sat hearkening and watching her face; and when she had made an end, he said: "Now shall I ask none other boon of thee, though I long sore for it: but best it is that we sunder straightway, else maybe I might yet be for hindering thee."

Therewith he stood up, and Birdalone also, and he looked on her eagerly, and said: "I am now to bid thee farewell, and it is most like that I shall never see thee again, wherefore I will ask thee yet to let one thing come from thy mouth; for I deem thee the dearest of all women I have ever seen."

"What shall I say?" said Birdalone, smiling on him kindly; "must thou needs put the word in my mouth? Thou hast been friendly with me here when need was to me of friendliness; wherefore I say, I would I might see thee again, and thou better bestead than now thou art."

The young man's face brightened and he said: "Spake I not that thou wert the dearest of all? This was even the word I would have put in thy mouth. But now see thou, one goeth on from one thing to another, and I must now ask thee, is there aught which thou hast a mind to give me ere I depart, some keepsake which I durst not ask for?"

She flushed red and said: "I will with a good heart give thee my bow and arrows for a keepsake; whereas the old carle told me that ye be ill furnished of shooting-gear."

And she would have taken her bow from her back, but he laughed aloud, and said: "Nay, nay, I will not have that; for there be those who gird them to a sword and know not how to use it, but few will cumber their shoulders with bow and quiver who cannot shoot therewith; I deem it like that thou art a fell bowman. Keep thy bow therefore, and if thou wilt go without any other gift, even so be it."

And he made as if he would turn away; but she put forth both her hands and took his in them, and lifted up her face and kissed him kindly, and then turned away to her ferry;

while Otter stood still and said in a merry voice: "Now is it better than well, for thou art in all ways what I would have thee, and there is nought like unto thee." And therewith he turned away and departed ere Birdalone had stepped into the Sending Boat, and she blushing like a rose the while. Then she did due sacrifice to the wight of the witch-ferry, and sped on her way without any hindrance.

CHAPTER XIII. BIRDALONE COMETH TO THE ISLE OF THE YOUNG AND THE OLD.

AMIDST all this had worn some hours, but yet it was barely noon; wherefore it was yet dark by then Birdalone made the Isle of the Young and the Old; so she stepped out of the boat, and lay down on the grass and abode the dawn sleeping. And she awoke with the clatter of shrill voices, and she rose up and looked, and lo a multitude of children all about her, both men and women children, and, as it seemed, from five years old upward to fifteen. They cried and crowed merrily when they saw her stand up, and pressed on her to see her the nearer and to touch her hands or her raiment. They were but little clad, and the younger ones not at all, but were goodly younglings and merry. So great was the noise they raised, that loud were the thunder which had not been hushed thereby; and Birdalone stood looking on them smiling, and knew not what to do.

Anon she turned to a tall thin lad of some fifteen winters, and said unto him: "Wilt thou now take me unto the house, and the place where dwelleth the old man?" Quoth he: "I neither know of an old man, nor rightly what it means, the word. Am not I old enough for thee? I am the oldest of these here. But belike thou art hungry; wherefore if thou come to the place where we sleep a-nights, and where we shelter us from the storm and the rain when need is, I will give thee to eat; for we have both bread and milk and cheese, and raisins of the sun."

So he took her hand and led her along, and asked her by the way concerning her armour and weapons, and of the fashion of battle, and she told him thereof what she would.

Thus came they to the place where erst had been the cot under the ruin of the great ancient house; but now was gone all that ruin and the great grey walls, though the cot was left; and all about it were low bowers built of small wood and thatched undeftly. But the lad smiled when he saw it, as if the sight thereof made him happy; and he said: "All these have we made since I have dwelt here, and no other home have I known."

And he led her in to the cot, and set her down to eat and to drink, and through the open door she could see the children swarming, and they that were nighest thrusting each other this way and that to catch a sight of her.

Now she said: "Fair child, how gattest thou this victual, if there be no older folk to help you?" Said he: "We dig the ground and sow it, and the wheat comes up, and we reap it in harvest, and make bread of it; and we have goats and kine, and we milk them, and turn the milk with a little blue flower, which is fair to see. And there are in this isle little hills where the grapes grow plenty; and some we eat and some we dry for store. Lo thou, such be our ways for victual. But tell me," said he, "thou sayest old, and I know not the word: art thou old?" She laughed: "Not very," said she, "yet older than thou."

Said the lad: "Thou art fair and dear to look on, and thy voice is sweet; wilt thou not abide with us, and teach us what it is to be old?" "Nay," said she, "I may not, for I have an errand which driveth me on; wherefore I must be gone within this hour."

Forsooth, she was growing eager now to be done with her journey and come to the House under the Wood, whatever should befall her there. Moreover she deemed it would not be restful to her to abide among all these restless children, with their ceaseless crying and yelping: if rest she might, she

309

would rest, she deemed, in the Isle of Increase Unsought, if there were no ill things abiding there.

Wherefore now she arose, when she had sat hearkening the sound of the lad's prattle for a while, for as to the sense thereof she might not heed it over much. The youngling would not leave her, but led her, holding her hand, down to her ferry again; she kissed him in thanks for his meat, and he reddened thereat but said nought. All the whole rout of little ones had followed her down to the water, and now they stood as thick as bees on a honeycomb on the bank, to watch her departure. But if they were keen to see her doings before, how much keener were they when it came to the baring of her arm and the smearing of the Sending Boat. To be short, so keen were they, and pushed and shoved each other so sturdily, that more than one or two fell into the water, and Birdalone was frighted lest they should drown; but they swam like ducks, and got on to the land when they would, which was not so very soon, for some of them hung on to the gunwale of the boat, and hove their faces up to look over into it, and left not hold till the ferry was fairly under way and beginning to quicken its speed.

So left Birdalone the isle, and nought befell her on the way to the Isle of Increase Unsought.

CHAPTER XIV. NOW IS THE SENDING BOAT GONE.

IT was as before that Birdalone came to the shore of the isle while it was yet night; but the wizard keel was so loathsome to her, that she stepped out of it and laid her down on the land for what was left of the night; yet hard she found her bed, and neither grassy nor flowery.

For all that, she slept, for she was weary, and it was broad day and not very early when she awoke. She stood up trembling, for she foreboded evil, so near as she was to the abode of her old mistress; and she looked up to where in time past was the fair and wicked house, and saw that all was changed indeed: for no longer was the isle goodly with meadow and orchard and garden, but was waste and bare, and nought grew on it save thin and wiry grass, already seeding even ere June was born, and here and there hard and ugly herbs, with scarce aught that might be called a flower amongst them. Trees there were yet, but the most of them stark dead, and the best dying fast. No beasts she saw, nor fowl; nothing but lizards and beetles, and now and again a dry grey adder coiled up about a sun-burned stone. But of great carrion flies, green and blue, were there a many, and whiles they buzzed about her head till she sickened with loathing of them. All this she found on her way as she went up toward the place where erst was the great perron. But when she came to the top there was no sign either of the stairs or the house, or aught that ever was builded: there was nought but the bare bent top, ungrassed, parched by wind, scorched by sun, washed by rain.

She wandered about the isle, to places where she had not been herself, but which she deemed she might have known by the telling of the Green Knight's tale, had there been no change since those days; but now was all changed, and the whole isle was a mere waste, and withal poisonous of aspect to her mind, as if many corpses lay underneath the wretched stones of it. Nevertheless, though it seemed so evil unto Birdalone, she lingered on it, wandering about till she was to-wearied, for she had no will to depart at such time as she would be like to come to her old abiding-place by night and cloud: wherefore she dallied with the time, and came not back to the haven of her ferry till it was nigh sunset, and the westering sun was in her eyes when she came there; and she said to herself that this was the cause why she might not see the Sending Boat.

So she cleared her eyes and looked on the thin grass awhile, and then down over the edge of the land, and still she saw not her boat. She turned pale, and a pang of anguish went to her heart; but she walked a little east, deeming that

311

perchance she had erred as to the place of the haven on that dull and empty shore; but yet there was no boat. Then she turned back wild with terror, and sought where erst she had missed it, and found neither boat nor the world's end. And she deemed that there might be some devilish malice of the wight of the Sending Boat, to torment her with fear, and she walked along the land's edge up and down, and down and up, further each time, and still there was no boat.

Then she stood still and strove to think and might not, nor might she do aught but spread abroad her hands and moaned in her agony; for now indeed she felt herself in the trap; and she said that all her past life of hope and desire and love and honour was all for nought, and that she was but born to die miserably in that foul ruin of an isle envenomed with the memories of bygone cruelty and shame.

But in a little while she came somewhat to herself, and she said: At least this hideous land shall not mock my dying anguish: I will give myself to the water and let it do with me as it will.

Therewith she cast off her helm and hawberk first, and her weapons, and her pouch with the treasure that could buy nought for her now, and thereafter all her raiment, till she was as naked as when she first came aland there that other time. Again she moaned, and put up her hand to her bosom and felt a little gold box lying there betwixt the fragrant hills of her breasts, which hung to a thin golden thread about her neck; and a thought came into her mind, and she stooped adown and drew from her pouch flint and fire-steel, and then opened the said golden box and drew thence the tress which Habundia the Woodwife had given to her those years agone, and all trembling she drew two hairs from it, as erst she did on the Isle of Nothing, and struck fire and kindled tinder and burnt the said hairs, and then hung the golden box with the tress therein about her neck again; and she said: O Woodmother, if only thou couldst know of me and see me, thou wouldst help me!

Thereafter she sought along the bank for bread which

she had taken from her store that morning, and she found
it, and compelled herself to eat of it for the strengthening of
her body, and then she stood and abode tidings, and by then
the sun had just sunk below the rim of the lake, and the
stars began to twinkle; for the night was cloudless, and
exceeding fair, and very warm.

No visible token came to her, but her heart grew stronger,
and she seemed to see herself yet alive and in hope on the
other side of the water; and she said: Who wotteth what
Weird may do, or where the waters may bear me? and there
is no swimmer stronger than I.

So then without more ado Birdalone slipped into the
water, which lay before her as calm and plain as a great
sheet of glass, and fell to rowing with her arms and her legs
as though she were but swimming from Green Eyot to the
mainland, as so oft she had done in the other days.

CHAPTER XV. SHE SWIMMETH THE WATER AND HELP COMETH.

ON swam Birdalone, not as one who had a mind to
drown her for the forgetting of troubles, but both
strongly and wisely; and she turned over on to her
back, and looked on the stars above her, and steered herself
by them thitherward whereas she deemed was the Land under the Wood. When she had been gone from the evil isle
for an hour or so, there rose a fair little wind behind her,
which helped her forward, but scarce raised the water more
than a little ripple.

Still she swam on, and it was some three hours ere she began to weary, and then she floated on her back and let the
wind and water have its way with her; and now the night
was as dark as it would be ere dawn.

Thus it went for another hour, that whiles she swam on
and whiles she floated; and now her heart began to fail her,
and the Great Water was no longer unto her a wet highway,
but a terrible gulf over which she hung fainting.

313

PART VI
Chap. 15
Nevertheless she did not give up doing what she might: she floated supine a long while, and then, when she had gathered a little strength, turned over again and struck out, still steering her by the stars. But she had scarce made three strokes ere her arms met something hard and rough; and at first in her forlornness she deemed she had happened on some dread water monster, and for terror of it she sank down into the deep, but came up presently blinded and breathless, and spread abroad her arms, and again they came on the thing aforesaid, and this time found that it was nought alive, but the bole of a tree sitting high out of the water. So she clomb up on to it with what might she had left, and sat her down, and saw in the dim light that it was big, and that there was a fork betwixt two limbs reaching up into the air, and she thrust herself in between these two limbs and embraced one of them, so that she might scarce tumble off; and a great content and happiness came over her that she had thus escaped from the death of the deep; but therewithal weariness overcame her, and she slept, whether she would or not; and the bole went on over the waters no slower than might have been looked for, whether it were by the pushing on of the south wind, or by the hand of Weird that would not have her die.

Long she slumbered; for when she awoke it was broad day and the sun was shining high in the heavens, and she cleared her eyes and looked around, and saw before her the land, but yet blue in the offing. And the tree-bole was yet speeding on towards the shore, as if it were being drawn there by some bidding of might.

Now indeed grew Birdalone happy, and she thought if any had helped her it must have been the Woodmother once again; and she said to herself that she should soon meet with that helper; nor heeded she that she was naked and unfurnished of any goods, whereas she deemed indeed that it was but to ask and have of her friend.

For a while indeed she knew not whither she was wending, and if her face were verily turned toward the Land
314

under the Wood; but as the morning wore the blue distance
began to grow green, and then she saw that a great wood
was indeed before her, and thereafter, as it cleared yet more,
she knew the land she was nearing for the meadows of the
House under the Wood, and it was not long thence ere she
saw clear and close Green Eyot and Rock Eyot, though
the house was yet hidden from her by the green shores of
the first of those two isles.

Shortly to tell it, her tree-bole floated with her past the
outer ness of Green Eyot, and came ashore in that same
sandy bight where erst she was wonted to make her body
ready for the water. She stepped ashore all glad to feel the
firm warm sand underneath her foot-soles, and as one drunk
with joy she was when the tall flowery grass of the latter May
was caressing her legs as they shook the seed-dust off the
bents, and smote the fragrance out of the blossoms; and she
might scarce at first lift her eyes from their familiar loveliness.   Glad she was indeed, but exceeding worn and weary
with the long voyage, and all the longing and fear and hope
which had encompassed her that while. She lifted up her
eyes but once, and saw the witch's house standing where it
was wont, but no shape of man moving about it; then she
turned aside to a little brake of thorn and eglantine in the
meadow hard by, and laid her down on the grass in the shade
thereof, and almost before her head touched the ground she
fell asleep, and slept there long and peacefully.

CHAPTER XVI. BIRDALONE FINDETH HER WITCH-MISTRESS DEAD.

IT was some while after noon when she wakened, and the
sun was shining bright and hot. Somewhat she felt the
burden of fear upon her, even before she was fully come
to herself, and knew not what it was that she feared; but
when she called to mind that it was even the meeting with
her old mistress, her flesh quaked indeed with the memory
of bygone anguish, but valiantly she arose and faced the

315

dwelling of the witch despite her naked helplessness. As she went she looked up unto it, and saw no smoke coming from the chimney, but marvelled little thereat since it was not yet cooking-time and the weather hot. She drew nigher, and saw someone sitting on the bench without the door whereas the witch was wonted; and her heart beat quick, for she saw presently that it was none other than her mistress. Moreover, near to her stood three of the milch-kine lowing uneasily and as in reproach, even as such beasts use when their udders be full and they desire to be milked.

Birdalone stayed a minute, and her legs nigh failed her for fear, and then because of the very fear she hastened on till she came within ten paces of the said witch; and sore she missed her bow and arrows, and the cutting blade of her feigned squirehood, lest the carline should arise and come raging and shrieking at her.

Then spake Birdalone in no feeble voice, and said: "Dame, I am come back unto thee, as thou seest, in even such plight as I fled from thee; and I have a mind to dwell in this land: what sayest thou?" The witch neither moved nor spake at her word; and the kine, who had held silence when she first came up, and had turned from her, fell to their peevish lowing again.

Birdalone drew a step nigher, and said: "Dost thou hear me, dame, or art thou exceeding wroth with me, and art pondering what vengeance thou wilt take on me?" Still no answer came from the carline, and the kine kept on lowing now and again. Once more Birdalone drew nigher, and spake loudly and said: "Tell me at least, is it peace between us or unpeace?"

But now when she looked she saw that the eyes of the witch were open and staring, and her lips white, and her hands hard writhen; and she cried out and said: "Is she dead? or will she waken presently and be at me? surely she is dead." And she put forth her hand and touched her face, and it was stone-cold; and she found that she was dead beyond any question.

Then was a great weight lifted off her heart, and she turned about and looked on the meadows and up to the trees of the wood and down to the rippling stream before her, and fair and sweet and joyous were they gotten unto her; and she looked at the kine who were drawing up towards her, and she laughed merrily, and went to the outhouse hard by and took forth a milking-pail and a stool and fell to milking them one after the other, and the beasts went off down the meadow lowing in a changed voice, for joy to wit, this time. But Birdalone knelt down and drank a long draught of the sweet warm milk, and then arose and went swiftly into the house, and saw nought changed or worsened so far as she could see. There was her own bed in the corner, and the mistress's, greater and much fairer, over against it; and the hutch by the door wherein the victual was kept: she opened it now, and found three loaves there on the shelf, and a meal-tub down below, and she took a loaf and broke it and fell to eating it as she walked about the chamber. There was her bow standing in a nook beside the hutch, and the quiver of arrows hanging on the wall above it. There was the settle lying athwart from the hearth; and she smiled, and fitted her wrists to the back of the carven bear which made its elbow, whereto the witch was wont to tie them when she chastised her.

Then she went to the coffers that stood against the wall behind it, and threw up the lid of one of them, and found therein a smock or two of her own, yellowed by the lapse of time, and her old grey coat, ragged as it was when last she wore it, and now somewhat moth-eaten withal; and she drew forth both smocks and coat and laid them on the settle. Then she opened another coffer, and therein were gay and gaudy gowns and gear of the witch's wear; but lying amongst them, as if the witch had worn them also, her green gown and shoon which her own hands had broidered. But she said: "Nay, ye have been in ill company, I will wear you not, though ye be goodly, at least not till ye have been fumigated and hallowed for me."

317

Therewith she turned back to the settle and did on her old smock and her ragged grey coat, and said: To-day at least will these be good enough for to-day's work. And she knit her brow withal, and walked with a firm step out-a-doors and stood a while gazing on the dead corpse of her enemy; and she thought how that here was that which once was so great a thing unto her for the shaping of her life-days, and which so oft came to her waking thoughts after she had escaped from her hands (though, as aforesaid, she seldom dreamed of her a night-time), and moreover an hour ago she yet feared it so sore that she [scarce] might stand for the fear of it—and now it was nought but a carven log unto her.

But she told herself that the work was to be done; so she dragged the body away thence, and across the brook, and a little way into the meadow, and then she went back and fetched mattock and spade from the outhouse, where she knew they lay, and so fell to digging a grave for the corpse of her dead terror. But howso hard she might toil, she was not through with the work ere night began to fall on her, and she had no mind to go on with her digging by night. Wherefore she went back into the house, and lighted candles, whereof was no lack, and made her supper of the bread and the milk; and then sat pondering on her life that had been till the passion arose in her bosom, and the tears burst out, and long she wept for desire of others and pity for herself. Then she went to the bed she had been erst wont to, and laid her down and fell asleep. And her mistress walked not, nor meddled with her peace; nor did Birdalone so much as dream of her, but of her mother and Master Jacobus in the fair city of the Five Crafts; and in her sleep she wept for thinking of them.

CHAPTER XVII. OF THE WITCH-WIFE AND THE SENDING BOAT.

WHEN morning was, Birdalone awoke, and felt a weight upon her heart, and called to mind the task which lay before her. So she arose and clad herself, and went straight to the grave begun, and toiled hard till she had digged it out deep, and sithence she dragged the witch thereinto and heaped the earth upon her. Then she bathed her in the nighest pool of the brook, and went back into the house and made her breakfast on the bread and milk, and it was then about mid-morning. Thereafter she went about the house, and saw to the baking of bread, and so out to the meadow to see to the kine and the goats, and then stored the milk for making butter and cheese, and did in all wise as if she were to dwell long in that stead; but thereafter she rested her body, whiles her thought went wide about. But she said to herself that she would not go up to the Oak of Tryst to meet the Woodmother that day, but would abide the night, in case aught befell that she should tell her.

But when the sun was getting low she roused herself and went out, and walked about the meadow, and hearkened to the birds' song, and watched the kine and the goats as they fed down the pasture; and now a soft content came over her, that all this was free unto her to hold in peace, and to take her pleasure in, as much as one lone child of Adam might do.

At last she wandered down to the sandy bight of the lake and stood gazing on Green Eyot, where the osiers and willows were grown wild and long in all these years, and she said that she would swim over to it on the morrow. But now her feet took her eastward thence toward the haven of the Sending Boat amongst the alders; for in her heart she would fain know if there were any tidings for her.

So she went softly along the path by the water, where she had sped so swiftly that last time, and came at last to the creek-side, and looked down on to the water somewhat timorously. There then she saw what she deemed was the very boat itself lying as she had known it; but when she looked again she saw that it lay from stem to stern all loose staves with the water betwixt, and the thwarts and ribs all sundered and undone, so that never again might it float upon the waves. Then she said in a soft voice : "Art thou dead then, as thy mistress is dead ? was it not so that thou wert at the point of death, and she also, when thou failedst me at the Isle of Increase Unsought?" No voice came to her as she spake; and she said again: "Must I then bury thee as I have buried thy mistress ? Nay, that will I not until thou compellest me; belike in a short while little of the staves of thee shall be left now that the life is out of thee. Let thy ghost and hers foregather if ye will."

As she spake the last word, she saw a stir about the stem which lay furthest in up the creek, and while she quaked with failing heart, lo ! a big serpent, mouldy and hairy, grey and brown-flecked, came forth from under the stem and went into the water and up the bank and so into the dusk of the alder-wood. Birdalone stood awhile pale and heart-sick for fear, and when her feet felt life in them, she turned and stole away back again into the merry green mead and the low beams of the sun, pondering whether this evil creature were the fetch of the wight who drave the ferry under the blood of the sender.

So she hastened back again to the house, and lit a fire on the hearth, and fell to cooking her somewhat of grout to her supper; and she watched the fire, thinking withal: Now if some poor soul be abroad, they may see the smoke and seek hither, and I may comfort them with food and shelter and converse; or when night darkens, they may see the litten windows and come to me; wherefore shall the fire burn yet and the candles be lighted, for as warm as is the evening, even as if it were Yule-tide and the snow deep without, and the wind howling in the woodland trees. And therewith she wept for longing of them that she loved.

But in a little she dried her tears, and reproached herself
320

for her much softness; and she ate her supper when she had
lighted a candle (for it was now dark), and again sat looking
at the hearth, till she said: Now am I getting soft again, and
who knows but my softness may tempt the ghosts to come
in to me. I will give my hands somewhat to do.

Therewith her eye caught sight of the rents and rags of
her old grey gown, and she smiled somewhat ruefully as she
called to mind her gallant knight's array, which lay now on
the shore of the evil and ruined isle; and her goodly attire of
the days of the Five Crafts; and the rich raiment wherein
her friends of the Castle of the Quest had clad her. Then she
arose and sought needle and thread and some remnants of
green cloth, and did off the ragged coat and fell to patching
and mending it, and so sat at her work in smock, sewing till
the night was old and she was weary and sleep overcame her,
and she lay down in her bed and slept dreamlessly till the
sun was high next morning.

CHAPTER XVIII. BIRDALONE BETAKETH HER TO THE OAK OF TRYST.

NOW Birdalone arose and bathed her and broke her
fast, and then went about her work with the beasts
and the dairy; but all that time seemed long to her
till she had bow in hand and quiver on back, and was wending her way to the Oak of Tryst; and swift were her feet,
and her heart beat quick with hope of pleasure.

Forsooth no long tarrying had she, for scarce had she set
her down beneath the oak, ere the Woodmother came forth
from the thicket even as the first time when Birdalone saw
her, and presently she had her arms about Birdalone and
was kissing and clipping her. Then they sat down together
in the shade of the great tree, and the Woodmother made
much of her friend with few words and those but simple,
while Birdalone wept for joy.

At last spake Birdalone: "Woodmother, my dear, I look
in thy face, and I see thee that thou art nowise changed, so

that thou callest to my mind the Birdalone that met thee here when she was straying from the House of Captivity like to a bird with a string to its leg."

Habundia smiled on her and said: "So it is that now thou lookest older than I. Rounder and fuller is thy body, and thy limbs greater and fairer, and thy flesh sleeker; lovelier art thou in all wise, and such as I have thought of thee during these years: save that thy face is grown wiser and sadder than might be looked for."

"Mother," she said, "I am grown older than I should be by the tale of the years, for I have had joy and grief, and grief and joy, and grief again; and now that the years have worn, the grief abideth and the joy hath departed, save this joy of thee and the day of the meeting I have so often thought of."

Said the Woodwife: "Were I to hear the story of thee, I deem it most like that I would fain buy thy joy with thy grief, both that which has been and that which is to come. And now I will ask thee right out to tell me all thy tale, as much as thou canst; and all thou canst tell to me, who am thine other self: and I wot moreover that thou hast not told of me to any whom thou hast met in the world since we were last together: is it not so?" "In faith and in troth so it is," said Birdalone.

Said Habundia, after she had looked hard on Birdalone a while: "Now there is this I find in thee, that though thou callest me woodmother still, thou art not my daughter as thou wert erewhile, nor I thy mother: and I know not whether to be glad or sorry thereof, since thou art even as much my friend as ever thou wert. But much do I rejoice herein that thou hast not told any one soul of me."

Said Birdalone: "That part of the tale I shall tell thee is how I have found my mother in the flesh, and loved her sorely; and then I lost her again: for she is dead."

Quoth the Woodwife, smiling on her lovingly: "Then should I be even more thy mother than erst I was: there will be something else in thy tale, sweetling."

322

Then Birdalone flushed very red, and she smiled piteously in Habundia's face; but then she put up her hands to hide the change therein which the anguish of longing wrought, and her shoulders shook and her bosom heaved, and she wept bitterly; but the Woodwife still looked on her smiling, and said softly at last: "Yea, how sweet it were to be grieved with thy pain."

But in a while Birdalone grew calm again and the very smile blossomed out in her face, and they kissed together. Then Habundia rose up and looked on her, and said at last, and laughed out withal: "One thing I must needs say, that thou hast not fetched thee raiment of price from the knighthood and the kings' houses. Or have I not seen thy grey coat of old time, while thou wert living amidst the witch's cruelty?" "Yea forsooth," said Birdalone; "thou needest not to ask this."

"Verily not," said Habundia, "nor why thou art not clad in the fair green gown which thou didst broider: for whiles I have seen the witch flaunting it on the wooden ugly body of her, and thou wouldst not wear it after she had cursed it with her foulness. Is it not so?"

"Yea, it is even so," said Birdalone; "dost thou love me the less therefor?" Habundia laughed again: "Were I a man of Adam's sons," said she, "I might make thee many words on the seemliness of thy short coat, and the kindness of it, that it will be for ever slipping off one or other of thy shoulders. But now am I at least enough thy mother, and thou art dwelling even so much in my house, that the next time we meet (and that shall be to-morrow) I shall fetch thee raiment which shall make us forget that thou camest back again to this land as naked as thou didst depart thence."

Birdalone reddened and hung down her head, but the Woodmother sat down beside her and kissed her and said: "But now forget all save thy tale, and tell all as closely as thou mayest, for I would lose nought thereof."

"Yea," said Birdalone; "and where shall I begin?"

Said Habundia: "I know nought thereof save the begin-

Y2   323

ning, that thou fledst away naked and escaped the witch; and the ending, to wit, that the Sending Boat failed thee at the last of the Wonder Isles, and that thou calledst on me not wholly in vain; whereas the witch was dead, and therefore there was nought to stay me from sending thee one of my trees and the wight thereof (whom belike I may show to thee one day) to save thee from the bottom of the deep water."

At that word Birdalone threw herself on the Woodwife and clipped and kissed her, and thanked her for the helping with all the dearest words she might. But the Woodmother laughed for joy, and stroked her cheeks and said: " Now I deem thee my daughter again, whereas thou thankest me with such sweet passion for doing to thee as a kind mother needs must without any thought thereof. And I bid thee, my dear, never again to go so far from me as that I may not easily help thee and comfort thee from out of my realm wherein I am mighty. And now tell me all in thy dear speech."

Therewith Birdalone began her story without more ado, even as ye have heard it afore. Yea and many more things than we can set down did she tell, for fullfilled she was with the wisdom of the Wood. And between whiles the Woodmother fed her with dainty meat and drink, such as Birdalone had never erst tasted the like of. And by then she had got so far as her flight from the Isle of Increase Unsought, the sun was set and the twilight begun. And the Woodwife said: "Now shalt thou go home to thine house; and have no fear of witch or evil thing, for I am not far from thee and will watch over thee. Sweet is thy tale, my daughter, and dear are thy she-friends; and if ever it may be that I may do them any pleasure, fain were I; and that especially to thy Viridis, who meseemeth is both sweet and wise even as thou thyself art. Nay, dost thou begrudge my loving her?"

"Nay, nay," said Birdalone, laughing; "but I rejoice in it. And hereafter when I tell thee how sorely they paid for helping me, I will bid thee to love them yet more than now thou dost."

324

Therewith they parted, and Birdalone came to her house; and on the way she made as it were a feigned tale in mockery of her old trouble, that there would be the witch-mistress awaiting her to whip her. So that when she came to the door she was half frighted with her own mock, lest the witch might now at last have taken to walking.

But all was quiet when she entered with the last of the twilight, and she rested that night in all peace, as in the best of her days in the Five Crafts.

CHAPTER XIX. BIRDALONE IS CLAD IN FAERY RAIMENT.

NEXT morning Birdalone tarried about the house as little a while as she might, and then went hastening up to the wood; and when she came within sight of the Trysting Tree, lo! there was Habundia before her, and the hands of her busy turning over goodly raiment, so that it was well-nigh as if the days had gone back to the time of the Captivity, and the sitter under the oak was Birdalone herself dealing with her half-finished gown.

Joyously they met and embraced each other, and then spake the Woodwife: "Now, thou darling of the world, I have been no worse than my word, and if thou durst wear web of the Faery thou shalt presently be clad as goodly as ever thou wert down there amongst the knighthood: and then thy tale, my dear, and if it may be, the wisdom of the barren wood-wife set thereto."

And therewith she laid on Birdalone's outstretched arms the raiment she had brought with her, and it was as if the sunbeam had thrust through the close leafage of the oak, and made its shadow nought a space about Birdalone, so gleamed and glowed in shifty brightness the broidery of the gown; and Birdalone let it fall to earth, and passed over her hands and arms the fine smock sewed in yellow and white silk, so that the web thereof seemed of mingled cream and curd; and she looked on the shoon that lay beside the

gown, that were done so nicely and finely that the work was
as the feather-robe of a beauteous bird, whereof one scarce
can say whether it be bright or grey, thousand-hued or all
simple of colour. Birdalone quivered for joy of the fair
things, and crowed in her speech as she knelt before
Habundia to thank her: then in a twinkling had she done
off her beggar's raiment, and then the smock clung about
her darling nakedness, and next the gown was shimmering
all over her, and the golden girdle embraced her loins as
though it loved them worthily; and Birdalone looked to the
wood round about her and laughed, while Habundia lay in
her place and smiled upon her with gentle loving-kindness.

But in a little while was Birdalone sobered: for the
thought of how fair she should look to the eyes of her
beloved when she was shown unto him on the day of days,
thrust her light and eager pleasure aside; and she took up
her shoes from the ground (for she had not done them on),
and sat down beside the Woodwife and fell a-toying with
the marvel of them; and thus without more ado began her
tale again, whereas she had left it last even, when she had
told of how the Sending Boat was speeding her over the
waters toward the Isle of the Young and the Old.

CHAPTER XX. BIRDALONE TELLETH OF HER LOVE.

LONG they sat there that day, and until the sun was
down, and by then had Birdalone but little to tell of her
story, for she was gotten therein to the days of the
Five Crafts. Many times had she wept and turned to
Habundia for solace as she told, not without shame, but
without any covering up, all the tale of her love for Arthur
the Black Squire, and how she was surprised by the love of
him, and of his wisdom and grace and loveliness. And the
Woodmother was ever as sweet and kind unto her as could
be; yet might another than a lover have seen that much of
all this was strange unto her, and she looked upon Birdalone
326

as a child who has broken her toy, and is hard to comfort for
the loss of it, though there be a many more in the world.

But when it grew dusk as aforesaid, and it was time to part, she spake to Birdalone, and said: "True it is, my child, that thou hast lived long in these six years' time; neither do I wonder at the increase of thy beauty, and the majesty thereof; for fair is the life thou hast lived, although thou hast been grieved and tormented by it at whiles. And now I know what it is for which thou longest; and herein again will I play the mother unto thee, and seek about to fetch thee that thou wouldst have; so be not over anxious or troubled; and thou mayest be good herein, as my fair child should be; for this I have noted in thee, that Love is not so tyrannous a master but that his servants may whiles think of other matters, and so solace their souls, that they may live despite of all."

Now was Birdalone arisen, and stood before her friend confused and blushing. But Habundia put her two hands on her shoulders and kissed her, and said: "Go home now and sleep, and come again to-morrow and let us hear the last of thy tale; and when that is done, maybe I shall be able to do something for thine avail."

So they parted, and on the morrow Birdalone came again and told the remnant of her story, which was not so long now that the Black Squire was out of it. And when she had done, Habundia kept silence a while, and then she said: "One thing I will tell thee, that whereas erewhile it was but seldom indeed that any son of Adam might be seen in the woodland here, of late, that is, within the last three years, there be many such amongst us; and to our deeming they be evil beasts, more pitiless and greedy than any bear; and but that we have nought to do with them, for they fear us and flee from us, we should have destroyed them one and all. And now that I have heard all thy story, it seemeth unto me not so unlike but these may be the remnants of the bands of the Red Hold, and that they have drifted hither fleeing before the might of thy friends of the knighthood. Where-

fore now, trust me that I will look into this, but I must
needs be away from here for a little; so hold thy soul in
patience though thou hear nought of me, and dwell quietly
at home for seven days' space, and then come hither and
find me. Farewell now, my child!"

So they kissed and departed; and Birdalone went home
to the house, and wore the days thereafter doing what was
needful about the stead, and wandering through the meadows, and swimming the waters about Green Eyot; and the
days were not unrestful unto her.

CHAPTER XXI. HOW THE WOODWIFE EN-
TERED THE COT, AND A WONDER THAT
BEFELL.

BUT when it was the sixth day since those two had met,
Birdalone arose in the morning and stood in the door
of the house, and she looked toward the bent which
went up to the wood and saw one coming down it, and knew
it for Habundia clad in her huntress' raiment and bearing
something over the left arm, for her bow was in her right
hand. So Birdalone ran to meet her, and embraced and kissed
her and was merry over her, and said: "Dear mother, thou
farest far from thy fastness to-day." Said Habundia: "There
is nought in the meadows now save the neat and the goats
and thou; of none of that folk am I afraid. But mayhappen
thou shalt be afraid to come with me into the depths of the
wild-wood, for thither would I lead thee."

"I will be afraid of nought with thee beside me," said Birdalone. "But come now and look upon the house that I have
won for me." And she took her hand and led her along; and
the Woodwife said no more till they were across the brook
and standing by the porch.

Then said Birdalone: "Thou hast a green gown over thine
arm; is that also for me?" "Yea certes," said Habundia;
"the old rag which thou hast on thee, and which thou lovest
so sore, is not fine enough for my company; and the glitter-

328

gown I gave thee may be too fine for the thorns and the briars,
and moreover thou mayst be over easily seen if thou bear that
broidered sunshine mid the boughs. Wherefore go in now
and do on this other coat, though the Faery have made it, and
then come out to me with thy bow and thy quiver, and I shall
find thee sandal-shoon and girdle withal."

"Nay, Woodmother," said Birdalone, "hallow my house
by entering it, and eat a morsel with me and drink the wine
of the horned folk ere we go our ways."

Habundia shook her head and knit her brows somewhat
as she looked hard on the house; then she said: "I know not,
Adam's daughter; I have little to do with houses, and doubt
if a house be safe for me. And this one that the witch builded!
and belike she buried some human being at one of its four
corners. Tell me, fair child, sawest thou ever here at night-
tide the shape of a youngling crowned with a garland straying about the house?"

"Nay, never at all," said Birdalone. Said the Woodwife:
"Then maybe thou hast hallowed it with the wisdom and love
of thee, and I may venture; and moreover I note that it is all
builded of tree and the grass of the earth; and thou art free
to use them by my leave. But if aught befall of my coming
under thy roof, heed it not too much; but think, whatsoever
my aspect may be, I am thy Woodmother and Wisdom-
mother that loveth thee. And I bid thee also wish with all thy
might that my aspect may not change to thee. Also, if I eat,
thou wert best not to sign the meat as Adam's sons are wont.
Lead in then: for now am I grown wilful, and will enter whatever betide."

Birdalone marvelled at those words, but she fell to wishing strongly that her friend might not lose her lovely youthful shape either then or ever, and she took her hand, which
trembled somewhat, and led her over the threshold; and
when they were under the roof herseemed that the Woodmother dwindled in a wondrous way, though her face was as
sweet and her limbs as shapely as ever; and she laughed shrilly
yet sweetly, and spake in a thin clear voice: "Birdalone, my

dear, wish strongly, wish strongly! though thou shalt see nothing worse of me than this." And she was scarce three feet high, but as pretty as a picture.

Thereat indeed was Birdalone affrighted, but she wished all she might, and stooped down to kiss this little creature; and therewith the Woodwife seemed to wax again as great and tall as ever she was, and her voice came full and strong again, as she laughed and said: "Now is it all over for this time, and I see how well thou lovest me; and I pray thee love me no less for this wonder thou hast seen in me. But now it were better that I never go under a roof again." And she took her arms about Birdalone and clipped her lovingly; and glad was Birdalone to feel her so strong and solid again.

Then they sat to the board and ate simple meat of bread and cheese and wood-berries, and drank milk withal; and the Woodmother was merry, and the smiles danced over her face as she looked on Birdalone with all loving-kindness, so that Birdalone wondered what was toward; but so light-hearted and happy she grew, that she deemed it might be nought save good.

But when they had eaten, then Birdalone did off her old coat, which she said was meet enough for her daily toil, and did on the green hunting-gown and the sandal-shoon, and girt her with the fair girdle which Habundia had fetched her, and drew up the laps of her gown therethrough till her legs were all free of the skirts. And Habundia looked on her and laughed and said: "Now are these white and smooth legs as bad as the gleam-gown for the lying hid; but it may no better be, and thou must draw thy skirts down and stumble, if needs must be, when we come to the ambushment."

Birdalone reddened as she laughed at the word, and took down her bow and hung her quiver at her back and thrust her sharp knife into her girdle, and forth they went both of them, and were presently past the bent which went up from the meadows and in amongst Habundia's trees.

330

CHAPTER XXII. BIRDALONE WENDETH THE WILDWOOD IN FELLOWSHIP WITH HABUNDIA.

NOW as they went their ways lightly through the wood, spake Habundia and said: "Birdalone, my child, fair is the gold ring with the sapphire stone that the third finger of thy right hand beareth; seldom have I seen so fair a stone as that deep blue one; hangeth any tale thereby?" Said Birdalone: "Did I not tell thee thereof, Woodmother, how that my beloved who is lost gave it unto me the very last time I saw him—woe worth the while!" "Nay," said Habundia, "I mind not the tale. But deemest thou he would know it again if he saw it?" "Yea surely," said Birdalone, hanging her head; "for when first he gave it, the gift was not to me, but to another woman." And she held her peace, and went on with hanging head and all the glee faded out of her a while.

At last she turned to Habundia, and said: "I have now bethought me to ask thee whither we be going and on what errand; for at first I was so glad at heart, I know not why, and it was so merry to be wending the wood with thee freely, that I had no thought in me as to whither and wherefore. But now wilt thou tell me?"

Said the Woodwife: "How if I were to tell thee we were going a-hunting?" Birdalone said: "Then I should ask thee what like the quarry were." "And suppose it were men?" said the Woodwife.

Birdalone turned somewhat pale. "My mother," she said, "if we be going against some of those men of the Red Band, I am not happy over it. I am no warrior, and fear strokes." Said Habundia, laughing: "Yet art thou a fell archer; and thou mayest shoot from an ambush of the thick leaves, since June is in to-day." "But neither would I slay or hurt any man," said Birdalone, "but it were to save me from present death."

Habundia looked on her with a sly smile and said: "Well

maybe though we take cover and get within wind of our
quarry thou shalt not need to speed an arrow to him. Have
patience therefore. For this is a strange beast which I have
marked down; he is not ill to look on, and his voice, which
we may well hearken, for whiles he singeth, is rather sweet
than surly."

"What meanest thou, mother?" said Birdalone, growing
red and then paler yet; "what man is it? since thy calling
him a beast is a jest, is it not?"

"Nay," said Habundia, "I neither name him nor know
him: only I deem him by no means to be one of the Red
Band. For the rest, he may be a man in a beast's skin, or a
beast in a man's skin, for aught I know; whereas he seems,
so far as I have seen him, to be not wholly manlike or
wholly beast-like. But now let us hold our peace of him till
we be come nigher to his haunt."

So they went on their way, and Birdalone said but little,
while the Woodwife was of many words and gay. They
made all diligence, for Birdalone was not soon wearied, and
moreover as now she was anxious and eager to see what
would befall, which she might not but deem would be something great.

They went without stay till past noon, when they were
come to a little shady dale wherethrough ran a clear stream;
there they rested and bathed them, and thereafter sat under
the boughs and ate the dainty meat which the Woodwife
provided, howsoever she came by it; and when they had
rested a while, the Woodwife turned the talk once more
unto Arthur the Black Squire, and would have Birdalone
tell her all nicely what manner of man he was; and Birdalone was nothing loth thereto; for had she her will she had
talked of him daylong.

CHAP. XXIII. NOW IS BIRDALONE BROUGHT TO SIGHT OF ARTHUR.

NOW they go on again, no less speedily than before, and rest but little, until it was hard on an hour before sunset. And now Habundia began to go warily, as if they were come anigh to their journey's end and the thing that they sought. They were come by now to a long bent of the forest well grown with big-boled oak-trees, not very close together, so that short fine greensward was all underneath them; and Habundia went heedfully from bole to bole, as if she would be ready to cover herself if need were; and Birdalone went after her, and was now flushed of face, and her eyes glittered and her heart beat fast, and her legs trembled under her, as she went running from tree to tree.

So came they nigh to the crown of the bent, and before them were the oak-trees sparser and smaller as they went down the further side, which seemed by their sudden shortening to be steeper than the hither side; and betwixt them showed the topmost of thorn and whitebeam and dogwood, intertwined with eglantine and honeysuckle and the new shoots of the traveller's joy. There the Woodwife put forth her hand to bid Birdalone stay, who came up to her friend and stood before her eager and quivering: and anon came the sound of a man's voice singing, though they could hear no words in it as yet amidst the rustle of the trees and the tumult of song which the blackbirds and throstles raised in the dale below them.

Then spake the Woodwife softly: "Hearken, we are right and the time is good, our beast is giving tongue: now below us is the bent-side steep, and goeth down into a very little dale with a clear stream running amidst; and therein is the very lair of the thing that we are hunting. Wherefore now let us slip warily down between the bushes till we get close to the bottom, and then belike we shall see the very creature quite close, and we shall then consider and think what we shall do with him."

333

Birdalone had no voice wherewith to answer her, but she
stole quietly along by her side till they came to the bank of the
dale and plunged into the thicket that flourished there, and
fell to threading it, making them as small as might be. But
ere they had gone but a little way the wordless song of what
was below had ceased, and they heard the sweet tingle of the
string-play, and the Woodwife stayed her to hearken, and
the smiles went rippling over her face and she beat time with
her fingers; but Birdalone, she stared wild before her, and
would have scrambled down the bank straightway at all haz-
ards, for that string-play was a melody of the Castle of the
Quest; but Habundia withheld her by the arm. And then
suddenly the music died, and there came up a voice of wailing and lamenting, and Birdalone put her hands and held the
palms tight against her ears, and was at point to cry out aloud
herself; but Habundia drew a hand of her down and whispered into her ear: "Child, child, make thyself strong and forbear, and then perchance joy may come to thee; hold thy
peace and come softly along with me!"

So Birdalone forbore, and strove with her passion, though
the sobs rent her bosom for a while; and by then the loud
lamenting waned and was done, and the sound of sobbing
came up from below, as it had been an echo of Birdalone's
grief.

Then Habundia drew her on again till they saw the level
of the dale and its stream piecemeal betwixt the leaves, and
they had a glimpse of a man on the hither side of the stream;
and again they went lower, till they were well-nigh on a level
with the greensward of the dale; and as Birdalone knelt with
head bent low, and her hands covering her eyes, the Woodwife put away from before her the thick leaves of a hazel-
bush, and whispering said: "Child, child! look forth now
and see what is before thee, and see if thou knowest him, or
if he be strange to thee, and thy mother hath done nought
for thee when all is said."

Birdalone looked up, pale and wild-eyed, and into the dale,
and saw a man sitting on the grass by the stream-side with

his head bowed down on to his knees and his face covered
with his hands; he was clad but in two or three deerskins
hung about him, with a strip of skin for a girdle, wherein
was thrust a short sword; his brown hair hung down long
and shaggy over his face. He was beating the earth with
his feet and writhing him about over them. And Birdalone looked, and her breath well-nigh failed her. For presently he sat more quietly and lifted up his head, and she saw
his face that it was Arthur, her beloved, and now she durst
not move lest he should spring up and flee away; and the
mingled pain and longing within her was sweet indeed, but
well-nigh deadly.

Now his hand sought round to his harp, and he took it in
his arms and fondled it as it were, and his fingers went among
the strings, and anon the voice of it came forth, and it was
nought changed from the last time it spake, and Birdalone
hearkened breathlessly, till the melody died again and Arthur
looked about him and raised his face as a dog when it fares to
howl.

Then Birdalone gave a great cry, and leapt forth out of the
thicket and stood on the greensward with nought betwixt
them two, and she stretched out her arms to her beloved and
cried out: "O! no, no, no! do it not, I beseech thee, lest I
deem that thou art all changed, and that the man and the dear
heart beloved of thee has gone out of thee and left thee but
a beast in a man's shape!"

He leapt up as she spake, and thrust forward his head and
looked fierce at her, and cried out: "What! art thou come
again? This is the second time I have seen thee, thou image
of her that hath tormented me so long: of her that left me in
my most need and hid herself away from me. Hah! a man,
sayest thou? Did I not strive with it, and hold my manhood
so long as I might; and at last it might no longer be, and I
became a beast and a man-slayer—But what avails it to talk
with thee, since thou art but the image of her that hath wasted
my life. Yet perchance of the image I may make an end since
I may not lay hand on the very destroyer herself—and woe's

335

me, how I loved her! yea, and do still; but not thee, O false image!"

And forthwith he drew the blade from his girdle and sprang forward at Birdalone; and she cowered and cringed, but moved not else. But therewithal the Woodwife came leaping through the bushes, and she nocked an arrow on her bended bow, and threatened him therewith, and cried out: "Thou man-beast, I will slay thee if thou hurt my child and my dear; so forbear! Nay, I tell thee more, unless thou make her as glad at the sight of thee as I meant her to be, I will in the long run slay thee—so look to it."

He laughed and said: "What! there is another image of the love that wasted me, is there! Nay, but by the Hallows this new-comer is the first one, and the one who chattered at me is the second. Or is it this, that all women now have the semblance of the evil one that has undone me, and there is nought else left?"

And he stood staring at Birdalone and moved not a while; and she stood with her hands before her face, cringing before him. Then he raised his arm and cast the weapon far into the bushes of the bank-side, and then came forward and stood before Birdalone, and drew down her hands from her face and stared in the eyes of her, holding her by the two arms, and he said: "Thou hast forgotten now, belike, how fair a life we two might have lived if thou hadst not fled from me and spoiled me.

"And thou! by the looks of thee, for thou art sleek and fair, though this moment thou art pale for fear of me, thou hast lived a happy life through all these years, with many a merry thing to think of: and dost thou deem that my life was happy, or that I thought of any merry thing, or of anything save my sorrow? Dost thou doubt it? go ask the good spears of Greenford, or the Riders of the Red Hold, and the field of the slaughter! If there was little joy there, less was there elsewhere."

He let go of her therewith and stood trembling before her, and she bowed down and put palm to palm and held

336

them out to him as one who prays; and she knew not what PART VI
she did.   Chap. 23

Then he cried out with a lamentable cry and said: "O
woe's me! for I have frighted her and scared the wit out of
her, so that she knows not who I am nor what I would; and
I would pray to her and beseech her to pity me and not depart from me again or mock me with images of herself."

Then he went down on his knees to her, and he also joined his hands to pray to her; but it seemed as if she was
stricken to stone, so wholly she moved not. But for him, he
sank his forehead to earth, and then he rolled over and his
limbs stretched out, and his head turned aside and blood
gushed out from his mouth. But Birdalone shrieked out
and cast herself on his body, and cried: "I have found him
and he is dead! he is dead, and I have slain him, because I
was a timorous fool and feared him; and he was coming to
his right mind and knew me for what I was!"

But Habundia came and stood over them, and drew up
Birdalone, and said: "Nay, nay, be comforted! for now he is
thus, and the strength is gone out of him for a while, we may
deal with him. Abide, and I will fetch the blood-staunching
herb and the sleepy herb, and then we will heal him, and he
will come to his right mind and be a man again."

Therewith she hastened away and was gone but a little;
and meanwhile Birdalone knelt down by her love and wiped
the blood from him, and caressed his sword-hardened hands
and moaned over him. But when the Woodwife came back
she put Birdalone aside once more, and knelt down by the
Squire and raised his head, and laid the blood-stauncher to
his mouth and his heart, and muttered words over him,
while Birdalone looked over her shoulder with her pale face;
then the she-leech fetched water from the stream in a cup
which she drew from her wallet, and she washed his face, and
he came somewhat to himself, so that she might give him
drink of the water; and yet more he came to himself. So
then she took the sleepy herb and bruised it in her hands and
put in his mouth and again said words over him, and pre-

xx.z   337

sently his head fell back and his eyes closed and he slept
peacefully.

She stood up then and turned to Birdalone and said: "Now, my child, have we done all that we may do, save that we shall bring him to a place where the dew and the sun shall not torment him and sicken him; for he shall lie thus till the sun comes up to-morrow, or longer; and fear not: for when he awaketh he shall be in his right mind, and shall know thee and love thee: this I swear to thee by the earth and the sun and the woodland."

Said Birdalone, trembling yet: "O mother, but may I kiss him and caress him?" "Yea surely," said the Woodmother, smiling in her face, "but be not too long over it, for lo! the last of the sun, and it were better that he be under cover ere the twilight falls."

Birdalone knelt down by her love quietly at that word, and fell to kissing him softly, and laid her cheek to his, and called him gentle names such as none can tell again without shame, till the Woodwife laid her hand on her shoulder and said kindly and sweetly: "Rise up now, for thou must make it enough for this present: thou shalt have time enough hereafter for more and much more."

So Birdalone arose and said: "How shall we bear him to his place? Shall I not take him by the shoulders and thou by the legs? For I am stronger than thou after all these years."

Laughed the Woodwife: "Nay, little one," said she; "thou knowest me not utterly as yet. Thou shalt not bear him at all, nor any part of him; I am strong enough for more than that; see thou!" And she stooped down and took him up in her arms as if he were a little child, and stepped off lightly with him; but looked back over her shoulder and said to Birdalone: "But thou mayest walk by me and hold a hand of him as we go, though it will hinder me somewhat; but I know thine heart and would pleasure thee, my child."

Birdalone ran up to her and thanked her and kissed her, and took Arthur's left hand, while Habundia bore him on down the dale and out of it, and still along the stream till

338

they came to a place where it was narrow on either side thereof, and a sheer rock came down so near to the water that there was but a strip of greensward three yards wide betwixt water and rock; and in the face of the rock was a cave wide enough for a man to enter by stooping somewhat. Therein the Woodwife lightly bore Arthur, and Birdalone followed; and they found the cave dry and roomy within; there was a bed therein of dry heather and bracken, and thereon Habundia laid her burden, and said: "Now, my child, there is nought to do but abide till he comes to himself again, which may be some time to-morrow; and be of good cheer, for he will come to his right self, but he will be weak and humble; but I shall have meat and drink ready for him. Now if thou wilt be ruled by me, thou wilt keep out of the way when he awakens; moreover, be thou not scared if I meet his awakening with another shape than that which thou hast known of me: for sure it is that it will trouble his wits overmuch if again he seeth the two of us alike. But fear not; for thy sake, my child, I will take no ugly shape, though it may well be less beauteous than thine."

"I will do what thou wilt, mother," said Birdalone, "for I see that thou art helping me all thou mayest; yet I beseech thee let me sit by him till the time of his awakening draweth nigh."

The Woodwife smiled and nodded yeasay on her, and they sat down, both of them, beside the sleeping man, and the day died into the night as they sat hearkening to the ripple of the brook and the song of the nightingales.

CHAPTER XXIV. THE WOODMOTHER CHANGETH HER FORM.

WHEN the morrow came, there yet lay Arthur sleeping peacefully, and Birdalone awoke from the slumber which had at last fallen on her, and looked about her and saw not Habundia in the cave; so she arose and bent over Arthur and kissed him, and so went

forth and stood in the door and looked about her. And she
was still dim-eyed with her just departed slumber and the
brightness of the morning sunlight, and she scarce knew
whether it were a part of a dream, or a sight that was verily
before her, that she seemed to see one coming across the
brook toward her, stepping heedfully from stone to stone
thereof: a woman stricken in years, but slim and trim and
upright, clad in a gown of green cloth, with a tippet of some
white fur. When she was come on to the greensward she
spake to Birdalone in a sweet voice, but thin with eld, and
gave her the sele of the day; and Birdalone was somewhat
afraid to see a new-comer, but she greeted her, drawing back
a little from her shyly. But the old woman said: "What
maketh thee here, my daughter? Dost thou not know that
this is my land and my house, and that I am said not to be
unmighty in these woods?"

"I pray thee pardon me if I have done amiss," said Birdalone; "but here have I a sick friend, a young man, and I
would pray thee suffer him to abide here in this cave a little
longer; for there hath been also another friend, a woman,
but she hath gone out while I slept, belike to gather simples;
for she is wise in leechcraft, and is tending the sick man. I
pray thee humbly to suffer us lest we lose our friend."

As she spake, she heard the carline chuckle softly, and at
last she said: "Why, Birdalone, my dear, dost thou not
know me after all these years? Look on me again, look! and
thou shalt see that I am not so much changed from what
thou sawest me last night. I am still thine image, my dear,
only I was the image of what thou wert, and now am I the
image of what thou shalt be when two score years and ten of
happy life have worn for thee. Tell me, am I now aught like
to thy mother in the flesh?"

"How hast thou frighted me, mother," said Birdalone;
"I thought that my friend had forsaken me, and that perchance the new-comer was another witch like unto the old
one, and that I was never to be at rest and happy. But as to
my mother in the flesh, nay, thou art not now wholly like

340

unto her; and sooth to say I shall be fainer when thou hast PART VI
thine own shape of me young back again; for I love thee not Chap. 24
so much as now thou art."

The Woodwife laughed: "Well," she said, "thou shalt not
see over much of me in this shape; and that the less because
of something I shall now tell thee: to wit, that I have been
thinking the matter over, and I would have thee leave us
twain together alone before the young man awaketh. I would
have thee get thee home and abide him there: it shall not be
long I promise thee; and this also, that he shall come home
to thee sound in body and whole in limb."

Birdalone's countenance fell, and she said: "Why this
second mind, mother? why, I pray thee?" Said Habundia:
"I fear for thy love lest he be not strong enough to open his
eyes upon thy face; but after he hath been a day in the
woods, and I have spoken to him diversely and cheered him
with the hope of meeting thee, he may well be strong
enough to seek thee for a mile's length, and find thine
house first and then thee. So now wilt thou obey me? Nay,
if thou must needs weep, I will be gone into the thicket till
thou hast done—thou wilful!"

Birdalone smiled through her tears, and said: "I pray
thee pardon my wilfulness, mother, and I will depart without turning back into the cave."

"Nay," said Habundia, "there is no need for so much
haste as that: I will in now, and do my leechdoms with the
sick man. But do thou go across the stream, thou barefoot,
and thou wilt find on the other side, by the foot of the
quicken-tree yonder, honeycombs and white bread and a
bicker of wild goats' milk. Bathe thee then if thou wilt, and
bring those matters over hither; and then shalt thou go in
and kiss thy mate's sick face with thy fresh one, and thereafter shall we sit here by the ripple of the water and break
our fast; and lastly, thou shalt go in and kiss again and then
take to the road. But tell me, deemest thou surely that thou
canst find it again?"

"Yea, surely, mother," said Birdalone; "I am wood-

341

woman enough for that; and now I will do all thy will."
And therewith she stepped out lightly on to the greensward,
and sought up the stream till she found a smooth-grounded
pool meet for her bath, and when that was done, she fetched
the victual and came back to the Woodwife; then they two
sat down together, and ate and drank while the water rippled
at their feet. But when they were done, Birdalone gat her
into the cave again, and kissed the sleeping man fondly, and
came forth lightly and stood a moment before the Woodwife, and said: "Tell me this at least, mother, when shall he
be there?"

"To-morrow," quoth the Woodwife; "and, for my part,
I would keep thee within doors and abide him there, lest
there be trouble. For he may not yet be as strong as the
strongest."

Birdalone hung down her head and answered not, but
said presently: "Farewell, Woodmother, and be thou
blessed." Then she took up her bow and betook her lightly
to the woodland way, and the Woodwife stood looking at
her till the thicket had hidden her, and then turned back
and went into the cave.

CHAPTER XXV. THE WOODWIFE HEALETH AND TENDETH THE BLACK SQUIRE.

SHE stood over Arthur for a minute or two, and then
stooped down and whispered a word in his ear, and presently he stirred on the bed and half opened his eyes,
but straightway turned on his side, as if to gather sleep to
him, but she took him by the shoulder and said in a clear
voice: "Nay, knight, nay ; hast thou not slept enough ? is
there nought for thee to do?"

He sat up in the bed and rubbed his eyes, and his face was
come to its wholesome colour, and his eyes looked out quietly
and calmly as he looked about the cave and saw the Woodwife standing by him ; and he spake in a voice which was

somewhat weak, but wherein was no passion of rage or wood-
ness: "Where am I then? and who art thou, dame?" She
said: "Thou art in a cave of the woodland, and I am for one
thing thy leech, and meseemeth thou desirest to eat and to
drink."

He smiled and nodded his head; and she fetched him
the milk, and he drank a long draught, and sighed thereafter, as one who is pleased; and she smiled on him, and
fetched him the bread and the honey, and he ate and drank
again, and then lay down and fell fast asleep. And she suffered
his slumber for two hours or so, and then awoke him again;
and again he asked where he was and what was she, but she
said as before. And said she: "The next thing thou hast to
do is to arise, as thou well mayest, and take this raiment,
which is fair and clean, and go wash thee in the brook and
come back to me; and then we will talk, and thou shalt tell
me of how it was with thee; and peradventure I may tell thee
somewhat of how it shall be with thee." As she spoke she
went to a coffer which stood in a nook of the cave, and drew
forth from it a shirt and hosen and shoon, and a surcoat and
hood of fine black cloth, and a gilded girdle and a fair sword,
red-sheathed, and said: "These may serve thy turn for the
present, so take them and don them, and thou shalt look like
a squire at least, if not a knight."

So he arose as one in a dream and went out; but as he
passed by her she saw something gleaming on his breast, and
noted that it was Birdalone's fair sapphire ring which hung
about his neck; so she smiled and said under her breath:
"Crafty is my dear daughter! But that shall save me some
words at least." And she abided his return.

Anon he cometh back clad in the fair raiment, with the
sword by his side; and the Woodwife smote her palms together and cried out: "Now indeed thou art fair and wellliking, and a fair lady might well take pleasure in beholding
thee."

But his brow was knit, and he looked sullen and angry,

343

and he said: "What is all this play? and where gattest thou this ring which I found e'en now about my neck? And who art thou, and why have I been brought hither?"

His eyes looked fiercely on her as he spake, holding out his palm with the ring lying thereon. But the Woodwife answered: "Many questions, fair youth! but I will tell thee: the play is for thine healing and pleasure, whereas both sick hast thou been and sorry. As to the ring, it is thou hast got it and not I. But I will tell thee this, that I have seen it on the finger of a fair damsel who haunteth the woodland not far hence. As to what I am, that were a long tale to tell if I told it all: but believe this meanwhile, that I am the Lady and Mistress of hereabouts, and am not without power over my folk and my land. And as to why thou wert brought hither, I brought thee because I had no better house handy for a sick man to lie in."

Then Arthur stood a long while considering the ring that lay on his palm, and at last he put his hand on the Woodwife's shoulder, and looked into her face beseechingly, and said: "O mother, if thou be mighty be merciful withal, and have pity on me! Thou callest me a youth, and so I may be in regard to thee; but I tell thee it is five long years and there hath been no other thought in my heart but what was loathsome to me, and it hath worn and wasted my youth, so that it waneth and withereth and is nought. O, if thou be mighty, bring me to her that I may see her at least one time before I die." And therewith he fell down on his knees before her and kissed the hem of her gown and wept.

But she drew him up and looked on him with the merry countenance of a kind old woman, and said: "Nay, nay, I am not so hard to be won to thy helping that thou needest pray so sore and weep: here need we tarry no longer, and if thou wilt come with me we shall go seek the damsel who bore this ring: though how it should come to thee why should I know? Neither do I know if the said ring-bearer be the one woman whom thou needest. But I will tell thee at once that she is a dear friend of mine."

344

Then Arthur threw his arms about her, and kissed her cheeks and blessed her, while she laughed on him and said: "Nay, fair sir, if thou wilt do so much with the withered branch, what wilt thou with the blossom of the tree?" And he was abashed before her, but hope made his heart to dance.

So the Woodwife took up her bow, slung her quiver at her back, and girt her short sword to her, and then led him forth, and so into the thicket out of the dale and forth into the oaken bent, and lightly she led him thereafter through the woodland.

CHAPTER XXVI. THE BLACK SQUIRE TELLETH HIS TALE.

AS they went Habundia said to Arthur: "Now shalt thou talk and tell for the shortening of the way, and let us know somewhat of thy story. But first I must tell thee, for thou mayst not know it, so witless as then thou wast, that yesterday we found thee down in the dale yonder, playing the string-play sweetly indeed, but otherwise dight like a half beast more than a man, so that we wondered at thee and pitied thee."

Arthur knit his brows as if he strove with some memory and might not master it; then he said: "Thou sayest We— who then was the other?" Said Habundia: "I had a dear friend with me." Quoth he: "And did she pity me also?" "Yea," said the Woodwife, "else scarce had she been a friend to me." "O let us on swiftly," said Arthur, "so long as the time may be!" And they quickened their pace and ate up the way speedily.

Presently spake the Woodwife again: "Now for the tale of thee, fair sir; yet will I shorten it somewhat by telling thee that I know thy name, that thou art Arthur the Black Squire of the Castle of the Quest." He stared at that word, and said: "How knewest thou this? how couldst thou guess it, who hast never seen me erst?" "A friend told me," said she; "too long it were as now to tell thee thereof. Rather do thou tell

345

me how thou didst fare when ye found thy friend gone from
the castle when ye came home from the winning of the Red
Hold."

Arthur stared astonished, and said: "What is it? Dost thou
verily know my love? or art thou a sorceress and knowest
somewhat of me by spell-work?" "I am somewhat more than
a sorceress, mayhappen," said the Woodwife; "but heed it
not, since I am thy friend to-day, but tell me what I ask, that
I may have all the tale of thee; it will serve for the shortening of the way." Said Arthur: "And who but I needeth it as
short as may be? so stand we not loitering here, and I will
talk as we wend on speedily."

On they sped therefore, and said Arthur: "How did I
fare? as one stunned, mother, and knew not what had happened; and when I heard their babble of how she had done
wrong here and right there, I was driven half mad by it, so
that I hastened back to the Red Hold, and became the captain of Greenford, to hunt down their scattered foemen; for
I said to myself that needs must I rage and slay, and that
were worser amongst my friends than mine unfriends. What
then? that business came to an end; though all the ill men
were not slain, but all were driven away from the parts of
Greenford; and sooth to say they durst not come anywhere
nigh where they heard of me. Then became each day like every
other, and the thought of my hope and my despair ate mine
heart out, and I was of no avail unto any.

"Now it so happened, amidst my many battles and chases,
I had hunted the bands of the Red Hold into the northwest
marches of the woodland; and I noted that even they, howsoever hard bestead, and the worst of men to boot, would
scarce at the first be driven into the thickets thereof, though
at last, whether or no they have made covenant with the
devils there I know not, they have betaken them to the depths
of the wood and have borne off women from the dwellings
and got children on them, and are like to breed an evil folk.
That then I noted that this Evilshaw was a dwelling loathed
and desert, and little like it was that any would meddle with

346

me there. Three years had worn since I was cast away at the Castle of the Quest by her that loved me, who must needs sacrifice both her and me to the busy devil of folly; and I also deemed that if I sought for her I should not find her; and yet more forsooth, that if I found her she would be as hard unto me as when she fled from me. And as for me, I was gotten hard and crabbed, and no man, if his heart would let him, would have aught to say to me. So I gat me away from the Red Hold, as I had from the Castle of the Quest, and I gave out that I would enter into religion, and forbade any man to follow me. Neither did any desire it. First of all I set me down at the very outskirts of the woodland, and raised me a bower there, rude and ill-shapen. Few folk came anigh me, and yet some few, charcoal-burners and hunters of the edges of the wood and such-like. These deemed me a holy man, whereas I was but surly. Somewhat also they feared me, whereas in some of their huntings or goings and comings after prey I had put forth all my strength, eked out by the lore of knighthood, which was strange to them. One man there was of them who was fashioned of the minstrel craft by nature, and who forgathered with me specially till we became friends, and he was a solace to me with his tales and his songs of a rougher people than I had been wont to deal with. But when I had been in that place for two years he died of a sickness, and I was left lonely, and my soreness of heart fell upon me till I scarce knew what next I should do. So I fared away yet deeper into the wildwood, taking with me the harp which my friend had given me before he died. It was summer, and I wandered about ever deeper into the wood, until belike I had scarce been able to win out of it if I had tried. At last, when the autumn came, I built myself again some sort of a bower in a clearing of the wood wherein was water, and the resort of plenteous venison.

"What befell next? My mind is not over clear concerning it all, for I was now becoming more of a beast than a man. But this I know, that some men of the bands whom I had chased happened on me. They knew me not for their old foeman, but of their kind it was to torment and slay any man whom they might lightly overcome. Yet was not the battle so over light but that I slew and hurt divers of them ere they got me under and stripped me and bound my hands and tormented me, after the manner that the devils shall do with them when they go to their reward. Yet somehow I lived, though they deemed me dead, and I crawled away thence when they were gone; and somehow I was healed of my body, but I was confused of my wit thereafter, and now can call to mind but little of what befell me as I strayed from place to place; save that I remember I was hapless and heart-sore ever: and also meseemeth that I saw visions at whiles, and those who had been in my life before these things, their images would come before me to mock me, as I sat singing whiles and whiles playing the string-play (for my harp I bore ever with me); and whiles I bewailed me, and called for help on them that would not or might not help me. And now I may not even tell the years of my abiding in the desert, how many they be. But I pray thee let us on more swiftly yet."

Said the Woodwife: "Thou hast told me but little of thy life, Black Squire, but it is enough maybe; and I see that thou mayst not tell me more because thou hast thy mind set on what may betide thee when this day is over. But thou must know that thou hast come into the wood of Evilshaw, wherein, besides those savage men who quelled thee and their like, there be uncouth things no few, and wights that be not of the race of Adam; wherefore no great marvel is it that thou sawest visions, and images of them that were not by thee."

"Yea," said he, "but one vision had I that confused and overcame me more than all others, and meseemeth that came to me not long ago. For first I saw the shape of her that my soul desireth ever, and it wept and lamented for me; and then for a little I seemed as if I were coming forth from my confusion of wit, when lo! there issued from the thicket another image of my beloved and blamed me and threatened me: God wot good cause there was of the blame.

348

But tell me, mother, since thou callest thyself wise, what
may this portend?"

The Woodwife laughed: "Since I am wise," said she, "I will foretell thee good days. And now we will talk no more of thee or thy love or thy sorrow, but since thou wilt so fiercely devour the way, I will tell thee a tale or two of this wood and its wights to save us from over-much weariness."

So did she, talking and telling as they went; and she went on a pace before him, and howsoever long or hardly he might stride he might not overgo her. And so fast they went, that they were within a little way of the Oak of Tryst a good while before the sun had set, though they had set out from the cave three hours after the hour when Birdalone and the Woodwife had left the House under the Wood on the yesterday. They had come to a steep rock that rose up from a water's side, and there the Woodwife bade stay, whether Arthur would or no, and she made him eat and drink, bringing the victual and wine from out of a cleft in the said rock. And she held him there till the night was come and there was a glimmer of the rising moon in the east, and he was ill at ease and restless; but still she held him there till the moon rose high and shone upon them, and the shadows of the oak-boughs lay black all around.

Then she bade him arise, and led him on to the Oak of Tryst, yea and somewhat beyond it toward the Great Water. Then she spake to him: "Black Squire, I am now come home, and will lead thee no further; I was deeming that we should have slept in the wood a good way from this, and then would I have brought thee on thy way to-morrow morning; but the eagerness of thine heart hath made thy feet so speedy, that we be here somewhat rathe, and yet I am not ill-pleased therewith." Then she turned him about and said: "Look down the bent and tell me what thou seest." He said: "I see the boles of goodly trees, and betwixt them the gleaming of a great water."

She said: "Go thitherward then while the moon is yet at her brightest, and thou shalt presently come to wide meads lying along the water, and a stream running through them. Enter then into the meads and look about thee, and thou shalt see a little house (there is none other nigh) standing just across the said stream; go up thither boldly and crave guesting from whomsoever thou shalt find there, and maybe things shall go after thy mind. More than this I may not do for thee. Farewell then, and if thou wilt thou mayst meet me again; that is to say, that which is verily me: but it is like that this shape which hath been striding on with thee day-long thou shalt not see any more."

He looked on her wondering, for she seemed to grow goodly and stately before his eyes. But even as he stretched forth his hand to take hers, she turned about suddenly and fared into the wood out of his sight, wending full as swiftly as might have been looked for. Then he drew his sword and turned his face from the wood, and went down toward the water.

CHAPTER XXVII. SIR ARTHUR COMETH TO THE HOUSE UNDER THE WOOD.

SO came Arthur into the meadows, and went eagerly but warily over the dewy grass. And here and there a cow rose before him and went bundling down the mead a little way, and the owls cried out from behind him, and a fox barked from the thicket's edge. Then he found himself on the stream-side, and he stayed and looked from side to side, and lo! on the other side of the stream a little house that looked familiar to him as a yeoman's dwelling in the builded lands, and the thatch thereon shone under the moon and its windows were yellow with candle-light; and so homely it seemed to him, that he thrust his sword into the sheath and lightly crossed the brook, and came to the door and laid his hand upon the latch and lifted it and shoved the door, and all was open before him.

His eyes, coming from the night, dazzled with the bright light of the candles, but he saw a fair woman rising up in her

place, and he said: "May a traveller in the woodland be
welcome here to-night, dealing with all in all honour?"

But the woman came toward him holding out her two hands, and ere he could cry out that he knew her, she had thrown herself upon him, and had cast her arms about him and was kissing his face, and murmuring: "O welcome indeed! welcome, welcome, and welcome!" And so sore did his past grief and his desire move him, that he was weak before her, and held down his hands and let her do.

And both those were breathless with wonder and joy and longing; and they stood aloof a little in a while and looked on each other, she with heaving bosom and streaming eyes, and he with arms stretched forth and lips that strove with his heart's words and might not utter them; but once more she gave herself to him, and he took her in his arms strongly now, so that she was frail and weak before him, and he laid his cheek to her cheek and his lips to her lips, and kissed her eyes and her shoulders and murmured over her. And then again they stood apart, and she took him by the hand and led him to the settle, and set him down by her, and herself by him; and a while they said nought.

Then she spake as one who had come to herself and was calm, though her heart was aflame for love: "Tell me, love, when thine hand was on the latch didst thou look to find me here in this house? for thine hand it was that waked me; I heard not thy foot before the threshold, for I was weary and slumbering. Alas! that I lost the sound of thy feet!"

He spake, and his voice sounded false unto him, as if it came from another's mouth: "I wot not; the woman that led me nearby seemed to bid me hope." Then he said: "Nay, the sooth is that I should have died if I had not found thee here: I have been sick so long with hoping."

Again were they silent till she said: "I would that I had heard thee crossing the brook. But the Woodwife bade me look for thee no earlier than to-morrow; else had I time enough; and I would have made the house trim with the new green boughs, and dighted our bed with rose blooms;

351

and I would have done on me my shining gown that the Woodwife gave me." For indeed she was but clad in her scanty smock and nought else.

But he laid his head on her bosom and kissed her all about, and said: "Nay, my own love, it is well, it is better." And she murmured over him: "O friend, my dear, think not that I had will to hide me from thee. All that is here of me is thine, and thine, and thine."

And she took his hand and they arose together, and she said: "O friend, I fled from thee once and left thee lonely of me because I deemed need drave me to it: and I feared the strife of friends, and confusion and tangle. Now if thou wilt avenge thee on me thou mayest, for I am in thy power. Yet will I ask thee what need will drive thee to leave me lonely?"

He said: "The need of death." But she said: "Mayhappen we shall lie together then, as here to-night we shall lie."

CHAPTER XXVIII. FAIR DAYS IN THE HOUSE OF LOVE.

ON the morrow it was sweet times betwixt those twain, and what was hard and fierce of their love they seemed to have put behind them. A dear joy it was to Birdalone that day to busy herself about the housekeeping, and to provide whatsoever seemed now, or had seemed to her in her early days, to be dainties of their meadow and woodland husbandry, as cream and junkets and wood-fruit and honey, and fine bread made for that very occasion.

Withal she was careful as a mother with a child that he should not over-weary himself with the sun of the early summer, but rather to follow the brook up into the wood and lie adown in the flecked shadow, and rest him wholly as if there were nought for him to do but to take in rest all that was done for his service, both by the earth and by the hands and nimble feet of Birdalone. And as she was wilful in other ways of her cherishing, so also in this, that for nought in

that daylight would she go anywise disarrayed, nay not so
much as to go barefoot, though he prayed her thereof sorely,
and told her that fairer and sweeter she was in her smock
alone than in any other raiment. For in the morning she
went in her woodland green let down to her heels, and when
the day wore towards evening, and the wind came cool from
over the Great Water, then she did on her wonder-raiment
which the Woodwife had given her, and led Arthur over the
meadows here and there, and went gleaming by the side of the
black-clad man along the water's lip. And they looked forth
on to Green Eyot and Rock Eyot, and stood by the shallow
bight where she had bathed those times; and they went
along to the dismal creek where the Sending Boat was wont
to lie, and where yet lay the scattered staves of it; and then
along the meadow-land they went from end to end, resting
oft on the flowery grass, till the dews began to fall and the
moon cast shadows on the greensward. Then home they
fared to the house, and again on the way must Birdalone
feign for their desport that the witch was come back again
and was awaiting her to play the tyrant with her; and Arthur
fell in with her game, and kissed her and clipped her, and
then drew his sword and said: "By Allhallows I shall smite
off her head if she but lay a finger on thee."

So they played like two happy children, till they came to
the door of the house, and Birdalone shoved it open, and
they two looked in together and saw nought worse therein
save the strange shadows that the moon cast from the settle
on to the floor. Then Birdalone drew in her love, and went
about lighting the candles and quickening a little cooking-
fire on the hearth, till the yellow light chased the moon away
from the bed of their desire.

CHAP. XXIX. THOSE TWAIN WILL SEEK THE WISDOM OF THE WOODWIFE.

AGAIN next day was their life such as it had been the day before; and as they lay in cool shadow of a great oak, Birdalone fell to telling Arthur all the whole story of her dealings with the Woodwife, and how that she had so loved her and holpen her, that through her love and her help she had escaped the witch and her snares, who would have turned her into a half-devil for the undoing of manfolk. And how that the said Woodwife had never appeared to her but as an image and double of herself, save on the time when she played the leech to him. Then she told him how all had gone when the Woodwife had sought him out for the fulfilment of their love, and of the dreadful [day] when they had come upon him out of his wit and but little manlike.

Then she asked, would he, within the next day or two, that they should go see the Woodwife together and thank her for her help, and bring him within the ring of her love and guarding; and he yeasaid it with a good will.

After this she would have him tell her of how things had gone with him since that evil day when he had come home from the Castle of the Quest and found her gone. So he told her somewhat, and of his dole and misery, and his dealings with the foemen of Greenford; but yet scantly and as one compelled; and at last he said:

"Dear love, since thou art cossetting me with all solace of caresses, I pray thee remember my trouble and grief, how sore they were, and do with me as with a sick man getting well, as I wot surely thou wouldest do; and do thou that which is at this present the softest and merriest to me, and that forsooth is, that thou shouldest talk and tell, and I should hearken the sweetness of the music, and only here and there put in a word to rest thee and make thy tale the sweeter."

She laughed with love on him, and without more ado fell to telling everything she might think of concerning her days

354

in the House of Captivity, both when she was but a bairn,
and when she was grown to be a young woman; and long
was she about the tale, nor was it all done in one day; and a
multitude of things she told him which are not set down in
this book.

In the evening when they were going again to and fro the
meads, it was other talk they fell on, to wit, of their fellows
of the Quest, both of Sir Hugh and the three lovely ladies:
and now was Arthur nought but kind when he spake of Atra,
nor spake Birdalone otherwise; but she said: "I shall now
say a hard word, yet must thou bear it, my loveling, since we
twain are now become one, and have but one joy together
and one sorrow. Deemest thou that Atra is yet alive?"

"Sooth it is," said Arthur, "it may well be that I have
slain her." "And what may we do by her if ever we fall in
with her alive?" said Birdalone. "I wot not," said Arthur;
"some would say that we have done penance for our fault,
both thou and I; and what other penance may we do, save
sundering from each other? And by God above I will not."
"By thine head and thine hands I will not," said Birdalone.

So said they; but therewith their eyes told tales of the fair
eve and the lovely meadows, and the house, the shrine of the
dear white bed less sweet to them than erst: but then presently Birdalone stayed her love, and took her arms about
him, and each felt the sweetness of the other's body, and joy
blossomed anew in their hearts.

Then fell Arthur to telling of the deeds and the kindness
of Baudoin, whom never again they should see on the earth;
and they turned back home to the house, and on the way
spake Birdalone: "This is what I would we should do:
whereas I have sought thee and thou me, and we have found
each other, whereas ye sought me when I went astray in the
Black Valley of the Greywethers, and before, when ye three
sought your own loves, now I would that we should seek our
fellows and have joy in them, and thole sorrow with them as
in days gone by."

Spake Arthur: "Dear is the rest with thee in this wilder-

ness; yet were it a deed of fame, and would bring about a day
of joy, might we find our friends again, and knit up the links
of the fellowship once more. But thou the wise and valiant!
belike thou hast in thine head some device whereby this might
be set about."

Birdalone said: "Simple is my device, to wit, that we ask
one who is wiser than I. Let us tarry not, but go to-morrow
and see the Woodwife and talk with her concerning it."
Then she smiled upon him and said: "But when thou seest
her, wilt thou be aghast if she come before us in my shape of
what I was five years agone, or six?"

"Nay, nay," he said, "thou art not so terrible as that; not
very far do I run from thee now." And therewith they kissed
and embraced, and so entered the House of Love.

CHAP. XXX. THEY HAVE SPEECH WITH HA-BUNDIA CONCERNING THE GREEN KNIGHT AND HIS FELLOWS.

WHEN the morrow was they arose and went their
ways toward the wood, and Birdalone in her hunter's coat, quiver at back and bow in hand. They
came to the Oak of Tryst, and Birdalone was at point to call
on the Woodwife by the burning of a hair of hers, when she
came lightly from out the thicket, clad as Birdalone, and her
very image. She stood before them with a glad countenance,
and said: "Welcome to the seekers and finders." But Arthur
stepped forth and knelt before her, and took her right hand
and kissed it, and said: "Here I swear allegiance to thee, O
Lady of the Woods, to do thy will in all things, and give thee
thanks from my heart more than my tongue can say."

Quoth the Woodwife: "I take thine allegiance, fair young
man, and mine help shalt thou have henceforward." Then
she smiled and her eyes danced for merriment, and she said:
"Yet thy thanks meseemeth for this while are more due to
the wise carline who brought thee through the woods two

356

days ago, and only left thee when the way was easy and clear to thee."

"Lady," said Arthur, "I know now how great is thy might, and that thou canst take more shapes than this only; and humbly I thank thee that for us thou hast taken the shape that I love the best of all on the earth."

Said the Woodwife: "Stand up, Black Squire, and consider a little what thou wouldst have me do for thee, while I have speech with mine image yonder." And therewith she came up to Birdalone, and drew her a little apart, and fell to stroking her cheeks and patting her hands and diversely caressing her, and she said to her: "How now, my child, have I done for thee what I promised, and art thou wholly happy now?"

"O yea," said Birdalone; "if nought else befell us in this life but to dwell together betwixt the woodland and the water, and to see thee oft, full happy should we be."

"Nevertheless," said Habundia, "art thou not come hither to ask somewhat of me, that ye may be happier?" "So it is, wise mother," said Birdalone; "grudge not against me therefor, for more than one thing drives me thereto." "I will not grudge," said the Woodwife; "but now I will ask thy mate if he has thought what it is that he will have of me." And she turned to Arthur, who came forth and said: "Lady, I have heard thee, and herein would we have thee help us: There were erst six fellows of us, three carles and three queans, to whom was added this sweetling here; but one of them, to wit the Golden Knight, was slain, and for the rest—"

"Yea, I know," said the Woodwife; "my child here hath told me all; and now ye wot not where they are or if they be yet alive, all or any of them. Now is it not so that ye would seek these friends, if it were but to greet them but once, and that ye would ask of the wise Woodwife help to find them? Is there any more of the tale?" "Nay, lady," said Arthur. Said she: "Well then, that help shall ye have, were it but for the sake of that little Viridis whereof my child hath told me. Wherefore abide tidings of me for a fourteen days, and seek

357

not to me ere then; and meantime fear not, nor doubt me, for many messengers I have, and ever may I do somewhat if the end of the tale is to be told in these woodlands: and I deem these friends will not be hard to draw hither, for it is most like that they be thinking of you and longing for you, as ye for them. And now I will depart on my business, which is yours, and do ye be happy to-day in the woodland, and to-morrow in the meadows and by the water; and let no trouble weigh down your happy days."

Therewith she flitted away from them, when she had kissed them both. But when she was gone they fared away together deep into the wood, and were exceeding merry desporting them, and on their return they gat them venison for their meat, and so came back to the House of Love when the moon was up and shining brightly.

CHAPTER XXXI. HABUNDIA COMETH WITH TIDINGS OF THOSE DEAR FRIENDS.

WORE the days thenceforth merrily; and one day it was delight in the wide meads, and another they went a long way west along the water-side, and so into another meadow-plain, smaller than their home-plain, which Birdalone had never erst come into; and three eyots lay off it, green and tree-beset, whereto they swam out together. Then they went into the wood thereby in the heat of the afternoon, and so wore the day, that they deemed themselves belated, and lay there under a thorn-bush the night through.

Another day Birdalone took her mate over on to Green Eyot and Rock Eyot, and showed him all the places she was used to haunt. And they had their fishing-gear with them, and angled off the eyots a good part of the day, and had good catch, and swam back therewith merrily. And Birdalone laughed, and said that it seemed to her as if once again she were ransoming her skin of the witch-wife by that noble catch.

358

Divers times also they fared into the wood, and thrice
they lay out the night there in some wood-lawn where was
water; and on one of these times it happed that Arthur awoke
in the grey dawn, and lay open-eyed but not moving for a
little; and therewith he deemed he saw the gleam of war-gear
in the thicket. So he kept as still as he might, but gat his
sword out of its sheath without noise, and then leapt up suddenly, and sprang thitherward whereas he had seen that
token, and again saw armour gleam and heard some man
crashing through the underwood, for all was gone in one
moment. So he woke up Birdalone, and they bended their
bows both of them, and searched the thicket thereabouts
heedfully, arrow on string, but found nought fiercer than a
great sow and her farrow. So came the full day, and they gat
them back to their meadows and their house; but thereafter
were they warier in going about the woodland.

In all joyance then wore the days till the fifteenth, and in
the morning early they went their ways to the Oak of Tryst,
and had no need to call Habundia to them, for presently she
came forth out of the thicket, with her gown gathered up
into her girdle and bow in hand. But she cast it down and ran
up to Birdalone, and kissed her and clipped her, and then she
took a hand of Arthur and a hand of Birdalone, and held
them both and said: "My child, and thou dear knight, have
ye still a longing to fall in with those friends of yours, and to
run all risk of whatsoever contention and strife there may be
betwixt you thereafter?" "Yea certes," said Arthur; and
even so said Birdalone.

"Well is that then," said the Woodwife; "but now and
for this time, ere I help you, I shall put a price upon my
help, and this is the price, that ye swear to me never wholly
to sunder from me; that once in the year at least, as long
as ye be alive and wayworthy, ye come into the Forest of
Evilshaw, and summon me by the burning of a hair of mine,
that we may meet and be merry for a while, and part with
the hope of meeting once more at least. And if ye will not
pay the price, go in peace, and ye shall yet have my help in

359

all other matters that may seem good unto you, but not in this of joining your fellowship together. How sayest thou, Birdalone, my child? How sayest thou, Black Squire, whom, as meseemeth, I have delivered from a fate worse than death, and have brought out of wretchedness into bliss?"

Spake Birdalone: "Had I dared, I would have bidden thee to swear to me even such an oath, to wit that thou wouldst never wholly sunder thee from me. How then may I not swear this that thou biddest me, and that with all joy and trustiness?"

Spake Arthur: "Lady, had I no will to swear this oath for thy sake, yet with a good will would I swear it for my true-love's sake who loveth thee. Yet verily of mine own will would I swear it joyfully, were it for nought else save to pleasure thee, who hast done so kindly by me, and hath given me back my manhood and my love, which else I had miserably lost."

Spake the Woodwife: "It is well again; join hands then, and swear as I have bidden you by the love ye bear each other."

Even so they did, and then the Woodwife kissed them both and said: "Now do I deem you Earth's very children and mine, and this desire of yours is good, and it shall be done if I may bring it about; yet therein the valiance and wisdom of you both may well be tried. For this have I found out by my messengers and others, that your friends are alive, all of them; and they have thought of you in their inmost hearts, and have long determined that they must needs go seek you if they are to live lives happy and worthy. Furthermore, their Quest hath drawn them hither to Evil-shaw (nor say I that I have been nothing therein), and they are even now in the wood. But ye shall know that peril encompasses them; for they fare but a few, and of those few be there two traitors who are minded to deliver them to the men of the Red Company, unto whom three women as fair as your she-friends were a prize indeed. Wherefore the Red Folk are dogging them, and will fall upon them when they

360

find the occasion. But I shall see to it that the occasion shall
be in time and place where they shall not be unholpen. Now
what ye have to do for your parts, is to waylay the waylayers,
and keep watch and ward anigh the road they must needs
take, and to fall on when need is. But this again I shall see to,
that your onset fail not.

"But now ye may say: Since thou art mighty, why
shouldst not thou thyself take our friends out of the hands
of these accursed, as thou couldst well do, and we to take no
part therein? My friends, this might indeed well be; but
thou, Birdalone, hast told me the whole tale, and how that
there be wrongs to be forgiven which cannot be made right,
and past kindness to be quickened again, and coldness to
be kindled into love, and estrangement into familiar friendship; and meseems that the sight of your bodies and your
hands made manifest to the eyes of them may do somewhat
herein. Yet if otherwise ye think, then so let it be, and go ye
back to the House under the Wood, and in three days' time
I will bring you your four friends all safe and sound."

Now they both said that they would not for aught that
they should have no hand in the deliverance of them; so the
Woodwife said: "Come with me, and I shall lead you to the
place of your ambush."

Then all they went on together, and fared a long way
west and toward the place where erst they two had found
Arthur; and at last, two hours before sunset, they came to
where was a glade or way between the thickets, which was as
it were a little beaten by the goings of man-folk. And the
Woodwife did them to wit, that the evil folk aforesaid had
so used it and beaten it, that it might just look as if folk were
wont to pass that way; whereas it was not very far from their
chiefest haunt and stronghold. A little on the north side of
this half-blind way, and some ten yards through the thicket,
the ground fell away into a little dale, the bottom whereof
was plain and well grassed, and watered by a brook.

Thither the Woodwife brought the twain; and when they
all stood together on the brook-side, she said to them:

"Dear friends, this is your woodland house for this time, and I rede you go not forth of it, lest ye happen upon any of those evil men; for nought have ye to fear from any save them. Here amidst these big stones, which make, see ye, as it were a cavern, have I stowed victual for you, and armour therewithal; because, though both of you are in a manner armed, yet who knoweth where a shaft drawn at a venture may reach."

And from the said stones she drew forth two very fair armours, helm and hawberk, and leg and arm wards; and they were all of green, & shone but little, but were fashioned as no smith of manfolk could have done the like.

"This is thine, Sir Arthur," said the Woodwife, "and thou wilt wear it like as it were silk; and this thine, my child, and thou art strong enough to bear such light gear. And I charge you both to do on this gear presently, nor do it off till ye have achieved the adventure. And now this is the last word: here is a horn of oliphant which thou shalt wear about thy neck, Birdalone; and if thou be sore bestead or thy heart faileth thee, blow in it, yet not before the onfall; and then, whether thou blow much or little, thou shalt be well holpen.

"Now be not downcast if nought befall to-night or to-morrow, or even the day after; but if the third day be tiding-less, then at sunset burn a hair of my head, Birdalone, and I will come to you. And now farewell! for I have yet to do in this matter."

With that she kissed Birdalone fondly and embraced Arthur, and went her way; and those twain abode in the dale, and slept and watched by turns, and all was tidingless till the morrow's dawn; neither was there aught to tell of on that day and the night that ended it.

CHAP. XXXII. OF THE FIGHT IN THE FOREST.

LIGHT was growing on the dawn of the next day, and the colours of things could be seen, when Birdalone, who was holding this last watch of the night, stood still and hearkened, deeming that she could hear some noise that was neither the morning wind in the tree-boughs nor the going of the wild things anear them in the wood.

So she did off her helm to hear the better, and stood thus a little; then she turned about and stooped down to Arthur, who was yet sleeping, and put forth a hand to rouse him. But or ever she touched him, broke forth a sound of big and rough voices and laughter, and amidst it two shrieks as of women.

Arthur heard it, and was on his feet in a moment, and helmed, and he caught up his bended bow and cast on the quiver (for Birdalone was already weaponed), and without more words they went forth swiftly up the bank and through the thicket till they were looking on the half-blind way, but under cover, and there was nothing before them as yet.

There they stayed and hearkened keenly. There were no more shrieks of women, nor heard they any weapon clash, but the talking and laughter of men went on; and at last they heard a huge and grim whoop of many men together; and then thereafter was less sound of talking, but came the jingle as of arms and harness, and Arthur whispered in Birdalone's ear: "Stand close! they have gotten to horse, and will be coming our way. Nock an arrow." And even so did he.

Therewith they heard clearly the riding of men, and in less than five minutes' space they saw three big weaponed men riding together, clad in red surcoats. And they were so nigh that they heard the words of their speech. One said to the other: "How long shall the knight hold out, think ye?" "O, a week maybe," said the other. "Meseems it was scathe that we stayed not a while to pine him," said the first man. "Nay," said the second, "we be over-heavy laden with bed-gear to tarry." And they all laughed thereat, and so went on out of hearing.

But then came four on together, whereof one, a gaunt, oldish man, was saying: "It is not so much how long we shall be getting there, but what shall betide when we get there. For this is not like lifting a herd of neat, whereof sharing is easy; but with this naked-skinned, two-legged cattle, which forsooth ye can eat and yet have, there may well be strife over the sharing. And look to it if it hath not begun already: we must needs dismount three of our best men that these white-skinned bitches forsooth may each have a horse to herself, or else would they be fighting as to which should have a damsel of them before him on the saddle—curse the fools!"

Laughed out they who were about him, and one young man cast a jeer at him the meaning whereof they might not catch, and again they laughed and that deal passed on. And next came a bigger rout, a half score or so, and they also laughing and jeering; but amidst them, plain to see riding a-straddle, their ancles linked together under the horses' bellies, their hands bound behind them, first Atra, black-clad as erst; then Aurea, in a gown of wheat-colour; then Viridis, green-clad. Atra rode upright, and looking straight before her; Aurea hung her head all she might, and her long red hair fell about her face; but Viridis had swooned, and was held up in the saddle by one of the caitifs on each side of her. They were but little disarrayed, save that some felon had torn the bosom of Viridis' gown, and dragged down the cloth so that her left shoulder was bare.

Arthur looked, and drew at the caitif who went afoot beside Atra, and Birdalone at him who went by Viridis, for she wotted whitherward Arthur's shaft would be turned. The loose of the two bows made but one sound; both men fell stark dead, and the others huddled together a moment, and then ran toward the thicket on either hand, and they who ran north, two of them saw not Arthur, because of his green armour, ere they felt the death which lay in his sword. And then he brake out amidst them, and there were three of them on him: yet for no long while, whereas their weapons bit not on the armour of the Faery, and his woodland blade sheared

364

leather and ring-mail to the flesh and the bone; mighty were his strokes, and presently all three were wallowing on the earth.

Even therewith the seven who had passed on had turned back and were come on him a-horseback; and hard had it gone with him, despite of his might and his valour and the trustiness of Habundia's mail. But meanwhile Birdalone had run to Viridis, who had fallen a dead weight aside of her horse, and lay half hanging by the bonds of her ancles. Birdalone swiftly cut the cords both of her feet and her hands, and drew her off her horse as best she might, and laid her down on the grass; and then ran to Arthur sword aloft, just as his new battle was at point to begin.

But as she ran it came into her mind in a twinkling that her sword would be but weak, and the horn hung about her neck. Then she stayed her feet, and set the horn to her lips and blew; and the oliphant gave forth a long singing note which was strange to hear. But while it was yet at her lips one of the caitifs was upon her, and he cried out: "Hah the witch, the accursed green witch!" and fetched her a great stroke from his saddle, and smote her on the helm; and though his sword bit not on that good head-burg, she fell to the ground unwitting.

Yet was not the Woodwife's promise unavailing, for even while the voice of the horn was in the air, the way and thickets were alive with men-at-arms, green-clad as those twain, who straightway fell on the caitifs, and with Arthur to help, left not one of them alive. Then went some to Viridis, and raised her up, and so dealt with her that she came to herself again; and the like they did by Birdalone, and she stood, and looked about confusedly, but yet saw this, that they had gotten the victory. Some went withal to Aurea, and cut her bonds and took her off her horse and set her on the ground; and she was all bewildered, and knew not where she was.

But Arthur, when he saw Birdalone on her feet, and un-hurt by seeming, went to Atra, and cut her bonds and loosed her and set her on the earth, all without a word, and then

stood before her shyly. Came the colour back into her face
therewith, and she flushed red, for she knew him despite his
outlandish green war-harness, and she reached out her hand
to him, and he knelt before her and took her hand and kissed
it. But she bent over him till her face was anigh his, and he
lifted up his face and kissed her mouth. And she drew aback
a little, but yet looked on him earnestly, and said: "Thou
hast saved my life, not from death indeed, but from a loathsome hell: I may well thank thee for that. And O, if my
thanks might be fruitful to thee!" And her bosom heaved,
and the sobs came, and the tears began to run down her
cheeks. And he hung his head before her.

But in a while she left weeping, and turned about her face
and looked round the field of deed; and she said: "Who is
yonder slim green warrior who hath even now knelt down
by Viridis? Is it not a woman?" Arthur reddened: "Yea,"
said he; "it is Birdalone." "Thy love?" she said. He said
swiftly: "Yea, and thy friend, and this time thy deliverer."
"So it is," she said. "It is five years since I beheld her. My
heart yearns for her; I shall rejoice at the meeting of us."

She was silent, and he also a while; then she said: "But
why tarry we here in idle talk when he is yet bound, and in
torment of body and soul; he the valiant, and the kind and
the dear brother? Come, tarry for no question." And she
stepped out swiftly along the green road going westward,
and Arthur beside her; and as they went by Viridis, lo!
Aurea had wandered unto them, and now was Birdalone
unhelmed and kissing and comforting her. Then cried out
Atra: "Keep up thine heart, Viridis! for now we go to fetch
thee thy man safe and sound."

So they went but a little way on the green road ere they
came to Sir Hugh bound hard and fast to a tree-bole, and he
naked in his shirt, and hard by lay the bodies of two stout
carles with their throats cut; for these honest men and the
two felons who had betrayed them were all the following
wherewith the Green Knight had entered Evilshaw. And as
it fell, the traitors had been set to watch while the others
366

slept; and sleeping the caitifs found them, and slew the said men-at-arms at once, but bound Hugh to a tree that he might be the longer a-dying; since none looked for any but their own folk to pass by that way. All this they heard afterwards of Hugh.

But now the said Hugh heard men going, and he opened his eyes, and saw Atra and a man-at-arms with her; and he cried out: "Hah, what is this now, sister? a rescue?"

"Yea," she said, "and look thou on the face of the rescuer; and there is another hard by, and she is a woman."

Therewith was Arthur on him and cutting his bonds, and when he was loose they fell into each other's arms, and Hugh spake: "Now then at last doth life begin for me as I willed it! And hast thou my sweet she-fellow, Birdalone, with thee?" "Yea," said Arthur. "How good is that!" said Hugh. "And yet—if it might but be that Baudoin were yet alive for us to seek!"

Then he laughed and said: "These be but sorry garments wherewith to wend along with dear and fair ladies, brother!"

"Nay," said Arthur, "that may soon be amended, for yonder, where sword met sword, lieth raiment abundantly on the grass."

"Fie on it!" said Hugh, laughing; "shall I do on me the raiment of those lousy traitors? Not I, by the rood! Thou must seek further for my array, dear lad!" So they all laughed and were glad to laugh together. But Atra said: "It is easier even than that, for thine own fair garments and weapons shall we find if we seek them. Sooth to say there was none left to bear them off, save it were this man, or Birdalone his mate."

With that word she looked kindly on Arthur, and again they laughed all three; though forsooth they were well-nigh weeping-ripe; one for joy, and that was Hugh; one for memory of the days gone by; and one for the bitterness of love that should never be rewarded: albeit dear even unto her was the meeting of friends and the glory of forgiveness and the end of enmity.

CHAPTER XXXIII. VIRIDIS TELLETH THE TALE OF THEIR SEEKING.

NOW came they back to where were the three others and Viridis was quite come to herself and ran to meet her man, and he took her in his arms and caressed her sweetly; and then he turned to Birdalone, and spared no sign of friendly love to her; and Arthur, for his part, did so much for Aurea and Viridis. No long tale there was between them for that while, for they would busk them to be gone. But first they dug a grave for those two poor men who had been slain by the felons, and prayed for them. As for the caitifs who lay slain there, one score and two of them, they left them for the wolves to devour, and the tearing of the kites and crows, nor meddled they with any of their gear or weapons. But they speedily found Hugh's raiment, and his pouch, wherein was money good store; and they found also rings and ouches and girdles, which had been torn from the damsels in the first rage of their taking.

First though, when they had gathered together such horses as they needed, and let the rest run wild, Birdalone brought her she-friends down into the dale, and did them to bathe in a pool of the stream, and tended them as if she were their tirewoman, so that they were mightily refreshed; and she made garlands for them of the woodland flowers, as eglantine and honeysuckle; and herself, she bathed her, and did not on her battle-gear again, but clad her body in her woman's array. Then she brought forth victual and wine from Habundia's store, and set it out on the stream-side; and thereafter she went up the bent to the green way and fetched down Hugh and Arthur, and brought them to the ladies, and bade them note how trim and lovely they were gotten again, and again it could scarce be but that kisses and caresses were toward; and in all content and love they took their breakfast, though bitter-sweet unto Atra had been the holding of her hand by Arthur and the kissing of her cheek, albeit not for worlds had she forgone it.

368

So there they abode merrily for some three hours, whereas the day was yet young; and they asked and told each other much, so that the whole tale, both of the seekers from the world and of the seekers from the water-side, came out little by little. Now of the last ye have heard what there is to tell, but for the others Viridis took up the tale, as erst she did with the dealings of the Knights of the Quest in the Isle of Increase Unsought; and it seemed by her tale that Hugh and the ladies, though they were living happily and prosperously in the land of the Green Mountains, wherein Hugh had wealth enow, yet the thought both of Arthur and of Birdalone would not out of their minds, and often it was that they thought of them, not as friends think of friends of whom they are content to know that they are yet alive and most like thriving, but as friends think of friends whose absence cuts a shard out of their lives, so that they long to see them day by day. Wherefore it came to this at last, after much talk hereof, that Hugh left his possessions and his children (for he had two women-bairns born of Viridis) in the keeping of trusty folk, and took with him Viridis his wife, and Aurea and Atra, and they set out to seek those twain the world over till they should find them.

And first by the rede of Atra they fared to Greenford, and there tarried a month, and sought tidings of many, and heard a word here and there whereby they deemed that Birdalone had passed therethrough some little time before. So they went thence to the Castle of the Quest, and found it in such plight as ye have heard, and it went sore to their hearts to behold it and to be there. But therewithal they happed upon Leonard the priest, and he was rejoiced beyond measure to see them, and told them all that ye have heard concerning Birdalone's coming thither and departing thence; and he told them therewith about those hauntings and sendings in the hall of the castle, and that they came to an end the very day that Birdalone departed thence in the Sending Boat. But for the last three days there had been

visions therein; but being questioned he was loth to tell
thereof, so they forbore him a while.

At these tidings they were sore moved, and they talked
the matter over betwixt themselves (and Leonard also was
in their redes), and they must needs deem that either Birdalone was cast away, or that she had come to her old dwelling, the House under the Wood, and belike had fallen into
the hands of the witch once more, and thereat were they sore
downcast; and yet somewhat it was, that they had heard sure
tidings of her; though meanwhile of Arthur had they heard
nought.

While they talked this over, Atra, who had been somewhat silent, spake and said: "Here are we brought to a stop
with the first tidings which we have heard, whereas we know
no manner of wending the Great Water. This seemeth evil,
but let us not be cast down, or die redeless. Ye have heard of
what sayeth Sir Leonard of these hauntings in the hall, and
how that they have come back again; wherefore why should
we not sleep in the hall this night, those of us at least who
have not so much fear as not to note them well, to see if we
may draw any avail from them? How say ye? For my part I
will try the adventure, whatever may come of it."

Now they all yeasay it, though Aurea was somewhat
timorous, albeit she would not be parted from the others;
so when night came there they made their beds and lay down;
and the end of it was, that a little before midnight Atra
waked the others, and did them to wit that by her deeming
something was toward; and presently they were all four as
wide awake as ever they were in their lives: and next, without any sound that was strange, there came the image of a
woman on to the dais, clad in green like to an huntress of
ancient days, her feet sandalled, her skirts gathered up into
her girdle, so that her legs were naked; she had a quiver at
her back, and a great bow in her hand.

Now to all of them save Atra this appearance seemed to be
the image of Birdalone; but she told her fellows afterwards,
that to her it seemed not to be altogether Birdalone, but

370

rather some other one most like unto her, as it were her twin-sister.

Gazed the image kindly and sweetly on them, so that they beheld it without fear; and it seemed to them that it gave forth speech; yet not so much that the sound of words was in the air about and smote their ears, as that the sense of words reached the minds of them. And this was the tale of it: Ye, who are seeking the lost, have done well to come hither, and now shall ye do well to wend the straightest way to the dwelling of the wildwood, and that is by way of the western verge of Evilshaw the Forest. Greenford is on the way. Wayleaders ye shall get; be wise yet not prudent, and take them, though they be evil, and your luck may well avail.

Therewith the image vanished away as it had come, and Leonard, who with the others took the appearance for an image of Birdalone, said that it was such as he had seen it the three last days. So they lay not down again, but departed for Greenford without tarrying, and rode the other end of the short night through till they came to Greenford. But Leonard would not with them; and Hugh behight him, if he lived and did well, to come back somehow to the Castle of the Quest, and so re-do it that it should be no longer desolate.

So to Greenford they came, and spared not to do folk to wit that they would ride a pilgrimage in Evilshaw, and were fain of wayleaders; and there they dwelt a day or two, and many would let them of that journey, which, said they, was rather deadly than perilous only. But on the third day came to Sir Hugh two stout carles well-weaponed, who said that they knew well all the ways that led to Evilshaw, and the ways that went therethrough, and they offered themselves for a wage to Sir Hugh. Now these said carles were not over fair of favour, but seemed somewhat of ribalds, nor would Sir Hugh have taken them to service in his house at home; but he called to mind that it were more prudence than wisdom to spoil his journey and lose the occasion of finding his dear friends for the hasty judgment of a man's face and demeanour, wherefore he waged these two men, and they set out for the western edges of Evilshaw.

Many towns and thorps they passed through, and everywhere, when men knew whither they were bound, they letted them all they might in words; but little heed they paid thereto, whereas they were all fixed in their rede that nought was to be done save the finding of their friends, and that their life-days were spoiled if they found them not. And moreover, each one of them, but especially Atra and Viridis, had dreams of the night from time to time, wherein they seemed to see the green-clad woman, were she Birdalone or another, beckoning and bidding them to enter the Wood of Evilshaw.

As to those two wayleaders withal, whether it were that they got used to their faces, or that their ways and manners were nought uncourteous or fierce, they doubted them less and less as time wore; all save Viridis, whose flesh crept when they drew anigh her, as will betide one who comes across an evil-looking creeping thing. As for Atra, she now began to heed little the things about her, as if her heart were wholly set on the end of the journey.

But now at last were they come so far that they had no choice but to use the said wayleaders, for they were gotten to the edge of Evilshaw. So they entered it, and those two led them by half-blind ways and paths amongst the thickets, and fumbled never with the road.

Five days they went thus, and on the fifth evening they lay down to sleep in the wood, and it was the turn of those two hirelings to keep watch and ward, and they woke not the next morn save with the hands of the Red Felons at their throats, so that Hugh was bound, and his two trusty men who came with him from the Green Mountains were slain before a stroke might be struck.

This was the end of Viridis' tale, save that she told how that it was she that had uttered those two shrieks which Arthur and Birdalone had heard from the thicket; and that she had so done when the two false wayleaders laid hold of her to drag her away from her man, who stood there before

372

her bound to a tree that he might perish there, whereon the
two caitifs had smitten her into unwit that they might have
no more of her cries.

Now when all this had been told, and they had abided
awhile in the fair little dale, and had said many kind endear-
ing words of friendship, they went up on the green way again,
and took what of the horses they needed and trussed their
goods thereon (and Birdalone would not leave that brave
armour which Habundia had given her), and they dight
others for their home-riding, and the rest they turned loose
into the woods, and so rode their ways, Birdalone going ever
with Atra, and Arthur by Aurea; but Viridis must needs
have Hugh within reach of her hand all the way.

Good speed they made, so that ere the night had fallen on
them, though the sun was set, they had come to the House
under the Wood; and there again was joy and wondering of
the new-comers, and merry feasting on such simple victuals
as were there, and good-night and rest in all contentment in
the house where erst had Birdalone tholed so many griefs
and fears.

HERE ENDS THE SIXTH PART OF THE WATER
OF THE WONDROUS ISLES, WHICH IS CALLED
THE DAYS OF ABSENCE, AND BEGINS THE SEV-
ENTH PART, WHICH IS CALLED THE DAYS OF
RETURNING.

THE WATER OF THE WONDROUS ISLES. THE SEVENTH PART: THE DAYS OF RETURNING.

CHAPTER I. NOW SHALL BIRDALONE CHOOSE THE LAND OF THEIR ABODE.

WHEN the next day was, they arose and were glad, and it was to them as if the sun of the early summer had arisen for nought save to shine on their happy day. And they went about from place to place whereas tidings had befallen Birdalone; and she served them one and all as if she were their handmaid, and they loved her and caressed her, and had been fain to do all her will did they but know it.

In this wise wore day after day till June began to wane, and then on a time came Hugh unto Birdalone, and spake unto her and said: "All we have been talking together, and I am sent to ask thee what is in thy mind as to abiding here or going elsewhither. For now that we be come together again, not for all the kingdoms of the world would we sunder; and above all, none of us would leave thee, O my sister. But if thou wilt come with me to our land under the Green Mountains, there is for thee a pleasant place and a fair dwelling, and honour from all folk, and our love that shall never leave thee; and I, and Arthur my brother, we shall win fame together amongst the knighthood, and thou shalt be proud and glad both of him and of me."

She said: "And if I may not go with thee thither, what other way is there to escape the sundering?" Said Hugh: "This, that thou choose in the world what land liketh thee for a dwelling-place, and we will go with thee and leave thee never, and thou shalt be our Lady and Queen." Then he laughed and said: "Yet, our lady, I have left behind me under the Green Mountains certain things which I love, as two fair women-children, and a squire or two whose fathers

374

served my fathers, and whose children I would should serve
my children. And moreover I have left there certain matters
of avail, my wealth and livelihood to wit. Wilt thou begrudge
it if I must needs go fetch these, and bring them to the land
where thou dwellest, through whatever peril we may have
to face?"

"Dear art thou," she said, "and my very friend! but tell
me: how sorry wouldst thou be to leave thine own land and
follow after me for the sake of one who is neither thine own
true-love nor of thy kindred?" Said he: "Not so sorry that I
should grudge against thee thereafter. Moreover if that much
of sorrow came to me, I should deem it not ill, lest I grow so
over happy that the luck rise up against me and undo me."

She said, smiling on him kindly: "Meseems that I am over
happy, whereas I have such dear cherishing of noble friends.
But now I will tell thee all, and maybe thou wilt love me the
less for the telling. In these woods here, and Lady and Mistress of them, dwelleth one who is not of the race of Adam.
And she helped and cherished me and gave me wisdom when
I was tormented and accursed, and she it was who saved me
from the evil witch, and gave me the goodhap to meet your
loves and to fetch you to their helping; and twice hath she
saved me from mortal peril otherwise. And she hath found
me my love, thy brother Arthur, and delivered him from
unwit and wanhope; and she it is who drew all you hither
unto us, and who delivered you from the felons who had
mastered you. And I have sworn unto her that I would never
wholly sunder me from her; and how shall I break mine oath
and grieve her, even had I the will thereto, as God wot I have
not?" And she wept therewith.

But Hugh kissed her and said: "Birdalone my dear, why
weepest thou? Didst thou not hear my word, that thy people
should be my people, and thy land my land, and that whither
thou goest I will go? Dost thou not trow me then? Or how
deemest thou I may tear thy friend Viridis from thee, when
she hath just found thee? But tell me, hast thou in thy mind
any dwelling-place other than this?"

"Yea," she said: "I may not depart very far from this Forest of Evilshaw lest I grieve my Wisdom-mother overmuch. But if one go westward through the wood, he shall happen at last, when he cometh forth of it, on a good town hight Utterhay, which lieth on the very edge thereof. There was I born, and there also I look to find three dear and trusty friends to whom I owe return of their much kindness. It is a noble town in a pleasant land, and thou and my lord Arthur may well win both honour and worship and lordship there. And wholly I trust in thy word that thou wilt not grudge against me for dragging thee thither."

Therewith she gave him her hand, smiling on him, though there was yet trouble in her face. But he took the hand and held it, and laughed merrily and said: "Lo now! how good it is for friends to take counsel together! What better may we do than go with thee thither? And how greatly will Viridis rejoice when she heareth of this. Now will I go and tell her and the others."

"Go then, dear lad," she said; "but as to the matter of thy fetching thy children and livelihood hither, that may be not so hard nor so perilous as thou deemest ; and thou shalt go about it whenso thou wilt, and the sooner the better, and we shall abide thee here as long as need may be." And therewith he went his ways to tell Viridis and the others of this rede which they had come to between them.

CHAPTER II. BIRDALONE TAKETH COUNSEL WITH HER WOODMOTHER.

ON that same day went Birdalone to the Oak of Tryst and called her Woodmother to her, and she came glad and smiling, and kissed and embraced Birdalone, and said unto her: "Now I see that thou art well content with this last matter I have done for thee, whereas thou art come to crave a new gift of me."

"How knowest thou that?" said Birdalone, laughing. Said Habundia: "Wouldst thou have come to me so soon

otherwise from out of all that happiness?" "I have come to
tell thee of my rede," said Birdalone, "and to ask thee if
thou art like-minded with me thereon." Said the Woodwife:
"And what is thy rede, my child?" "Woodmother," said
Birdalone, "we deem that it were good for us all to go
down into Utterhay where I was born, and to take up our
abode therein."

Said the Woodwife: "This rede I praise, and even so
would I have counselled you to do; but I abided to see if it
should come from out of thy breast, and now even so it hath
done; wherefore I understand thy wisdom and rejoice in
thee. And now crave thy boon, my child, and thou shalt have
it without fail."

"Yea," said Birdalone, "that will I, and the more that it
is a simple one and easy for thee to do. Thou knowest that
Hugh the Green Knight hath come with my she-friends
seeking us all the way from Under the Green Mountains,
and he hath left there goods that he needs must have and
folk whom he loves; and now he would go back thither, and
fetch all that away hither, and see to his matters as soon as
may be. And I would have thee counsel us what to do,
whether to build a barque, as perchance we may get it done,
and sail the lake therein to the Castle of the Quest or thereabout, and thence to ride to his land; or else to take thy
guidance and safe-conduct through the wood, and to bring
his folk back the same way."

Said the Woodwife: "As to the way by water, I may help
you little therein, and meseemeth that way be many traps
and wiles and many perils; wherefore I bid you try it not.
But let the Green Knight come up hither to this tree to-
morrow before noon, all horsed and armed and arrayed, and
there shall he find three men armed in green gear, horsed
well, and leading two sumpter-beasts with them; and they
shall be his until he giveth them back unto me. But if he
doubteth any thing betwixt the wood's end and Under the
Green Mountains, let him wage what folk he will besides, for
these my men will have money enough of his with them.

377

But by no means let him send them away till he hath done
with the wood altogether, both betwixt here and the western
dwelt-land, and here and Utterhay, save thou be with him.
But while these be with him, both he and whatsoever money
he bringeth shall be sure from all peril whiles they be in the
wood. Now, my child, was not this the boon thou camest up
hither to ask of me?"

"Yea verily," said Birdalone; "yet also I came up hither
to praise thee and thank thee and love thee." And she threw
herself into Habundia's arms and kissed and caressed her,
and Habundia her in like wise.

Spake the Woodwife: "Thou art the beloved child of my
wisdom; and now I see of thee that thou wilt be faithful and
true and loving unto me unto the end. And I think I can see
that thou and thy man shall do well and happily in Utterhay;
and the Green Knight also and thy she-friends. And whatsoever thou wilt of me that I may do for thee or thy friends,
ask it freely, and freely shalt thou have it. But this I will bid
thee, that the while the Green Knight shall be gone about
his matter, thou shalt come hither to me often; and thy
friends also thou shalt bring to me, that I may see them and
talk to them and love them. And specially shalt thou bid
Atra unto me; for meseems she is so wise already that I may
learn her more wisdom, and put that into her heart which
may solace her and make her to cease from fretting her own
heart, and from grief and longing overmuch. And I were
fain to reward her in that she hath forborne to grudge
against thee and to bear thee enmity. For I know, my child,
not from mine own heart, but from the wisdom I have
learned, how hardly the children of Adam may bear to have
that which they love taken away from them by another, even
if they themselves might in the long last have wearied of it
and cast it away their own selves. Go now, my child, and do
thy friend to wit what I will do for him."

Therewith they parted, and Birdalone fared home to the
house, and found the fellowship of them all sitting by the
brook-side, and talking sweetly together in all joy and hope

of what their life should be in the new land whereto Birdalone would lead them. Straightway then she told them of
Hugh and his journey, and how well he should be guarded
in the wood both coming and going. And they thought that
right good, and they thanked her and praised her, and took
her into their talk, and she sat down by them happily.

CHAPTER III. THEY JOURNEY THROUGH THE FOREST UNTO UTTERHAY.

ON the morrow in due time Birdalone, going afoot,
led Sir Hugh, all-armed and horsed, to the Oak of
Tryst, and there they found the three men-at-arms,
well-weaponed and in green weed, abiding them. They did
obeisance to Sir Hugh and he greeted them, and then without more ado he kissed Birdalone and went his ways with his
wayleaders, but Birdalone turned back to the house and her
friends.

Next day Birdalone brought her three she-friends unto
the Trysting Oak, and showed them to the Woodmother,
and she was kind and soft with them; and both Aurea and
Viridis were shy with her and as if they feared her, but Atra
was frank and free, and spake boldly. And thereafter when
Birdalone went to meet her Woodmother, Atra would go
with her if she were asked, and at last would go alone, when
she found that Habundia was fain of her coming, so that there
were not many days when they met not; and the Woodwife
fell to learning her the lore of the earth, as she had done aforetime with Birdalone; and Atra waxed ruddier and merrier of
countenance, whereof was Birdalone right glad, and Arthur
yet more glad, and the others well content.

So wore the time till Hugh had been gone for twenty and
three days, and as they walked the meadows anigh the house
about undern, they saw a knight riding down the bent toward them, and presently they knew him for Hugh, and
turned and hastened to meet him, so that he was straightway
amidst them, and on foot. Dear then were the greetings and

379

caresses betwixt them, and when it was over, and Birdalone had led away his horse and dight it for him, and had gotten him victuals and drink, and they were all sitting on the grass together, he told them how he had fared. He had done all his matters in the Land Under the Green Mountains, and had given over his lands and houses to a man of his lineage, his cousin, a good knight, and had taken from him of gold and goods what he would. Then he had taken his two bairns and their nurse, and an old squire and five sergeants, whereof one was his foster-brother, and the others men somewhat stricken in years, and had departed with them. Sithence he had come his ways to Greenford, and had held talk therein with the prior of a great and fair house of Black Canons, and had given him no little wealth wherewith to re-do the Castle of the Quest what was needed, and for livelihood of four canons to dwell there, and Leonard to be their Prior, that there they might remember Sir Baudoin their dear friend daily in the office, and do good unto his soul. Sithence he had ridden to the Castle of the Quest with the said Prior of St. Austin, of Greenford, and had found Leonard, and had settled all the business how it was to be done. Thereafter he had returned to Greenford, and gathered his folk, and got him gone, under the guidance of Habundia's folk, by castles and thorps and towns the nearest way to the edge of Evil-shaw. And they had come to the Forest and ridden it six days without mishap; and when they had come to the Oak of Tryst once more, the wayleaders said that it were well if all they together tarried not much longer in the Forest; wherefore they had brought them to a fair wood-lawn, and there they encamped, and were there as now. "And," said Hugh, "there are they abiding me, and it is in my mind that this very eve we go all of us and meet them there, if ye may truss your goods in that while; but as to victuals, we have plenty, and it needeth not. And then to-morrow shall we wend our way as straight as may be toward the good town of Utterhay."

All they yeasaid it, though in her heart maybe Birdalone
380

had been fain of abiding a little longer in her own land; but
she spake no word thereof. And they all set to work to the
trussing up of their goods, and then turned their backs on
the Great Water, and came up into the woodland, and so to
the camp in the wood-lawn. And there had Viridis a joyful
meeting with her babes, and she gladdened the hearts of Sir
Hugh's men-at-arms by her kind greeting; and they rejoiced
in meeting Aurea and Atra again, and they wondered at Birdalone and her beauty, and their hearts went out to her, both
the old men and the young ones. But Habundia's men looked
on it all like images of warriors.

There then they feasted merrily that evening. But when
the morrow was come they were speedily on the way toward
Utterhay; and the wayleaders guided them so well and wisely, that by noon of the fifth day they were come forth of the
wood and on to the bent that looked down upon the town of
Utterhay. There turned to Hugh the three wayleaders, and
spake: "Lord, we have done thee the service which we were
bidden; if thou hast no further need of us, give us leave."

Said Hugh: "Leave ye have, and I shall give you a great
reward ere ye go." Said the chief of them: "Nay, lord, no
reward may we take, save a token from thee that thou art
content with us." "What token shall it be?" said Hugh.
Quoth the wayleader: "That each of us kiss the Lady Birdalone on the mouth; for she it is that is verily our mistress
under our great mistress."

Laughed Hugh thereat, but the men laughed not; then
spake Hugh: "This must be at the lady's own will." "Even
so," said they.

Then Hugh brought Birdalone thither and told her what
was toward, and she consented to the kiss with a good will,
and said to each of the men after they had kissed her: "Here-
with goeth my love to the Mistress and Queen of the woods;
do ye bear the same unto her." And thereafter those wayleaders fared back into the woods.

Now they gather themselves together and go down toward
Utterhay, and make a brave show, what with the sumpter-

horses, and the goodly array of the four ladies, and the glittering war-gear of the men-at-arms; and Sir Hugh and Sir Arthur displayed their pennons as they went.

All this saw the warders on the wall of Utterhay; and they told the Captain of the Porte, and he came up on to the wall, and a many with him; and when he saw this bright company coming forth from the wood, he bade men to him, two score of them, all weaponed, and he did on his armour, and rode out a-gates with them to meet those new-comers; and this he did, not because he did not see them to be but few, but because they came forth out of Evilshaw, and men doubted if they were trustworthy.

So he met them two bowshots from the gate, and rode forward till he was close to the wayfarers; and when he beheld the loveliness of the women and especially of Birdalone, who wore that day the gleaming-glittering gown which Habundia had given her, he was abashed, and deemed yet more that he had to do with folk of the Faery. But he spake courteously and said, turning to Hugh, who rode the foremost: "Fair sir, would ye tell unto the man whose business it is to safeguard the good town of Utterhay what folk ye be, and on what errand ye ride, and how it is that ye come forth from Evilshaw safe, in good case, with pennons displayed, as if the said wood were your very own livelihood? Forsooth to say, hitherto we have found this, that all men dread Evilshaw, and none will enter it uncompelled."

Thereto answered Hugh: "I hight Sir Hugh the Green Knight, and am come from Under the Green Mountain; and this is Sir Arthur, called the Black Squire, but a knight he is verily, and of great kindred and a warrior most doughty. And he hath been Captain of the good town of Greenford west away through the wood yonder a long way, and hath done the town and the Frank thereof mickle good service in scattering and destroying the evil companies of the Red Hold, which Hold we took by force of arms from the felons who held it for the torment and plague of the country-side.

382

"Now as to our errand, we be minded to dwell in your
good town of Utterhay, and take our part with your folk,
and we have wealth enow thereto, so as to be beholden to
none; and as time goes on we may serve you in divers wise,
and not least in this may be, that with a good will we shall
draw sword for your peace and the freedom of them of Utterhay."

When the Captain heard these words, he made obeisance
to Sir Hugh, and said: "Fair sir, though we be here a long
way from Greenford, yet have we heard some tale of the
deeds of you, and surely the Porte and all the folk shall be fain
of your coming. Yet I pray thee be not wrath; for there is a
custom of the good town, that none may enter its gates coming from out of this Forest of Evilshaw, save he leave some
pledge or caution with me, be it his wealth, or the body of
some friend or fellow, or, if nought else, his very own body.
Wherefore if thou, Sir Green Knight, wilt but give us some
sure pledge, then will I turn about and ride with you back
and through the gate into Utterhay; and doubtless, when
the mayor hath seen you and spoken with you, the said pledge
shall be rendered to you again."

Ere Hugh might answer, came Birdalone forth and said:
"Sir Captain, if I, who am the lady of the Black Squire here,
be hostage good enough, then take me, and if need be, chain
me to make surer of me." And she drew near unto him smiling, and held out her hands as if for the manacles.

But when the Captain saw her thus, all the blood stirred in
his body for joy of her beauty, and he might but just sit his
horse for his wonder and longing; but he said: "The Saints
forbid it, lady, that I should do thee any hurt or displeasure,
or aught save the most worship I may. But thy hostage I
will take, Sir Knight, if thou be content to yield her, whereas in an hour belike she shall be free again. And now fare we
all gateward again."

So then they all rode on together, Birdalone by the Captain's left hand; and as they passed by the poor houses with-

out the wall, she looked and saw the one which had been her mother's dwelling, so oft and so closely had she told her all about it.

Thus then they entered Utterhay, and the Captain led them straight to the Mote-house whereas the Mayor and the Porte were sitting; and much people followed them through the streets, wondering at them, and praising the loveliness of the women, and the frank and gallant bearing of the men-at-arms.

So they lighted down at the Mote-house and were brought to the Mayor, and when he had spoken them but a little, and had come to himself again from the fear and abashment that he had of them, he showed himself full fain of their coming, and bade them welcome to the good town, and took them into his own house to guesting, until folk might dight a very goodly house which the Porte did give unto them.

But some two hours afterwards, when they were housed in all content, as they sat in the hall of the Mayor, which was great and goodly, talking and devising with worthies of Utterhay, there entered two fair and frank-looking young men, who went straight up to Birdalone, and the first knelt down before her and kissed her hand, and said: "O our lady, and art thou verily come to us! O our happiness and the joy of this day!"

But when she saw him and heard him and felt the touch of his hand, she bent down to him and kissed him on the forehead: for she knew him that it was Robert Gerardson.

Then the other man came up to her as if he also would have knelt to her, but his purpose changed, and he cast his arms about her body and fell to kissing her face all over, weeping the while, and then he drew off and stood trembling before her; and she, all blushing like a red rose and laughing a little, and yet with the tears in her eyes, said: "O Giles Gerardson, and thou, Robert, how fain I am to see you twain; but tell me, is your father well?"

"Yea verily, our dear Lady," said Robert, "and it will be unto him as a fresh draught of youth when he wotteth that

384

thou art come to dwell amongst us; for so it is, O Lady beloved, is it not?" said he.

"Yea forsooth, or even so I hope," said Birdalone. But here be other friends that ye must needs know, if we come to dwell together here in peace; and then go and fetch me hither your father."

Therewith she presented them unto Arthur and Hugh and the three Ladies of the Quest, and all they greeted them kindly and in all honour; and the Gerardsons loved and worshipped them, and especially the lovely ladies, the she-friends of their lady.

And whiles they were about this, in cometh old Gerard himself, and when Birdalone saw him at the door, she arose and ran to meet him, and cast her arms about him as if she were his own daughter; and most joyful was the meeting betwixt them.

CHAPTER IV. OF THE ABIDING IN UTTER-HAY IN LOVE AND CONTENTMENT.

NOW when seven days were worn, the Mayor made a great feast at his house, and thither were bidden all the men of the Porte and other worthies, and great merchants who had come unto their town; and the said feast was given in honour of these new-comers, and that day they sat on the dais, and all the guests worshipped them and wondered at their beauty; and nought was spoken of for many days save the glory and hope that there was in this lovely folk.

But the next day after the feast were they brought to their house in all triumph; and it was as fair as might be thought of, and there they dwelt a while in rest and peace, and great recourse there was there of Gerard and his sons.

But ere the winter was over, ere Yule was fully come, were Hugh and Arthur and Gerard and his sons taken to the freedom of Utterhay; and thereafter spake the chief men of the Porte and the masters of the crafts unto the two knights by the mouth of the Mayor; and he told them, what already they partly knew, that the good town had of late gotten many enemies, whereas it was wealthy and not very strong, and that now two such warriors having come amongst them, they were minded to strengthen themselves, if only they two would of their gentleness and meekness become their war-dukes to lead them against the foemen. But the two friends [answered] that it was well their will to dwell there neighbourly, and do them all the help they might, and that they would not gainsay the worship they offered them nor the work that should go with it.

With that answer were all men well content and more: and then the Mayor said that the mind of the Porte it was to strengthen the walls and the gates, and to build a good and fair castle, meet for any earl, joining on to the wall by the face that looked west, that is to say, on to Evilshaw; and that liked the war-dukes well.

So when spring came it was set about, but it was five years adoing, and before it was all finished the war-dukes entered into it, and dwelt there with their wives and their friends in all honour. And a little thereafter, whether they would or no, the men of Utterhay had to handle weapons and fare afield to meet the foe with the valiant men of the crafts, and what of waged men they might get. And well and valiantly were they led by their dukes, and they came to their above, and gained both wealth and honour thereby; and from that time forward began the increase of Utterhay under those two captains, who were unto them as in old time the consuls had been unto the Roman folk, save that they changed them not year by year as the Romans were wont.

So wore the days, and all those friends dwelt together in harmony and joy; though the wearing of time wrought changes amongst them. For Robert Gerardson began in no long while to look on Aurea with eyes of love; and at last he came to Birdalone and craved her leave to woo the said lady, and she granted it with a good will, and was fain thereof, whereas she saw that Aurea sorely lacked a mate; and

386

scarce might she have a better than was Robert; so in process of time they two were wedded and dwelt together happily.

Forsooth Birdalone had been fainer yet might she have seen Giles Gerardson and Atra drawn together; but though they were dear friends and there was much converse betwixt them, this betid not, so far as we have heard.

The old Gerard dwelt happily amongst them all for fifteen years after they had come to Utterhay, and then fell asleep, a very old man.

As to the wood of Evilshaw, it was not once a year only that Birdalone and Arthur sought thither and met the Woodmother, but a half-score of times or more, might be, in the year's circle; and ever was she kind and loving with them, and they with her.

But of all those fellows it was Atra that had longest dealings with the Woodwife; for whiles would she leave Utterhay and her friends and fare lonesome up into Evilshaw, and find Habundia and abide with her in all kindness holden for a month or more. And ever a little before these departures betid would she fall moody and few-spoken: but she came back ever from the wood calm and kind and wellliking.

Amidst all these comings and goings somewhat wore off the terror of Evilshaw; yet never was it accounted other than a daring deed to enter it alone without fellowship; and most had liefer that some man of religion were of their company therein. Or they would bear about them something holy or blessed to hold the evil things.

Now when all this hath been said, we have no more to tell about this company of friends, the most of whom had once haunted the lands about the Water of the Wondrous Isles, save that their love never sundered, and that they lived without shame and died without fear.

SO HERE IS AN END.

NOTES

These notes are primarily intended to facilitate understanding of the structure and conventions of the romance, and to introduce readers to the pleasures of Morris's clarity of language, richness of narrative effect, and wisdom of implication. Changes between the full MS and the printers' Fair Copy are far too numerous to catalogue here, unless they show a significant strengthening, or change of intention. Chapter-titles after page 174 were mostly supplied after Morris's death, by May Morris and Sydney Cockerell; the 'first MS' has few.

The seven Parts are given as sub-headings; the numbers before each citation are those of the chapter within that part, and of the page in this edition. B= Birdalone, H= Habundia; all other names are given entire.

PART I

1,1 *as tells the tale* An emphatically non-authorial opening, as if the romance were a folktale or legend. Morris was bored by the egotistical sublime and the self-conscious author.

1,1 *walled cheaping-town* Two capitalist principles are evoked with great economy : conflict and mistrust, competition and profiteering. See the following note.

1,1 *Utterhay* 'farthest hedge'. Hedges were the edges of towns in early medieval Europe, protecting citizens from the wildwood. The name reinforces the emphasis of 'walled', and since the town is surrounded by woods the capitalist principle of alienation from or subjection of external nature is also implied.

1,1   *Wood* In Morris a source of beauty, natural abundance and its analogue, spiritual health. This wood's spirit becomes the hero's foster-mother. Utterhay's fear of the Wood indicts Utterhay.

1,1   *the Goddesses of the Gentiles* Medieval Christianity adopted and sanctified a few 'pagan' gods and diabolized others; the Jews diabolized all foreign deities. It is tempting to imagine Artemis or Aphrodite becoming wood-spirits, but in a more northern interpretation 'Gentiles' are the Gens of the gothic or celtic tribes, with goddesses of power, pride and glamour like Frigga or the Valkyries, the triple Morrigan or the ladies of the Sidhe.

1,1   *Faery* Not 'fairies', miniature sprites like Peaseblossom and Mustardseed, or Tinkerbell, but dangerous non-human powers like Spenser's Faerie Queene, Thomas the Rhymer's Elf-Queen, Tolkien's elven lords, with an intimate relationship to wild nature and the extra-natural.

1,1   *Evilshaw* The name makes explicit the ironies about the citizens' attitude to the wood, both Christian and superstitious, in the surrounding paragraphs.

1,2   *alien* Stranger, but a deeper irony is developing. More truly alien than the shape-changing witch is the poor young mother starving in a prosperous town.

1,4 *poulaine* Probably an error for 'poularde' or 'poulet', a young cooked fowl; 'poulaines' are usually shoes.

1,5 *the saying of a low mass* Typical Morris irony, using the medieval phrase for 'a short time' to interrogate the pious cowardice that allows the witch to escape with the stolen baby.

1,5 *nought worser than herself* Again a medieval stereotype phrase, this time for safe travel, re-energized. It would be rare for this woman to meet anyone literally wickeder than herself.

2,6 *whoso might be sorry, the child was glad* Common medieval antithesis for being engrossed, here reminding us of the desperate mother.

3,7 *Of Skin-Changing* The witch, like many of Morris's power-women, has specific perception-magic as well as her other skills.

4,8 *Birdalone* This unusual epithet-name poetically identifies the hero with nature, where solitude is not irreconcilable with joy, and specifically with the wild life of the woodlands.

5,10 *seventeen* the MS 'sixteen' seems more plausible; the witch's training in seduction and witchcraft ought to begin early.

5,10 *were but a part* The untypically ornate clause produces an error. This should be 'were not but a part', that is, 'were not merely a part'. All editions preserve this error.

5,12 *god now damned* Morris was well-read in comparative religion and the Christian processing of older European theologies. See 1,1. 'God' is capitalized, like 'Faery', in the MS and Fair Copy.

5,12 *woman of the Faery* H, as the genius loci of Evilshaw, is like an elf-queen in some respects.

6,13 *maybe someone may be coming* The double 'may' merely toys with the prospect: the witch is reluctant to embark on the program of training, even though it was part of her initial intention in stealing the child. It is difficult, if not impossible, to bind human love and desire, though physically Birdalone was an excellent choice.

6,14 *rue it only once, to wit, lifelong* Morris was always alert for such striking medieval phrases; this one threatens either unremitting punishment or incipient death.

7,15 *say her name* It is already established that the witch rarely (if ever) uses B's name; H does so as a 'godparent' to the girl.

7,15 *the shape of a young woman* Natural abundance is fulfilled by taking the shape of a maiden, both complete and potential ('dawn and meridian in one', in Dickinson's phrase). Her oak wreath is not for modesty but is the signature of the forest, corresponding to the green gown lying across B's lap.

7,16 *two children whom the earth loveth* A lovely pagan image of unfallen harmony between nature and humanity. Compare the deer facing each other in B's embroidery.

7,16 *mirror* B is ignorant of many civilized French terms, but the antagonism between the witch-wife and the wood-woman gives an ironic edge: these speakers are natural in their nakedness and frankness, and H is B double, her mirror-image. However, the only reason B has not met a mirror is because the witch did not wish there to be one; it is by no means unnatural for a teenager to be curious about her own body.

7,17 *the promise of the earth* A mythic aspect of this crucial meeting, which is also a medieval-style decorative set-piece (the erotic description of fair women) and a ritual self-acceptance by B which, in the context of her broidering her first gown, completes a necessary stage of her Bildungsroman.

7,17 *is not stayed by thy girdlestead* An ungraceful ambiguity: either the hair does not stop at her hips ('at' replaces the cancelled 'by' in the MS, but 'by' reappears in the Fair Copy) or it is not hindered by her hips.

7,17 *thine imaginer* H's commendation of the master-worker God, designer of humans, is detached as if she herself were from a different source. See 7,19, on 'the children of Adam'.

7,18 *the folly of love* H never understands love, or sorrow, or most other human emotional experiences.

7, 19 *so alike we are* Instead of studying individual psychology, romances slate episodes and characters one upon another to make a single evolving personality. The doubling in this episode is repeated throughout B's fostering; H always appears in B's image (though once very small and once grown old). Doppelgangers, alter egos and shadows are major non-naturalistic conventions.

7,19 *the children of Adam* The Faery might well see humanity as late-comers, of limited capacity yet accorded great privilege. H finds us fascinating, though irrational.

7,19 *Habundia* Morris knew both *La Roman de la Rose* and Chaucer's translation of it, where Dame Habonde stands for natural abundance, generosity and spontaneity, but is narratologically associated with a woman's inner nature and with the right true end of physical love. One of Morris's favourite books, Grimm's *Teutonic Mythology*, uses Habundia as the name of the 'Nature Goddess of the North'. 'Habondia' is invoked in witchcraft, especially if the spell has a sexual purpose, as long as it involves natural ingredients.

7,20 *by way of Weeping Cross* Often as 'Whipping Cross', this is grim medieval humour for the hard road of punishment, playing on 'Cross' as crossroads. There is at least one actual Weeping Cross in England, in the old Staffordshire.

8,21 *masterful* Meaning 'exultant' rather than 'domineering', but the witch is waiting for her authority to be challenged.

8,22 *Or what sayest thou?* Not inviting objections but expecting enthusiastic agreement or thanks: 'What d'you think of that?'

9,23 *A pity of it, to leave it!* In the MS, 'Thou, who so longest to be quit of it, wilt thou ever live to long for it all?' A Morris hero loves the physical world, what is, even if it must be left behind for other realities.

9,24 *so little and low* Awareness of mortality, of the shocking possibility of premature death, goes with the love of life. Death is not a consummation to be wished. This passage presages the dangerous rite of passage when she returns to the house under the wood by swimming, VI,15,313–4.

10,25 *a huge serpent* The nightmare serpent is not a mere tale to frighten the child but the spirit of the Sending Boat.

11,28 *her face changed horribly* The fury and subsequent fit create a distance between B and the witch, which in its turn introduces the skin-changing punishment.

11,29 *a little flasket* No satisfactory source has been adduced to me for this skin-changing drink. Anointing with the grease of the appropriate animal is sometimes met with, but the imaginative consent of the changer is usually essential, even in the comic transformation of *The Golden Ass*. The berserk and ulfhedinn traditions of northern warriors who feel themselves transformed into ferocious animals were of course well-known to Morris. The whole of this amazing transformation is introduced in the Fair Copy; in the verse text and the MS proper, there is merely a savage beating. Math's punishment of his relatives Gwydion and Gilfaethwy in *The Mabinogion* is the closest analogy I have found.

11,29 *thy guilt will be required of me* Presumably by the spirit of the Sending Boat, or higher powers which consent to the witch's transactions with it.

12,31 *the glory of dominion* The witch's version of courtly love and power over male admirers (later enacted by her sister) is more like Miss Havisham's than Marie de France's. Dickens' influence is pervasive in Morris.

12,32 *Eld...Hell..Death* This diabolic trinity expresses the savage gender-pessimism that can alone account for the witch's bitter Havisham-like witchcraft as an anti-natural choice. Its Christianity is problematic, since 'Hel' was the name of Loki's daughter, loveless queen of the underworld, in Norse mythology.

12,32   *grace* Secular 'grace and favour', not the religious term, but the blessing of having a human form again may seem divine.

13,33   *tears* Like the rest of the Faery, changelings and demons, H cannot weep human tears.

13,35   *looking anxiously on her* H cannot understand B's compassion for the witch, but fears she has been 'beguiled'. This human pity is added late to the Fair Copy text.

13,35   *a serpent holding his tail in his mouth* The worm Ouroboros stands for the paradoxical relationship between cyclic eternity and linear time, which should outclass the manipulations of the witch-sisters. It gives invisibility by removing the ring-wearer from temporal sight, as does its descendant, Tolkien's One Ring.

13,35   The comparison with the natural wind suits H's kind of magic, and the simple rhymed charm contrasts with the witch's ornate ritual binding-spell (15,40).

15,40   *barren white skin* This is the witch's shape when away from her house; her colouring and her flat chest contrast strikingly with H and B.

15,40   *she sang in a crow's croak* The spell is a complex interweaving of southern rhyme and metre with northern alliteration. Morris knew both Old English and medieval alliterative verse (he translated *Beowulf*) and the more difficult skaldic measures of Old Norse charms, spells and drottkvaett. This dark chanting is appropriate to the ritual blood-sacrifice or payment-from-self it accompanies.

15,40 *red raven-wine* A fine kenning for blood. Morris was, it seems, never happy with this spell (see notes on the variants, especially II,8,81). In the MS the first three lines read,

> The red raven-wine now
> Hast thou drunk, stern & prow;
> Dwell not then, but wake!

The Fair Copy retains 'prow', though all editions have 'bow'.

16,42 *book of the earth* Wise Women teach heroines like this in most of Morris's romances. Their natural magic is quietistic, descriptive and celebratory; if it affects others, it is only in their perceptions (both witches use enforcement and acquisitive magic). At the end of the romance H teaches this wisdom, her heritage and dominion, to Atra.

16,42 *forgotten is the wisdom* The story-teller disclaims any profundity, though the audience cannot be prevented from hoping that 'the tale of its learning' is itself worth learning.

16,43 *thou seemest changed* The book of the earth is affecting B already, prompting the witch to both unease and a back-handed admiration.

17,44 *her mother (as now she called her)* Their bond is now intellectual as well as a general fostering.

17,45 *from the teeth outward* 'As a matter of course, without real passion'. In 19,47 the phrase connotes 'avoiding the expression of their deeper feelings'.

18,47 *yet once wert thou more like unto us* This is not a generalization about human beings developing away from Faery, but in the singular. B, as a child, was naturally less ethical than she is now becoming; the Woodmother's teaching has effects on the children of Adam different from its effect on herself. Though H cannot weep, yet loving B has made her capable of sadness.

20,49 *half-dead briar-rose* The natural thorns, rather than the manufactured scissors or bodkin, align B with nature even in the binding-magic. Her blood-letting is her rite of passage into the adult world, not only by analogy with menstruation but in parting her from her good and evil foster-mothers.

20,51 *Then wake and awake!* Morris was still concerned about this third line. In the MS it is 'Awake then, awake!' as at II,8,81.

20,51 *back over the flood* B does not remember the witch's counter-spell when she tries to return from the Castle (VI,8,291) to the house under the wood.

20,51 *O child! O child!* Though she is carrying a heavy sword, the witch's 'prayer' is almost as sincere as her subsequent curse.

PART II

2,54 *lightly and merrily* Although the ladies are slaves, Aurea and Viridis, at any rate, seem sufficiently at one with their fate to be but little cast down by it.

2,54 *Now she comes....* In the Fair Copy this present-tense change is continued with the –ed of 'asked' over-written with –s, though this may not have been legible to the printers. The MS uses past-tense throughout the passage.

2,54 *a servant to servants* Morris often sounds a little like the Authorized Version of the Bible, or its predecessors. Here the echo is a very apt one.

2,55 *more manlike* The Queen, though human-born, is a spiritual alien, from her continual dependence on the Water of Might.

2,56 *Aurea* The golden one. Viridis, the green one, and Atra, the black one, make up one of the few Latin-based name-groups in Morris. The heraldic effect of their sisterhood, names and clothing sets off B's nakedness and complex personality. It also establishes that their individualities are subjugated not only to their enforced servitude but to their roles in the story of their male lovers' heroism. Since 'other names we have not now' they may have abandoned their Christened names because of the meanness, pride and malice of their families. Viridis' colour is summer, Aurea's harvest, and Atra's winter. B, naked, is spring.

2,56 *Viridis* In the MS, until p. 63, the less euphonious 'Virida'.

3,58 *standing there alone* The splendour of the palace is set off by B's naked and quivering figure.

3,58 *the Lady-witch* She resembles the Witch under the Wood as an indulged younger sister might resemble her indulgent older sister, but also naively parade her difference.

3,59 *thou hast stolen thyself from her: thou art a thief* Morris delighted in *Huckleberry Finn*, where a similar irony shocks Huck when he hears Jim propose to steal his own children, 'that belonged to a man I didn't even know'.

3,59 *the House of Death* The Queen's obsessive fear of mortality has become a fear of all change, and a hatred of the natural life and beauty of the women around her. B's arrival is the first step in the destruction of the superficial loveliness of this house.

3,60 *and what is prison?* The idea of imprisonment is an obscenity in itself, to a free imagination like B's – and the inhabitants of Nowhere in *News*. Appropriately, it is a French-derived word. B's language and perspective are simple, direct and intensely Northern; see I,7,16. Atra's answer is radical and forthright.

4,61 *pillar of red marble* Combined with the polished floor, this associates cruelty with exotic, refined opulence. The torture-rooms of Utterbol in *The Well at the World's End* have a Red, a White and a Black Pillar to chain victims to. Here the great chest's torture instruments are the more menacing because unseen.

5,64 *She hath no pity* How can the upper classes believe that the poor, the servant class, feel respect and sympathy for each other, let alone that they develop class solidarity?

5,65 *the Isle of Increase Unsought* Morris despised the smug, helpless, selfish ruling classes of England, who wore, ate, drank, dwelt in, drove and played with the products of the labouring classes they despised, reviled, feared and imprisoned in ignorance. These maidens, coming from the gentry, aren't useful workers who can turn nature into 'dinner and supper', but they wish to love and help B; their Queen has no such good intentions.

5,65 *mishandling or pining* In the MS, a Latinate cadence 'oppression and torment'. Old English is more appropriate to B.

5,65 *a tyrant and a fool* This sharp and uncourtly reaction is partly caused by B resenting her earlier fear of the Queen. The Greek word 'tyrant' extends her rhetoric.

5,66 *they who long for us* Another erotic tableau, like that in which H presented B's body to her. Here the naked teenager is educated by two older women acquainted with love and sex, and explicitly aroused by their excitement.

5,66 *the sons of Adam* In the MS 'the world of men'. An elegant reminder that B comes from outside male humanity, and is more like H than her informants.

5,66 *as surely as death* This sombre phrase hints at Atra's temperament, and, more subtly, at her prophetic insight.

5,67 *oppressed by the sweetness of longing* Medieval romance offers many male heroes aroused by the idea of love, but B is the first female hero to respond in this way. The MS text had been far less beautiful: 'and now for the first time she felt the shame of her nakedness, for erst when she stood before the Witch Lady it was but fear, and the despair of her helplessness.' The revision from embarrassment to celebration of female sexuality is typical of Morris.

6,68 *the Black Squire* Arthur is immediately set apart from other knights as more vulnerable, with more potential for change and suffering. Atra stands out from her companions because their bright garments are more conventionally pretty, and this too increases the tension about Arthur. Hamlet, blackclad amid wedding finery, is an ancestor, but the name and style of Tristan provides a closer relative, especially since Arthur's blazon is black, sprinkled with silver tears. See notes to IV,10,160 and V,7,205.

6,68　Morris had no sentimentality about medieval life, as is shown by Froissart poems like 'The Haystack in the Floods'. The limitations and cruelties of aristocratic life-style, as shown in Atra's story, are as clear as those of mercantile Utterhay. B can be stolen because her mother was poor, the maidens because their families are caught up with feuds and jealousies – and they themselves idle and vacuous. Failures in human fellowship give power to the witch in 'good town' and 'great family' alike.

6,69　*long and deftly, and...none heeded him* A pleasant comic touch. Morris was an earnest public speaker, but despised mere parliamentary eloquence. The king may be right, but no decree can resolve the situation, however deftly it is expressed.

6,70　*old barons* The French term implies division, self-importance and local family self-indulgence. The king uses the English 'thanes' to remind his contentious audience of their allegiance.

6,70　*churl or earl* A common medieval phrase for 'low and high'. Ursula, the yeoman heroine of *The Well at the World's End,* claims defiantly that once both words meant the same thing, a man.

6,70　*let rear* He had it built. To 'put hand to pouch' and spend freely is the lot of the Victorian father of the bride, but there is a difference between paying to have the pavilion built and building it. Morris's work ethic asserts that what you work on you value – both in itself and (by transference) for your own sake – and when you work you value yourself, both as craftsman and as an active imagination. The product of work is a Thou, not an It.

6,71 *to wear through the day as we might* Their idle, privileged life, as well as their emotional and familial tensions, make the maidens vulnerable. They are bored and 'wearied' because they have no self-expressive function, but are passive prizes, waiting to be won. B's active femininity contrasts directly, but there is also the ironic hint that the cruelty of the witches was valuable. Service and even humiliation have necessitated that they develop skill, intelligence, and loving cooperation.

6,73 *the great God himself* The witch's sarcasm challenges the nexus between aristocracy and clergy, which created the smug world which had entrapped the maidens for her.

6,73 *edge-friend* A kenning for sword, sax or knife: an ally when she seemed to have none, and effective because of its edge.

6,76 *lazy sorrow and shameful ease* Echoing the idleness theme, but Atra is too modest. They have endured their servitude bravely and are risking savage punishment.

8,79 *to clothe thee from our very bodies* The ritual clothing of B is another erotic tableau, because it partially strips the ladies, but mainly because it invites the audience to imagine her disrobing again before the knights. B's response to these, her first fancy clothes is also partly a response to the ladies who have just removed them.

8,79 *Wherefore be good to me* This plea distinguishes Atra from the others. This gentle foreshadowing of her future troubles and need for B's help is made more emphatic in her 'passion' at the end of the chapter.

8,80 *Baudoin*.... The male names have personal rather than conventional connotations, unlike the ladies'. Baudoin is from the Old English Baldawine, 'bold friend'; its Middle English form Baldwin was one of Charlemagne's paladins. A popular Crusading name (of kings of Jerusalem and Constantinople), it was also borne by a rebel Morris might have preferred, Baldwin of Redvers. The French form of his name identifies Baudoin, though admirably knightly, with the sterile aspects of romance.

Hugh.... Although with Norman and crusading associations, the name derives from either the Celtic 'Hu', 'Huw' ('inspired' or 'fire', as in the green boughs bearing flames which are his dashing motif) or the Norse 'Hugu' ('thought', as in his natural married chastity, which makes him take thought and defeat the Queen).

Arthur.... For any contemporary of Tennyson, a name resonant with nobility, wisdom, and ill-luck in erotic matters. The Celtic origin connects with 'arth' ('bear') and 'gwr' ('hero'), and bear-people figure largely in Morris romances. His temperament is intense and somewhat withdrawn, and his moral life chequered as Baudoin's or Hugh's could not be; his sexual availability to the Queen, quite apart from his male corner of the love-triangle with B and Atra, may be compared to Arthur's availability to his half-sister Morgause.

8,80 *speech-friends* Betrothed lovers; those who are 'spoken for' or have spoken their feelings and been accepted.

8,81 *southward* B varies the spell to avoid being carried back to the Witch. In the Fair Copy the last couplet is set out as a quatrain.

8,81 *and the sun arose as they looked, and his path of light flashed on B's golden gown* This lovely echo of Browning's quatrain of male self-indulgence, *Parting at Morning*, inverts its satire: B's healthy eagerness for 'a world of men' contrasts finely with Atra's dreadful foresight in the following sentence.

9,82 *voyage* The second and third lines of this chapter were set up in the wrong order in this *Collected Works* text.

9,82 *new and strange hope* B's speculative attraction towards males recurs just before she meets her first, the next morning. However, being cut off from change, neither the three-year-old nor the very old man are much more than 'images' of men.

9,83 *rather glad* In the MS 'not pleased' is first bracketed then deleted, presumably because of its dysfunctional ambiguity.

9,84 *rabbits* B is not civilized, even though clothed, and the rabbits respond to her natural kinship with the wild.

9,86 *welcome as the very spring* The Isles, trapped in midsummer, have no cycle of seasons, so the conventional greeting gains new significance: B is the very spring, the new beginning.

9,86 *thou hast brought hither somewhat less than peace* The old man intends primarily to compliment her beauty, which will excite and disturb wherever she goes, but it may be that he also expects her arrival to portend his death, as with the solitary men living successively under the cliffs in *The Wood Beyond the World*: the new arrival would be the successor. However, he is right in that B's journey dooms the Queen.

9,87   *it was overgrown with ash-tree and quicken-beam, and other berry-trees and key-trees* The Fair Copy, providing 'great and flourishing' trees growing in the walls, makes the ruin so much more ruinous.

9,89–90   *Fair child....* These four paragraphs of conversation are well revised from the confusing MS passage, in which the old man seems to imply successions of children as well as old people: 'these be taken away & others put in their place, before they may change any deal.' The arbitrary fantasy of the unchanging children, like the old man closed in his own selective amnesia, is far more effective.

9,89   *wax they will not* The prohibition of change and ageing resembles the eponymous *Glittering Plain*, another preserved weariness of spirit that falsifies human experience.

10,92   *she must needs go forward* A complex idea, uniting the dynamics of story structure with determinism: now the protagonist has set her hand to the plough, there is no turning back. Morris certainly knew King Arthur's definition of kingship that ends 'The Holy Grail' (lines 901–7), a rich expression of this idea. However, folktale protagonists must often complete a specific series of tasks in a specific order: monsters must be destroyed, tests passed, talismans acquired, stages of experience completed, as structural principles. Whether directly or through Morris and his disciples, this convention has become typical of late twentieth-century quest-romance and sword-and-sorcery fiction. In this case, there is no evidence that B's scrupulousness is necessary to guarantee her journey's success.

10,94 *new tidings* The king perpetually 'waked' by the Queens may not have caused their entranced state; they have focused their misplaced courtly mourning, their ritualized passion, upon him. The inbuilt parody of the Sleeping Beauty motif implies that they might all re-enter life if he did; however, he is undoubtedly dead, with change and hope fossilized around his body. B is a humble peasant girl stumbling into an aristocrat's story.

11,95 *the pride of that ferry* B has intuited the evil will of the Sending Boat, that longs to dominate those who accept its blood-bargain. Later she thinks of having to 'content its greedy soul with her blood' (11,98).

11,96 *war-swales* In the MS, one of the rare illegible words, perhaps 'alluses', occurs here.

11,97 *the steel which had been her bane* Presumably the bloody sword borne by the king on the previous Isle.

11,98 *nay, whether* This sentence and the question that follows, emphasizing that the Queen's rule is over 'images', replace the less interesting fear in the MS that 'perhaps she should find on the next isle some witch awaiting her with prison and whips'.

12,101   *sending* An apparition, usually identifiable with and controlled by the will of the sender. This transaction, since H wears B's image, is cooperative rather than binding magic. The Sending Boat, by contrast, maintains its form by feeding on her.

PART III

1,103   *builded* The just-completed castle is not a tower of strength, but of courtly-love devotion. Like many castles in Malory, it is dedicated to a single obsession; it faces away from its country and people towards the open lake. The garrison, in the absence of the lords, is neither shrewd nor confident; the problems of a culture defined by the assumptions of its upper-class males are obvious throughout Parts Three and Four.

1,105   *we are bound by oath* Sir Aymeris is obsessed with oaths and duty; his inorganic formalism cannot cope with the simple fact that B is starving and exhausted. Her word is her bond, but her spiritual faith is in the pagan H, not the crucified Christ by whom Aymeris swears. Since she is meeting her first males, but is well acquainted with female power for good and evil, the idea of a male and suffering God intensifies her alienation.

1,105   *religious* Leonard the chaplain; like Aymeris he represents male supremacy and its French- and Latin-based rhetoric, as in technical terms like 'castle', 'quest', 'castellan', 'chaplain' and 'religious'. B, being female, is forbidden the comfort of 'raiment', 'cushion', 'comfort', 'victual', 'venison', 'solar' and 'screen'. As to conduct, the castellan uses 'suffer', 'pardon' and 'gracious', and the priest twice 'makes obeisance'. Later, Leonard teaches B the Castle's reality through words like 'custom', 'mischief', 'battle', 'chamber' and 'matin'.

1,106 *with God nailed thereon* Not irony, but showing the literalism of the castle's faith.

2,108 *The Castle is called in this countryside, the White Ward by the Water; but within there we call it the Castle of the Quest* Leonard discriminates precisely between English and Norman-French languages and perspectives. Later he uses the French words for food animals: 'venison, or it may be beeves and muttons for our victualling'; much in the spirit of *Ivanhoe*, the story invites us to recognize that this language of the plump diners is not that of those (like B) who work outdoors with animals.

3,112 *pass her by?* Cancelled are two untypical experiments in coyness. B wishes, in the MS, 'Would that I were fairer fashioned of my body!', and a cancelled replacement in the Fair Copy is similar: 'if I were but as fair of body....'

3,112 *goddess of the Gentiles* See I,1,1. Like the reference to the Faery in the nearby description of Viridis' smock (3,111), and her effect on Aymeris and Leonard, this invites readers to anticipate B's impact on the knights.

4,113 *a cleft heart of red* In the MS, close to stereotype: 'a device of a heart cleft through with an arrow'.

4,113 *silver tears* In the MS, 'golden tears'.

4,114 *oak-wreath* Suiting his outdoor tan, and linking with his later woodland life and H's acceptance of him – and contrasting with B's eglantine.

4,116 *a new sweetness* The hints about B's response to Arthur are not insistent, but neither are they obscure.

4,117 *and so beauteous* Just as ladies appear in quest-romance as 'so beauteous' decoration, baits and rewards for knightly heroes, so knightly prowess is decoration to B's story. Even more deeply delightful, she is sexually attracted to one of them! This scene balances the earlier triptych of B's arraying.

5,120 *Come then, thou Thomas unbelieving* The erotic application of St Thomas' famous comment on the wound in Jesus' side is startling (though B would not have recognized the reference).

5,122 *my kindred all greedy about me* Like Aurea's 'niggard' guardian, Viridis' relatives are not noble or knightly but mercantile in their vices. The gifts and tokens of the lovers are generously playful not because of their noble birth but because they are lovers.

5,123 *this first time* The tension between B and Arthur develops in this first private interview, and alert audiences will treasure his manifest discomfort, especially when B describes it as 'Thou art out of heart as now'.

5,123 *I was verily her lover* Arthur's past tense contrasts vividly with B's 'if thou be...'. The flat circumstance of his tale, culminating in the bathetic citing of the fords' names, provides an equally poignant contrast with the open sexuality and affection in the other two tales. Two parallel narratives as preamble and contrast to a more important third forms a time-honoured story-telling convention (compare Lear's older daughters' love-declarations with their sister's 'Nothing', or Cinderella trying the shoe after her ugly sisters).

5,124 *lest ill-luck come thereof* This shrewd touch of foreboding, added in the Fair Copy, implies the similarity of Arthur to Atra. The ring figures in a minor misunderstanding later in the story.

6,126 *whereas the said ladies be all beset with sorceries* The MS has the feeble, 'though wherefore I wot not'.

6,126 *'Moreover,' said the Black Squire* This speech again shows Arthur as much more aware of physical female reality, especially B's reality, than his fellows. In the MS it had been given to the Green Knight, ending at 'therewith' and joining immediately to the Green Knight's speech 'It were not so ill done...' that now follows. The revision is typical in its filling out a character from what had been primarily a flat, or actant, role.

6,126–7 *a goodly and great town hight Greenford* Merely 'the cheaping-town' in the MS, and only '15 miles hence'.

6,127 *dwarf-wrought gold* Well-wrought ancient gold was naturally assumed to be the work of the legendary master-smiths.

7,128 *he sought her company ever* This passage, like most of the many revisions to this whole chapter, reinforces any expectations of love between Arthur and B the audience may have developed.

7,128 *deemed that her sweet friend would love her the better if she babbled not of her* The MS is feeble: 'feared they would not trow in the tale, and so she might win a little scorn of them.'

7,129 *B glanced on him wistfully ere she went on with her tale* Added in Fair Copy to confirm that B is in love with Arthur.

7,129 *O I pray thee pity me for the sundering* In the MS he only says, 'But needs must I'. Here the plea is both a declaration of love and an echo of Atra's entreaty to B – though his idea of pity was probably very different.

7,130 *no less well than the others* This understatement becomes a brighter irony once the Fair Copy revisions, especially those in the two adjacent notes, confirm her to be in love with Arthur.

7,130 *And then she spoke it in a soft voice that she would indeed pity him for the sundering, yea, and herself, also* Again added in Fair Copy.

8,130 *who hight Leonard* He is not named in the MS at this point, nor Sir Aymeris in the next paragraph. When it becomes necessary to name him in Part IV, the MS gives 'Lawrence' (see V,1,185 for the aptness of 'Leonard'). As with folktales, Morris usually avoids giving personal names to minor actant roles – or even major ones at times. In *The Wood Beyond the World*, everyone that Walter meets 'beyond the world' (except his rival Otto) is unnamed.

9,131 *Rather sunrise than sunset it seemed, as verily birdalone* Added in Fair Copy; this reminder of her name's literal meaning occurs when she is in her finest array, amid the largest assembly of her life (and mainly of males), but about to be more isolated, by the knights' departure, than ever before.

9,132 *it shall be a light thing for me to die for thee* Baudoin is not fey, but Fate seems to take him at his word, see V,4,196.

9,132 *and all her body yearned toward him to solace him* In the MS 'she wept not, but sore she longed to comfort him'. The Fair Copy's very fleshly response is especially striking in the context of the Christian males all swearing on the Cross.

9,133 *the Rood* The less archaic 'Cross' of the MS has been altered, as with 'Tree' and 'Rood' throughout this scene, perhaps to give Morris's Christian contemporaries a chance to adopt a more detached, Nowherian view of the Castle's established faith.

9,133 *the sweetness of that moment* Arthur's tender use of her name and his care for her safety touch her, but the implications are much wider. Her previous life's solitude and present social centrality to such a splendid occasion, her sense of having achieved her promise to the ladies, and her delight in the masculine beauty and admiration of the 'Champions', contribute. This wars against her physical longing for Arthur and his incipient departure (which is his precise subject), and her half-stifled fears about the love-triangle that must ensue when he and Atra return. But there is another irony: his instructions are the more confining because he is quite unconscious of the limiting paternalism of the arrangements he is proposing. She, because of her love for him, is gladly assenting to an arrangement that will eclipse her whole personality and make her very ill indeed. Being in love limits her perceptiveness drastically!

9,133 *the Red Knight* It seems curious that such
virtuous, heroic and pious Champions have endured
being almost cheek-by-jowl with a vicious, cruel, and
implacably evil warrior-sorcerer, their precise
antonym, who seems to do far more harm to
humanity in the area than they can do good. But the
Castle of the Quest faces out toward the empty
Lake....

10,134 *in a strait black coat and with unshod feet*
Her choice of sober, understated clothing befits a
tense occasion, but also reaffirms both her bond with
the Black Squire and her half-conscious desire to
replace Atra, black-clad and barefoot at their parting.

10,134 *smite the head off her* The MS adds '& then
were we all free', which makes Hugh somewhat too
naive.

10,134 *His eyes flashed and his brow knitted, and so
fierce he looked that B shrank back from him* Not in
the MS. Fair Copy revisions are often brilliant in
both style and psychology, but some run the risk of
softening B too extravagantly. However, she is trying
to be a lady, to respond to the expectations she has
accepted from both the knights and their courtly
environment.

10,134 *yet must we so fashion our carving...die with
her* In the MS, '& yet I wot not what web of charms
& sorcery she may spread for our feet; whereas we
might do more wisely, & meet guile with guile'. The
revision retains his air of wisdom, while avoiding any
reference to 'guile'.

10,135 *northern* In the MS 'northward', as at
VI,8,291, and responding to B's 'southward' at

II,8,81. The Fair Copy again presents the spell's last couplet as a quatrain.

10,136 *saying to herself that the sundering was easier to bear than she had deemed* All this sentence has replaced the more conventional emotion of the MS: 'Then she turned away, sobbing and weeping as she went, & came to her chamber.' The text's gentle irony is psychologically far more precise.

PART IV

The early chapters of this Part are very closely re-worked in the Fair Copy; they were of course the last that the author was spared to revise. Most of the reworking includes expansion, to establish the oppressive normality of life in the Castle, and B's increasing alienation and depression within it. Having once been forbidden entry into the Castle, she is now forbidden egress.

1,137 *Now came B to herself...* The whole first paragraph, and the next sentence, replace the single sentence in the MS: 'After a while she arose, & the women came to her & attired her somewhat more seemly, but for all their words & their flatteries she would wear nought [save] black while her friends were away from her.' The text reminds us that B is unused to being dressed and would be embarrassed to be found lying on the floor by them. Her response is not extreme: she has experienced only two partings previously, neither from a lover.

1,137 *peevishly, and was sorry for it thereafter* Added in the Fair Copy and evoking B's emotional confusion well.

1,138 *hope deferred* Added in the Fair Copy, this reference to Proverbs 13:12 ('Hope deferred maketh the heart sick') distances Leonard from B's untutored emotion, while implying his heartsick, forbidden desire for her.

1,138 *gone into another land with as many of his folk as be not needed for the warding of his hold* The MS claims that the sorcerer is 'away as now serving in our Lord's host!' The rich implications for Crusade historians are rather too distracting for B's story. The text emphasizes Leonard's half-instinctive tempting of her, inviting an alliance with her against the 'old and straitlaced' castellan.

1,138 *peril* B here derives a major French word from Leonard. The Castle's conventions are given linguistic weight by words like 'countenance', 'remember', 'departure', but most derive from the priest and his implied religious norms. This speech is B's serious attempt to induce the ladylike weaknesses of fear and obedience in herself, to make herself worthy of Arthur's and the Castle's protection.

2,139 *lessons... question... embroidery... master* Words define and confine B. After all, she's only a woman! The skill-words are used without contempt, because skills such as reading, writing and embroidery must be respected, but they all contribute to B's neurotic prison, forcing her responsiveness and crafts-manship for the first time to combat the misery of idleness and frustration. B's skills, built upon hard work, are only slickly described by southern indoor phrases like 'marvellous fine' and 'apt scholar'.

2,140 *Sir Aymeris* 'Sir Aymer' in the MS and Fair Copy, is 'Aymery' here and at 3,142.

2,140 *she must have wept, sleeping* Her body insists on being restive, however cool she strives to be in her waking life.

2,140 *Catherine* Morris rarely gives minor characters names. Here B is reaching out towards normality and human contact, only to find them insufficient as counterbalances to love.

2,141 *neither boat nor burning mountain* This sounds proverbial for 'nothing either commonplace or remarkable', but I know of no other occurrence. The irony is that B would be far more excited by the commonplace boat.

3,143 *but the Red Knight is not the only foe, though he be the worst* Added, like much in this chapter, in Fair Copy. To mention him by denying that he is a danger is to foreshadow him.

3,143 *pearl of great price* From Matthew 13:45–46, where it stands for the soul's right of entry into the kingdom of heaven. B is the soul of the castle; in nineteenth-century 'medieval' stories like *Christabel* and *The Eve of St Agnes* the maiden's abduction, seduction, flight or expulsion bereaves the Castle of its soul.

3,144 *Nay, nay, thou shalt not kneel to me* This heavily revised conversation shows the castellan and B hard at work establishing this new courtly-love lady's constraints.

4,145 *vain longing* Fascinated by love and the absence of her beloved, B blames herself for her instinctive struggle against her prison. In the MS she once goes so far as to try to think like a Christian about a reward in heaven: 'And oft she wondered if this misery would buy her any delight in the world to come'.

5,147 *and yet she blamed herself* Another attempt to think like the lady the Castle (and, she assumes, Arthur) requires.

5,148 *Oh! but thou art beautiful, O earth, thou art beautiful!* Like Ellen's famous exclamation to the stones of Kelmscott in *News from Nowhere*, a thanksgiving for the natural world. But Ellen has merely been confined in a boat; B has been imprisoned in the male-centred life of a Castle lady and the obsessive love-longing of a courtly-love heroine.

5,149 *The Black Valley of the Greywethers* The desolate beauty of Iceland has a role in most of Morris's romances, where the hero's quest and his love-relationship (if they can be distinguished from each other) come to a climax. The chilling grandeur and immensity of this *locus amoenus* also has a distant, violent and mysterious history, of appropriately titanic proportions, so both time and space instruct tiny humans to scorn the self-importance and triviality to which we are addicted. The contrast with the shiny new Castle and its pretence that Christian and upper-class male standards are the measure of all things could hardly be more emphatic, as B's immediate response makes clear.

6,151 *and if that be not enough* The priest is obviously divided against himself, because of his unpriestly passion for B, and his lovesickness tempts him to tempt her by preaching this most ungodly mystery. In the MS, implausibly, he makes the temptations much more even-handed as to gender, 'or if it be a quean such goodly swains will be brought to her, so sweet of tongue and so lovesome, that it will be hard for her to naysay them.'

6,151 *is lost for ever* Mere greed is distinguished from soul-yearning by the Stony People's temptations, but the major test is of courage, a firmness of spirit without which all pining, noble or base, is futile. B is a hero, Leonard is not.

7,152 *unless it be that the trier of the adventure is some one fated above all others thereto; as forsooth thou mayst be* Added in the Fair Copy, and a valuable reminder, at this low point in B's story, of the principle of the hero as a lucky protagonist.

8,155 *she deemed she had a thing to crave* In the MS, evasively, 'though what it was she hoped for she knew not in good sooth'.

9,159 *that he may come back now at once and loving me* This eager and immediate demand is a superbly specific contrast with the passive and patient MS prayer, 'that one day I may be happy with him & he with me'. Having three parts, all of which are granted unconditionally, it resembles the folktale tradition of the three wishes. Introducing the Black Knight with eerie appositeness, it also tempts B to think he is offered in place of the fulfilment.

10,159 *and at first it was in her mind that this was the very chieftain come alive for her* The phrase 'for her' is usefully ambiguous. The MS is feeble: 'and she was sore afraid at first.'

10,160 *whereas now thou art within reach of my hand* The mingled relish and menace of these words, from the first male B has had good reason to mistrust, is added in Fair Copy revisions.

10,160 *hairless save for a little lip-beard* In the MS he is heavily bearded, and correspondingly less sophisticated and memorable.

10,160–1 *wherefore may we call him the Black Knight* Not in the MS, this phrase indicates the richness of Morris's revision process. This dashing fellow, the false answer to B's prayer, is now constructed as Arthur's alter ego or shadow. B has been reduced to courtly-love proportions by her long misery in the Castle of the Quest, so the temptations of a Guenevere-like sexual triangle are now appropriate to her. Sir Thomas exemplifies fantasy 'slating', where characters are not only complete in their actant roles but also component parts of a whole story's 'psychology'. The problems of keeping faith with his earlier vow (to his liege lord) or rejecting it as immoral and unnatural because love compels him to make a later, superior vow, are ruthlessly exemplified in Sir Thomas. The 'Black Squire', with no more wit or courage than he, survives his analogous situation because his pledges of knighthood have led him to consort with more moral and merciful people. The sacred and ancient place (see IV,5,149 above) is usually the scene of a turning-point in the love-relationship of the hero. Here, Arthur is absent – on a quest his life and emotions have outgrown – and so the magical place throws up, as it were from its own violent history, a dangerous (or at best ambiguous) shadow or stand-in. Arthur shows himself fully aware of the potential of this doubling in Part V, chapter 4.

10,162 *up the dale, or down it and out of it; it is all one unto me, so long as I am with thee* The MS merely has 'it is nought unto me'. Fair Copy revisions of the Black Knight's speeches construct this cool shrewd persistence, and the wit that forces B to recognize it.

11,162 *fighting for* The causes for which men fight, and those for which they must die rather than yield, are an abiding concern of Morris. It was Britain's threatening of war in the Balkans that began his career of public political activity, and his last sizeable poem, *The Pilgrims of Hope* (1885–86) is a celebration of the heroism of the Paris Communards.

11,163 *and though he said not so right out, yet let her wot that, youth as he was, he was of the battle* This Fair Copy addition keeps the battle distanced or tapestried by foregrounding B, the intradiegetic audience, and the question of whether the subtle teller is being modest or devious.

11,164 *ordered rings* Morris was fascinated by stone circles such as Avebury, and by the more recent Teutonic tradition of Things, Witans or Moots: assemblies meeting in doom-rings. To combine them gives a grave and sombre effect.

12,165 *thou wouldst have thy pleasure of me* B's frankness about her awareness that the Black Knight is capable of raping her, challenges him to similar frankness and does much to obviate the possibility.

12,166 *'Let that pass,' she said, and blushed not* The duel between her natural and straightforward approach and the Black Knight's male amalgam of flirtatious flattery and knowing menace is the last episode that Morris completed. It energetically re-expresses the ironic constraints of courtly love conventions upon B's integrity. Now that her love for Arthur no longer disguises these constraints, she resists them with the same swift seriousness she had displayed in exploring the Isles.

14,173 *'tis blessed bread to him* This witty description of his kinsman carries the hint of black-mass depravity.

14,173 *the Red Hold* Its menace and legendary cruelty, like that of Utterbol under Gandolf's regime and the Castle of the Scaur under the rule of 'the she-bear of the crag' (both in *The Well at the World's End*), is the more eloquent for never being described in detail.

14,174 *so help me God and All-Hallows!* The Black Knight has been brought up in the Christian faith, which has not hindered him from working for and fearing the Red Knight, who would be 'Death and the Devil' to B. Fortunately, he later swears by her hands, a more pagan and amorous oath he is unlikely to break.

14,174 *not though I give my life therefor* Though he knows the Red Knight's ruthless temperament, his declaration is not much closer to the truly fey than Baudoin's vow (III,9,132). The fey mood that descends upon him when they leave the Bower in the Dale is different, and the result of the Red Knight's psychic invasion.

14,174 *And what shall befall me if I come to the Red Hold? What is the Red Knight, and what would he do with me?* The last words of the Fair Copy, revised from the less immediate MS: 'And what should have befallen me at the Red Hold? What is the Red Knight, & what would he have done with me.'

15,178 *Nay, if I take thine hand, I shall take thy whole body* The menace of the Black Knight's sexual awareness, evident in her suspicion that he was not very far off when she was bathing, remains, and even intensifies as he struggles with himself.

16,180 *such dolts they are, that they will ever be worshipping the mere shadows of them, and turn away from flesh and blood* This scorn of the Champions is partly inspired by jealousy, but there is some truth in the implication that these virtuous lovers have been ineffectual in serving both virtue and B, supremely real as she is in flesh and spirit.

16,181 *be a man and not a wild beast* This tantrum of despair foreshadows Arthur's madness. It also embodies the thematic ironies of the shifting relationship between beast-nature, 'natural' human responses and 'civilized' complexities of conduct (including virtue, vice, and ambiguous states where consciousness is divided against itself). B is demanding that he choose between passion, reverence and simple good behaviour, hoping he will choose the third.

16,184 *HERE ENDS THE FOURTH PART...* There are no tailpieces to the Parts from now on in the MS, but they are easy to supply.

PART V

1,185 *THE TALE OF THE QUEST'S ENDING* More than one quest is in fact ended; the three ladies are rescued from the red-clad Queen and B from the red-clad Knight. However, there can be no true analogy between the unwilling passivity of active male heroes and B's search for an active role for herself.

1,185 *Sir Leonard* Still 'Lawrence' in the MS. His name is apt, meaning 'hardy (or brave) lion' in Germanic tongues. As a sixth-century Christian convert, his patron saint devoted his life to helping and sometimes freeing prisoners, as this Sir Leonard helps B in her benevolent male-world prison, though he is also, as a celibate priest, an agent of it.

1,185 *Sir Aymeris* In this chapter the naive rigidity of the castellan is seen at its most futile. The name may be a Norman-French variant on either Almeric or Almeris, a Germanic name meaning 'work rule', or Aylmer or Elmer, equally Germanic, from Aethelmaer, 'noble-famous', or Hjalmar, 'helmed warrior'. As one who thinks with his helmet, or his rule-book, most of these etymologies are appropriate.

1,187 *the first coming thither of B* The contrast between the two landfalls at the same steps is both significant in itself and agonizing for Leonard. The single girl turned away was the fulfilment of the Castle's only real purpose, and the thronged boat that seems like that fulfilment is in reality defined by that same, now absent, female figure.

2,189 *our dear ladies* However beautiful and beloved, wise or courageous, ladies must be bundled out of the way when action calls. The 'sweetlings' go obediently, pausing only for the ironic ritual that reinforces their passivity, commanding their champions to go and do what they are in any case resolved to do.

3,190 *but four hours after* May Morris seems to believe there is some error in the chronology at this point, but since we are to imagine B's prayer granted with absolute precision Arthur cannot be far from her when she makes it.

3,190 *they had never erst come into the dale but a very little way* On the next page this is contradicted by the sergeant claiming to be 'more at home in the Black Valley than ye be; heed ye not wherefore'. Morris would have corrected such minor inconsistencies had his Fair Copy extended so far, but the hint that the sergeant too has his story, mostly outside the frame of B's story, is typical of the circumstantial and egalitarian charm of the late romances.

3,191 *the dale was full of thick white mist* Mist, fine weather and storm may be natural, but are more probably summoned by the ill-will of the Stony People (now 'evil wights') or by the Red Knight's weather-magic. If the latter, the results are much against his interest: oft evil will shall evil mar.

3,192 *another night in the Black Valley* The third night in a place of power is likely to be the climactic one.

4,194 *three hours after noon* A careless repetition of a phrase from the previous chapter.

4,195 *round about her neck was hung a man's head newly hewn off* This 'shaming' accuses the woman of sexual guilt with the beheaded male.

4,196 *Sir Thomas of Estcliffe* He has not previously been named. In Morris romances, characters are frequently only referred to by the title of their role, as with the Squire, Sergeant and Red Knight in this scene. However, the individuation of the Black Knight at this point has two effects. He can now be distinguished from the Black Squire, since Arthur is present, and his personal name works on Arthur's imagination, giving more personal and intimate dimensions to his jealousy.

4,196 *my dead friends* The plural is correct: B is concerned to defend Sir Thomas against association with the Red Knight.

4,196 *the hand of Fate it is that led thee* The vows and deaths of both Sir Baudoin and Sir Thomas justify this assertion, which has nothing in common with the Christian trappings of Baudoin's vow and everything else about the surface life of the Castle. The romance's patterns of ritual magic, incorporating similarity, contiguity, association, perception, binding and foreknowledge, also all seem to imply that Christianity is irrelevant.

5,198 *If that be gain* Arthur cannot help challenging Sir Aymeris' sentimental attitude to B. The cold, judgemental tone, and reference to B in the third person, imply an imperfectly repressed anger and jealousy. His quasi-cynical 'I scarce know in what quarrel' doubts whether B was worth fighting for.

6,200 *thy friend who is lost, and who shall be thy friend no more* Viridis assumes B means the dead Baudoin, but B explains she means herself. The term 'lost', applied to a woman, implies moral guilt such as she knows Arthur imputes to her.

6,200 *So is it fated* Atra recognizes the irony in all their situations, and her own misery and potential for savage response.

6,201 *when a man loveth a woman* Viridis may be sweetly pretty, but she can be forthright. As the most affectionate of the group, she is the first to bear witness to the facts of love.

6,201 *I am not a proper minstrel* The MS does not include 'not', and the self-mockery of 'a proper minstrel' does not require one.

7,202 *B TELLETH THE TALE OF HER WANDERING* An affirmative romance counterpart to Morris's great 'Defence of Guenevere'.

7 202 *there was none lacking save Baudoin* The supposed 'Happy Ending' of the male quest is made bitterly irrelevant when the tableau is of two men and four women.

7,202 *a black coat* Mourning for Baudoin, but also, consciously or not, alignment with Arthur's colour (see III,10,134). Atra and Arthur of course are wearing black too, if the others are not.

7,203 *which should make me whole again* B neither accuses the Castle's male-defined culture, nor admits that she was lovesick for Arthur, but there is sufficient accuracy in her diagnosis.

7,203 *Weird* Not capitalized in the MS, B's term encompasses both Fate and neutral chance or hap, such as when 'She would liefer have gone back to the castle by the shortest way' (IV,5,147), but instead sees the mountains for the first time, and hears about the Valley.

7,203 *Arthur spake not* Leonard's betrayal seems to prove either his intentional falseness to his vows or B's powers of seduction. How horrible if she were merely a *femme fatale*, the enemy of all manly virtue, enthralling Arthur along with all other males!

7,205 *a red surcoat* The connotations of blood, murder, pride, passion and self-indulgence, and their skill at bringing a blush to the cheek of the young person, align the Red Knight with the Queen of the Isles, whom her friends have confronted. However, he is far more intelligent, and does not depend on external aid. As a parody of knightly vows and qualities he is also connected with the Red Knight (the mentally unhinged Pelleas) of Tennyson's 'The Last Tournament', the nadir of ill-faith and violence in *Idylls of the King*. This 'idyll' culminates in the treacherous murder of Tristram, a dark, cynical, pessimistic, amorous knight, by his viciously treacherous kinsman King Mark, in the presence of Isolt, the woman they both desire. The similarity is obvious. Again, Tennyson's Red Knight has founded an obscene parody of the Round Table, whose members are whores and whoremasters, torturers and murderers, as with the Red Hold. His howling, neurotic contempt for King Arthur is a hysterical analogue to the Red Knight's accusations against the amorous purity of the Champions of the Castle of the Quest. Incidentally, his heraldically incorrect blazon of 'a shower of blood upon a field noir' is rather similar to that of Morris's Arthur, a shower of tears, argent, on a field sable. The misery and frustration with which Arthur leads the assaults on the Red Hold may also relate to the impassioned atrocity in which King Arthur's young Round Table knights slaughter that Red Knight's followers.

7,205   *wood-wife* Woman of the woods, because of the bow, but the Red Knight's limited clairvoyance may also have detected the influence of H upon B.

7,206   *by Red Peter* St Peter is known as an impulsive saint, but he is not traditionally red-haired or particularly concerned with women's legs. Such a blasphemous incongruity would have amused the Red

Knight, as would the phallic slang meaning of 'peter'. However, his self-indulgent, rattling speech contains no other overt obscenity, so the probability is that he turns even saints into his own hot, blood-stained but unblushing image.

7,207 *True Thomas* The Red Knight's use of the title of Thomas the Rhymer is typical of the man's careless brilliance. First, it accuses Sir Thomas of treachery, and there is weight and menace in the mockery; second, it implies that just as the poet spent seven years in Faerie serving the Queen of Elfland for the reward of 'the tongue that can never lie', so Sir Thomas, serving B three nights in the wild, has gained the same inconvenient gift!

7,210 *all the sweetness of life seemed departed* This dreadful state is the end-product of B's experience of a world of male prowess, and the Red Knight before whom she stands helpless is the genially vicious embodiment of Might is Right, the Fort Main.

7,211 *the hand of Weird* Arthur emphatically accepts the terms B herself had used for the forces of both fate and chance.

7,212 *the Millers* To 'mill' is, in Victorian slang, to fight fiercely. However, the Red Knight's sardonic humour would have delighted to coin the term from the famous quasi-Biblical lines of the moralistic Longfellow (translated from von Logau),

The mills of God grind slowly
But they grind exceeding small.

The Red Hold's Millers would torture body and spirit in such excruciating detail that both would be ground exceeding small.

7,212   *Furies...Graces* Similar triplings of old and young women are powerful in the Fellowship of the Dry Tree at the Castle of the Scaur in *The Well at the World's End*. Sir Thomas had pointed out that women are likely to be far more cruel to a girl prisoner than men would be. Their nicknames mock classical tradition, as the Millers may mock Christian tradition.

7,212   *hounds that love man's flesh* Traditionally, a dog that has tasted human flesh or blood can never be trusted. A specific reference may be to the seven bloodhounds of Shelley's post-Peterloo satire *The Masque of Anarchy*. In the MS, 'man's-flesh'.

7,212   *the men of ancient days* Myth, Scripture, history and legend all interpenetrate in the imagination of those who dare great deeds and comparison with the heroes of the mighty past. Beowulf, for example, fights a Son of Cain in Grendel.

7,213   *my man shall rejoice in Paradise* Not many of Morris's characters believe in a personal afterlife in heaven, but the rhetoric of Christianity is essential to the Castle and its ladies. Aurea's faith is intensely literal.

7,213   *the deed shall be better yet* Atra takes on the role of Valkyrie, not only in response to vision but as antidote to the darkened future and the misery, jealousy and despair she expects will be her lot. In the next chapter she tells B of her conscious wish that Arthur should die in battle, that they might mourn him together rather than resent each other as rivals.

7,213   *prevent thee* Hugh's most Latinate usage for 'forestall', 'anticipate' or 'say it first' is appropriate for the Castle at its most masculine and intrepid.

8,215 *Minorites* Morris naturally preferred the humbler Friars Minor, Franciscans, to the Dominicans: they 'knew not the road to Rome, now how to find the door of the Chancellor's house' (*The Well at the World's End*).

8,215 *I speak the word, and the hope springeth; the word is spoken, and there abideth desire barren of hope!* The moment that divides speaking from spoken is a common theme in Victorian poetry, most brilliantly in Browning's 'Two in the Campagna', and survives into the twentieth century in the colder tones of T.S. Eliot: 'Between the emotion/and the response/ Falls the Shadow.' Here the effect is complex: the bitter falling away contrasts harshly with the sentimental sexlessness of the mural, reminding Atra that, whatever happens, there is no cure for the one love of one's life. She can only hope to be able to hope for a heaven where desire is transmuted into loving-kindness.

8,215 *I will crave somewhat of thee* The promise she exacts echoes her early prayer to B (II,3,79) and is an attempt to transform desire into 'loving-kindness'.

9,217 *Hugh spake and said* As the only happy lovers in the group, he and Viridis take on themselves much of the fellowship's emotional load, in itself a maturing process.

9,218 *Sir Arthur here stayed us* Arthur's cool judgement in the first tests is not only based on wisdom: his mind is no longer obsessed with Atra as the object of his quest. He can advise, 'let not the anguish of love steal all your wits', but the third test proves that he had been eloquent on a point in which his own conduct would ill bear examination, because

B is in question. This episode, in the darkest part of the night before the summer dawn, foreshadows Arthur's later madness.

9,222 *who is the Black Squire's* In the MS the 's' is omitted. A better emendation would be 'the Black Squire's friend'.

9,224 *though the woman was hateful and thick-hearted and cruel, yet she was become fairer* The Queen is the true *femme fatale,* determined to tyrannize over the imagination of one (or all) of the knights. Since she sets out to entrance Arthur, it is not surprising that his suspicions of B are so fierce when he returns to the Castle. He also has a very uneasy conscience because he was beguiled into the Queen's bed.

9,225 *to see aught ugly in our servants now unseen* The satiric aspect of the romance reminds us that the ugly drudgery of the servant and working classes of Victorian England was usually hidden from the well-bred, charming and cultured nobility and gentry of that society.

9,229 *before the others* Since Hugh is the narrator, 'us' or 'us others' would make more sense. The error is in the MS.

9,229 *I am shamed for ever* Arthur's sexual sacrifice evokes many stories in which the hero's one true love prefers death to sexual dishonour in the villain's arms. Since the hero of this story, and this particular villain, are female, this male sex-object's vulnerability and shame are sharply interrogated. Should a male choose death rather than sexual dishonour? B, captured by the Red Knight, expects to be forced to make this decision, but she resolves healthily to hope on while she may, just as Ursula, enslaved by the Lord of Utterbol in *The Well at the World's End*, resolves to endure all rather than despair. As with Walter being charmed and compelled into bed with the powerful Lady of *The Wood Beyond the World*, and forbidden to touch the Maid to whom he is pledged, males must experience sexual passivity to achieve psychic wholeness. However, the hermaphroditic aspect of Arthur's character is not well suited by this experience; he transforms his shame into jealous suspicion of B. Presumably he would have conducted himself with more impulse and less guilt and shame if his affections had still been fixed upon his first love, Atra.

9,231   *clad as a hunter* The virgin huntress and Amazon stereotypes are both evoked by this elaborate 'painted show' of the Queen.

9,232–3   *I unclad myself* The motif of vulnerable nakedness, usually associated with B, is here a form of virtuous deception.

9,233   *the ancient blade betwixt my side and her place* Traditional assertion that the knight will refrain, because of honour, a vow or a curse, from sex with the bed's other occupant. Hugh's touching faith in the tradition is justified, because the enemy is stupid enough. The comedy of the narrative here adapts, subtly and precisely, archetypal images of phallic aggression (the sword) and female passive reception (the ambry and the crystal flask) into what seem like their opposites.

9,233   *both for thyself and thy loveling* The witch foolishly admits that she has Viridis (and presumably the others) under her hand, which she has previously denied.

9,233   *a tide of war* In wartime theft from the enemy is morally as well as tactically justified. Hugh's lack of guile and open sexual rejection completes the otherwise fruitless subtleties of Arthur, and sends the witch off in a malevolent tantrum.

9,233   *white like to water* That is, clear, not an opaque white. The story's whole palette is medieval, as Morris's wordhoard necessitates; see the 'grey' edges of the sword above.

9,236   *Water of Might* This eau-de-vie seems more powerful, because more concentrated, than in *The Well at the World's End*, but its effects are temporary. Its benefits include physical health, healing and beauty, heightened perception, confidence and self-esteem, but it does not change or strengthen character or self-mastery, or affect the politics of desire. Though the Queen's indulgence in it is evil, it is not evil in itself. It is because she uses it to make herself feel sexually irresistible that Hugh can find it, and her foolish over-use makes it a drug upon which the body becomes dependent: the withdrawal effects are dreadful. Since her paradise is keyed to her own well-being, it also collapses when her beauty is deconstructed.

10,242   *red water* Presumably the same lead-protected liquid that the witch had forced on B (I,11,29); B did not note its colour.

10,242   *I deemed it was poison, and was glad* This statement comes strangely from a Morris character of any worth, even if helpless and obscenely tortured. But after a paragraph Viridis does recover her courage: 'there came upon me the desire of life.'

10,244   *I whom he desired was not the poor wretched creature chained there in her nakedness* But the three who survive this ordeal are not quite the same afterwards, neither pretty spoiled maiden, nor humiliated serf, nor tortured prisoner, but admirable survivors of all three experiences.

10,244 *whereof thou didst tell us* B in fact told the Champions, not the ladies.

11,249 *belike for a little while both those twain were happy* The honesty of their conversation is healthy, but it cannot remove their awareness of the emotional tangle they share with Atra, or the likelihood of their being parted, perhaps by death in battle.

13,252 *Wall-wolf* Like many kennings (and riddles), an example of Aristotle's metaphor of analogy 'as that to flocks so this to walls', in this case. 'Stone-fretter', later, may be thought of as either distressing, scarring or playing musical chords upon the walls.

13,252 *the Poison-jar* Surely the tower where the Apothecary conducted the evil experiments of his art.

13,253 *and that with all the good-will of my heart* B combines her natural honesty and her Castle-taught shamefastness to express her apprehension about what will be her first completed sexual encounter. The added pressure of her unredeemed promise to Atra is hardly needed, and neither embroidery nor calligraphy can quite relieve all her tensions. Arthur may express any uncertainty or nerves by dealing and receiving blows and wounds, besieging some satisfyingly villainous villains in a satisfyingly strong castle – and no one supposes he is a virgin....

13,254 *and now if I do amiss again, even if it be at his bidding* Morris scorns the double standard of sexual conduct. B's bitter irony shows its power over female self-respect.

13,255   *the Good Lord* B rarely attempts to sound
Christian, but the Castle people would never have
understood about H as a power to lead her *away*
from love.

14,256   *Weird* As a power operating on both B and
Atra, Weird begins to sound like a love-god.
However, B knows that her own choice has led her to
escape the Castle before Arthur's return.

PART VI

1,258   *THE DAYS OF ABSENCE* B's refuge in
mercantile life does not prevent her drawing hearts to
her, but her purposeful and skilled pursuit of a trade
offers more imaginative consolation than the aesthet-
ically graceful pastimes for Castle ladies.

1,259   *as for their condition* They are common
mounted soldiers; a knight would need lance, shield,
long-sword, body-armour, visored helmet and
protective padding.

1,260   *Gerard of the Clee* Both his personal name,
'spear-hard', and his name of origin, 'from the cliff'
connote tough dependability.   Later, his sons are
referred to by the other major surnaming convention,
the patronymic 'Gerardson'.   Gerard's knightly form
would have been Gareth.

1,261   *the City of the Five Crafts* Cancelled phrases
from the MS describe Five Crafts as a seaport.   The
city's name, its possession of a Frank, and the
alternative destination, 'the City of the Bridges and
the Liberties thereof', indicate immense social distance
from the war B has just left, where the Castle of the

Quest opposes the Red Hold. There seems no Baronial authority around Five Crafts at all, and it is probable that it will have disappeared very soon from about Greenford, with the Hold reduced and the Castle abandoned.

1,262–3 *Utterhay...Evilshaw* Gerard's origin tempts the audience to expect a return by land, but instead it foretells a meeting.

2,363 *the wildness of the shepherd-music* The contrast between her Castle-taught courtly-love songs and this peasant music evokes both tears and thought 'of the wild world withal, and all the ways of its many folk'. Both emotion and wonder are beginnings of her healing, not from the wounds of love but from the privilege of the Castle life.

3,264 *cried out with joy* Though cities may be filthy and corrupt, there is beauty in urban community, as B intuitively recognizes.

3,265 *the great lords and ladies of the land, and the rich burgesses, and especially by the high prelates* The three estates that reap the benefits of human work, art and craft. This is not a just society, though by no means unendurable. Morris & Co. had a similar clientèle, especially early in its trading life.

3,265 *by St. Lucia!* 'How blind I am!', since Lucy is patron saint of the blind.

3,266 *[gain]* This word is added in pencil to the MS probably by May Morris's hand: the square brackets in the *Collected Works* edition indicate it as an emendation.

3,267 *Jacobus* Not necessarily Jewish, since it was the common Latin form of James, the name nonetheless has associations with business skills and success, coupled with capacity for love and willing service, from the Old Testament story of Jacob. The beautiful thirteenth-century book, *The Golden Legend*, by Jacobus de Voragine, was a major early publication of Kelmscott Press.

3,267 *hearing the name from thy mouth* Leading gently to the recognition scene by use of B's well-developed intuitive faculty.

3,269 *that ye have heard at the beginning of the book* Dramatic irony is invited by this honest reminder: the audience foresees what the characters do not yet see.

3,270 *by St Ursula* It is not clear why this saint is sworn by; she is not generally associated with embroidery.

3,271 *My child* The simple poignancy of this reunion is prevented from sentimentality by the dramatic irony principle (see 3,269), and also by B's mind turning back to the fellowship, wishing one at least of them could share her joy.

4,272 *Audrey* A fine name for a wronged woman of skill with cloths and silks. St Audrey, properly Aethelthryth or Etheldreda, was a Suffolk princess who became abbess of Ely and has a charming ribbon-ceremony associated with her feast-day. Because the poor hung their ribbons up too, 'St Awdry's lace' produced the degraded word 'tawdry'.

4,272 *Of these, forsooth, were but two that anywise troubled her* Three, in fact, since both Robert and Giles Gerardson love her, as well as Jacobus. This error is not merely a slip based on, say, the omission of a more abstract word after 'these', since the next paragraph refers clearly to Master Jacobus as 'The second wooer that troubled her'. Morris would certainly have corrected this, since the Gerardsons are very distinct in verbal and general presentation when they declare their love (6,281–2).

5,276 *the witch-wife was speaking* B's fascinating dream gives her enemy the arguments she is most intensely attracted to.

5,276 *the pillow wet with her tears* The verb 'was' is pencilled into the MS after 'pillow', but not adopted in any text.

5,277 *that it might be loved as it deserved* Her response to her own naked body completes the process of prompting her to leave the city.

5,278 *not unseldom do women use the custom of going arrayed like men* This seems implausible; men of the Castle would say the idea was appalling, if not impossible. It is, however, a motif of romance and romantic comedies, and an excellent test of female courage in a role for which they were allowed no training.

5,279 *good* portable property, the origin of the modern 'goods'.

6,281 *the day before yesterday* An obvious error, since they have travelled five days since that conversation. Other MS errors are corrected in pencil about this point.

7,285 *waste is that house now* The Castle of the Quest was only built for the Quest, which determined both its isolated position and its strained and courtly atmosphere.

7,286   *something uncouth* Not merely ill-mannered, but beyond rational understanding, frighteningly unnatural. Apart from an easily explicable dream, all B's experiences since the death of the Red Knight have been non-magical.

8,288   *I did as biddeth Holy Church in all wise* The apparitions are unimpressed by Leonard's Christian exorcism. Though no one in the romance speaks out against it, and the narrator refers to 'Holy Church' with reverence (10, 296), Christianity seems in general impotent against either witch, sorcerer or wood-magic.

8,288   *There be two of these things* Since the all-male chivalric company that had the Castle built is now dispersed and the conventions to which it had related are quite deconstructed by B's superior ethic and spiritual energy, it is fitting that its ruins should be haunted by malevolent and beneficent female power-shapes.

8,289   *a fetch of my witch-mistress* How intentional the sendings are cannot be known. The witch can perhaps locate the Sending Boat, but not control it. She may seek to challenge B, or terrify others, with her own image, or with the wailing image of B, but surely not with the singing image, which may be due to the abiding influence of H. Leonard cannot know of H, who always appears in B's image. B herself never finds out the reason or reasons for the haunting; one plausible possibility is that the Sending Boat is itself trying to call its two most recent customers, tapping memories from their blood.

8,290   *I have never told any* This is not strictly true, but Sir Thomas is dead.

8,290 *to let me…and let me go* The two 'let' verbs, in opposite senses, in a single sentence, are a stylistic blemish Morris would not have missed. In the next sentence the verb 'let blood' also appears.

9,293 *we know what things they be which thou bearest* Edenic innocence, not of facts but of their experiential application, is worthy of respect but also of avoidance. If B were to demonstrate what weapons are, the 'innocent' race must either forbid them, and her, or take them up and use them. When the inhabitants of Nothing 'become great' (10,296) they will no longer be 'Innocent Folk', as in *The Well at the World's End*. This isle implies mild humour about Morris's Utopia 'Nowhere'.

10,296 *their very own Lady and Goddess* This is not naive euhemerism: B has once summoned up a goddess's pure aspect there, and that aspect is exactly her own. The Isle's inhabitants praise and are defined by natural abundance, and B's human beauty ratifies their faith, so she becomes their patron saint.

11,297 *the God of Love turned warrior* Sunlight reflecting from armour gives the hero a solar 'glory', warm and life-enhancing, whether virile or feminine. As a hermaphroditic vision, B seems like the young Apollo to the adoring females on the Isle of Kings, and Venus rising from the waves to the dazzled males of the Isle of Queens. Goldmane and Sunbeam, the lovers who marry at the end of *The Roots of the Mountains*, have solar attributes, as has Goldilind the Fair, the princess Child Christopher weds, and Golden Walter, hero of *The Wood Beyond the World*.

11,298 *Now do all we give ourselves to thee as thy slaves to do as thou wilt with* The women, convinced that the only role of a woman is submission, deny wholeness and self-acceptance. They hope to be a hero's houris in a male-centred courtly-love cult, and their disappointed jeering at B is a neurotic female self-imprisonment such as Morris saw in many women of his own day.

12,301   *I need fear naught on this Isle of Queens save women like myself* Considering the reversal of previous conditions on the last two Isles, B's logic is untypically poor.

12,302   *God of Love* B is bold to joke on this matter. See 11,298.

12,302   *Louis Delahaye* B's epicene appearance prompts her to choose a foppish French by-name. Its meaning, 'from the hedge', hints at bastardry, but also at Utterhay, her birthplace.

12,304   *Goddess of Love* Antony's theological fantasy is more convincing than B's. A single woman among these marooned males might well have started a courtly-love cult such as had previously ruled the castles of the two isles, or even played the men off against each other to accrete power like the dead Queen of the Isles.

12,305   *Antony* Named more probably for St Antony of Padua, saint of those who look for lost property, than for the ascetic hermit St Antony the Great!

12,305   *Otter* A fine Norse name, associated with conflict over treasure, as in the *Volsungasaga*. The two Otters in Morris romances are both warriors; in *The House of the Wolfings* Otter epitomizes honour and dies because of the passions of others, but in *The Well at the World's End* he works for a bad lord, then finds a better.

13,309 *how gattest thou this victual* The innocence
of children is also ignorance, but the children are far
from starving. It is clear they do not yet eat fish,
goats or rabbits, but what kind of society they
develop is unpredictable. Like the grown people on
the earlier Isles, they do not know how they came to
the island, but they have resilience and possibility;
their response to B is promising. They lack education,
judgement, concentration and patience, but ask
bravely 'teach us what it is to be old'.

14,311 *no longer was the isle goodly* There is
eventually no such thing as a free lunch. The cosmetic
beauty of the house and Isle is lost, for the real
harvest of cruelty and unashamed greed is a nature
sickened to death.

14,311 *she saw not her boat* The bargain between the
wight of the Sending Boat and its passengers seems to
be at an end, either because of the boat's contact with
the poisoned Isle or, more probably, because the
witch, the original blood-signatory, has just died.

14,312 *she was as naked as when she first came
aland there* This visual completion of the circular
pattern of journey displays the surface of the
convention, but in fact she has not finished her story.
She is simply forced to return home with no promise
of even the simplest reward.

14,312 *the tress* There are worse places than
Nothing, but this Isle is probably beyond H's healing.
Still, H's hair is physically identical with B's, so prayer
to the external power is also a demand of courage
from herself.

15,313 *a terrible gulf over which she hung fainting*
This vertigo is the nadir of B's relationship with

nature. Awareness of the void, the depths, steals all thought of nature, beauty, faith, hope or love.

15,314 *by the hand of Weird* The tree is H's sending, but only useable if B refuses to let herself die. B can believe in a Weird that 'would not have her die' or in the wind she can feel. Later, she feels that the tree is drifting shoreward 'as if drawn there by some bidding of might', but this is only a simile. Her first swimming 'strongly and wisely' is a prerequisite of being helped.

16,318 *the corpse of her dead terror* B accepts and buries her childhood fear, thus accomplishing the self-acceptance that continuing to flee from the witch could never provide. Her shadow of fear has been greeted, and it is now impotent to mar her conscious life.

17,320 *Art thou dead then* The serpent is an embodiment of the boat's spirit, not dead but dismissed by B's words.

17,321 *the rents and rags* The feeling that she has come full circle is more circumstantial now, but the contrasts with her previous fine clothes are alive in her mind.

18,321 *even as the first time when B saw her* This is ambiguous: is she young and naked, as then, or is she simply approaching in the same way? The latter seems more probable.

18,322 *thou hast not told of me to any* Again B has forgotten that she told Sir Thomas 'somewhat of the Woodmother' (IV,16,183).

18,323 *how sweet it were to be grieved with thy pain* H remains fascinated by human emotions, especially by grief; feeling for B's emotions, she seems to be drawing closer to the human.

18,324 *whereas the witch was dead* The witch must have had real power, to forbid the Woodmother to float a tree in the lake....

19,325 *yellow* The solar associations are much more radiant than the 'black', Arthur's colour, cancelled in the MS.

20,327 *than any bear* An ominous comparison, since Arthur's name associates him with that animal, but apt for the 'evil beasts' H is talking of. The largest and most dangerous animal in ancient Western Europe, and as famous for adopting an aggressive two-legged stance as berserk warriors were for adopting the animal's fearless ferocity, the bear has a special place in folklore and imagination.

21,329 *hallow my house* H is invited to be a patron saint of the house, but thinks herself almost the opposite. Later she decides that B has hallowed the place with her wisdom and love.

21,329 *belike she buried some human being at one of its four corners* Ancient binding-magic to prohibit Other races from entering a human building, as in the children's song 'London Bridge is Falling Down'.

21,329 *sign the meat* Make the sign of the cross to bless it.

21,329 *dwindled in a wondrous way* This brilliant threshold effect is made the more striking by the Victorian convention that fairies were tiny 'little people' like Titania's servants – or Tinkerbell. *Puck of Pook's Hill* and *Rewards and Fairies*, Kipling's Edwardian exorcism of Tinkerbell, show the gulf between Adam's children, using 'cold iron', and folk of the hills, using 'oak, ash, and thorn' wood-magic.

21,329   *I note* Not H's kind of language; possibly mis-written for 'I wot'.

22,331   *fair is the gold ring* H pretends not to recall the story of the ring, and the narrator certainly doesn't. B says Arthur gave it to her on their last meeting, but this is not in the text: he is wearing it for Atra, 'as a token of my grief for her grief' and so he could not well give it to B.

23,332   *he may be a man in a beast's skin* This plays lightly on Arthur's name and more gravely on the question of his sanity.

23,335   *the dear heart beloved of thee* An error for 'of me': B is saying that his heart is beloved of her.

23,335   *the second time* He has seen H in her habitual B shape.

23,335   *I became a beast and a man-slayer* Male love-madness is associated with the historical character of Arnaut Daniel as well as the legendary heroes Lancelot and Tristan, and others whom desperation turns vicious, as with Morris's questers in *The Earthly Paradise*, III,49:

> So with the failing of our hoped delight
> We grew to be like devils....

23,337   *and blood gushed out from his mouth* Though Lancelot comes to mind, the power of this episode goes further than any literary resemblance. His debasing and madness begin to free Arthur from the vows of his youth, but he also alters to a non-knightly reality, aligning himself with B, when the blood-vessel bursts. The inter-acceptance of the lovers as male and female will involve the spilling of her blood, and his helplessness in the wildwood, and his madness, equate with B's passivity as a Castle lady, and her spiritual sickness.

23,337 *the blood-staunching herb* Female care heals the bloody sign of Arthur's spiritual menstruation, his entry into total (rather than gender-specific) humanity.

29,354 *[day]* This emendation is written on the MS in pencil by, I take it, May Morris.

29,355 *by God above* Arthur still swears like a Christian. B's matching oath 'by thy head and thy hands I will not' relates more intimately to their having become lovers.

31,360 *Earth's very children and mine* They are blessed in becoming, for a little while, noble savages, excelling in a secret woodland world of unfallen beauty and activity.

31,360 *The Red Company* The strong antipathy of green to red, of natural and human mutuality to unnatural bullying selfishness, produces a third red menace to set beside the Scarlet Queen and the Red Knight's Red Hold. But these are out of their element in the greenwood, and seem merely perverse, temporary and rejected.

32,364 *wheat-coloured* Aurea's gold is a little muted now, but still connotes autumn harvest.

32,364 *the armour of the Faery* Just as elven armour is, in Tolkien, lighter and better even than dwarven, so H's gift is more effective than sturdier material.

32,365 *Hah the witch, the accursed green witch!* He takes B for H, who is rightly to be feared, and whom evil men hate.

32,366 *the Green Knight* The phrase sits eloquently beside Hugh's helplessness in the greenwood, while Arthur and B wear H's green armour. His green is bright heraldic vert, the colour of summer meadows, not the shadowy shifting green of woodland.

33,373 *good-night and rest* There is no indication of the sleeping arrangements, an unusual reticence in the romances.

PART VII

1,375 *Thy people should be my people, and thy land my land, and that whither thou goest I will go* Appropriately for the joining together of alienated companions, Hugh is paraphrasing closely the vow of Ruth to Naomi, the Book of Ruth 1:16.

3,380 *Black Canons* Presumably Dominicans, though Leonard and Atra had both referred previously to the local abbey as belonging to the Friars Minor, the Franciscans, and being little rather than 'great and fair'.

3,381 *like the images of warriors* H's 'men' are of Faery, not sons of Adam, as were the ambushers who came so speedily to B's horn-call in VI,32,365.

3,382 *Porte* 'Door', but applied by French merchants to the Ottoman Empire's central office or vizierate, and hence to any urban administration charged with defending the city gates.

3,383 The crucial role of women in binding together alliance – and houses, tribes and whole peoples – is a major theme of medieval romances. Similarly, the Hall-Sun in *The House of the Wolfings* changes her name to Ransom in token that the defeat of the Romans has begun a new, stronger, tribal union. The heroine of *The Story of the Glittering Plain* is called Hostage, and is restored to Hallblithe on the Isle of Ransom, to testify to his alliance with the reiver islanders. At the end of *The Roots of the Mountains* both The Bride and Sun-Beam make intertribal marriages; later they strengthen the bond by fostering each other's children. Nevertheless, to have B simplified into such a symbolic role between two male groups is markedly anticlimactic.

4,386 *[answered]* Another square-bracketed May Morris emendation.

4,387 *they lived without shame, and died without fear* A strongly fatalistic romance which does not subscribe to a religious faith must evoke a clear, emphatic 'happy ending' without offering an 'ever after'.

GLOSSARY

Abbreviations:
/=from, D=Dutch, Eccl.=ecclesiastical, F=French,
G=German, Middle High German or Teutonic,
L=Latin, ME=Middle English, Mod.=post–1660
English, OE=Old English, OF=Old French, ON=Old
Norse, Sc.=Scots, Ren.=Renaissance (1400-1660
English)

Acre n. ploughland, tilled field, OE, I,3
Adown adv. downwards, OE, III,4
Adventure n. chance, risk; *or* hazard, perilous enter-
prise, OF/L, IV,3
Aland adv. to land (opposite to aboard), OE, II,3
Alboun adj. ready, ME, V,13
All Hallows n. the saints; *or* All Saints' Day, OE, VI,4
Aloof adv. afar off, distant, ME/D, IV,10
A many adj. a great many, several, OE, I,11
Ambry n. cupboard, wall-safe, Eccl.L, V,9
Angle n. fishhook *or* rod-and-line, OE, I,14
Anigh prep./adv. close, near, Mod. archaism 1773, II,5
A-night-tide adv. by night, ME, I,17
Anlace n. girdle-knife, two-edged dagger, ME, IV,10
Arras n. hanging tapestry with figures, ME/F town,
II,11
Array v. adorn, clothe, *or* prepare for action, OF, III,6
Array, Arrayal n. adornments, clothes *or* battle
formation, OF, III,6
Ashlar n. dressed stone, squarehewn stonework,

ME/OF, II,4
As now adv. for the moment, ME, I,3
At all adventure adv. at random *or* recklessly, OF/L, VI,1
At point to adv. about to, on the point of, ME, VI,13
Aumbrye = *ambry* see above.

Balefire n. open-air bonfire *or* funeral pyre, OE, IV,16
Ban v. summon by proclamation, ON, I,17
Bane n. agent of death, doom, OE, I,12
Barque n. ship, F, VII,2
Base-court n. castle's outer courtyard, OF, II,11
Basnet n. steel helmet with visor, OF, V,9
Bawdekin n. rich embroidered stuff, *usually* gold on silk, OF (*from* 'baghdad+kin'), II,9
Bed-gear n. female captives (kenning: women regarded as sexual objects), OE, VI,32
Bedizenments n. adornments, vulgar finery, Mod/D, V,9
Behight adj. promised, vowed, OE, I,1
Belike adv. possibly *or* probably, ME, I,1
Bent n. wiry grass *or* slope *or* moorland, OE, II,10
Beset v. beseige, surround, OE V,12
Bestead adj. in difficulties, usually 'hard bestead', ON, I,7
Bestial n. cattle, OF VI,1
Betake (oneself) v. go, consign (oneself), ME, IV,1
Betide v. befall, happen, ME, I,6
Be-timbered adj. wooded (possibly erroneous, from *Beowulf* 'built of wood'), OE? II,9
Bewray v. divulge, expose *or* accuse, betray, ME, I,5
Bicker n. beaker, ME, VI,29
Bight n. bay *or* curve, OE, I,1
Birdalone adj. solitary, M, I,4

Blent adj. blended, Ren., II,5

Boon n. gift *or* prayer, OE, VII,2

Boot n. advantage *or* bargain, OE, IV,15

Bower n. cottage inner room *or* boudoir *or* arbour, booth, *or* leanto, OE, III,2

Brake n. thicket, ME, II,9

Brunt n. heat of battle, onset, ME, V,13

Burg n. fortress *or* walled town, OE, IV,9

Burgess n. freeman of a town (*later* a magistrate), ME, IV,16

Burgreve n. town governor, OE, VI,1

Busk v. clothe or get things ready, prepare busily, ME/ON, VI,33

But adv. merely, only, OE, II,5

But if conj. unless, OE, I16

Buttery n. provision store *or* liquor store, OF, III,1

Byrnie n. corslet, mailcoat, OE, III,4

Caitif, caitiff n. villain, baseborn rogue, ME, IV,32

Carl, carle n. man, male, *usually* workingclass, OE/ON, II,5

Carline, n. woman, *usually* old woman, ON, II,6

Castellan n. governor ('constable') of a castle, L, III,1

Catch n. prey (not necessarily fish), OE, I,16

Cates n. delicate food, *usually* shop-bought, OF, II,2

Certes adv. certainly, OF, I,16

Chaffer n. bartering, trade, OE, I,1

Chapfallen adj. crestfallen (chap=chops, cf. 'his face fell', 'his jaw dropped'), Ren, IV,1

Chapman n. merchant, OF, I,1

Chattel n. commodity *or* possession, OF, I,5

Cheapeners n. dealers *or* bidders, OE, I,1

Cheaping n. market, OEI,1

Chief n. head *or* upper third of a shield, ME/OF, III,4

Churl n. peasant, *usually* male, OE, II,6

Cleave v. cling, hang (*from* clifan, clifian, *not* cleofan, cliofan, *meaning* split, cut), VI, 7

Clemm v. pinch with hunger, starve,? ON (*still* Northern dialect), I,12

Clip v. embrace, hug, OE, III,5

Close n. enclosed field, F, I,2

Clottered adj. clotted OE (of milk, ME), VI,9

Clout n. cloth, rag, OE, III,4

Coal-blue adj. blue-black, OE, II,4

Compass v. manage, F, IV,4

Coney, cony n. rabbit, ME/OF, III,v

Cot n. hut *or* small house, cottage, OE, III,2

Cote-hardie n. close-fitting garment with sleeves, OF, III,9

Crabbed adj. cantankerous, irritable, OE, V,13

Craft n. guild of craftsmen in the same skill, ME, V,13

Dastard n. coward, ?ME (first in Malory), IV,12

Deal n. amount, portion *or* business, OE, I,7

Debonnaire adj. courteous, gracefully friendly, OF, III,8

Deer n. any animal(s), *usually* mammalian, OE, I,v

Desert adj. desolate, uninhabited, ME/OF, II,10

Device n. design *or* figure, *usually* a heraldic emblem, ME/OF IV,10

Dight adj.& v. (past) dressed (food *or* people), E, I,1

Disport n. pleasure, amusement ME/OF, IV,3

Do v. cause to, OE, II,3

Do make v. get made, OE III,5

Do off v. take off (clothing), OE, II,12

Do on v. put on (clothing), OE, IV,1

Doom n. judgment, legal decision, ON, II,2

Doom-ring n rign of stones where debates and trials were held, ON, V,3

Do to wit v. make known to, explain to, OE, V,8

Doubt v. suspect *or* fear, L, VI,8

Draught n. drawing, sketch *or* drink, ME/?OE, VI,3

Due adj. appropriate, ME/OF, II,8

Edge-friend n. knife *or* sword (a kenning), OE, II,6

E'en adv. just, exactly, OE, I,18

Egg v. urge *or* persuade, ON III,6

Eglantine n. sweetbriar, wild dog-rose, OF, III,3

Eke v. prolong *or* augment, increase, OE, II,9

Eld n. old age, OE, I,12

Elder n. old man, *usually* community leader, *or* older person *or* flowering shrub, OE, II,9

Elf n. faery, unchristened being, OE, I,7

Endlong adj. from end to end, lengthwise *or* at full length (*often* with 'overthwart'), ME, II,4

Environed adj. surrounded, OF, I,1

Erewhile adv. a little while ago, formerly, OE, III,6

Erst adv. first *or* before, earlier, OE, I,17

Eyen n. eyes, ME, I,3

Eyot n. islet (Morris MSS consistently spell 'eyott'), OE, I,2

Faery n. elves, non-mortal spirits associated with wild nature and magic *or* the realm they dwell in, ME/?OF, I,1

Fain adj. eager, full of longing *or* glad, well-pleased *or* fond , making an affectionate fuss , OE, I,7

Fair-writer n. calligraphist, scribe, OE, IV,3

Fall on v. attack, OE, VI,31

Far and far adv. a long way, very far, ME, I,7

Fare v. go, travel, OE, I,7

Fashion v. construct, shape, OF, II,9

n. appearance, build, shape, OF, II,9

Fathom n. depth *or* breadth, OE, III,10

Favour n. appearance, OF, II,6

Fell adj. dangerous, fierce *or* fatal, OF, VI,22

Fence n. defence, swordsman's guard *or* the sport of fencing, OF, VI,12

Fetch n. a witch's familiar *or* the wraith *or* double of a human being, OE, VI,17

Flaggy adj. flagging, sagging, ON, II,3

Flasket n. bottle, flask, ON, I,11

Flockmeal adj. in a crowd, OE, III,9

Flyting n. rebuke *or* dispute, OE, I,13

Foison, n. abundance, plenty, OF, II,5

Footpace n. dais, platform (*not* walking-pace), ME, II,4

Forbear v. give up, let alone (*rarely* restrain oneself), OE, I,17

Force n. waterfall, ON, IV,15

Fordone adj. exhausted, OE, I,5

Foregather v. associate, OE, III,8

Foreseeing adj. prophetic, OE, II,5

Forgat v. (past) forgot, OE, I,13

Frank n. free trade area guaranteed by city or castle, G, VI,1

Franklin n. freeman, householder (not 'nobility' or 'gentry'), ?OF/?G, VI,7

Frist n. delay, respite *or* period of truce, OE, II,6

Fulfilled v. (past) filled out *or* filled up, ON, I,18

Gainsay v. deny *or* refuse, OE, II,5

Gallantly adv. generously, thoroughly *or* very easily, with aplomb ME, I,4

Gamesome adj. merry, sportive, OE, IV,16

Gangrel adj. vagabondish, vagrant, wandering, ON, III,2

Garth n. fenced yard, field enclosure, garden, ON, II,11

Gat v. (past) got *or* gained, OE, I,4

Gear n. equipment, possessions *or* clothing, OE, III,6

Ghyll n. deep glen *or* its stream (Wordsworth's spelling, 'gill' is more traditional), ON, II,11

Gild n. trade-association, 'guild' of craftspeople, OE, VI,3

Gin n. entanglement, trap (*from* 'engine'), OF, V,9

Gird at v. nag, rail at, Ren. (OE sense was to strike or push), I,4

Girdlestead n. waist (kenning: place of the girdle), OE, I,7

Girt adj. fastened, belted, OE, II,6

Girt with adj. wearing, OE, II,6

Gleeds n. coals of fire, live coals, OE, II,5

Glooming n. evening, twilight, OE, II,11

Gobbet n. fragment, small piece (*usually* of meat), OF, II,1

give the Go-by v. avoid (*usually* while travelling), OE, I,4

Goodhap n. good luck, OE, I,19

Goodly adj. handsome, in good condition, OE, II,4

Greywethers n. standing stones (kenning: like grey sheep), OE, IV,5

Grizzled adj. grey, *usually* of hair, *thus* old, OF, III,1

Grout n. groats, wholemeal porridge, ON, VI,17

Guile n. deception, trick, OF/G, V,9

Halling n. tapestry hangings, OE, II,11

Hallow v. bless, consecrate, make holy, OE, II,6

Haply adv. 'as it may chance', perhaps (*not* by chance, accidentally), ON, IV,1

Harbour n. safe place, shelter, OE, II,3

Hard by, Hard on adv. close to, OE, I,1

Hards n. coarse hemp *or* flax, OE, V,9
Hardly adj. with difficulty *or* boldly, vigorously, OE, IV,2
Hauberk n. mailcoat *or* neckpiece of mail, OF, IV,10
Have will v. prefer, wish, OE, I,4
Havings n. possessions, OE, V,14
Hawberk = *hauberk* see above.
Haysel n. hay harvest *or* haying season, OE, I,8
Hazelled field n. marked-out challenge-ground for public duels, ON, II,6
Head-burg n. helmet (kenning: head's fort), OE, VI,32
Heretofore adv. before, OE, I,16
Herse n. barred cage, grate *or* portcullis *or* harrow, F, V,9
Herseem v. seem to her, ME, III,2
Hight v. (past) called, is called, OE, I,1
Himseem v. seem to him, ME, V,1
Hind n. doe, OE, I,12
Hold n. fortress, OE, II,11
Holpen adj. helped, with help, OE, VI,31
Hosen n. socks, stockings, OE, VI,9
Host n. army, crowd with shared purpose, OF, V,8
Hosting n. assembly, gathering, OF, V,8
Howso adv. however, whatever, OE, I,4
*Husbandr*y n. domestic tasks, household management, OE, VI,28

Ill adj. bad, wicked, ON, III,8
    adv. badly, unpleasantly, ON, III,8
Imagery n. statuary (*rarely* pictures and tapestry figures), L, II,10
Increase n. gain, harvest, profit, L, II,5
Instant adj. insistent, pressing, L. IV,12
Irk v. irritate *or* bore, weary, ON, I,5

Jack n. sleeveless 'coat of fence' with quilting or metal plates, worn by foot-soldiers, OF/G, III,4
Joyance n. pleasure, rejoicing, OF, IV,4

Kale-blade n. cabbage-leaf, ON, II,2
Keel n. ship, boat, OE, III,6
Key-trees n. ash, maple, sycamore and their relatives, OE, I,9
Kilt v. tuck up (skirts), ON, II,9
Kindly adv. naturally, harmoniously, OE, III,3
Kine n. cattle, cows, OE, V,2
Kinned adj. related, OE, VI,1
Knot n. posy of flowers *or* small crowd, OE, V,12

Laded adj. loaded, OE, I,1
Landwight n. creature of the place (genius loci) *or* creature of earth (eg. kobold), OE, IV,6
Latten adj. made of tin (*or* light copper) alloy *or* brass, OF/G, I,7
Leads n. roof (of lead, as of church or castle), OE, IV,3
Leaguer n. seige *or* beseiging force, D, VI,1
Learn v. teach, OE, IV,3
Leash n. bunch, group, set *or* pair (of hounds), OF, II,1
Leech n. doctor (*thus* 'leechcraft', 'leechdom'), OE, VI,23
Leman n. lover ('leof-man'), sweetheart, ME, v,9
Lendings n. loans, things borrowed, OE, II,8
Let v. hinder, obstruct *or, rarely,* leak, let out *or, more rarely,* allow, permit, OE, II,8
Let-pass n. pass, permit, OE, VI,1
Lewd adj. illiterate (=lay), uneducated *or* artless, tasteless *or* base, immoral, OE, V,1

Licorous adj. lecherous, sensual *or* bon-vivant, OF, IV,11

Lie on v. depend on, OE, III,1

Liefer adv. more readily, rather, OE, IV,5

Lift v. steal, *usually* cattle, ON, VI,1

Light adj. frivolous *or* dishonest, immoral, promiscuous, OE, III,6

Lightly adv. easily, quickly, readily, OE, I,1

Like adj. likely, OE, III,1

Linden n.lime-tree, G, V,9

Litten adj. lighted, Mod. archaism, VI,17

Loathly adj. ugly, unpleasant, OE, VI,1

Lonely adj. alone, *not usually* sad, isolated, ME, III,7

Look to have, look to see v, expect, ME, I,17

Lout v. bow low, courtesy, ME, V,9

Low mass n. abbreviated, unaccompanied celebration of the mass, ME, I,1

Mail n. chest, coffer, ME, V,9

Main n. most important one *or* ocean (= 'main sea'), ME, IV,6

in the Main adv. mainly, mostly, usually, ME, IV,6

Make nothing of the work v. fail, admit defeat, be frustrated, ME, I,10

Manchet n. small loaf of roll of bread, OF, II,2

March n. frontier, border, debateable land, ?G, II,6

Matins, Matin-song n. daybreak mass *or hence* dawn, OF/L, III,2

Maul n. hammer *or* war-hammer, L, V,3

Mayhap, mayhappen conj. perhaps, maybe, OE, II,9

Mazer n. drinking-bowl, cup, G, II,9

Measurely adv. restrainedly, moderately, slowly, ME, I,5

Meat n. food of any kind, OE, I,2

Mere adj. absolute, complete, ME, I,7

Meseemeth, meseems v. seems to me, 4
Mickle adj. great, OE, V,3
Milch- adj, milk-yielding (*of* cows, goats), OE, II,9
Minded adj. inclined, intending, ME, VI,1
Minish v. diminish, lessen, OF, VI,4
Minorites, Friars Minor n. Franciscan monks, friars, L, V,8
Mishandling n. brutality, maltreatment, ME, II,5
Mote (or moot) n. assembly, public meeting, OE, II,6

Natheless conj. nevertheless, OE, II,12
Naysay v. refuse (*also* n. refusal), ON, II,9
Neat n. cattle, oxen *or* bull, cow, ox, OE, III,4
Ness n. headland, promontory, ON, I,20
Newel n. pillar of stairwell, L, II,4
Niggard adj. mean, miserly, ME/OF?, III,5
Nigh adj. close, nearby, OE, II,15
Noble n. gold piece, F, I,1
Nock v. notch, string an arrow, G, V,7
Noise n. herald, trumpeter, OF, V,1
Noseling adv. face-downward, nose-first, OE, VI,12
Nowise adv. in no way, not at all, ME, I,3

Offing n. about to impinge *or* off-shore, OE, I,4
Oliphant n. elephant, *hence* horn of ivory, OF, VI,31
Onfall n. onset, attack (*of* disease), OE, VI,31
Ort n. fragment, scrap, G, II,11
Othersome n. some others, OE, I,1
Ouch n. brooch, clasp *or* buckle, ME/OF, V,9
Out-a-gates adv. outside, ON, IV,1
Out-gates n. exits, ways of egress, ON, V,3
Outgoing n. escape, way out, OE, I,7
Overcast adj. overthrown, OE, V,9
Overthwart adv. across, athwart *or* opposite, ON, II,4

Palfrey n. saddle-horse, *usually* for ladies, L, IV,5
Pennon n. small flag, *usually* for lance-head, L, VII,3
Perron n. platform at the head of stairs, F, II,3
Piece of work n. elaborate fuss, laborious or ostentatious reaction, ME, II,6
Pine v. afflict, torment *or* languish, suffer, OE, II,5
Pined adj. afflicted, made to suffer, OE, V,9
Plashed adj. pleached, interwoven (of arbours, hedges), OE, III,5
Play n. game *or* performance, ME, I,7
Pleasance n.secluded walking-place, OF, III,5
Plenishing n. furnishings, furniture, OF, II,9
Postern n. small back or side door, OF, IV,7
Potherbs, herbs *or* vegetables grown 'for the pot', OF, 1,2
Poulaine n. pointed shoes, erroneously used for table fowl (*usually* dressed and cooked=poulard, poulet), F, I,1

Quean n. female, woman, OE, II,5
Quern n. millstones, OE, I,5
Quickbeam = *quicken-tree,* see below.
Quicken v. become pregnant *or* come alive, OE, I,16
Quicken-tree, quicken, n. mountain ash, rowan, service-tree, OE, II,9

Ransack v. search thoroughly, ON, I,15
Raven-wine n. blood, *usually* on battlefield (kenning: the drink ravens appreciate), ON, I,15
Rate v. carp at, scold, ME, I,4
Rede n. advice, policy, wisdom, OE, I,7
      v. advise, counsel, OE, II,5
Reek n. fumes, smoke, steam, OE, III,9
Reiver n. cattle-thief, plunderer, robber (also 'reaver'), OE, III,9

Religious n. monk *or* nun, OF/L, III,1

Ribald n. knave, rough rascal, OF, I,1

Riding-reek n. dust-cloud from horses, OE, III, 4

Rive v. cleave, split, tear apart, ON, V,13

Rood, the Cross, OE, III,9

Rose-leaf adj. smooth and clear, *usually* of a woman's skin, OE, III,5

Rout n. mob, rabble, ME, IV,14

Runagate n. deserter, fugitive, renegade, Ren. (from Spanish), VI,7

Runaway n. escaped slave, ME, II,2

Sallet n. round helmet, F, II,11

Sax n. short sword or knife, OE, 1,2

Scantly adv. meagrely, scantily, ON, III,5

Scathe n. pain, harm, ON, IV,7

Screen n. partition between dining-hall and entrance-hall, ME/OF, IV,1

Scrip n. wallet, satchel, pouch, ON, I,1

Seeming n. appearance, ON, II,6

Sele of the day n. morning greeting, ME, IV,14

Sender n. witch or sorcerer, OE, I,15

Sending n. apparition, OE, II,12

Shamefast adj. bashful, modest, constrained, OE, III,8

Shaper n. designer, maker, OE, III,6

Sharp of the hand n. edge of the palm, OE, I,9

Shaw n. wood, copse, OE, I,1

Sheepwalks n. pasture for sheep (not trails made by them), OE, VI,1

Slot n. track, spoor (from deer hoofprints), OF, V,3

Slug-a-bed n. sluggard, oversleeper, Ren./ON, I,12

Sluttish adj. slovenly, with unclean habits, ME, III,3

Smart n. sharp pain, OE, I,13

Smock n. woman's underslip, petticoat, shift, OE, I,6

Solace v. console, entertain, OF, I,20

Solar n. sunny private family room in a castle, L, V,2
Somewhat n. something, OE, I,16
Somewhence adv. from somewhere, OE, V,3
Sooth n. truth, OE, I,2
Sore adj. painful *or* great, OE, II,5
Sorry adj. sad, OE, I,2
Sort n. group, set *or* kind, species, OF, VI,7
Speech-friend n. declared lover, OE, II,8
Spell-work n. sorcery, magic, OE, VI,26
Spur n. haste *or* knight's spur, OE, II,6
SS collar n. necklace designed in repeated S-shapes, ME, III,6
Stanchions n. stays, supports, OF, II,4
Stark adj. strong (*also* adv, intensely, completely), ON, I,3
Stave n. barrel-board *or* musical *or* poetic unit, ON, IV,9
Stay v. delay *or* stop *or* nourish, OF, II,4
Stead n. place (*usually* farm) *or* aid, assistance, ON, I,17. v. place, establish *or* aid, help, ON, V,3
Stonecast n. stone's throw, OE, I,20
Stopple n. stopper, ME, I,11
Stour n. fight, pitched battle, OF, VI,1
Strait adj. narrow, confined, OF, I,1
Straiten v. narrow down, limit, OF, IV,9
Strand n. beach, shore, ON, II,9
Strike v. take down, dismantle (tents, gibbets), OE, II,10
Stringplay n. string music (*usually* harps) ON, VI,26
Stripes n. beating, lashes, punishment, D, I,6
Stuffs n. cloth, lengths of material, OF, III,6
Sumpter n. baggage horse, pack-animal, L, III,4
Surcoat n. outer coat for both sexes (*but* often over armour), OF, III,4

Sure adj. trustworthy, OF, III,10

Swain n. young man, *usually* as wooer, ON, II,6

Swale n. timbers used in fortification, ME, II,17

Swathe n. line of mowed grass *or* its breadth, OE, I,13

Sweetling n. darling, sweetheart, OE, I,13

Sweet water n. potable, freshwater, OE, I,13

Swink n. physical labour, hard work, OE, 1,4

Tabernacle n. booth *or* ark, sacred repisitory, Eccl. L, II,10

from the teeth out adv. superficially, insincerely (opposite of 'from the heart'), ME, I,19

Thane n. warrior freeman heading a family, liegeman to a king, ON, II,6

Therefor prep. for it, OE, II,6

Thereout adv. out of there, OE, II,4

Thole v. endure, ON, I,4

Thorp n. hamlet, village, ON, VI,1

Thrall n. slave, ON, I,4

Throstle n. thrush, ON, VI,23

Thrums n. thread-ends (in weaving), ON, V,9

Tide n. season, time, ON, IV,2

Tillage n. news, information, OE, II,10

Tilt-yard n. practice-ground for jousting, ME, I,16

Tippet n. cape, short cloak, OE, VI,24

Tiring-woman n. lady's maid (for attiring), OE, III,4

To- prefix, very much, a great deal, OE, I,11

Toward adj. at hand, beginning, imminent *or* appropriate, timely, welcome (opposite of 'untoward'), OE, I,16

the Tree n. the Cross, Rood, OE, III,9

Treen adj. wooden, OE, VI,9

Trim adj. neat *or* neatly built, OE, III,4

Trow v. believe in, ON, I,10

Tryst n. secret, *or* appointed, meeting-place, ME, I,13
Twain n. two, OE, VI,33
Twiggen adj. made of twigs (*usually* birch), OE, I,4
Twig-shower n. beating, birching (kenning), OE, I,15

Ugsome adj. hideous, loathsome, Sc., IV,5
Unartful adj. unskilled *or* unskilfuly made, OE, II,9
Uncouth, adj. strange, incomprehensible *or* alien, unholy, unkent, ON, VI,7
Undo v. defeat, destroy, OE, II,5
Unfriend n. enemy, ME, IV,12
Unhap n. misfortune, ill-luck, ON, III,5
Unkenned, unkent adj. occult, ominously mysterious, uncouth, unholy, Sc., IV,5
Unminished adj. not devalued, unmarred, OF, V,7
Untold adj. secret, unspoken *or rarely* countless, ON, III,9
Unwont to adj. not used to, OE, III,4

Vavasour n. feudal tenant, ranked below barons, OF, VI,7
at a Venture adv. at random (*not* 'aventure' *or* 'peraventure'), OF, VI,31
Villein n. peasant *or* serf, OF, VI,7

Wade n. ford, ON, III5
Wage v. employ, hire, OF, III,5
Wain n. cart, wagon, OE, VI,1
Wakers n. chief mourners at a wake, OE, II,10
Wall-nook n. alcove, niche, OE, II,7
Wand n. stick, twig, ON, VI,9
Wanhope n. despair, hopelessness, ME, II,4
Ward n. guard, protective building *or* position, OE, III,2

War-horn n. ceremonial, rallying, summoning horn, OE, II,6

War-swales n. ?timber fortifications added to stone walls, ?OE, II,11

Watering-places n. where flocks and herds are brought to water, OE, VI,1

Wattle-work n. interlaced branches and stakes forming walls *or* fences, OE, III,2

Wax v. grow, increase, ON, I,3

Way n. path, road, ON, I,1

Way-beast n. road animal (*usually* ass *or* horse, *not* military), OE, I,1

Way-warden n. road-guard, watchman, ME, I,1

Way-worthy adj. fit to travel, OE, VI,1

Wear v. be used up, last, pass (*of* time), OE, I,4

Weather v. pass to windward of (*in* sailing), ON, I,19

Weird n. fate, the Fates, ON, V,7

Well-favouredly adv. charmingly *or* enthusiastically, handsomely, ME, II,9

Wend v. journey through, travel, ON, I,2

Whatso pron. *or* adj. whatever, OE, I,1

Wheedling adj. enticing, persuasive, tender, touching, ?OE, II,2

Whenas adv. *or* conj. when *or* if, OE, I,3

Whereas conj. *or* adv. because, seeing that *or* where, OE, I,2

Whereto pron. to where, OE, I,1

Whet v. sharpen ON, II,5

Whilom adv. at one time, once upon a time, OE, I,1

not a Whit adv. not at all, not a bit, II,9

Whyso adv. *or* pron. why, whyever, ON, II,2

Wicket n. gate, small door, ?OF, II,7

Wife n. woman (*no* implication of marriage), ON, I,1

Wight n. man *or* active spirit, ON, IV,5

Will v. want, wish, ON, I,5

Wind v. blow (a 'wind instrument'), OE, III,2

Window-work n. crisscross patterning, lattice-work, ON, II,11

in no Wise adv. not at all, ON, I,4

in such Wise adv. in that way *or* in the same way, ON, II,5

Wit n. sense, ON, II,9

to Wit conj. that is, ON, I,1

Withal adv. also, too, ON, I,1

Without adv. conj. *or* pron. outside *or* forgetting, ignoring OE, III,2

Wont n. habits ('of wont' = normally, 'wonted' = accustomed), ME, I,4

Wood-cattle n. deer (kenning), OE, I,4

Wood-neb n. outlying ara of forest (kenning: beak of forest), OE, V,3

Wood-reeve n. forester, OE, I,1

Wot v. consider, guess *or* know, OE, I,1

Would v.(past) hoped, wished, ON, I,4

Writhen adj. twisted, wrung, OE, VI,16

Wroth adj. angry, ON, II,6

Wrought adj. made, shaped (*usually* of metals, metathesis of 'worked'), ME, III,6

Yea-say v. agree, assent (*also* n.), OE, I,1

Yeoman n. commoner owning land, ON, VI,7

Yet adv. nevertheless *or* so far, still, OE, I,4

Yore n. history, the past, OE, IV,6

Youngling n. child, novice, OE, II,9

THE WILLIAM MORRIS SOCIETY

The life, work and ideas of William Morris are as important today as they were in his lifetime. *The William Morris Society* exists to make them as widely known as possible.

The many-sidedness of Morris and the variety of his activities bring together in the *Society* those who are interested in him as designer, craftsman, businessman, poet, socialist, or who admire his robust and generous personality, his creative energy and courage. Morris aimed for a state of affairs in which all might enjoy the potential richness of human life. His thought on how we might live, on creative work, leisure and machinery, on ecology and conservation, on the place of the arts in our lives and their relation to politics, as on much else, remains as challenging now as it was a century ago. He provides a focus for those who deplore the progressive dehumanization of the world in the twentieth-century and who believe, with him, that the trend is not inevitable.

The *Society* provides information on topics of interest to its members and arranges lectures, visits, exhibitions and other events. It encourages the reprinting of his works and the continued manufacture of his textile and wallpaper designs. It publishes a journal twice a year, free to members, which carries articles across the field of Morris scholarship. It also publishes a quarterly newsletter giving details of its programme, new publications and other matters of interest concerning Morris and his circle. Members are invited to contribute items both to the journal and to the newsletter. *The William Morris Society* has a world-wide membership and offers the chance to make contact with fellow Morrisians both in Britain and abroad.

Regular events include a Kelmscott Lecture, a birthday party held in March, and visits to exhibitions and such places as the William Morris Gallery, Red House, Kelmscott Manor and Standen. These visits, our tours and our short residential study courses, enable members living abroad or outside London to participate in the *Society's* activities. The *Society* also has local groups in various parts of Britain and affiliated Societies in the USA and Canada.

For further details, write to:
The Hon. Membership Secretary
Kelmscott House
26 Upper Mall
Hammersmith
London W6 9TA